MY HAIRY LIFE

MY HAIRY LIFE

a novel

Jayne Mead

Full Court Press
Englewood Cliffs, New Jersey

First Edition

Copyright © 2012 by Jayne Mead

Published in the United States of America
by Full Court Press, 601 Palisade Avenue
Englewood Cliffs, NJ 07632
www.fullcourtpressnj.com

ISBN 978-0-9849536-4-6
Library of Congress Control No. 2012934589

Editing by Arlene Pollack
Book Design by Barry Sheinkopf for Bookshapers
(www.bookshapers.com)
Author Photograph by Linda Erickson
Colophon by Liz Sedlack
Cover art courtesy istockphoto.com

THIS NOVEL IS DEDICATED
TO THE MEMORY OF MY HUSBAND,
BOBBY CURTIS

May he rest in peace.

Acknowledgements

I would like to thank my mother, may she rest in peace, for her unconditional love; my father, for introducing me at a very young age to such great writers as Tolstoy, Hugo, Dostoyevsky, and Balzac; my sister, Rose Blum, for her enthusiastic and encouraging response to everything I have ever written; and my brother, Mark Nachtigal, for his support.

Also thank you to my sons, daughters-in-law, and my adorable grandchildren, my *raison d'être*.

I would like to thank Barry Sheinkopf, of Bookshapers.com, for entering my life just when I needed him.

And thanks to the following songwriters whom I quoted in this novel: "Ya Ya," by Lee Dorsey and Clarence L. Lewis, sung by Joey Dee; "Don't Let Me Be Misunderstood," by Benjamin Bennie, Sol Marcus, and Gloria Caldwell, sung by Nina Simone; "Spinning Wheel," by David Clayton-Thomas, sung by Blood, Sweat, and Tears; "Son of Suzy Creamcheese," by Frank Zappa, sung by The Mothers of Invention; "I Still Miss Someone," by Johnny Cash, sung by Joan Baez; and "The World is Falling Down," lyrics and song by Abbey Lincoln.

1

OUT OF THE BLUE

IT'S GETTING VERY LATE, *and I must tell this story now while it's still fresh in my mind and my thinking is still sharp, even as I am filling my lungs with pot, blowing the pungent, heady smoke out my bedroom window. Overnight, I have left the turmoil, clutter, hysteria, and shame that had resided within my inner life for so long— left the chaos of daily life, its echoes still within earshot, its texture familiar and resounding. My past is right behind me, and I have entered, kicking and screaming, a new realm, a third act. This inevitable act is shockingly different, and there is no way to connect all the past tension to the person who is me today, or the non-person I will inevitably become.*

I have slipped and fallen down a well-polished banister, into another space, another part of the house that I had never considered entering. Old age is not for the faint of heart, I've heard people say, and I say it myself, often. Magazines no longer speak to me. Their offers of 501 ways of making oneself younger and sexier, their myriad tips on improving my self-image, self-confidence, marriage or career, are irrelevant to me now. I do not need to lose weight or comb my hair in the latest fashion. Television does not address me. Commercials cannot tempt me to purchase flirty bags, feminine products, a new iPhone, or darker, thicker eyelashes. I am at last invisible: an old lady limping along with arthritis, thinning hair, saggy knees, bunions, and false teeth.

Suddenly it is all over, except for one last look over the shoulder. This is what I want to tell you:

BEING AN EXTREMELY HAIRY female not only fucks with the mind but is a full-time preoccupation, necessitating constant vigilance, attention to detail, creativity, stubbornness, frustration, and tedium. Worse yet, though a woman who is hirsute may appear pretty and otherwise feminine and normal at first glance, at closer range she may be seen as a freak. If she's thin-skinned, sensitive, and hungering for approval, she has to ensure that the second glance never happens. That was what I had attempted to achieve: *no second glances.*

Assuring myself that I appeared normal became my *raison d'être*, my *calling.* There must be women who can ignore others' curious looks, pity, or negative comments—women to whom physical appearance is low on their list of priorities. Perhaps they possess unique talents, wisdom, fortune, and fame, riches that can compensate for anything or everything, particularly a cosmetic flaw. Maybe their ideal backgrounds have prepared them to cope, perhaps even thrive, despite adversity— particularly an adversity that, compared to all the possible hardships in life, could be considered trivial.

I was not such a woman. I was not blessed by good fortune or strength that could have tipped the scales in my favor and rendered hirsuteness a nuisance instead of a calamity. Being hirsute struck me as a unique curse that became my biggest challenge in life, my Achilles heel, my nemesis, my secret. To avoid being seen the way I was, I had to channel time and energy onto the Sisyphean task of ridding my body of unwanted hair that, by its nature, always, no matter how hard and how long I worked at it, quickly recovered, multiplied, and thrived, claiming back its right as a *bona fide* feature of my skin.

DAYDREAMING IN SOPHOMORE CIVICS class, tuned out during a discussion of which I understood virtually nothing, I gazed out the large window on my left, noting the leafless trees, the bright incongruous sun that did not warm, the cold blue skies of my first American winter.

I could almost feel the November cold that was so unlike any cold I had ever known or conceived possible, I was amazed by its intensity, that cold that seeped inward like icicles melting through skin, freezing blood and bone.

As I daydreamed, I absentmindedly tugged on some coarse, short hairs on my chin. That motion of tugging and twisting the new hair shafts felt rather pleasant, a frisson of arousal accompanying the touch. Then it hit me, like a gust of wind, or, rather, like the sinking feeling when the realization of bad news hits its target: *Dear God, I have hair on my chin!* Furtively examining my face in my compact mirror, right there in class, I was stunned to realize what in fact I had already known just below consciousness: A fine mustache was casting a shadow upon my upper lip, and sideburns were framing my face, as if in my sleep I had been liberally infused with hair-growth hormones gone awry, altering my fifteen-year-old girl face into one resembling that of an effete, adolescent boy on the precipice of maturation.

That eventually I might sport a full beard, if I were to let nature follow its course, was a thought I couldn't bear. No, not me. There was nothing otherwise masculine about me: I was beginning to grow breasts; my body was small, girlish; my facial features were feminine; I had no interest in boys' play, nor could I even throw a ball. I didn't envy boys and had never longed to be one. When I was introduced to the concept of "penis envy," I simply couldn't buy it; it was a laughable idea, dreamt up by a man who didn't understand women. Every morning of my life I could have recited the reverse of the Jewish prayer, thanking God for not making me a *man*. Developing a masculine trait, particularly one as obscene as hairiness, would render me a social pariah, a freak, and an object of ridicule, I knew. Hair on the chin, in addition to elsewhere, would make me appear either goat-like or an avatar from prehistoric times, a primitive forerunner of modern men and women, a freak of nature dressed in twentieth-century clothing.

I had to destroy the hair before anyone noticed, and I had convinced myself that the whole world would not only notice, but would exile me from polite society like a modern-day leper. Children would chase me down the street calling me names: *"Hey, monkey!" "Hey mister!"* and I would have to run and hide and cry for shame.

It was not as if I hadn't known all along that I was hairy: it didn't suddenly spring into my consciousness. Yet, I was not prepared; I had not imagined the *scope* of this affliction. I certainly never thought that hair would grow on my face, obvious and grotesque for the whole world to see! I was fifteen years old, and my world was changing; I could do little but howl at the moon.

IN AN EARLY MEMORY, I am sitting on the floor next to my iron bed in the back room, looking at a picture book, my legs splayed out, half-consciously noting the dark, curly hair on my knees and legs. I was not shocked or surprised: conscious awareness of one's body and self is probably a gradual process, and more than likely I had then returned to my book without giving my legs further thought; yet the memory became impressed upon my mind, reserved in the long-term file together with significant events and poignant moments, to be recalled many years later, the texture, pattern, and sense of that memory fresh and keen, as if captured, kept, and nurtured in the mind like a prized heirloom.

Hairy legs were unaesthetic, the opposite of beauty, and unacceptable, but there were no options. Girls in Israel, particularly girls in my age group, didn't shave their legs, and if they did, I would not have known. The idea had never entered my head. Moreover, my thin arms were covered in abundant dark, long hair as well, a fact I took in stride even though I always visualized the hair erased, gone from my skin as if it had been washed off by the rain or burned by the sun. In my mind's eye I could see the skin clearly, glowing and smooth, just like my mother's, or like my cousin's soft hairless arms, which I would pretend were mine. But of course, unwanted hair endures like a bad case of the croup or an autoimmune disease, seeking its own immortality, resisting modern medicine. There was nothing a girl in my position could do about it.

As with any autoimmune infection, more and more skin became affected, until almost every inch save the palm of my hands and the soles of my feet was covered in growth. If I had any doubts about this abnormality, the cruelty and candor of my peers affirmed my own observation. During an outdoor gym class in third grade, while we were working on abdominal exercises on floor mats, a girl nearby pointed at me and merrily shouted, *"The lady has hair under her arms,"* and everyone, including the teacher, burst out laughing, trying to see my armpits, while I, shamefaced, lay flat on my mat, concentrating on a gray cloud in the sky that was shaped like an eagle, my arms tight against my body, as I strove to hold back an avalanche of tears. It was a wonderful distraction for the class, but an *"I wish I were dead"* moment for me. I was too shy to come up with some witty retort that would silence them and soothe my injured ego.

That comment from my Israeli classmate had been made in Hebrew, before my family emigrated from Israel to New Jersey when I was an underdeveloped fourteen-year-old teenager.

Now, after years of non-use, I have forgotten Hebrew almost entirely. On rare visits back to Israel, I learned that I had retained my accent but spoke in broken Hebrew, unable to recall even simple, everyday words. Yet I remember that girl's exact expression: *"La giveret, yesh kvar saarot ba'yadayiim."* I could have gone home and told my mother or used my father's razor to shave my underarms, but I did neither; instead, I stopped lifting my arms whenever, in the oppressive Israeli summer heat, I had to wear a sleeveless blouse. Initially, avoiding a movement that had never before required conscious thought felt awkward and ungainly to me, as if I were missing a body part; but within a short time, it became second nature—so much so that, whenever I saw others lifting their arms, I cringed, as if the action were either illegal or universally tabooed. But none of my peers had hairy armpits, and they could stand on their heads without looking freakish. Soon, I grew pubic hair, but that was just for me to know, a private matter, and therefore did not cause me any angst or shock. At age twelve, I told Varda, my best friend, "I can't remember a time I didn't have pubic hair"; and she, a year younger but already wearing a bra, confided, "Yes, me, too."

If I stood on my tiptoes on the toilet seat, I could see my reflection in the bathroom mirror that my father had hung too high. As a preadolescent, I had no conception of what my body should look like, but it seemed to me that it looked pretty good. Was that really *possible?* Although I had no breasts yet, I appeared curvy and feminine, and I liked what I saw. I had long, thick hair that my mother usually braided; my waist was small, and my legs long. I looked at my reflection every time I had a chance; in hindsight, it was probably the only time in my life when I actually admired my body and enjoyed looking at it.

Varda and I could talk about anything, particularly as we felt our bodies developing and changing, and I was not yet dismayed or guarded about my hairiness. Actually, although a year younger than I, Varda had already developed breasts and gotten her period, while I was still skinny and flat, not menstruating or needing a bra, but having hairier legs. We'd go for our Friday evening walks from our slum, Abu-Kabir, to the sycamore-lined streets of Tel Aviv, and boys would whistle at her, size her up and down, and often make passes. She in turn was always prepared with a witty retort. Those Friday night walks were precious, as they marked a time in my life when I felt most adult. That lovely time would soon end: we were immigrating to America.

Yes, it was finally happening. After years of daydreaming, years of tagging along with my parents to formidable-looking office buildings, my mother in high heels and her best blue taffeta dress, my father in a top hat, the paper work was finally completed. Something called an *affidavit*—a word tossed around at home in conjunction with the process and which I thought sounded peculiar, and rather un-English—finally came through, and an actual date in June was set for our departure. Unfortunately, my father had yet another love affair to conduct that spring, this time with Varda's mother. When my mother got wind of it, all hell broke loose. She forbade me to have anything to do with the girl who had been my best friend since age two, and I was forced to sneak out to see her. Varda was already seeing boys and, from time to time used me as a go-between--that is, until our geographical move put an end to our friendship, and an end to my father's latest affair as well. That affair would cause my mother a lifetime of bitterness and pain. Varda's mother would forever be referred to as the *kurva*, Polish for "whore," even after the lady grew old and fat, and even after her death.

But while Varda and I were still friends, it dawned on us that I could yank out the hair on my arms and legs by their roots, and, just as with weeds, the hairs would be gone forever. Somewhere we found tweezers, and Varda and I sat on the crumbling stone steps by the eucalyptus tree, which led to a neighbor's house, and plucked away.

Although we had lived next to these neighbors through my entire childhood, there was little interaction between the two families. They were from Portugal and spoke only Ladino. The father's name was Albert. He and his family, including the small children, minded their own business. One of the babies had bad legs and had to wear a long brace between her feet. We saw each other on those horrid occasions when someone from the health department would come to the neighborhood, gather up all the kids, make us stand in line, and force a spoonful of revolting cod liver oil down our throats.

I was invited into the neighbors' house only once. They were preparing dinner, and something pungent and flavorful was sizzling in the frying pan, the smell almost making me faint with hunger and craving. I was given only one slice of bread spread with something green that was spicy, wonderful, and utterly strange to me. They laughed when they saw my obvious pleasure, for they knew that European Jews cooked only bland and tasteless food, a fact that was a source of amusement to Jews from Spain and Africa. I never learned the name of that mysterious green spread, but I would think about it a great deal in the years to come.

Sitting there on the stone steps, we rarely saw anyone emerge from the house, and so Varda and I took our privacy for granted. The days were hot and balmy, the tree branches seemed tired and heavy as the heat beat down endlessly, and the fields were barren; grass, anemones, and weeds turned as dry and lifeless as straw under the endless summer sun. From time to time, plumes of gray sand dust blew from the desert, displacing the last possible rustle of a branch, settling over rooftops, stones, pathways, branches, gutters, hair, until air seemed to be a distant memory from another life.

Varda and I acted out our fantasies by the evergreen eucalyptus, making up role-playing games, she always the beautiful princess, I always the thief who loved her, who risked life and limb for her kiss. I didn't like playing the male role, but Varda argued that, since she was younger and more feminine, it had to be so. Plus, my legs were hairier.

"Keep pulling them out by their roots!" Varda reminded me. "Then they'll never grow back, and you'd be able to play the queen."

I did follow her advice that summer, and there was much satisfaction in the process.

We were in our own world for hours, always ignoring the adults' urgent advice: "Girls, go in the house. The heat and *hamsin* will give you sunstroke!"

But long before the foliage in the fields blossomed once again, as the November rains and hail poured down in biblical fury, the hair on my limbs grew back more tenaciously, darker, sharper, and masculine-looking. They say that shaving or plucking does not make hair grow thicker, but there was evidence to the contrary right on my own body.

THERE WERE OTHER THINGS to worry about. A recurrent theme, the leitmotif of my childhood, was my mother's sobs, recriminations, sorrows, and regrets. She had her own mother to complain to, but between the two of us there were no boundaries or secrets. Her laments over her lost beauty and lost opportunities were like daggers through my heart. One theme surpassed all others and never ceased being a topic of obsession and rumination: the thinning of her hair. She had had long, thick brown hair that was a source of pride, but suddenly it had begun falling out, like dried-up leaves from a late autumn tree. She would say to me, "My hair was so thick; I had trouble running a comb through it. *Now* look—it's falling out. It's almost gone!"

After much discussion and repeated analysis with my father —who, incidentally, was just as mortified as she: having a bald wife would reflect poorly on him—she concluded that the source of her distress was the hairdresser who had talked her into having a "permanent." She looked at herself in the mirror, combed her fallen mane, gathered the stray dead shafts from the bathroom floor, and wept, day after day, year after year.

My father not only empathized and mourned her lost tresses with her, but went so far as to threaten the hair salon owner. I wouldn't have been surprised to learn that he had *murdered* that man. Quick-tempered as he was, I had seen my father get into fistfights with some neighborhood men; once he even dragged a guy out of the back of a truck and pummeled him severely, all the while smoking a cigarette. He had boxed professionally in Austria around the time I was born, after the war was over, ostensibly for financial reasons but no doubt for pleasure as well.

As for his reaction to my mother's tears, his empathy and charity did not accompany his anger; he solved the problem for himself by forcing her to wear a wig for most of her life.

Since my mother was barely five feet tall, he also forced her to wear high heels. Later in life she had two or three bunion surgeries and tossed all her high-heeled shoes in the recycle bin. Much later, the wigs, hated and maligned as if they were living symbols of her lost charms, were tossed out as well. As it turned out, she ended up with short, thin hair which she dyed a reddish blonde. She would constantly look at her image in the mirror and, rather pleased, say to me whenever I visited, "See, I got a little hair left! I don't look so bad, right?"

Actually, my parents worried a lot about *my* looks as well. There was much ado about my appearance, the subtext being that if my looks were damaged, so would be my prospects for finding a husband.

There was quite a fuss when I came down with a case of impetigo that spread over my body and face. My parents, freaking out, dressed me hastily in the middle of the night and whisked me off to the doctor's home as if I had contracted smallpox rather than a garden-variety childhood infection.

"Dear God, *help* me!" my mother cried, wringing her hands. "Her *face*! She has lesions on her *face*! Oh, my God! Her face is ruined!"

My father, pale and taciturn, looked at me as if I were a disgrace, something that needed to be disposed of at once, a daughter who was about to impose shame on the whole family.

After reassuring my parents that I would recover completely, the doctor advised them to avoid frantic middle-of-the-night visits for non-emergency crises. Somewhat calmed, we left his office. But my parents were not reassured that night, and my father vowed to murder the doctor if my face were to end up pockmarked!

Indeed, I wound up with tiny scars on my forehead that in time faded to almost nothing--but from the *measles*, not the impetigo. For that, my parents were furious, as they considered the superficial scars to be *my* fault: I had refused, out of sheer stubbornness, disobedience, and stupidity, to heed their warnings and avoid scratching my face!

I wasn't a daring or athletic child and never broke a bone, but I did end up with an unsightly, large, permanent scar on the lateral aspect of my leg. While in bed sleeping early in the dawn hours of a weekday morning, I had been stung by a scorpion, which left me almost faint with pain that radiated up my leg and thigh and felt as though my blood had been filled with lye. I shrieked, my mother shrieked, and the neighbors came running. Estrella, the Jewish-Portuguese woman who lived right next to us with her husband and two kids—Moshiko, a boy my brother's age, and Vickie, a couple of years younger than I, was the first to run in, still in her pajamas. All those years I had never been to their house, strangely enough, except for the few times when I came to tutor Vickie in Hebrew. The women who lived on the other side, by the eucalyptus tree, rushed in as well.

"Where does it hurt?" asked one of the women while I stood in my underwear screaming at the top of my lungs.

"All over! All over!" I howled.

"The poison is spreading! You better get her to the doctor at once!" the women advised my mother, who, in the chaos, had been ambling about aimlessly, weeping, trembling, tugging at her clothes in her woe, pulling out precious hair.

When we arrived at the clinic, the doctor was not in yet. The nurse asked me to point to the bite. She left the room briefly, returning with a bottle of some tincture that did not look ominous. It wasn't a needle, to my relief, but as she applied the tincture to the site, I was stunned by the burning sensation; it felt as if she had lit my skin on fire, and after a moment I resumed screaming, louder than before. I felt bitten twice that morning. She wrapped a dressing around my leg, suggested I stay out of school, and left me with a three-by-one-inch translucent scar where hair never grew.

When my father came home from work that evening, my mother and I, competing for his attention, breathlessly related our story, while his eyes narrowed, his face paled, and his hands clenched into fists. Without a word, he crouched down under the bed, found the offending creature, and with his bare hands seized it and crushed it to death. But luxuriating in my father's sympathy and love was short-lived.

"Because she screamed bloody murder and said the poison was spreading, I had no choice but to take her to the clinic," my mother explained.

"Nah, *what* poison? Nonsense," he mocked. "She would have been okay without the hysteria; instead, now she is going to have a scar on her leg for the rest of her life!"

"But we are so lucky," my mother said, attempting to calm and appease him. "Thank God it didn't bite her on her face!"

"Thank God!" The sheer thought of a burn mark on my face was too awful to imagine. Even saying it out loud was dangerous, an invitation to the Devil.

MY PARENTS' ANXIETY AND vigilance concerning my looks continued to escalate as I was maturing into my preteen years. I was blamed for my overbite: "Stop pushing your teeth out with your tongue," my father repeatedly admonished, though I had no idea what he was talking about. I ended up wearing braces for about two years. There was nothing remarkable about that—practically everyone in school wore them—but mine were removed prematurely, before we left for America, since the assumption was that the treatment would be continued by American orthodontists. However, once in the States, my parents learned that orthodontists were expensive. They cursed the Israeli dentist for his poor advice and ultimately decided that I looked presentable enough.

I didn't want to start life in America with braces in my mouth. I had not forgiven my father for the time he punished me for forgetting to bring the braces to a dental appointment. Reaching the office, I realized that I had forgotten the braces. The dentist was amused and scheduled me for another appointment. I rode the bus home, sitting by the window, enjoying the sights. On the way, I noticed a restaurant named California and fell into a reverie about my future in the United States, almost unable to believe my good fortune.

When my father returned from work, he seemed in a good mood, gave my cheek a little squeeze, then asked, "So, what did the dentist say about your progress?" When I explained and justified my absent-mindedness, his face turned dark, his eyes hostile, his breathing fast and shallow, and he launched into a tirade that was part anger, part violence, part mockery, part frustration, and complete abhorrence towards me, the recipient of all that unjust fury. The evening that had started so well was totally ruined, and the adjectives that he hurled at me—*idiot, moron, stupid*—hit like ripe tomatoes exploding on impact.

I had actually witnessed such a scene once before: my father tossing ripe tomatoes at my mother's direction—not hitting her, but bloodying the kitchen walls, the book I was reading, Shlomo's head, and my new patent leather shoes.

THE CONCERN OVER MY looks didn't stop with my face. In sixth grade we were examined for scoliosis, and the nurse sent my parents a note about my uneven posture. My parents were convinced that I would develop a hunchback by the age of thirty if I did not sit up straight and walk properly with my back erect. All their recriminations fell on deaf ears; I couldn't change my posture even when I was forced to join exercise classes for that purpose. My mother took me to several classes, and then assigned the chore to my crippled grandmother, who loved the movies and had no trouble convincing me that it would be more fun to see *South Pacific* in 3-D than to attend a gym class.

But nothing compared to the drama that ensued from my mother's conviction that, like her, I was losing the hair on my head. At twelve years of age, I had two thick braids that extended to the middle of my back. I loved my hair; it was wavy and dark brown, not a mousy brown or dull blonde that I noticed on some girls. But when my mother washed it in the basin and then combed it out while I twisted and squirmed from the pull of the comb, she observed with increasing alarm that lumps of hair had come off my head into the basin, on the comb, on my shoulders, and on the towels. Unbeknownst to me at the time, my parents turned to others for advice, and a treatment plan was devised: My hair would have to be shaved off to prevent further loss and to allow new hair to take root and grow hardy and thick.

Somehow I was bribed and tricked into going to the barbershop, where the kindly barber attempted to soothe me with a green lollipop as he and my mother lifted me onto his chair. As if convicted of a crime I had not committed, I cried for mercy. In vain, I thrashed, screamed, and tried to get away, but the barber was stronger than I. My mother began crying as well, begging me to behave, to allow him to shave off my long hair, that it was being done for my benefit.

The scissors began shearing off huge chunks of hair. At once I closed my eyes and became a princess, dressed in a red velvet Victorian gown with sloping shoulders, low pointed waist, and voluminous golden skirts held up by crinolines. From the time I first held a pencil, I had loved drawing such pictures. I would draw and doodle constantly, particularly on notebook margins when bored in class. I became a ballerina in a pink tutu and pointy shoes, impossibly dancing on my tiptoes. I became a singer in a cabaret, sitting on the grand piano, my legs crossed, just like in the movies. But then I heard a man's gruff voice, and I became a bald and ugly girl, inconsolable, even as they wrapped a white kerchief on my newly shaved head.

When we left the barbershop, my mother took me to a bookstore and told me to choose any book I wanted. I found a hardcover of short American stories in Hebrew. The stories were all tragic tales of long-lost mothers, lost children, all types of loss. On the bus home, I read a story about a poor boy on a mission to find his mother in Argentina, where she had gone to become a nanny for a rich girl. Hungry, alone, scared of thieves or the police, he searched the crowded, noisy streets of Buenos Aires until he thought he'd found her. She was walking fast a few blocks ahead of him, and he had to run until he was out of breath; but when the woman turned around she was someone else, a stranger with cold, dark eyes.

At home my mother re-wrapped my bald head in a printed red scarf that I ended up wearing for the following two months. I was up-beat that evening, the nightmarish ordeal behind me, thinking that, as long as I had a pretty scarf on my bald head, nobody would know what was underneath it. I ran to a neighborhood boy's house to get my homework, and since the boy did not say anything about my head I thought I was going to be alright. The following day, I went to school wearing the scarf, like an old woman, and still nothing happened.

But a few days later, the rumors began:

"Look at her! She's bald!"

There were the usual snickers, ridicule, and harassment. Once on my way home from school, I was surrounded by a group of kids who demanded that I show them my bald head. I refused, of course, and held tightly onto my scarf, tears running down my cheeks. The children of Holocaust survivors were as cruel as children everywhere.

After a few weeks, I could feel stubble through the thin fabric, a reassuring sign, and began weaning myself off the scarf, which I had been wearing day and night up to that time. My hair grew fast, and before long I looked presentable. Varda came by unexpectedly one evening, stared at my short, bristly head, and exclaimed, "Wow, you *do* have hair!" I did have hair, but even in front of her I was still self-conscious and covered up immediately.

"You don't have to wear the scarf anymore," Varda declared.

"Yes, but, my hair is still so short," I mumbled. That was the beginning of the end of my bald period. My hair grew back, and my classmates lost interest in me.

Years later, I was surprised to hear my father say, "That barber was a complete idiot. There was no reason to shave her hair."

And my mother responded, "Yes, Yosef, you are right."

"I'd wring his head if I got a hold of him now," my father continued, and I believed him. It was all the barber's fault.

At a tour of the National Museum of Natural History in Washington, D.C., I saw suction cups displayed as relics of unscientific medical practices. I immediately thought I was back in Abu-Kabir, lying on my bed, flushed with high fever and surrounded by many neighbors in despair. Someone was applying the damned hot cups to my back while someone else was holding me down. My mother was crying and my father fuming with anger at my resistance.

For a stomach ache or constipation, or maybe even for a headache, the cure at home was an enema, a procedure for which I needed to be held down disgracefully, screaming, "Stop! Stop! I'm going to make *caca*! Stop!" to no avail. My brother was not spared that treatment either.

If I had a cold, I was not allowed cold water, the theory being that cold begets colds. For the same reason, I was not allowed to walk barefoot in winter. Rhinitis and various allergies plagued me my whole childhood, and although my parents sought medical treatment, I was the author of my own misery, according to my father, who knew *everything*. Sweets were blamed for causing catarrh, and for an itchy anus and the small white worms squiggling in my stool from time to time.

My parents did not believe in accidents or divine intervention. When I lost a pen, *I* was at fault, and only a spanking with my father's belt would teach me not lose anything again. Needless to say, I kept losing things all the time. Most nights before going to sleep I would take inventory of my stuff: count my books, check my school bag, go through my clothes, straighten out my shoes. There was no sleep unless I knew that all my belongings were intact. Then I would listen to my brother's regular breathing to make sure I didn't lose him either.

Food was another bone of contention. I hated my mother's cooking, and for good reason: Aside from the traditional Jewish foods, she had no cooking skills at all. Most evenings we ate bland soup. I would struggle with my bowl of barley or chicken or noodle or whatever soup she had cooked until the fat would congeal on top and she would then reheat it, place the bowl in front of me again, and expect me to consume the gray, unappetizing contents. Often I would throw morsels of food to the stray cats that slunk under the table, waiting for such an offering; but if my father caught me doing that, he would throw a fit.

There was no democracy in our household: You went to sleep when you were told, you wore what they gave you, and you ate what was on your plate and kept your mouth shut.

Clean clothes and a clean body were important values to both my mother and father, and I could get into big trouble violating them. At the same time, we lived with huge water bugs, crawling lizards, and overflowing sewers. I recall that there was a period of weeks when I went to sleep nightly unable to ignore the funky smell that rose up from the bottom of my bed. I thought it had something to do with the pillow and tolerated it as long as I could before telling my mother. When she looked under the bed, she found dead mice, and, as always, her response was to shriek, cry, and wring her hands. I ran after her down the street and across to the other one, where my uncle and cousins lived. When she spotted my father, she shrieked as if there was a death in the family, which of course there was: We had dead mice under my bed!

I DREAMED OF LIVING in a new house like those of many of the kids I knew, but our family remained in Abu-Kabir, in the dirty, squalid two-room house that the Arabs had abandoned prior to the Israeli government dumping us and some other penniless refugees in that place, where they didn't even bother to change the Arabic name Abu-Kabir, "Great Father," to Hebrew. The back room, where my brother and I, and sometimes my grandmother, slept, had an iron-barred window overlooking the neighbors' backyard. We had a wooden armoire, my mother's one prized possession, where all our clothes were stored, always smelling of mothballs. The front room, where my parents slept on the convertible couch, also contained our dining table and, much later, a radio console.

Over the couch hung a painting of foamy sea waves crashing on white sand. I could get lost in that picture for hours, riding the waves as if I were as weightless as a papier-mâché sailboat, basking in a primordial, life-filled ocean, not yet ready to come ashore. I never wondered how they had come upon that painting; it had always been there, like the small, depressing window on the western wall of the room just below the ceiling.

The kitchen and the bathroom were additions later built by my father, as were the ceramic tiles in that room. Before the tiles there had been just earth, where I could plant anemones or build sand castles—my own living room sandbox. All the walls were dirty and filled with graffiti produced by my brother and me. Oddly, my parents did not seem to mind the wall art; if anything, they found it amusing.

I WAS SIX YEARS old and we were going to visit my parents' friends, when my mother decided that I would look cute in a French beret. I did not want to wear it, and sitting on the bus with that silly thing on my head made me self-conscious, certain that everyone, all the tired and grumpy commuters, were staring at me and thinking, *She looks ridiculous.* I was not allowed to take the beret off that entire evening.

On another occasion, when I was still in kindergarten, my mother dressed me in a pretty, white, frilly dress and told me to play outside while the rest of the family was getting ready. I climbed down the stairs and played in the tall grass in front of our house. I pretended to be a farmer; the grass was wheat, and I was clearing the land for harvest. Suddenly there was a scream. "Yosef! Look at her! She got the dress all dirty!" Sure enough, green stains I had not noticed marred my formerly clean dress. I was dragged up the stairs and whipped with my father's belt while he held me in his lap.

"You won't be able to sit for a week," my father assured me, "and that's how you'll remember to keep your clothes clean!"

In hindsight it occurred to me that my screams must have been heard all the way down the street, but our neighbors, Holocaust survivors all, were people who had learned to mind their own business. We knew everyone, and everyone knew us. Our neighbors and we were more like a bunch of misfits attempting to live together in dilapidated Arabic houses, still in shock from the events that had brought us from all corners of the world to that hot, muddy mess.

Sonia Ostrovsky was raving mad. Every now and then she would have an episode of maniacal behavior, and her husband would call the men in white, literally, to take her away as we all stood in a circle and watched the show.

But it was a childless couple down the street that intrigued everyone the most: She had a beard, and he looked feminine, everything about him round and smooth. It was rumored that the Germans had experimented on them, but we children laughed at them behind their backs anyway.

Hanka was one of my father's girlfriends, as was Varda's mother, who had a number tattooed on her forearm. It was a confused, disordered, motley crew of European survivors who had only recently looked at death and the Devil directly in the face but now, in the land of Israel, complained about the heat, the government, the roaches, the sewage, the whores, the poor wages, the daughter-in-law, the Iraqi Jews, the unruly kids, the stupid schools, the cheating spouse, the dead mice.

WE ARRIVED IN THE United States in June 1961. I was wearing a two-piece ecru damask outfit consisting of a short-sleeved embroidered top and a very full, below-the-knees skirt, also embroidered in some kind of Gypsy or Israeli folk design. It was one of the most expensive outfits that had ever been purchased for me, and I hated it from the get-go. In photographs on the *S.S. Atlantic*, I look extremely ethnic, squinting in the bright sunshine, a flat-chested girl with thick dark hair, thin arms, and a faint mustache—a true fashion misfit among the throngs of confused humanity ready to start life anew. Standing on the ship's deck, waiting in long lines for what seemed forever that last day of our two-week ocean voyage, my younger brother Shlomo stared awestruck at the fast-moving traffic on the West Side Highway, as if we were two transplanted creatures from a foreign world, far away from home, not knowing where we were going, not knowing why. My parents, dressed in their finery, hustled us through the immense bureaucracy at customs. Once off the ship, my mother took stock of us and pronounced, "Wait till Ed sees us. The four ugly ducklings."

New York City welcomed us that breezy, sunny June day, as it had many other immigrants, promising everything imaginable but offering nothing for free. Uncle Ed, my father's brother, who had sponsored our whole journey, was waiting for us in the crowd, a thin, short, mustachioed man who had the demeanor of a person in charge, someone with everything under control. Quickly, impatiently, he spirited us out, bags and all, to his parked car, and off we went to Newark, listening to the adults jabbering away in Polish.

Newark was not *New York*, I quickly learned. It seemed that I had confused the names. I had thought we were going to live in New York, but alas, we were not. That was my first American disappointment: *Newark*, not *New York*. We crossed the Lincoln Tunnel, and for the life of me I couldn't imagine how we could be under water, although that's what my uncle told us. Soon we were in a gritty neighborhood looking at the industrial constructions, red brick factories, empty streets, run-down buildings. Eventually we came to a residential area replete with green lawns and gingerbread houses. "Look," my brother shouted, "these houses are just like the ones in cartoons!"

My reaction to Newark was diametrically opposite to that feeling of euphoria that had seized me upon walking the cobblestone streets of Manhattan: I felt dismay, and thought melodramatically—and it was a day for drama—*This ugly place will surely suffocate me!*

We moved in with the family, and I was assigned to share a room with my cousin Barbie. My aunt Nina, a kindergarten teacher and the type of woman who seemed to love motherhood, didn't take long to notice that I needed my legs and underarms shaved. It shocked me to realize that it could have been so simple: I could have been normal if my mother had been as capable and smart as Aunt Nina. But Aunt Nina was American, more or less, exuding confidence and sophistication—to my mind, at least—and she knew things that my own mother couldn't even imagine. To my mother I was pretty enough, and that was that.

IN 1962 THERE WERE very few foreign kids attending high school in that area, and so I was a mild curiosity at first; however, the novelty wore off fast. Because I spoke broken English and was by nature very shy, I receded into the background, just another face in a collage of strangers. I hated meeting all those new kids, as I was ashamed of having an accent and having to explain, from the second I opened my mouth, that I was new. . .from Israel. . .yes, Tel Aviv. . .been in the U.S. only a few weeks. . .liked being here very much. In truth, I really *didn't* like being there. My first impression of Newark stayed with me forever. I would never find a way out of those tree-lined, tony streets; I would never be welcome in the pretty gingerbread houses; I would remain an anomaly, sprung out of a distant country whose right to exist was suspect in the first place.

I would never fit in—sitting home, watching The *Ed Sullivan Show* and munching hard candy, or bowling, or eating tons of spaghetti and meatballs in restaurants, or going to backyard parties and talking about clothes. That's what we did that first summer at my uncle and aunt's house. I had little in common with my cousin Barbie and her friends, who had no idea what to make of me; I might as well have been an ancient hominid from Ethiopia, trying to blend in with the bobby-sox crowd doing the Twist.

"Get on the scale, Bracha; let's see how much you weigh." That request from Barbie and her pals seemed more like a taunt reeking of envy then the poorly expressed compliment it meant to convey.

"Wow, only 110 pounds. Boy, are you lucky!"

Lucky? I was stumped. What did my weight have to do with *luck?* I, who had never owned a scale, who had been tortured to eat when sated, forced to drink hot tea when I thirsted for iced water, who had never heard any of my Israeli friends speak of their weight one way or another, could not accept kudos for something over which I had no control or concern.

When my aunt refused a piece of cake, saying, "Oh, no, I am on a diet!" I could not connect the self-deprivation to anything rational.

That first American summer I was sent to adult English classes, where my classmates were from exotic places like Brazil, Shanghai, or Puerto Rico and were older than I. I wore second-hand clothes that my aunt had collected from friends and neighbors, learned to apply lipstick, and memorized the lyrics of diverse popular songs like "Crazy," "Moon River," and "Run Around Sue," intrigued by their unique love stories and the combination of melody, voice, and instruments that had the power to induce either total pleasure or two minutes of irritation.

In September, armed with more clothes than I ever had in my life but still speaking in halting broken English, I was sent off to my sophomore year in an all-American high school. As soon as I opened my mouth, someone would say, "Where you from?" and would look crestfallen when I answered, "From Israel." I thought they were disappointed in me for being Jewish. In due time, I began telling people I was from Austria. Since I was born in that country, it didn't feel too much of a lie, even though I had no emotional, linguistic, ethnic, or cultural connection with Austria or the rest of Europe. The high school kids often thought I was talking about Australia, and we left it at that, though I could not possibly imagine an Israeli first-grader not knowing the difference between the continent and the country.

In Israel I had read *The World of Suzie Wong* in Hebrew. When I saw the English version in the library, I pounced on it with excitement. Despite my poor vocabulary, I knew I could read the book because I had remembered every detail of the Hebrew text and thought it would be a fun way of improving my English. And it did. "What does the word 'sex' mean?" I asked Barbie.

"How can you read *Suzie Wong* and not know the meaning of sex," she giggled, and, as always, looked at me as if I were a complete moron.

The book not only improved my English but also gave me my new first name: Suzie—not because I had identified with the heroine, but because it was not *Bracha*, a name that in school forced others into numerous pronunciation hurdles, embarrassing tongue twisters, and puzzled expressions, leaving me feeling oddly guilty and ashamed.

My parents were sickened by my apparent rejection of a blessing they had bestowed upon me at birth, but everyone else never questioned me re-naming myself at age fifteen. I signed my homework with my new name, and my teachers began calling me Suzie immediately, as if they were relieved to never again have to mispronounce "Bracha." Eventually, Suzie became my legal name, and I had to live with that decision, always regretting not calling myself something more befitting my childhood identity, something like Barbara, Brenda, Bella, or even Barbie. Nevertheless, eventually I translated my last name from Holtz to Woods, and wore my new identity, Suzie Woods, like a coat of arms defending my background, showing off my good stock.

IN HINDSIGHT, IT SEEMED that I adapted to the new culture in no time, albeit not to the best the culture had to offer. Overnight, from a shy and aloof girl in mismatched outfits, I became one of those who were caught smoking in the bathroom or reading romance magazines in class. I made friends here and there. I started shaving my whole arms. It felt good sitting at the coffee shop where everyone hung out, flicking cigarette ashes into an ashtray with a long, extended, hairless arm. It was as if I were showing off to everyone, "Look at my arm. It's normal and hairless," as if I were convinced—and to an extent I was—that everyone was looking at my arms just to check out the hairiness level.

I would spend hours in the bathroom, shaving with my father's razor, and would end up with so many nicks and cuts that sometimes I looked as if I had walked through a glass door. With single-edged razors, it was quite a trick to get a smooth shave without a cut, particularly a cut on the shin, which could take off layers of skin, bleed as if a major artery had been cut, and leave a scar for weeks. And of course the stubble resurfaced immediately.

My arms and legs may have looked smooth but, close up, did not feel that way. It became second nature to recoil from another's touch lest they feel my shaven arms and guess my secret. My skin was off limits just as my underarms had been in the past. It also seemed so unnatural to me that others would allow themselves to be touched, and it made me jealous. The notion that my body would be repulsive to others was certainly in my mind, the same way that any distasteful flaw in another person could repel me. I would avert my eyes from a pim- pled face or grotesque features. I had to stay away from people like me and go to great lengths to lie to others and myself about my ap- pearance.

Hairiness took on a persona of its own: It was obscene, ape-like, primitive, reeking of testosterone and locker room perspiration. It was a thing that needed to be excised and destroyed. I required an arsenal of hair-fighting ammunition for that war of vanity and femininity against tough, male forces.

Bleaching and shaving could take up to two hours in the family bathroom. Bleaching my arms and face with Joleen Bleach Crème re- quired first mixing the cream with the powder and then applying the mixture with a small spatula. After much trial and error, I learned to leave on this noxious concoction for thirty minutes. During the first ten, the cream burned fiercely. I had to distract myself by jumping up and down, stretching, dancing, whatever. I used the little spatula to rub and re-rub the stuff over all the surface area until the itching that felt as if mosquitoes were feasting on my skin ceased.

After fifteen minutes or so, the procedure became tolerable but boring. The layer of the white mixture would dry up and flake off, and all I had to do then was to wait another fifteen minutes, seated on the toilet, until I could rinse all that mess off with warm water and soap. My skin would be red and blotchy for at least an hour afterwards, and the smell of bleach would bring tears to my eyes. Shaving my legs afterwards, I would lift each leg into the sink and work my father's razor against the growth of hair.

After a while my mother, father, or brother would start screaming at me to get out of the bathroom, and so, after all that work, I wouldn't get a chance to bathe the rest of my body properly. I would not feel fresh or tingly, but, blessedly, I looked almost normal—for a brief moment, it seemed. At any rate, I felt normal enough to face the American kids I would have to face in school day after day.

WE WERE SITTING IN the bleachers of the school gym for driver education class. The teacher was late, and everyone was chatting, laughing, hollering. I got out of my seat to go to the bathroom, and when I returned everyone held their noses. I sat down without looking left or right. A girl in a long ponytail spoke up in a high voice: "Someone give her a bar of soap, please!"

"Make it Dial," a guy chimed in, and everyone laughed, slapped their thighs, and practically rolled on the floor in hysterics until the teacher walked in and threatened them with detention.

I remained seated and said nothing. There was nothing to say. I never returned to that class, although the same kids were everywhere. I didn't get my driver's license either—not until many years later.

Before long, I was shaving my hands as well. Standing at the sink in the girls' bathroom, I noticed that they seemed to have grown hair almost overnight. Not only were they hairy, but each finger, below and above the knuckle, had sprouted hair as well. I looked around at the other girls for confirmation that what I was seeing was common, although I knew it was not, but *their* hands were smooth.

In those days, my junior year in high school, I spent much time smoking in the bathroom, getting caught, going to detention, and basically being a pain in the neck to the teachers. The other smokers and

I didn't become friends, but we passed the cigarettes around, sharing tokes the way we would eventually smoke pot. Many of the girls were black, a novelty to me who had not known black people in Israel. I was particularly curious about their hair texture. Was it soft? Hard? I couldn't tell, but there were none with hairy hands. That was a fact.

2

CUSHIM

ONE LATE-NOVEMBER EVENING, my friend Ann and I were hanging around the local pizzeria smoking Winstons, drinking Coke, repeatedly throwing dimes into the jukebox, and swaying to our favorite song:

> *Sittin' here la la, waitin' on my ya ya*
> *Uh-huh, alright*
> *Sittin' here la la, waitin' on my ya ya*
> *Uh-huh, she's outta sight*
> *May sound funny, but I don't believe she's comin'*
> *Uh-huh, uh-huh*

We started up a conversation with a tall, good-looking boy with teasing brown eyes.

"So you girls hang out here all the time?" he asked, looking at me. "You must really like pizza."

I confessed that I'd never had pizza in my life, and he cracked up laughing. He had a nice laugh, and a sexy voice.

"I'm gonna get us a pie," he said, and walked to the front to order.

"I think he's colored," Ann whispered as soon as his back was turned.

"*Colored?*" I was confused. "But he's so good looking."

"Well, he's mostly white, I guess—but there's something colored about him. Maybe he's a mulatto. Believe you me—you *don't* want to date a Negro!"

Ann was a very plain girl, almost homely. She had long brown stringy hair, bad acne, sad brown eyes, a crooked nose, thin lips, and protruding teeth. There was no feature in her whole presentation that could be complimented; in addition, she gave the impression that she carried her shapelessness with difficulty, as if it were a burden that needed to be hauled like a sack of trash.

"I don't know why anybody would go out with Negroes," I volunteered. "Seems to me white boys are better looking, although this one here is good-looking too."

Frankly, I thought she was jealous that the boy, Bobby, was making eyes at me.

Ann was not the first person in America to try to warn, educate, protect, advise, and inform me about colored people and their way of life. During dinner, in those early summer weeks of my attempting to adapt to and make sense of my new world, Uncle Ed explained that we must refer to Negroes as 'colored,' particularly in front of them. It was a strange notion: 'colored' to me meant *colorful*, and Negroes were not more colorful than whites.

"They are not like us," he declared officiously. "A Negro would rather eat nothing but peanut butter and jelly every day in order to afford a fancy Cadillac. They are dangerous people who would not think twice about stabbing you for a dollar."

He had our rapt attention. My parents looked worried, my brother puzzled; after all, that was not what they had taught us in Israel.

Turning his attention to me, Uncle Ed proceeded with his lesson. "Negroes smoke marijuana, cigarettes that make a person act drunk and crazy. And they will try to get you to smoke marijuana too, so that you get hooked and give them all your money—or worse. You and Shlomo stay away from the projects where they live. Don't go to the First Ward. Stay only in the Weequahic neighborhood, right here."

In Israel we had read *Uncle Tom's Cabin* as well as other classics, and learned about slavery and racism in America. My sensibilities had bristled at such injustice and cruelty. I'd always rooted for the underdog. I remembered reading somewhere in the Torah that even God referred to Moses' Midian wife Tsiporah as homely because she was a Cushite from the land of Cush.

Negroes in Hebrew were *Cushim*, a word that suddenly was thrown around by my parents quite often, although colored people had barely existed in our world, and my parents didn't know any *Cushim* up close. On the other hand, my brother and I made it a point to explore the dangerous parts of Newark where the Negroes lived. We liked buying junk on the streets whenever we had some change, and we were drawn to the music and laughter that emanated from the open windows.

After working with Uncle Ed for a couple of months in his downtown Newark liquor store and sweating bullets whenever a Negro entered the store, which was often, my father quit. He landed a job in his chosen profession, plumbing, at a small company that paid him cash under the table, as he was yet unlicensed.

Around Christmas time, only a few months after our arrival and a couple of weeks after quitting his job at the liquor store, he lost his wallet and a whole week's salary. When he came home, he looked ashen, like a person who had just been given a fatal medical diagnosis. He told my mother, of course, and she reacted in her typical manner—with tears, cries, and recriminations. Gloom descended upon our household, then escalated into the inevitable back-and-forth yelling, accusations, name calling: *varydka, kurva, shmuck, dupa*—ugly words traded back and forth between enemies airing their impotence, allowing their rage to explode unmodulated, unguarded, until their venom was spent and they felt relieved. Shlomo and I, unwilling witnesses, said nothing of course, but my brother's face mirrored my own growing panic. I wished that the ground would open up and swallow us whole.

But the story had a happy ending. The next day my father came home beaming: A Negro had found the wallet, contacted my father, and returned it with its contents intact. "I can't believe that he returned my wallet with every penny in it, especially since they looked so poor and could have used the money for Christmas," my father repeated at least a hundred times. He went on, "They live in this dilapidated building, and all those kids there looked skinny and hungry. I just can't believe it! I gave the kids a dollar each, and they were grateful."

"You know, Yosef, there *are* a few honest Negroes out there," my mother offered. "It was a miracle from God. God heard us. God took mercy on us."

But in the next breath, she added, "But, Yosef, you went out there to the projects! Thank God you weren't killed! Thank God they didn't attack you!"

"Well," my father explained, "I was scared. But what could I do? You should have seen the people, the streets, and the garbage. They live worse than animals."

IN MY HIGH SCHOOL it did not take long to notice that the colored kids hung out separately, and that tension between them and the white groups was palpable even to a stranger like me, who belonged to no group. But Ann, as my best friend, felt it her duty to clue me on facts about Negroes: They were malodorous, greasy, stupid, loud, and superstitious. In church they spoke gibberish, sang their African spirituals at the top of their lungs, so the whole street could hear, fainted, carried on, and got drunk. They had no morals and hated white people. The men loved white girls, and since their sexual appetites and organs were enormous, they were known to rape girls when given the chance. Only white tramps and white trash would go out with one. And, even if a Negro looked white like the boy in the pizzeria, he was *still* a Negro because he had Negro blood in him.

I did run into Bobby again, and I did willingly go into his apartment and, with his brothers present, drank Coca-Cola and listened to Chubby Checker, Johnny Mathis, and the Miracles on the hi-fi. No one attempted to rape me or take advantage of me in any way. When I left, we kissed on the lips and I gave him my phone number. He called the next day, and I grabbed the phone on the first ring, before Shlomo or my mother could get to it. I was not supposed to receive phone calls from boys. We chatted a little bit and then he said, "I just want you to know that I am Caucasian."

"You are *what?*" I exclaimed, the sound of the word 'Caucasian' striking me as strange and ugly.

"It means *white*. Don't you know that?" he asked.

"No. I know what 'white' means, but I never heard the word used that way before."

But I was in America, and I was learning.

THE BATTLES WITH MY parents were not only becoming more frequent, more urgent, those first few months after our arrival and during my sophomore year in high school, but had also taken a new direction: I, the obedient, bashful child, was quickly morphing into a sullen, angry, rebellious adolescent in this foreign land, where danger lurked behind every bush, where the reverse migration from the Holy Land to the Diaspora had wrought hitherto unimagined consequences.

To begin with, there was the whole business with the *shiksas* and *shkutzim*. As a girl, being friends with *shiksas* was not so bad, but then again, the friendship had to be closely monitored. It was understood that I was not allowed to date anyone not Jewish, now that they had uprooted me from Israel and brought me to this continent where *goyim* were a constant hazard.

In Israel, although I was not yet dating, my parents threatened that they would disown me if I dated an Iraqi, Syrian, Yemenite, or otherwise dark, Sephardic Jew. "They are all bandits," my mother had warned me more than once. But coming to America, things fell into perspective: A Jew was a Jew, after all.

But a *sheigitz* was an entirely different danger. It seemed to me that, in all the years that the move to America was being planned and arranged and anticipated, no one remembered that there would be *goyim* in the *Galut*. In their eagerness to get the hell out of the hellhole that was Abu-Kabir, they had overlooked a most obvious and grievous abomination—the possibility that their daughter would marry a *sheigitz*—and having committed that error, they took it upon themselves to watch over me night and day lest the worst happen and they would have only themselves to blame.

"If a boy asks me to go to the movies, what am I supposed to do, ask him if he's Jewish first?" I argued.

"No. You can tell by looking at him," my father insisted.

"Not *I. I* can't! I didn't grow up in Poland like you, and I can't tell the difference."

"Well, you better learn," my father retorted impatiently. "If you bring a *sheigitz* home and if you go out with one, I will personally beat you to death!"

I believed him, but it was true that, as a child, the notion that one could tell Jew and Gentile apart had mystified me. My mother told me that, before the War, when she was a girl on the way to her school, Polish children had chased her, beaten her, and called her "Sarah," an anti-Semitic slur back then.

I soon began to understand the differences between Jew and Gentile. I started noticing different speech rhythms, different facial expressions, and different traits. The tall blond, blue-eyed hunk that played on the football team and dated the most popular girls was not Jewish, but the dark, skinny boy with glasses who was headed to Harvard probably *was*.

MY PROBLEM WITH HIRSUTENESS, I concluded, could be attributed to my race—to a single gene that had mutated and propagated itself through thousands of generations of Jews, then found all the right factors and the ideal circumstances to manifest itself, grow, and prosper, at my expense. To be sure, there were probably female ancestors who not only carried that hairy gene but exhibited it as well; yet all my female relatives, the living ones whom I knew and the dead ones whose pictures I studied, looked smooth and feminine. Yes, everyone had silky skin; everyone had a feminine face—not one female with a *mustache* in the whole lot! I was on my own with *that* one.

But I held out hope. I reasoned that, in America, I should be able to find *someone* or some way to destroy the superfluous hair and restore the smooth, soft skin that should have been my birthright. It didn't seem like a long shot; after all, the whole world knew that doctors had done so much for humanity— invented antibiotics, vaccinated against virulent infections, removed cancerous growths, developed aspirin for headaches, destroyed the mosquitoes that carried malaria, fed children vitamins, and eliminated beriberi, scurvy, and all types of depressing diseases. I wasn't asking for too much.

I looked at every woman's face for comparison, hoping to find others in my predicament who would affirm that I was not too strange. Miss O'Brien, my English teacher, had smooth skin, with not a single wayward hair on her face. My civics teacher wore her blonde hair in a bun, and I could see she didn't have sideburns. I would scrutinize girls my age, and although I might rarely spot a slight mustache on someone, the hairiness level did not match mine by a long shot. Always keeping my problem in mind, I wore my hair long and loose so that it practically hid my face.

Eventually, I came across an article about electrolysis. I learned that electrolysis was a tedious, invasive, and painful process that involved inserting a needle into each individual hair follicle and delivering an electrical charge to each. I also understood that the procedure often required months of treatments at regular intervals, and that it could cost a fortune; but *whatever* the cost, I *had* to give it a try. There were hair depilatory products on the drugstore shelves, but those products seemed to coexist among personal hygiene items, among the displays of vaginal itching creams, dandruff shampoos, and Dr. Scholl's foot odor-eliminating powders. Hirsuteness or its treatment was not exactly a taboo subject; it was just under the radar, as unappetizing as fungal toenail disease or chronic hemorrhoids.

Usually I saved my milk money for cigarettes. I didn't get an allowance, and begging my father for money required ingenuity, patience, and perseverance. But somehow I managed to save up ten dollars and made an appointment with Merle, the electrologist.

I was nervous walking up the stairs to her office. It was a depressing building on West Market Street, which was fairly deserted at that time of evening, the office workers having long gone home. The elevator to the fourth floor creaked and grumbled as if it had a mind of its own, protesting having to work so late.

Six o'clock in the evening in Newark seemed like midnight in Israel; the short winter days were a challenge, not to mention the cold. But once I entered her suite, it was as if I had stumbled upon an oasis in the barren desert. The reception area teemed with exotic plants and flowers, and fish tanks housed placid, colorful fish and an ancient turtle. There were plaster statues, including a huge one of the Venus de Milo; interesting photographs, oil paintings, and posters took up all the wall space.

Merle emerged from the treatment area and welcomed me with a hug. She seemed an extension of her surroundings, a gypsy with a magic wand. Her hair was bleached platinum blonde, her face made up like a movie star's. She could have been thirty or sixty; I couldn't tell. She wore dangling earrings, jingling bracelets, and a long, flowing, romantic-type dress that did not reveal much but didn't hide her large, soft, rotund body. Her voice was mellifluous and high-pitched.

"Come in, honey," she said, and I followed her to the treatment area, another Garden of Eden, but with a chair like the one found in a dentist's office, except that, instead of a sink standing next to it, there was an apparatus with some dials and an electric cord—a lifeline, I hoped, to the world of feminine beauty.

She understood my problem despite appearing hairless herself—certainly not a candidate for her own treatment—and unlike someone who would choose to become an electrologist. I wondered how she had chosen that field; I thought that I could never do that for a living, as it would be admitting to everyone that I myself had a problem with hirsuteness. *Perhaps she has a hairy sister*, I mused.

In any case, she was receptive and easy to talk to, and so I felt a weight lift off me as I described my misfortune without shame or inhibition. I wanted a smooth face, without sideburns, mustache, or chin and neck hair. In an unhurried manner and in her mellifluous voice, she explained the procedure, almost easing me into a serene trance: She would remove each hair and its follicle by introducing a minute amount of current that would render the follicle dead. I would feel only a tiny shock, more like a pinch, and then she would tweeze away the dead hair. It seemed like a daunting task, but, if necessary, I was ready to suffer the pains of hell!

THERE I SAT VOLUNTARILY, subjecting myself to a needle that would prick me not once or twice but repeatedly over the course of a twenty-minute treatment. My history with needles was not reassuring: When I was about eleven years old, I'd had blood drawn for the first time and promptly passed out! While other kids in elementary school huddled together in front of the nurse's office waiting their turn for a vaccine shot, laughing and goofing around, happy to be out of the classroom, I had sat alone, scared and crying.

When we had been in the States only a few weeks, my aunt Nina took me for a glucose tolerance test, since I was spilling sugar in my urine and they wanted to rule out juvenile diabetes. As is often the case, this had been discovered during a routine medical clearance test performed by a doctor in Tel Aviv just prior to our emigration. I supposed America did not want lepers, Typhoid Marys, or otherwise medically undesirable immigrants entering its borders. My mother and I were examined at the same time, both of us naked but for our panties, and after the routine palpations, auscultations, and medical procedures, the elderly doctor suddenly lowered my panties and, for a brief moment, placed his hand on my hairy pubis. Then he did the same to my mother. It felt wrong, to be sure, but not as heart-stopping as the smallpox vaccination he performed afterward. Being completely unprepared for injections, I thought I would faint.

"Ha ha ha," my mother had laughed once we were out of the building. "What was *that* all about? Did he check to make sure that we have a *shmondo*?"

I don't know why Aunt Nina ended up taking me for the glucose tolerance test that the Israeli pervert had recommended, but I would guess that my mother, new in America and non-English speaking, was not up to the task. After being cajoled into drinking a horribly sweet concoction, I had to have blood drawn at intervals from both arms. My mind couldn't even wrap around the notion that such physical torture was about to be imposed on me.

"I didn't know you would do that," I sobbed, looking at the doctor as if he were a medieval sadist.

"Well, if we were to tell patients *that*, no one would show up, would they now?" reasoned the doctor in an understanding, empathetic voice. I survived the test, not giving a damn about diabetes, which I didn't have anyway.

Shortly after that ordeal, I had my first dental visit in America. Without warning or explanation, the dentist bent over me, aimed a huge needle right towards my open mouth, and, to my disbelief, plunged it right into my gums. I had never seen or heard of Novocain in Israel; whatever needed to be done was done without it, at least in my experience. Immediately I felt a wave of nausea and the sensation of losing control, losing consciousness, going under, as if life were draining away and nothing I could do would stop it. I fell into a black hole full of confusing, hurried activity and commotion that I couldn't decipher. Then, in what seemed hours but was only minutes or seconds, I was awake in the dentist's chair, trying to hold onto the dream, the strange images, if only to know what they were, but they were too obscure, too quick, fleeing away in a cacophony of colors, refusing to reveal their secrets.

I saw the worried face of the doctor and the pale face of my mother hovering above me. "She had a seizure," the dentist declared, and ordered an EEG and a bunch of other neurological tests. The EEG didn't hurt and nothing unusual was revealed; however, it had been very expensive.

"All that money for nothing," I heard my mother complain to my father, who was quick to agree: "The dentist was an idiot! *What* seizure? She *never* had seizures. She probably just fainted. She has a poor constitution, as you know."

"That's right," my mother agreed. "He probably just wanted to give his friends some business. You know all these doctors are all whores."

And there I was, reclining in Merle's chair, willingly surrendering without a qualm or doubt, as she was about to poke a needle into my face repeatedly! I was prepared to endure *anything* to look halfway normal. I felt a quick electrical impulse, just as she had described, and then she was tweezing out a bunch of sideburn hairs. After about twenty minutes she turned off her machine, wiped the area with witch hazel, and then handed me a mirror. My face was red but practically hairless. It was miraculous!

But—and there *was* a "but"—it all grew back before my next appointment two weeks later. When I questioned her about this, she sweetly explained the hair-growth cycle; in fact, she pointed to a large poster that described the stages of hair growth, depicted in colorful pictures and diagrams, and, like a teacher or mentor, admonished me to be patient. I had no choice; I would be patient with Merle and all the Merles who came after her for many decades—basically for my whole life.

DESPITE MY PRECOCIOUSNESS IN the hair department, I didn't get my period until I was almost fifteen. When I saw blood in my panties, I felt revulsion, and, not knowing what to do, I put on a second pair. My mother and a neighbor were out for an evening walk, and I decided to find them and tag along. It was necessary to inform her, although I didn't relish the idea, but I reluctantly whispered the news in her ear. She looked happy as she cheerfully explained, "You don't need two panties; I'll get you a rag when we get home."

"Please don't tell Father," I begged, remembering the first time I had tried on a bra and he had shouted from the other room, "Let me see it." The thought of the two of them discussing my period—of him even *thinking* about me so intimately—filled me with antipathy.

Later that evening, my father looked at me proudly and said, "So you are a woman now." Mortified, I directed a hateful look at my mother as I ran out of the room in tears, then buried my face in a book.

"Oh, I didn't tell him *anything*," my mother innocently insisted.

"He must have guessed," I countered.

TELLING MY MOTHER ABOUT my business with Merle was out of the question. Only once during that time did I remark to her, "Gee, I have a moustache," to which she replied, "What are you *talking* about? You *don't!*"

My father and mother never saw eye to eye about anything; yet, when it came to *me*, they seemed to be of one mind. An endless theme, the backdrop to my childhood, was their adult relationship—specifically, my mother's bitter recriminations and accusations concerning his infidelities and general meanness. *Kurva* (the Polish word for 'whore' I have already mentioned) was one of the first words I ever knew. Shouting matches, and bitter scenes between them, were not only routine but capable of taking place anywhere and at any time, without prior warning.

"The soup is too salty!" my father would declare upon tasting Friday's *Shabbat* boiled chicken soup.

"Not true. I didn't put but a smidgen of salt in it."

And they were off.

From over-salted soup, we would end up with salty tears on the oil-clothed table and angel food cake crumbs under our feet. Even the alley cats that were lured to our house by the cooking smells would rather have fled such a scene then hang around for a morsel of food. A fight could last late into the night, resume in the morning, and continue for days on end. Often it resulted in long periods of silence. My brother and I would be hired to relay messages, such as, "Tell him there is no money for ice or bread. He needs to leave me some money," or "Tell her to go to hell!"

Shlomo and I, despite all our experience, feared those fights, always anticipating some terrible ending. Huddled in a corner weeping, holding Shlomo's trembling body tightly against mine, I prayed for the night to be over, for silence, for Godly intervention. I would attempt to block out the noise by focusing on a lizard crawling upside-down on the ceiling, following its path, amazed that such a small creature could soldier on as it looked at the world topsy-turvy.

"If it weren't for *them*, I would leave you right *now!*" My mother would often scream out this trump card, pointing at us, her face smeared with tears and snot. And I *hated* her. Sometimes I prayed to God that she would *really* leave, that they would get divorced. But most of the time I felt pity for her, pity for me, pity for Shlomo—and anger and love for my father.

WHEN I WAS TWELVE, my father left Israel to visit his brother in England. At the same time, my school sent me for two weeks to a farm for undernourished children. I was terribly homesick throughout the two weeks and didn't gain an ounce, despite the sugary oatmeal breakfasts, tons of dairy, and lack of activity. But when I got home, a different sort of anguish—call it "homesickness"—began in earnest. My father was supposed to be back from England, but there had been no word from him. The whole neighborhood was in an uproar, juicy rumors brewing, kids laughing behind my back, old ladies saying knowingly, "He broke a glass over there!"

"What does it mean that he broke a glass over there?" I innocently asked my mother, only to receive a fresh burst of tears for an answer.

My grandmother explained, "They mean that he got married over there." My grandmother, always one to relish a good piece of gossip herself, would say to the neighbors, pointing at her palms, "Hair will grow *here* before he returns!"

My mother's weeping, and my own fears and longing, continued for two agonizing months, until he suddenly showed up bearing gifts like Santa Claus, smelling of cologne and good English soap. His arrival was heralded by a young boy who ran ahead of him up the street to our house, yelling like the town crier, "Your father is back! Your father is back!" We all dropped whatever we were doing and ran down the dusty street and into his outstretched arms. He was back, and all was forgiven! There were no apologies, only tears of joy.

Years later, I would learn from my uncle that my father had indeed considered abandoning all of us and making a new life in London but had had trouble finding a job. It had been my uncle, at the end, who convinced him to return to his wife and children.

MENARCHE WOULD SIGNAL THE beginning of sexual maturation, but I had already produced adult hair growth, albeit that of an adult male. Unfortunately, that was only the beginning of my intimate and sad relationship with superfluous hair.

Everything about me, all my secondary sex characteristics, were female. My dislike of my body was proportional to the outrageous hair growth. At that time, I was mostly concerned with visible hair that I could control by spending an hour or so in the bathroom attending to a new routine: I'd found Jolene, the bleaching product for face and arms. I shaved my legs as well as my upper thighs, and plucked or shaved my hands and fingers. In the dark I looked almost like any other person; there, I was shielded from being who I could not *possibly* accept myself to be: a masculinized female.

But I couldn't stay in the dark all the time, even though hiding could offer a semblance of comfort. It seemed to me then that my response to my physical shortcomings—that is, hiding and pretending—was the only solution. It had never occurred to me that some viable alternative existed somewhere.

Once, at a Howard Johnson's, on a rare occasion that my family took us out to eat, I noticed that our waitress looked young and pretty from a distance, but close up, when she came to take our orders, revealed a shaved face. I looked at her arms; they were obviously also shaved. My heart went out to her; but I could never shave my face and *still* walk around with a five-o'clock shadow. There was no way I could tolerate being the butt of a joke, the punch-line to someone's cruelty. I was a *girl*; I wanted to *look* like a girl. That I was considered pretty probably just added to the problem. Being hairy made me feel, not just masculine, but a primitive facsimile of a human female.

"Why you so hairy?" asked a boy who, when my long sleeves accidentally rode up, got a load of my unshaven arms. There was no answer, except perhaps to blush. Most people, one would imagine, are not that blunt or as direct as that boy, but for all I knew, they would want to ask the same question.

For a girl to be ugly was a bad thing, but to be *hairy* was *obscene*. What man would want a hairy woman? A pervert? A friendless hominid who was so misshapen and deformed as to hardly qualify as *human*? Even a *blind* man would recoil in repulsion upon touching a woman's shaved thighs or hairy nipples. Underlying all my hopes and wishes, ever since I can remember, had been a visceral longing for beauty. Just below the surface of self-awareness existed this Jungian dream, this hunger that was deeper than a hunger for bread or thirst for wine. There is beauty in a cloudless summer day, grace in the shape of a flower; one feels awe at the sight of a crescent moon, reverence at the reflection of a beautiful face. I wanted to dwell in the world of fairy tales; in stories that begin with "Once upon a time, in a far away country, there lived a beautiful princess . . . ." I hadn't been born to seek fortune or fame. I hadn't been born to find a cure for cancer, to have my name lauded in Stockholm; I had been born with an innate and burning desire to be a beautiful woman.

I knew, of course, that I was not unique in my quest for beauty; but I was hampered, not by acne, cellulite, pimples, too large or too small breasts, crooked teeth, or heft; instead, I had been deprived of beauty by a genetic accident, a flaw in the secondary sex characteristics that differentiate male from female. If I was not *totally* female, I was not even in the *running*. I couldn't be a contender. I would have sold my soul to the Devil for smooth skin if only he had made the offer. Had I been rich, I would have traded all my gold for even a *chance* of being smooth-skinned.

AT THE MOVIE THEATER Varda and I used to frequent on Saturdays, I'd pay more attention to the actresses' beauty than to the films' plots; and their beauty was so enticing—and *so* out of reach.

"Look, that's Elizabeth Taylor, the most beautiful woman in the world," Varda pointed out, and I wondered what it would be like to see the world through her eyes––to know that you are that gorgeous sunset, that work of art that everyone loves and admires. When you are beautiful, you are God's creation, you are on the side of the angels who play heavenly melodies; you are otherworldly; you are a goddess! And when you are a goddess, you don't need to be anything else.

Not being beautiful was different from being a freak—the bearded lady in a Coney Island sideshow who frightened children and amused adults. She was the self I had to keep hidden—tucked away with all the other small humiliations and unspeakable cosmetic rituals. She was Rochester's beastly wife locked up in the attic. She was everything evil and feral and dangerous that had to be suppressed at all costs, the ills in Pandora's Box which were to be vigilantly contained under lock and key.

It was up to me to show the world only that acceptable aspect of my physicality, to present to society the unthreatening persona, the sweet and pretty girl with the blue eyes who adored red ribbons, pink lace, ruffles, silk stockings, red lipstick, gold chains, and lovely jewelry encrusted with emeralds, rubies, sapphires, and diamonds. I had to reveal only the acceptable, the natural, the lovely femininity about which poets raved and that great artists depicted on canvas. All the rest—all things hairy, superfluous, itchy, creepy, and unwanted—had to be hidden where they belonged: under woolen covers and thick wraps.

To accomplish that, I had to maintain a level of diligence that kept me on guard at all times. No day or hour passed without my *idée fixe* ruling my emotions, activities, dress, sex life, friendships, self respect— or even interactions with strangers. The requirement to keep my hirsute status in abeyance, under cloaks and in the closet, kept me forever watchful and self-critical.

ANN HAD BEEN MY best friend from the time we met during my junior year in high school, but Pamela was a girl I loved, my first American friend, who taught me to smoke, dance, apply makeup, and even speak English.

I was with her the first time I saw snow.

"Oh, look, it's snowing!" she exclaimed when we walked out of her house and into the dark street lined with barren trees. I saw nothing, until my eyes adjusted to the gloom and then focused on the top of the street lamp: there, like tiny feathers, like pretty white moths attracted to light and frigid air, was snow!

The bitter December cold that very first winter in America took me by complete surprise. Sitting in the classroom and daydreaming, I just could not reconcile in my mind's eye the simultaneous existence of sunny skies and sub-zero temperatures. Winters were supposed to be gray and rainy, summers warm and dry; that's all I knew. When I was about eight years old, I learned that, when it was raining in Abu-Kabir, it was not necessarily raining all over the world, an odd revelation that I found hard to picture. I imagined an invisible wall separating rain and dryness, clouds and sunny skies. It had been hard enough to accept that, when I went to sleep in Abu-Kabir, American kids were getting up and going to school; yet, here I was in that new world, assimilating contradictions, not only in the weather, but in new sights, words, attitudes, food, dress, trees, flowers, as well as the myriad odd behaviors that only a non-native would notice.

I envied Pam's freedom and lack of supervision. Her older brother was away at college, and her parents were rarely home. Moreover, as Americans, they were not burdened by a ton of fears, not looking over their shoulders, not losing sleep over real and imagined catastrophes or all the disasters that my own parents took for granted and antici-pated would occur as surely as old age or the end of the world.

"They trust me," Pam explained.

"But you can stay out late without getting in trouble?"

"Sure. Why not?"

My bedtime was nine-thirty, no exceptions. Sleep was so impor-tant to my father that he even ordered Shlomo and me to our cots as our ship was sailing away from Haifa, when we had wanted to take one last look at the land, at the receding shores of home. Even that mo-mentous event was not as important as a good night's sleep.

Since Pamela did not have a curfew, we would spend most evenings at my house, lolling around on my bed, laughing, holding hands, chat-ting about school, other kids, sex, boys, queers, coloreds, television, popular songs, Harold Robbins novels, drug addicts—in short, typical teenage stuff that, to my thinking, proved that Pam was not only a fount of knowledge but also a model of sophistication and American beauty: tall, thin, blonde, flaunting a long ponytail and flirtatious green eyes.

My parents, particularly my mother, were of course suspicious of this friendship, as they were of *any* friendship I had ever had in my life.

"We don't care that you are friends with a *shiksa*," my mother and father explained in unison, striving to sound reasonable and loving, "but she is a bad influence. You should find other friends."

"Well, I like her, and it's not fair. I have no other friends, and you shouldn't tell me whom I should or should not see."

"We know what's best for you," they insisted. "In this country you have to be very careful, and we don't like her. She wears makeup, and she is slutty. She is not for you."

I knew better than to continue arguing with my parents, although I kept the argument going a while longer. It was easier just to go along with their rules and then sneak around behind their backs than to attempt to use logic. Once their minds were made up—particularly regarding my behavior—there was little chance that they would reconsider or relax whatever edict that was in dispute.

Many years later, I understood their objection to Pam: They viewed our hand-holding, secretiveness, and the affinity we had for each other in a sinister and suspicious light. They feared she was turning me into a lesbian.

Pam and I used to walk to school together. Ordinarily, I would stop by her house, which was only a couple of streets away from our apartment building, ring her bell, and wait for her to come down. A week or two after our friendship was formally broken up by my parents, when I stopped by her house she responded through the intercom that she had the flu and would be staying in.

Later that day, I started feeling sick myself. My throat felt sore, my head throbbed, and I felt dizzy and achy. When I asked permission to see the nurse, I knew without a doubt that this time I wouldn't have to fake illness. The nurse, a stern-looking woman in a white uniform, took my temperature and said, "You have a temp of 102.3, and I'm sending you home. Please let your homeroom teacher know."

Despite my cold, I was delighted to have a couple of hours to be with Pam. When I rang her bell, she answered her door wearing pink baby dolls and a smile that all but disappeared when she saw me.

"Look," she said, "I'm waiting for those boys we met at the movies last week. You know, I kind of liked Johnny; he's so cute. His friend has a car, and he's bringing him here."

"Well, I feel lousy anyway. I guess I might as well go home," I said, disappointed by the news and the lost opportunity to spend time with her. Besides, I remembered that Johnny's friend was unappealing, and I was scared.

"Oh, no, you don't have to leave." Pam shrugged as if she'd had an afterthought. "Stay. We'll fool around, have some fun."

I stayed. Within minutes, there was some commotion on the fire escape, and the two boys jumped in through the window like a couple of cat burglars. We all lit cigarettes. Sore throat or not, there was nothing like a Winston! We played records, danced for a while. Then Pam, in her baby dolls and high-heeled shoes, took Johnny's hand, and like some kind of a movie star, dramatically led him directly towards her parents' bedroom.

Suddenly I was alone with Sean, the ugly one, and to my utter dismay, he began pulling my arms towards Pam's room. He pushed me onto her unmade bed, threw the stuffed animals on the floor, and tried to put his tongue into my mouth as I was struggling to get free. I made it almost as far as the back door, my books in my arms, when Pam and Johnny came running out of the bedroom. Pam had only her lace panties on, and I noted her hairless thighs, her smooth skin. Johnny was still in his tight jeans and white T-shirt, looking relaxed, calm, confident.

"Sean, Pam, let me talk to her a minute, please," he suggested in a sexy, confident tone, and they took a step back to the kitchen.

"What's wrong, darling?" he murmured.

"Nothing. I just want to go home!"

"Please stay. Look, Pam knows us. It's cool."

"I don't care! I want to go home!" I was leaning against the wall, no longer scared but simply resolute.

He wrapped his arms around me and whispered in an impressive Elvis imitation, "We can change partners, honey. Pam wouldn't mind. Come with me." I could feel his body—lean, hard, demanding, sexy.

"Oh, no, I'm going home!" I insisted, and I did. I ran down the back stairs, out of the house, up the tree-lined street, around the corner, and up the stairs to our apartment. I was almost breathless, dizzy, sick, unable to think or make sense of the weirdness I had just left behind.

My mother was at the door, a peculiar look on her face that I couldn't read. "So, how was school today?" Her tone of voice exuded sarcasm.

"Okay. I'm sick. I think I have fever, and I want to lie down." Being sick was a good thing: it had never failed to elicit my mother's concern, love and tenderness.

"You are a *liar*! You are a damn *liar* just like your *father*!" The act was over, and she was in a frenzy. "The nurse called two hours ago to tell me you were on your way home. Where did you *go*, you tramp? Wait till your father gets here. I am going to make sure he *kills* you!"

With those words she marched off to the kitchen, where she continued her keening while throwing around pots and pans.

I knew that, when my father came home, there would be more music to face, but I wasn't too worried: After all, I was sick. Besides, I didn't have to tell them that I had visited Pam; I'd figure out some excuse. When he appeared, I was still dwelling on the unexpected and frightening earlier events.

My thoughts were jumbled and confused. I felt betrayed and anxious, yet thankful that I had escaped without being raped. I was beginning to doubt my memory, to wonder if I could have conjured up the whole scene, perhaps misunderstood Pam's and the boys' intentions; maybe I'd jumped to a conclusion too quickly. But I *knew*. I had hardly even felt a boy's kiss before, never felt a boy's erection—but I knew intuitively, knew what every girl knows in her bones: that I would have been, could have been, raped. Damn! My parents had been right after all!

But when my father entered my room, a murderous look on his face, with my mother trailing behind him, her lips pursed and her eyes red, I *knew* something bad, *very* bad, must have happened. It didn't take long for me to find out. Pamela's downstairs neighbor had called my mother and told her about the guys, except that she had embellished the story: Instead of describing the two blond boys as they were—which would have been bad enough—she had transformed them into Negroes. Colored boys. Pam and I had had sex with coloreds, whom she saw entering through the window. Moreover, she could hear the obscene activities through the thin walls, had been repulsed and aghast, and thought it her duty as a Jewish woman and neighbor to make my mother aware of the situation.

The histrionic onslaught of verbal abuse, warnings, threats, and recriminations lasted for hours, until they ran out of steam and took off to their room. Nothing that I said in my defense was of any use.

Later, in bed, I could hear them speaking together. "We'll take her to a doctor for an examination," my father said.

"What are we going to do?" cried my mother. "She is *lost!*"

"We'll tie her to the bed. We will not let her go *anywhere.*"

Quietly, I reached for a bottle of Tylenol on my night stand. I swallowed all the pills, all seven of them, and lay back down to sleep. There were no thoughts of suicide in my mind; I didn't expect to get sick; it was just a gesture that made sense at the time. Had there been more pills, I would have taken them all. I fell asleep, then woke up, fell asleep, woke up again, feverish and achy, for several days.

Then the crisis blew over, almost as if it had never happened. I began to believe that a severe case of amnesia had overcome my over-stressed parents—that I and I alone had broken their spirits, jinxed their minds, pushed them over the edge, and ruined their lives.

A few days later, my father turned to me during dinner, as we were eating chicken soup, and said gently, "Bracha, I want you to know that I realized that the *yenta* who called your mother that day was lying."

Did a fucking miracle *happen?* I asked myself in disbelief.

"Yes," my father went on, "I know the bitch was lying. I spoke with her and with Pamela's parents. I know you, Bracha, and I know you would *never* do such a thing. You would *never* have anything to do with *Cushim.*"

Yeah, right.

3

I WANT TO HOLD YOUR HAND

THE BEATLES BLEW IN. "I Want to Hold Your Hand" was huge. Bob Dylan became an unlikely star, and the president of the United States was assassinated on November 22, 1963. I was in my home economics class, as always in my own universe, trying to make sense of the teacher's advice: "When you go out on a date, girls, you must leave your wallets at home."

And what if the date doesn't have enough money, what then? I wondered, but in a million years I would not have raised my hand to ask that question. I was still a foreigner, and it was my place to *learn*, not *challenge*. Anyway, I had yet to have a real date. Suddenly, the principal made an announcement over the intercom: *Boys and girls, ladies and gentlemen, I have alarming news: We just received word that John F. Kennedy has been shot in Dallas, Texas. We don't as yet know his condition, and I am asking everyone to return to their homerooms. Let us all pray for our president. Let us pray for his safe recovery.*

For some reason, as I was walking into my homeroom, I couldn't wipe a stupid smile, like an involuntary tic, off my face. Despite, or perhaps because of, the stunning news, there seemed to be a lot of hustle and bustle, even a sense of excitement. After our homeroom teacher dismissed us, Ann and I walked to my house, she in tears and I trying to imagine an act that was completely unimaginable. At that moment, I *really* felt I was in America, where murders, revolutions, floods, earthquakes, and upheavals were all possible. Nothing like that could happen in Israel, I was certain.

As soon as we turned on the television, we learned that Kennedy was already dead. Transfixed, we watched the news, crying and hugging each other as the anchors on all three channels were uncharacteristically distraught, unshaven, at a loss for words. At some point, Ann suggested we go to church. "Let's stop at the synagogue first. It's on the way," I counter-offered. Just in case God got pissed off at me for treading where I did not belong, I would at least have some Brownie points to tip the scale in my favor!

I was a rare visitor to the synagogue and didn't expect that we would be walking into Sabbath services, where the usual songs and prayers in honor of the Sabbath and the Almighty were in progress. No mention of Kennedy. We stayed for an uncomfortable few minutes, then left stealthily and continued on Clinton Avenue toward the cathedral.

Even blocks away the cathedral stood out, its gothic beauty a relic from another era, magnificent yet awesome, a kind of house of worship where it would be easy to imagine horrific, medieval cruelties: Jewish children sacrificed for Jesus; blood flowing down the altar; robed priests and nuns kneeling before marble sculptures worshipping false gods.

Within, the mood was somber. Ann genuflected and crossed herself; I stood there like a dummy, as incongruous as an Orthodox rabbi at an Irish bar, hoping I wasn't noticed. When the congregation finished singing and the organist put her hands in her lap, the priest, without much preamble, turned to his rapt audience and began speaking in English, mourning Kennedy and offering an eternity of peace to all of us suffering from this collective trauma.

While he was speaking, I spotted a girl I knew from school who was dating a boy I liked. She was a couple of pews ahead, but even from that distance I couldn't help noticing her porcelain skin, and once again I was filled with envy. What I wouldn't have given to have her skin! For skin like that I would have been willing to take on the most mind-numbing and sickening occupations: elevator operator, public bathroom cleaner, checkout girl in the supermarket; I would have lit candles every Friday night; I would have given up cigarettes for Lent, or for Passover, or for Ramadan! *If only*. If only I could. While lost in my thoughts, the service ended and teary-eyed parishioners filed out of the church to return to their homes and turn on their television sets.

At home, like the rest of the world I watched the incredible un-folding of historical events, but my mind played games: Over and over it brought me back to the cathedral, to the girl two pews ahead, whom I envied with all my heart. I had to ask myself, *what kind of superficial inner life am I living? Why can't I channel all my energy and effort over hirsuteness toward a beneficial and laudable preoccupation?*

I felt I should sublimate the yearning for silky skin by, at the very least, attempting to pick up a worthwhile cause. I should study for exams; I should read Greek and Roman mythology, learn to speak Chinese or, at least, Spanish; I should involve myself in acts of goodness and charity. Furthermore, I should not permit myself to dwell on minutiae at every moment of my consciousness; such thoughts only di-verted my mind from issues that *really* mattered. Why couldn't I turn a bad situation into an opportunity? What was *wrong* with me?

As I watched television and tried to make sense of all the confu-sion—Lee Harvey Oswald being arrested and journalists screaming the news, their faces masked in sorrow and total disbelief—I remem-bered that it was getting late and I still had to tweeze my hands and feet.

ON TOP OF EVERYTHING else, I became boy-crazy. I could fall in love after a ten-second glance. Fearlessly and naively, I accepted rides from strangers who whistled at me as I walked by in a tight skirt, blowing smoke rings in the air, and would fall in love on the spot! I would imagine being married and having children with that person in the driver's seat, only to sink into immediate depression when nothing came of the short acquaintance.

I don't know why I was never abducted, tortured, raped, or killed; those thoughts never entered my mind! Once I hopped into a car with an older guy. As soon as we drove off, he wanted a blow job. When I refused, he became hostile and antagonistic, as if I hadn't given him what was rightfully his due. At the red light he ordered me to "get the fuck out" of his vehicle. I did.

I was scared of my parents, however. Boys were fun, even strange boys, but my parents never missed an opportunity to make my life hell. Whenever I was out of their sight, suspicion and distrust entered their minds. They would stare at me as if attempting to divine my thoughts, feelings, and recent activity, and would come up with questions and accusation out of left field, always putting me on the defensive. They believed in themselves and their ability to analyze and decipher each nuanced explanation from me, and could not accept fallacy in their conclusions. I was always *bad*. I was always on the verge of inflicting *sorrow* and *tragedy* upon them and myself. I could spend an evening bowling with a crowd of high school misfits and still catch hell when I walked into the house. My father would scream, "Who is that *sheigitz* who just dropped you off? Don't think we are blind!"

"It was a kid from school, who drove all of us home," I might counter truthfully; but reality had nothing in common with my parents' accusations.

Despite everything, I was drawn to adventure and to the streets.

I was afraid, but the world beckoned and I had to run toward it as fast as I could.

ON AN UNUSUALLY WARM April evening, after a particular close shave of my arms and legs and half an hour with Merle, I felt almost high with excitement. I had to get out and show off my almost normal me. I had to feel the warm air. I told my parents the usual, that I was going to study at Ann's house, and escaped the apartment as if it were a cloister. Three boys in a yellow Thunderbird stopped. "Where you going, good-looking?"

"To a friend's house to do homework."

"Can you take us with you? We'll help," offered the one in the back.

"Are you good in French? I teased.

"I'm practically a Frenchman," he laughed. "Hop in, and I'll show you."

He looked about nineteen and had long hair and a swarthy complexion. *He could be Jewish*, I thought briefly.

I got into the back seat, and he wasted no time feeling me up. "Wow! Body by Fisher!" he gushed, taking a swig out from the bottle of Southern Comfort the guys in front had been passing around.

"We need to find more chicks," complained the driver. He had an idea in mind and drove through Irvington and beyond, looking in vain for some willing girls. The evening started feeling like a drag, but the sweet hard liqueur started having an effect on me, the boy's hands under my shorts feeling as if they were about to ignite a fire. Yet I had to stop; it was going too far. In slurred speech, I managed to say, "I wanna go home."

"Why so soon, honey? Let's drive around. Look, the bottle is only half gone."

"My parents will kill me. It's late."

"Are you kiddin'? It's only ten o'clock!"

"*Ten o'clock!*" I shouted. "I was supposed to be home an *hour* ago!"

My panic was genuine; I was scared out of my mind, and the guys knew it and drove me straight home.

I chewed gum as I was flying up the stairs, taking the steps two or three at a time and hoping to mask the smell of cigarettes. Not having had much prior experience with alcohol, I had no idea that I was not only intoxicated, but that the sweet smell of Southern Comfort had clung to my clothes, hair, and body like a direct admission of guilt. As soon as my mother opened the door and took one look at me, she screamed, "She is drunk! Come over here, Yosef! Bracha is drunk! Oh, my God! At that, she began keening and hitting me simultaneously. My father jumped into the action and, without a word, struck my mouth with his fist and looked as if he were about to lunge for my throat. Tasting blood, I ran into the bathroom and locked myself in, leaving them cursing, threatening, and pounding on the door.

Cornered, I had to do *something* to make them stop. I had no desire to die or to seek attention. I just wanted to get *away*. With that aim in mind, I studied the items on the sink and in the medicine cabinet. I found my father's packet of single-edged razors, pulled one out, and began cutting. I felt relief sweep over me, knowing that whatever they could do or say, I could up the ante. The taste of blood in my mouth, and the sight of more blood and cuts on my wrists, were horrible. I vomited until there was nothing left in my stomach, and then I exited my sanctuary, holding both arms up like trophies, or more accurately like olive branches, begging for a cease-fire. I was sure that my parents would panic, call an ambulance or the police, do *something* to stop my imminent death. My mother, however, looked at me as though I had just lost my mind. "*Oy, vay is meier,* Yosef, she is *meshugane*! Look what she *did*! She is *nuts*!"

"Let's go to bed, Ruza!" ordered my father sternly. With those words, they both left me alone to dress my wounds and reflect upon my troubles.

The next day, no one spoke. There were chilly looks but no screaming—which was what I had hoped to achieve: no screaming, no yelling, no verbiage of any sort. I liked being in a quiet house; I liked passing the bread during dinner without having to say a word. End of topic. In very light moments, years later, my mother would refer to the incident as "the night Bracha came home *shikke*."

THEN THERE WERE MANY other situations that required scanty clothing, even when the weather was not as balmy as on that April night when I got drunk. Gym class offered myriad occasions for humiliations. My gym teacher's name was Mrs. Armstrong, a name I had never heard before and that I thought very appropriate to her career choice. I hated *everything* about gym: the smell of the locker rooms; the monotonous routines; team sports; but most of all I hated the short, old-fashioned bloomers we were supposed to don twice a week. I died a thousand deaths every time I put on those things that exposed my hairy upper legs, and, thus half-dressed, would have to prance about ungracefully in a feeble attempt to do what others in the class seemed to do effortlessly.

Equally thorny and complicated were warm days that required one to wear revealing clothing or bathing suits. Summer was a season for bare skin, for shedding layers of clothing that to me were much more than heavy garments for protection against the cold. Long sleeves, boots, coats were my *armor*, my protection against second looks, stares, laughter, questions, shame that made me feel as if I had screwed up somehow and deserved hairiness—as if my gross hairiness were the result of my own behavior, as if I were unclean. I felt as responsible as if I had knowingly unleashed a slimy, obscene virus, had permitted it to grow, multiply, and reside in my skin, in my cells, thereby creating ugliness where femininity should have been the rule.

I loved the Shore. In the old days we had lived only a short bus ride away from the soft white sand and warm, languid waters of the Mediterranean. The Atlantic Ocean, on the other hand, was nothing like my memories of home; I was shocked by the icy cold water the first time my toes touched the foamy waves, and disappointed with the granular brown sand; still, the salt air, the sun, the festive crowds, the waves, and the smell of fried food appealed to me like nothing else. My parents would decide upon an excursion to the Jersey Shore at least a few times during the summer, and, of course, I had to participate whether I wanted to or not.

My own preparations for the excursion had to be executed the night before in order for me to appear publicly in a bathing suit. Back then my thighs were not yet as hairy as they were to become, and so I just had to shave the tops of my legs and the backs of my thighs.

It had never occurred to me that there might be others in my position. I couldn't pass a single woman or girl without checking out her body for comparison, envying anyone with smooth skin and soft, fuzzy, blonde body hair on their extremities, all of which looked natural, feminine, and, for me, unobtainable. Instead of downy blonde hair on my upper legs, I had shaving bumps. Later on, when my legs became even hairier and I had to shave all the way up and around my pubic area, the bumps worsened, an indication that salt water had chafed and ravished my skin. I would leave for the Shore with my parents in the morning, go for a quick dip, and then cover up the excoriated areas for the rest of the afternoon.

Within my psyche, I felt completely like a girl—a girl cursed with a secondary male characteristic that diminished my femininity outwardly but never altered my inner feeling, my identification with my gender. If I had been as tall as a man, I would have had no choice but to accept it; but hairiness was worse: an invisible plague that could be concealed, but only temporarily; an affliction that demanded hours of privacy and effort to keep it from curious eyes. Since my problem crossed the border of what was gender appropriate, it seemed much worse to me than any other possible cosmetic flaw. I had been dealt a lousy hand, as if God, when he made me, had become distracted, too preoccupied with life-and-death issues. He had better things to do than attend to minutiae.

Once, a school friend, Elaine, came along with us on one of those dreaded shore expeditions. Right away, as she stepped into the back seat with me, I noticed that the tops of her feet were smooth while mine were shaved and stubbly. I was afraid Elaine would notice; but if she had, she didn't mention it. Whoever thought hair would also grow on *feet* and *toes*? By having to shave those areas, I felt I was losing my own self-respect. Years later, I watched Joan Rivers on television as she quipped, "Someone ought to tell Madonna to go home and shave her toes!" Of course, I didn't think that Joan was funny that night.

Elaine and I had a little spending money and bought Fritos and sodas, and then wandered off and away from my parents so that we could smoke our Winstons. The salty Fritos made my mouth dry and my lips parched, but they complemented the salt air. I would forever associate corn chips with sea breezes. It was work to light a cigarette on the dunes—the light winds kept putting out the small flames—but we kept trying, cupping a hand around the match. Smoking was wonderful, particularly in the early days: a moment of dizziness followed by sheer pleasure. Later, we went to the arcade area, and, to my dismay, in the shade my legs looked red, sore, disgusting! I noted the shaving bumps, the imprints of the razor, the scratches, and the soreness. I felt itchy and embarrassed. I was uncomfortable in my own skin and couldn't wait an extra moment to shower and dress.

In short, I could go with my parents to the shore, but not with friends, schoolmates, or boys. I would never be one of those girls who vacationed in the Caribbean or Bermuda, or rode to the shore in convertibles, one of their long legs extended over the side door, wearing bikinis and listening to rock 'n' roll, having a good time with their friends. Once, several years later, when I was in my early twenties, I chatted with a young woman about my age who was my roommate in the hospital when I underwent a minor gynecological procedure. She told me that she could never go to the beach spontaneously because she would need hours of preparation the night before. We compared notes. She said that she had learned to burn off the hairs on her belly. I never understood how she could do that without setting her whole body on fire, but I understood the impulse and believed she was telling the truth.

Bleaching became even more of a drag than it had seemed at first, mainly because unsightly dark roots on my face, arms, and between my breasts took only a couple of days to reappear. That meant that choosing what to wear for the day was not contingent upon the weather or the occasion but upon the state of my hairy arms.

As self-occupied as I was, I was aware that other girls had their own real or imagined defects to contend with and mull over. Fashion magazines were rampant with advice on how to choose clothes that would either conceal various unflattering features—flabby stomachs, skinny legs, large breasts, wide hips, short legs, big feet—or accentuate attractive assets. In magazines and television ads, girls were being coached on best ways to apply makeup properly, style hair, or wear slacks that would enhance and emphasize their positive features. Even various hair-removing products were on the market, but those were largely under the radar. Before the twenty-first century, little was said in polite society about depilatory methods. In those days it was common for television to advertise bras by demonstrating them worn over sweaters. Such were the mores of the times.

I consoled myself with the thought that, at least in the dark, I looked good, unlike obese or odd-shaped women; but I never let go of my conviction that my condition was unique and insufferable. Hirsuteness ran in the face of what was considered feminine and sensual. On the other hand, my self-involvement did not shield me from understanding that events in life occurred haphazardly: So many awful things could happen to adolescent girls that, by comparison, my hairiness would be no worse than a mole. At the same time, if I had not been the one to whom this happened, I would never have understood the dismay, the low self-esteem, the feeling of inadequacy that a physical defect could have on one's life.

LIKE MANY TEENS, I kept a journal in which I scribbled night after night, reviewing the day's events and ventilating my thoughts and feelings, as if expecting that, someday, I would become famous and my journal would be loved and adored by future generations. It would be like the diary of Anne Frank, except that I wouldn't have to die in a concentration camp. Writing was not only cathartic but also a compulsion, as were prayers and silent recitations of biblical poetry, from the erotic *Songs of Solomon* that I had memorized in elementary school to the song in *Exodus* sung by the newly-freed Israelites, celebrating God's greatness. Eventually, tired of the long nightly ritual, I gave myself an excuse to end the prayers, as I no longer feared God or believed that he was there listening. But it was a loss: I could no longer boast that I knew long and lovely Biblical passages by heart and, when my faith in a higher power faded like a childhood melody, the comfort of having my confidante, and that intimate and loving relationship, evaporated into thin air.

There was a story behind the recitations. I must have been in third or fourth grade when the teacher, who I knew disliked me, called on me to stand in front of the class and recite the passage in *Exodus* that she had assigned to us to learn by heart. I did. When I had finished, she said, "Go on," and I did. She continued to order me to go on, way past the assignment, perhaps waiting for me to flub the lines and stammer in shame; but I went on and on until the whole class stood up clapping and cheering, as if I had just performed a Nobel-worthy oration. It was the single most outstanding moment of triumph as a student in my entire life.

Without my own personal God, there was no one to turn to for succor and comfort. My diary became a refuge into which I could pour words and vent emotions until I would become sleepy and tranquil. With my childish and grandiose notions of fame always in mind, I not only wrote sentences as they came to me but also did not censor much, except, of course, the entire unflattering business of superfluous hair. Since I imagined that the diary would be discovered after my lifetime, it was cool to be a bit risqué, take advantage of the poetic license to which I felt entitled. In addition, I consulted a dictionary in order to learn new words, edit previous entries, and try to sound erudite. I didn't want to shame my eventual legacy, disgrace my offspring with my poor spelling and grammar. I wanted to leave behind a work of art as Ann Frank inadvertently had.

Naturally, all my battles with my parents were elucidated and analyzed with anger and disappointment. My mother drove me nuts. She wore a bright red coat that winter, and everywhere I went I saw red. All too often she would materialize almost magically, whether I was walking to the drug store on High Street or standing in some corner smoking a cigarette. Someone would ask me to meet him at Klein's department store, at the soda fountain at 12:30 p.m., and the first person I would encounter would be my mother, in red, like a matador ready to fight to the end. My small-statured mother scared me to death; I knew that she would tell my father everything before I'd even returned home, and the violent tirades and intimidations would erupt like an overflowing toilet bowl.

JACK, A FORMER GYM teacher, a short, stout, balding man in his fifties, was my driving instructor. Initially, my father had given me a few driving lessons, but soon enough his rages whenever I drove over twenty miles per hour made each lesson a nightmare. As a new driver, I was not brave, but he was *something else*. From the corner of my eye I could see him instinctively grasping the dashboard, white-knuckled and pale, then yelling, "Stop right now! Slow down at once!" as if we were about to crash and die—not to mention totaling his 1955 Pontiac, a used car that had already logged over a hundred thousand miles and could barely make it up small hills. It was a relief to have a professional instructor whose car was equipped with two steering wheels and two brakes. Jack was a calm person, prone to kidding around and laughing easily.

One late afternoon, my father and I were in the den watching television. The den was the site of many disagreements. Only the day before, he and I had been watching *Raisin in the Sun* when he, after appearing in deep thought, pronounced, "Well, the truth is that the whites are *right*: Once a house is sold to a black, the whole street becomes a slum, and then your own house is worth *nothing!*" Naturally I had a lot to say about *that*, and we screamed back and forth at each other. But on the next afternoon things were quiet. Outside, leaves were falling, and darkness was approaching fast. I had forgotten all about my scheduled lesson when Jack bounced through the door that had been left ajar and playfully said, "Okay, baby, put your shoes on and let's get on the way!"

"I'll only be a moment," I said apologetically, jumping up to get my shoes.

At this, my father, suddenly a madman, was already ahead of me. "*You son-of-a-bitch*," he bellowed, and jumped towards Jack, who appeared momentarily stunned. "*I am going to kill you right now!*"

Jack, regaining his composure, ran out of the house and, within seconds, was roaring down the street. I stood there aghast, leaning against a wall, as my father slammed the front door and approached me in a few quick steps before I had the wherewithal to size up the situation or make any sense of all I had just witnessed. Then his hands were around my neck. I could feel them squeezing. I wanted to say something, but I couldn't speak. I couldn't even think or breathe. It was already dark outside, and the den was lit only by the blue glow of the television set that continued showing the program we had been watching in black and white. What seemed like forever took, in fact, only seconds. Suddenly, he loosened his grip, and I sank to the floor as he walked out the door and drove off in his Pontiac. Later, he returned with my mother. She served dinner, and, silently, we ate the fried lamb chops and boiled noodles. At 9:30 p.m. I went to bed, as usual.

My father never said a word, and neither did my mother. There were no apologies from him, no soothing words from her. Both behaved as if their fury had been justified: They were good parents doing everything in their power to keep their only daughter from going astray. But there was a simple explanation to my mother's supernatural ability to appear wherever I happened to be: All that time, day after day, they had been reading my diary and keeping track of my activities. But as their English skills were minimal, they had confused 'flirting' with 'fucking'! I had written, "Jack, my driving instructor, is *flirting* with me."

MY ABILITY TO DATE normally was of course diminished by my parents' frequent reminders that they would kill me should I bring a *goy* home. Once, and only once, I brought home an acceptable date, a Jewish boy I had met at the park and who was cute and interesting and drove a convertible. I warned him that my parents were very strict, and he promised that he would come upstairs and reassure them with his gentlemanly behavior and above-reproach intentions. However, my father buried his face in a newspaper and my mother busied herself in the kitchen. The awkwardness was palpable, even as I attempted the usual introductions; aside from a grunt coming from my father, nothing was said. Mortified, I hustled the guy out of the place. It was an ordinary date with an ordinary boy, one who wanted only a couple of kisses before I went upstairs. Unfortunately, the movie did not end in time for me to be home by curfew, and my parents, because of me, "had to endure forty-five minutes of worry and sheer hell," I was informed as soon as I entered the apartment.

I HAD ONE WONDERFUL date with a handsome twenty-two-year-old on whom I had a crush. His name was Billy Austin. He was an all-American Ivy League college graduate, son of a well-known lawyer, who held a highly respected position in a bank and was on his way to a successful and lucrative career. Clean-shaven and well-dressed, as befit his country club upbringing, he was someone who could be any parents' ideal future son-in-law—*any parents but mine, that is:* he was not Jewish. Because he hated the corporate world and hoped to make it as an artist—a painter—our paths happened to cross, and when he asked me out to a Bob Dylan concert at Symphony Hall, I agreed immediately.

To be able to go on a late night date without my parents' knowledge required advanced scheming and conniving. For two weeks I calculated my moves and built a tower of lies that could stand up to their suspicious minds and close scrutiny, as if I were planning to either rob a bank or lead the Jews out of Egypt. And I succeeded.

Our seats at Symphony Hall were in the last row of the mezzanine, behind a guy who had some type of nervous tic that made his head bob up and down almost nonstop. But when the band came on and a live Bob Dylan began to sing, nothing else mattered. From where we sat, the performers were almost invisible, but the sound was something else, and I was sitting next to Billy thinking, *I love you.* Even a light brush of his arm against mine sent me into an erotic world, where each cell in my body came alive, firing electric currents, shivering in antici-pation.

I had never been to a rock concert before, and I was speechless. "Wow, that's the coolest band I ever heard!" I whispered.

"I was thinking the same thing," he whispered back. "You having a good time?" he asked, smiling.

"*Great* time. I want this to go on forever."

"Wow, Bob Dylan is a weird cat! But, man, he's good!"

With these words Billy leaned closer to me. He put his arm around my shoulders, and it stayed there for a good while. I didn't dare move. But then he reclaimed his arm and searched for my hand. When he touched it, I instinctively recoiled as if touched by a mortal enemy, as if my life were on the line. I had shaved my hands and fingers the night before, but I feared that they were already stubbly and coarse.

"Hey, Suzie," he whispered, surprise in his voice, "what's wrong? I just wanted to hold your hand in mine."

FREE

WHEN YOU ARE A *kid, an adolescent living at home, you are likely to tell yourself that whatever happens is worth it; it is something you will, in your old age, tell your grandchildren, the imaginary grandchildren on your lap who would love and admire you for being who you were: tough, daring, strong, one cool mama. You will let future generations know that you were not a stick-in-the-mud, but that you knew the score, you were hip, you were smart and witty, the kind of person you would meet only in novels, in films, in art.*

The sad truth is, now that I'm on the other side of the bridge, on the downside of the hill, looking, not at rainbows, but at unknown black holes, a silent eternity, I know that there was little to boast about. Actually, I would do anything to keep from letting anyone know about the brainless acting out, the dangerous deeds done for no lofty purpose, for no elevated goals, but for the mere thrill of the moment. Worse, the danger I courted and wooed like a lover was not tall and handsome, not clever or rich; it was only a vacant, nebulous has-been, a loser, a good-for-nothing distraction, no more worthy than a half-hour soap opera segment on a lazy weekday afternoon, good only for abusing time, for keeping a watchful self at arm's length.

I have never married. I have no children. I have no grandchildren, no one to tell my wild deeds to; but if I had had such an audience, I would have kept my mouth shut! Who in their right mind would want anyone to know? Who in their right mind would want to elicit sorrow and pity? Pity: A sad word, a sad emotion, a vast desert, a kiss of death to its recipient, the object of another's brief tear, a momentary dark thought. An unbefitting, unwelcome quiver of sensation best to be avoided. I don't want to be pitied; I want to be liked, admired, understood. I can relate to Nina Simone's lyrics:

> *I'm just a poor soul whose intentions are good*
> *oh Lord, please don't let me be misunderstood.*

Tensions at home seemed to worsen on a daily basis; they were un-tenable. My parents' fears for me, the fiery arguments, the constant threats, the intimidations and pleadings—all that strife engendered the opposite effect from the one they had intended. I didn't become a good girl. I didn't revert back to pre-America Bracha; furthermore, I said and did nothing to pacify and assuage their anxieties. I was be-coming someone they didn't recognize, a stranger dropped into their laps from an American Dream gone awry.

These two people, who had escaped Poland in their teens, met in Russia, and married at midnight in a secret Jewish ceremony, had no adolescence of their own on which to base their parenting. They were clueless, more in the dark in America than in the forests, work camps, and prisons in which they had spent their teen years. They were blind but thought they could see; they were unschooled but thought they had wisdom; they were innocent but believed that they had seen it all. Their bodies were in the New World, but their souls, their minds, their world view were back there, back on the cobblestone streets of Krakow, in a world where a Jew was a Jew and stayed put, and a daugh-ter was a girl who respected her father, waited for a husband, and knew her place in the synagogue balcony among the women, speaking in a language that was being forgotten, a throwback to the Diaspora, back in a time and space that had been annihilated, burned into ash.

After each battle with my parents I was overcome with guilt. Guilt was the predominant emotion that followed, preceded, and accompanied each and every act of deceit, dishonesty, and secretiveness that I felt I had to commit.

I felt particularly sad for my mother, the woman who had first endured a philandering husband and later had to suffer a wayward daughter. Her sobs, her tears, tore me apart; and yet I felt I had no other choice but to push past the limits that had been imposed on me, cut into pieces the ropes that had been tied to me. More than anything, I wanted to be free. *Free.* The word itself felt like milk and honey. In America, in my adolescence, I wanted to be free. My parents had survived the unimaginable, but their terrors, their nightmares, their fears were not mine; I was not afraid of the foreign land, the new language, the blond-haired boys with almond eyes, the church around the corner, the scent of poplar trees and evergreens. I was not only not afraid, but eager to embrace the exotic, brand-new temptations that beckoned from every corner. I was full of excitement, seeing and learning about the new world. I was discovering America, savoring each new flavor, becoming intoxicated with each new scent, lolling in a world of possibilities. No one could hold me back!

IT WAS A SERIES of everyday events that conspired to end the impasse between my parents and me and lead us to a crisis, then a resolution, and, finally, to an inevitable change in direction. I was already a senior. My grades the year before had been pathetic. I'd had to make up English and French in summer school. Then, for a purpose unbeknownst to me, in September I had been placed in a junior homeroom. Maybe it was their way to warn and degrade me at the same time. The academic demotion was humiliating, but on the bright side, with the demotion came a sigh of relief: I was no longer on the fast track to college, but to secretarial school, where I would learn business machines, accounting, typing, and stenography. Had they consulted me, they would have known that I had no interest in secretarial school, which sounded drearier than a future as a greasy spoon waitress. On the other hand, as I no longer had to struggle with French or physics or chemistry, life became easier, and I had more time for social activities and parties.

On a hot and humid day in September, a time when the heat should have already subsided, Ann and I were invited to a house party. It was sufficiently hot that smoking cigarettes seemed counterintuitive, but I smoked anyway every chance I had. While dressing for the party, the radio was on and I listened and swayed to "Honky Tonk," a record I loved. Once I heard it, the melody stayed in my head as if the needle were stuck on the same track. The tune had an extraordinary impact on me: It made me feel wild, wicked, wacky, and free as a butterfly.

At the party, everyone was drinking beer. I had never been to a party before and felt that I had finally reached an important milestone. Someone handed me a beer, and I guzzled it down thirstily and with relish. Then another, another, and another. I lost count. I could see Ann somewhere in the house, her face appearing pasted on, as if she had sprinkled it with flour, and I could hear her shrill voice admonishing me for *something*, wanting *something* from me, but I had no idea what that something *was*. And then she was gone.

Everything that happened after that had the quality of a dream, a *bad* dream that began in slow motion, then picked up steam, then made no rational sense, as dreams do, easily disregarding the laws of physics, creating jumbled scenes open for interpretation. You might be abandoned in one place, then magically transplanted to another; or you might be running from a killer, feel your knees buckle, then discover that you were actually safe and sound, taking a nice warm bath.

I was at the party—no, not at the party but in a bedroom. I was dancing, but there was weight on me; I was yelling, yet someone had his hand over my mouth. I was wearing white Bermuda shorts, but they were a bloody mess. Too many people were coming and going.

Now you are really *in a fine pickle*, I thought, and then the phrase struck me as hilarious and I couldn't stop laughing. "*A fine pickle!*" Who thought up *that* expression? I had no idea. I didn't know just yet that I had lost my virginity, which I was supposed to guard, to a stranger. Or strangers. Even worse, my mother would hear about it the next day.

I HAD NO IDEA what a hangover was and woke up feeling sick. My pillowcase was damp with snot and sweat, my panties bloody. I had my period and felt as if I had a very bad case of the flu. When I walked into the bathroom to vomit, my mother was at the door. "You whore!" she screamed. "You think I don't *know* where you were yesterday! You are a fucking whore! A whore like all of them!" And so it went, while I was throwing up, peeing on the seat, trying to keep my head from wobbling over and falling into the toilet bowl together with the gross yellow vomit that came up from somewhere deep in my bowels. My stomach was as empty as a pauper's pockets, but the vomit kept on coming in dry heaves, in revolting projectile outpourings that hit, not only their intended target, but also the walls, the tiles, and the green bathroom rugs that my mother had proudly bought at Korvette's.

When the nausea subsided and I could gather my wits about me, I began cleaning the floor with a dirty sponge that I found under the sink. But as relieved as I felt, the other verbal projectile outpourings from outside the bathroom kept on and on, rising in decibels, almost reaching a crescendo. "You whore! You miserable whore! You know how I *hate* you!" The vomiting had stopped, the nausea abated, I was finally on solid ground, but there was no end to the poisonous, ear-splitting lamentations, invectives, denunciations, and name-calling that flowed out of my mother's docile, small frame. I had to put an end to it. I had to stop the noise at any cost. I had to stop the cacophonous barrage of words that was pelting me like bricks, like stones meant to kill the wretched, adulteress, sinful part that my mother knew lurked within me. The part that complemented all my father's lovers, who didn't give a fuck about decency, who did not mind the hurt they inflicted, those whores that my mother had hated in Abu-Kabir, in the refugee camps, in the early years of marriage when she was still pretty and had a chance to flee and find happiness elsewhere. Like a Polack who could spot a Jew in a crowd, she could spot a whore among uniformed school girls. She knew me as well as she knew all the sluts, the *Kurvas*, who spread their legs, opened their mouths, stuck their tongues in her husband's mouth and made him groan with pleasure. She who had never loved anyone but her husband; who blushed when a man even looked at her with a hint of admiration; who was an honest wife, a good daughter, a loving mother, had been betrayed by fat, pimply, ugly whores, and had given rise to a daughter, a Jezebel, a wench like all the others. Her own daughter was that tramp, who at seventeen was no longer a virgin, a loose broad who should have never been born, never brought to America, never raised with so much love and tenderness. She herself had borne a female, a wanton thing with tits and cunt, a she-devil who seduced men; a witch with long nails and made-up eyes, a Lilith who dragged men into the burning pits of hell, who teased them with her charms until they lost control and gave up—for a paltry moment of sexual pleasure—the serenity of a God-loving, loyal wife forced to exist in the throes of pain, under piles of filth and groans of animalistic orgasms, for as long as God determined she would remain on the face of this Earth!

I never made a true suicide attempt. I never wanted to die. I feared death more than anything—but I opened the medicine cabinet and considered my options. My head was suddenly clear, and all my perceptions acute. One bottle attracted my interest. It was a bottle of iodine with the symbol of skull and bones. Compared to the clamor outside the bathroom, the iodine promised silence. I picked it up and drank the entire contents. I felt a burning sensation going quickly through my throat and chest. Pleased with myself, knowing that I had made an impact, I walked out holding the bottle, and, facing my ranting mother, calmly said, "Enough! You can stop now!" She did. She then looked at me as if I were a piece of shit, and screeched, "I'm going to call your father!"

She did call. "Come home, Yosef! Bracha drank poison! She has lost her mind!"

Shlomo, a silent witness to this melodrama, emerged from his room, his face puzzled, his eyes clouded with sleep, but he joined the fray at once.

"Boy, you are nuts!" he told me, ostensibly angry that his sleep had been interrupted, but, at the same time, unable to steel himself against this latest explosion—he, an unfortunate bystander caught in the wrong place at the wrong time, the unwilling object of the madness right outside his room! My mother was howling and shrieking on the phone with my father, bringing him up to date, venting her wretchedness and pain, pain that she did not deserve, pleading with him to leave work. When she hung up, her lamentations continued: "I never hurt anyone my whole life. God in heaven knows I don't deserve this punishment. I'm tired of this life of heartache. I will end it all! Yes, I will end it all! Take my own life!" She plopped down on the sofa, covering her face with her hands, her diminutive body curled into itself, and shaking as if in a fever. Keening, praying, wailing, she emitted sounds of primitive grief as if mourning the dead, keeping vigil over the corpse, as women before her had done from time immemorial.

Realizing in panic that she had no intention of calling an ambulance for me, I became crazed with fear of the poison. I should have known that she would await her husband's instructions; she would do nothing until his arrival as the legitimate head of household, as the commander in this latest tribulation.

Shamed and humiliated, I myself dialed 911, pleading for rescue, while from the corner of my eye I saw the derision on my brother's face, the smirk that said, *Yeah, some bullshit suicide* this *is!*

Just as I had hoped, my so-called suicide attempt achieved the desired results: I was taken out of the house by ambulance and brought to an emergency room, where everyone was sweet and kind, and addressed me in a courteous and respectful manner. They pumped my stomach, gave me a pelvic exam, assigned me a psychiatrist, and then set me loose under the guardianship of my uncle. At the time, I had no idea what he was doing there, but every time henceforth, he never stopped saying to me, "Oh, Suzie, you are doing so much better."

My father didn't yell at me. He drove me home, his affect and manner uncharacteristically calm. Even my mother was silenced. When we were in front of the house, I said adamantly, "I don't want to go home right now. Please drive me to Ann's house." And he did.

The next day I came to school, looked around, and decided I didn't belong there. I had no business being in that place where kids ran around cheerfully, teasing each other, laughing, making dates, fooling around. I was someone who had had a pelvic exam. I was soiled and damaged, ugly, hairy, foreign. I asked my teacher for a pass, then walked into my guidance counselor's office and told her I was quitting school.

"Well, Suzie, you are over sixteen and it's up to you, but your choices are going to be limited, you know," said Miss Roach. Up to that moment, I had always felt sorry for her for having such an unfortunate name, but when I met her cold beady eyes in her drab office, all my pity evaporated. "I don't know. But I'm sure I'll find something," I said, feeling very self-conscious about my accent.

"Maybe you can work in an office. Do you know the alphabet?"

Actually, I knew the alphabet as long as I could sing it. Otherwise, after the LMNOP, I got all the letters mixed up.

"Yes, I do."

"Okay. I think you should try to get a job as a file clerk."

I had hoped she would ask me some questions. I had hoped she would show an interest in my situation. I still had scars on my wrists from my drunken misadventure and hoped she would notice them and show some curiosity. Since I was the only foreign student and she had in the past been involved in my academic and social situation, she knew who I was. But after the brief exchange, she dismissed me, and I stepped out of her office during intermission, when the kids were off running from one classroom to another, jostling each other, pushing, shoving, running up and down staircases. A black girl in a red sweater yelled, "Andrea, wait for me! Hey, girl, wait for me!" And another girl in a yellow sweater, pleated skirt, bobby socks, and sneakers ran towards a group of boys as if she had not a care in the world. Over the intercom, the principal announced, *All students out of the hall. All students go into your fifth period. Teachers, close the doors.* And the kids scampered off.

Soon they would be home eating cookies and drinking chocolate milk. They would be on the phone chatting with friends, making dates, while their parents would look on with pleasure and pride. Their moms would have aprons on and would be preparing dinner. And *my* mother, *my* mother would be home with pursed lips and a hostile smile. No, no smile. She would be somewhere crying, wondering how she had ended up with a daughter like *me!*

I passed a garbage can and dropped in my books, notebooks, and various odd papers that had been very important only minutes before but were now as useless as an expired bus pass. In no time, I was alone. The walls of the school were gray, the clouds outdoors were gray, Miss Roach's door was shut, and I was officially a high school dropout.

THE PSYCHIATRIST HAD A freckled face, red hair, and thick lips. His white shirt was soiled and wrinkled and barely fit around his wide abdominal girth. The buttons looked ready to pop at any moment. He reminded me of the clerk in the doctor's office in Israel, the one who had patted my ass. I had no desire to speak to him. After a few sessions where I just sat there mute, daydreaming and squirming, I suddenly heard myself responding to his repeated question, "What is it you want?"

"I want to be free." My voice sounded hoarse, as if I weren't accustomed to using my tongue.

"What do you mean by *free?*"

"I mean that, when I go out, I don't have to look at the clock and worry about the time. I mean I don't want to be afraid that my parents will kill me if I'm late. I mean I want to be able to come and go as I please."

"You know," he responded thoughtfully, "if you live on your own and have a job, you'll still have to live by the clock. You'll have to worry about getting to work on time, getting enough rest, paying bills, meeting all kinds of deadlines. Is *that* what you want? You think you would be better off *alone?*"

"Yes, I would," I said without hesitation.

The thought that I could live alone had never occurred to me, and here was an expert, a psychiatrist I was being forced to see, bringing up this subject, this subject that made every neuron in my head tingle with hope.

But when I came home after the session, I stupidly boasted to my parents, "The doctor thinks I should move out." The two of them looked at me incredulously, then said the only thing I should have expected them to say: "That doctor is a moron!"

"We are not wasting more money on him!" my mother asserted with finality.

But a seed had been planted, and from that point on it was just a matter of time.

ALTHOUGH I WAS A high school dropout, I had no difficulty securing a dead-end job in an office downtown, and indeed I had to know the alphabet, file, type, and greet customers. My boss liked me, and the work was easy. The business, Credit Consultants, advertised itself as the ultimate solution to those losers who had gotten themselves in debt over their heads. The company offered the dubious service of consolidating the pesky bills into one easy payment that would come with a small fee. What they didn't explain was that most creditors wanted nothing to do with Credit Consultants, expected their money back as scheduled if not sooner, and had no incentive to deal with a third party.

There were two other girls in the office. Both of them wore skirts that came just below the knees but no stockings. I envied them. I had to wear nylons, worry about runs, and by the end of the day feel the pain that the garter belts had inflicted on my thighs. As soon as I got home, I'd carefully remove the offending garments one at a time. The garters left circular red indentations on my thighs. Still, I thanked God for nylons; there was no way I could walk around with my bare legs revealing ugly, stubborn dark stubble, rough to the touch, hard on the eyes. The nylons made my legs appear fairly decent. Even shaved, my legs were hideous. Pretty, smooth, tanned, bare, sexy, lovely naked legs could be mine, sort of, only in the dark.

NOT ONLY DID I have a job but a boyfriend as well. One bright day we were standing in front of the drugstore on Central Avenue where many kids hung out. We were just talking, but I was smoking a cigarette and blowing cool smoke rings when, to my dismay, I spotted my father coming towards us. I anticipated a scene, expecting my father to yell at me in Hebrew in front of my boyfriend, smack the cigarette out of my hands, and spirit me back to the house. But to my amazement, he did not stop or nod or say hello. In fact, I knew he saw me, but he barely looked at me. His pace neither slowed nor quickened.

Steadily, his head up, his face a dark mask, he simply walked on by as if he didn't know me. I immediately ran after him. When I caught up to him, I mumbled something about knowing the boy from school and being on my way home. I knew I smelled of smoke but was hoping that the combination of car fumes, restaurant cooking smells, buses, patchouli oil, incense, and ladies' perfumes would mask the tobacco odor and protect me from my father's wrath.

But he was uncharacteristically polite, gentlemanly, actually a very handsome man who wouldn't meet my eyes. "I'm in a rush," he said as we parted ways, I slinking into one of the department stores and quickly merging into the crowd of shoppers, making myself invisible, as he, tall and proud, marched on, looking for all the world like a spurned lover, a cuckold.

MY BOYFRIEND DICK, ALL things considered, played a fairly minor role in my life, despite the popular adage that a woman always remembers her first lover. I didn't love him, and there was absolutely no reason why he should have been the first, but for a time he was the prototype of the kind of man I liked: not a James Dean or a Marlon Brando, but a rebel in his own way. A high school dropout like me, he lived at home and dreamt of becoming a drummer, an artist. To that end he grew his greasy hair long, wore unwashed clothes, flaunted his pimples, and talked about nothing but music.

"Do you like Elvis Presley?" I asked in the car while we were driving around aimlessly and "Hound Dog" came on. I couldn't resist singing along and shaking my body to the beat. Back then, I didn't yet know that I couldn't carry a tune.

"No way, man," Dick moaned.

"So, who do you like?"

"The Beatles, the Stones, Indian music."

"*Indian?*"

"Yeah, Ravi Shankar, other cats like him."

He was hip. I felt I was at the forefront of something big happening, but like Mr. Jones, I had no idea what it was. I was running around with Dick and his friends, a bunch of guys in a rock 'n' roll band who smoked grass, made fun of squares, dug music, talked shit. They rehearsed in someone's garage and, to my ear, made wonderful music, jazzy and hot.

"What shall we call ourselves?" someone asked.

"The Prophets," someone suggested.

"No, too cliché."

Another cat looked around the garage and noticed a tomato crate.

"Yeah, man, how about Select Tomatoes?"

I liked that name, but I was just the chick, so my opinion didn't count.

"We can use a chick singer," somebody said, and looked at my boyfriend, the drummer.

"No, man," he drawled. "She can't sing."

Stung as I was by that comment, I never said a word about it; moreover, I never, I mean, *never* again, for the rest of my life, sang in front of another person, not even in the shower. But even if I didn't understand everything they were talking about, the fact that they talked music turned me on. These boys were not high school kids who worried about college. They laughed at all things I had thought most people considered important. For the first time since I had arrived in America, I had found kindred spirits, people who laughed at the ethos of the times, who mocked the mores and the attitudes that were supposed to matter.

I had thought I was alone, but I had found my brothers and sisters. I had found that I was not the only one who didn't give a damn about living in those lovely suburban streets, who saw no need to dress according to rules, to sit home on Sunday evenings munching chocolate-covered cherries and watching Ed Sullivan on TV.

I saw no point in education or cared at all about money, marriage, or a great job in some dreary office. The musicians revived some vague dreams that Varda and I had acted out in our childish ways: In our will to find something beyond the drudgery of everyday life, beyond the cooking, the cleaning, the working, and the struggling just for a chance to look at the sea, to have a seat on the promenade overlooking a sunset while eating a banana split or perhaps find abandon in a Dostoyevsky novel, we invented beautiful maidens and handsome pirates.

We knew who our parents were. The Holocaust had been crammed down our throats with mother's milk. The world hated us and hated our being in love with all those lovely things that were not supposed to be ours. And who *were* we, at any rate? What did it mean to be an Israeli girl, a shy Israeli girl who should have never existed in the first place, who should never have been born for a myriad of reasons, and who should never have sought anything but what the folks in the *shtetl*, long dead, long good and dead, considered important.

Who *was* I? Where were my grandfather, my grandmother, my aunts and uncles, people who peered at me from black-and-white photographs with their tentative smiles, their solemn faces? They were a bunch of illiterates who would never have understood me, or I them. They had romantic, evocative names: Hanka, Alla, Dora, Anya, like my beautiful paternal grandmother who, at eighteen, was captured on a postcard unsmiling, unaware that her future self would be dead before fifty, would in all likelihood be marched into the gas chamber hoping against hope for a shower but finding terror and death instead. She was my flesh and blood, my *grandmother*, yet a woman whom I could never know and whose existence was further back in time and space than years alone could account for. I became an American girl who smoked cigarettes, painted her lips red and her eyes black, and who spread her legs in the dark. I was an American girl who cared nothing about a tradition that had proved not simply useless but deadly, and deadly in a way that was more like a television melodrama than real life.

There were times when I forced myself to reflect, to think, to identify with my ancestors and their dire misfortunes. I tried to imagine myself in the ghetto, in a concentration camp, but to my shame, all I could think of was that I would not have been able to shave my legs, bleach my arms, or eliminate any facial or otherwise superfluous hair. I would have had hair around my nipples, and some fucking Nazi would have pointed me out as an example of an inferior race, a primitive race, more monkey than human. I wouldn't have lasted a day.

DICK WAS NO GIRL'S dream. We had met at a joint on West Market Street, Upstairs in the Downstairs. It was a small club, with a stage for live folk and rock musicians, a few tables, a basic menu of greasy hamburgers, and an area for dancing. I had persuaded my girlfriend Ann to come along one Friday, and although she had initially been reluctant, she finally consented. Her father drove us there. I had shaved my legs carefully before leaving home, but on the way I'd noticed the stubble on my lower legs and almost wanted to turn back. I knew that most girls shave their lower legs, but *their* legs did not wear a five o'clock shadow like mine did.

A beautiful blonde woman perched on a high stool at the entrance was collecting the cover charge. Her hair, straight and long, was parted in the middle, and her eyes were made up in black eyeliner, her lips painted white. She didn't smile or speak to anyone. When a customer arrived, she would look up from her novel and complete the quick transaction without a word. To me, she looked so hip, so cool, so much like Mary from the group Peter, Paul, and Mary. Although by then I was already seventeen, I felt very young and unsophisticated compared to her, but once in the dim lights inside, boys hovered around me, asked me to dance, and bought me sodas. For a while I became more or less a regular.

The first time I saw Dick, he was leaning against the cigarette vending machine in the back, near the restrooms. I observed that he was not dancing or moving to the music but rather listening intently. I was hoping that he would approach me and ask me to dance, but he did not, even as I walked to the bathroom and attempted to make eye contact. There was something about him that intrigued me. The Beatles were already on the scene, and he looked like one; but it was more than that: It was the slant of his body against the wall, the black clothes he wore, the disengaged expression on his face that turned me on. He was there because his friends were performing.

I was already listening to jazz giants: Mingus, Miles, Coltrane, Duke Ellington, and the music resonated with a part of me that wanted to escape the mundane, to look behind and under the melody, to find harmony and peace where others might hear nothing but chaos. The music made me feel as if I were turning inside out, shedding my skin, rolling into a ball, bouncing to a beat that brought me and all the others with me back to the beginning of time, where we belonged.

I had been exposed to jazz quite accidentally. When I was sixteen, my father had bought me a turntable, a hi-fi, which came with a promotional LP labeled Hi-Fi Jazz. It was an introduction, an indoctrination, an accidental encounter that was meant to happen. For the first time, I heard Sarah Vaughan and the syncopated rhythms of jazz.

Once, when my parents complained about the hellish din I was subjecting them to by playing a Coltrane side, "My Favorite Things," I thought I would surprise them with an Ella Fitzgerald album which I had only recently acquired, believing erroneously that they would love and appreciate Ella's elegant renditions of songs they must have heard before. The music was reminiscent of 1950s American music I had heard as a child blasting from my parents' radio, the centerpiece of our living room, while my mother was in front of the house washing clothes in the aluminum tub, then hanging them out to dry on the clothesline.

But my parents weren't impressed. Music was not their thing. It might have reminded me of Saturday evening strolls on the Promenade in Tel Aviv, when we stood outside the outdoor café, envying, at least from my perspective, the rich kids inside consuming great bowls of ice cream, and watching and listening to the entertainers who sang popular songs in English; but the music did not turn my parents on. Perhaps it created the opposite in them: a recognition that I was discovering something of my own that they perceived as a threat. I couldn't carry a tune, but I knew what I liked.

DICK AND I BEGAN dating, but in the peculiar manner that my home life dictated. Each date was based on lying and sneaking around on my part and complete bafflement on his. He had no idea what to make of my situation.

"I am on the way to Ann's house to do homework," I might announce with attempted coolness and composure.

"You are to be home no later than 9:30!" my father would at once retort authoritatively.

"But we have to study for a math test tomorrow. Ann is good at math and helps me."

"Be home at 9:30, no later, I said!" my father commanded.

Only a couple of hours were preferable to nothing. I would literally tremble with fear at the thought of being found out, but when Dick parked his car in a secluded lane in the park and we started necking, I thought only of the moment. I learned to dismiss the platitudes that I had picked up living in an environment of pre-sixties morality.

"Please let's go all the way," Dick would plead during those hot make-out sessions in the back seat of his Chevy.

"No."

"Why not? I really dig you."

"Why? Because I don't want to do it and have you lose respect for me."

"*I* lose respect for *you?*" Dick looked at me as if I had just stated that he was holier than the Pope. "How could I *possibly* lose respect for you?" he insisted.

Finally it happened. Dick convinced his best friend, another long-haired pianist who was married to a blonde, down-to-earth girl from Maine and who had a baby, to allow us to borrow the master bedroom that overlooked the railroad tracks and shook like a demon every half hour or so when a train rolled by. Making love for the first time felt strange, like falling from great heights, unable to breathe. I could feel him in me, and it felt good but odd, nothing like poetry but all-consuming, a deepness I had no idea was inside me that felt complete, fulfilled.

In the morning I was silent, brooding, overwhelmed with shame. I had a hard time facing everyone, particularly the girl from Maine. I was sure that I had left something revolting on the bed, though I wasn't sure what it could be, maybe some stain or smell or bodily fluid that would gross out Dick's friends and would make them never want to associate with me again.

Later I asked Dick, "Was I a virgin?"

He burst out laughing and said, "I don't think so." I waited until my period came and went before I saw him again. The second time was at his house. His parents were at work, and we sat out in the backyard smoking grass. When we both got very stoned, Dick asked, "Want to go to where it's at?" I nodded, and we climbed the stairs to his room. We had sex on his twin bed, and afterwards I felt nothing except shame and fear of pregnancy. We did not speak much to each other, did not share feelings, did not know how to address each other. It was easier to just end it without an excuse, phone call, or letter, as if it had never happened. Besides, by then I was planning my move away from home. Nothing in the world could compare to that milestone, to that watershed moment that I couldn't believe was really happening!

IN HINDSIGHT, IT SEEMS fantastic, almost miraculous, that these two people, my parents, who had watched and hovered over every move I made from the moment I was born—these two who for so long had fretted over real and imagined disasters—would very quietly agree to my moving out. The very same folks who screamed when I would show up half an hour late, who chased me up and down Central Avenue whenever they imagined I was out there doing something untoward, who sniffed me for cigarette smoke, alcohol, or marijuana when I came home after hanging out with my girlfriends or wherever I had been— those same folks, same mother and father, understood that they were no longer able to exert control over me. I had shown them that I was capable of upping my ante to the point of ingesting poison and coming to the attention of the authorities. I had proved that I was capable of creating crises of such magnitude that change was inevitable: the status quo could no longer be maintained, its foundation having crumbled, fallen apart, rotted like lifeless timber, like split off branches left out in the rain or allowed to bake in the sun.

As my foot was almost literally out the door, my mother said, "I did laundry today and have a clean towel for you in the bathroom," words that pierced my heart, making me feel like an immoral, wicked, selfish daughter who could not comprehend the extent of the damage and sorrow she was leaving in her wake. My father drove me to the rooming house where I was to live with three other girls and, on the way, instructed me, "Now that you are on your own, you are going to have to live with a pad and pencil. You have to watch every penny that you spend. You need to stay on a budget and remember that everything costs money. Nothing is free."

TRUE LOVE

EARLY ONE AFTERNOON ON a gorgeous spring day, I was walking home to see my parents and wish them a happy Passover. From where I lived, in two large rooms in the Iron Bound section, on the ground floor with the bathroom just outside and across the corridor, it wasn't too out of the way to pay them a visit. All my visits were motivated by guilt. I had no desire to see them or absorb the funereal gloom that shrouded the house like a curse, like one of those plagues inflicted by God himself on the Egyptians. Between them and me there was nothing to talk about. Whenever I showed up, the pretense around the dinner table was that everything had remained the same: My room was still down the hall, my clothes still hung in my closet, my hair brush still rested on the back of the toilet seat. Conversations were as trifling as background chatter among strangers on a bus—\not that in the past my parents would have discussed something like the latest Supreme Court nominee or the state of the theater, but ever since I moved out, topics of discussion had become as trite and safe as last year's snow. Occasionally, the latest bad news from Israel was analyzed and wept over, and there was always bad news from Israel, either familial or political; even so, such news, battered and weather-beaten by a distance of three thousand miles, lacked the luster, force, or immediacy that could ignite a true battle.

Because it was Passover, I knew that the house would be redolent of the warm and familiar aromas of the Seder and holiday meals. My mother, always proud of her cooking, and rightly so at such times, was especially capable when it came to her matzo ball soup, gefilte fish, pot roast, carrots with raisins, matzo stuffing, fruit compote, angel food cake, and almond macaroons, all delicacies laboriously and lovingly made from scratch, their recipes having been handed down by word of mouth from her mother and her mother's mother, all the way back a thousand years at least, to the beginning of the Jewish Diaspora in Eastern Europe.

On the way over, I ran into Carl, a guy I knew. He was twenty-five years old, "a quarter of a century," to quote his own words. He was tall, gangly, bearded, and shabbily dressed, with the reputation of being smart, an intellectual of sorts who read Kurt Vonnegut, Franz Kafka, Albert Camus, and other literary giants. Carl was interested in modern art and cinema, and he had a vocabulary that added credence to his reputation. He was not bad-looking, but he didn't turn me on. When he asked me to come up to his pad, I didn't hesitate, as it was still early. In his messy room, we sat on his unmade mattress, and after a few words, he rolled a joint. The pungent, heady smoke was strong, "Acapulco Gold," Carl explained, and it took only a couple of tokes for me to feel totally wasted.

I was amazed to see him able to stand up, look through his record collection, pick a Mingus album I recognized, and gingerly place it on his turntable, the needle right on the first track. Within seconds I was lost in the demanding, insistent hard bop rhythms of "Pithecanthropus Erectus," feeling part of a sacred realm, losing myself in it, coming back, knowing I had been in a faraway place for a long, long time, maybe years, but not able to pinpoint the place or the time. When the side ended and the spell was broken, Carl ambled over to the small refrigerator, removed two beers, and handed one to me. The cold liquid tasted heavenly going down my parched mouth and throat. After the grass, my mouth was as dry as the desert in which the Israelites implausibly roamed for forty years. Then I remembered: Passover! I had just violated the holiday. The beer was definitely not kosher for Passover, a holiday that, despite all, I still wanted to observe and respect. Remorse immediately displaced the high; nonetheless, I attempted to contain this emotion for a later time. There would be many occasions, I knew, to rue over spilled milk—or even unkosher beer.

Carl was on a trip of his own, it seemed. As I was going through my existential changes, he became amorous. "Let's ball," he proposed, nibbling on my ear lobe, a foreplay trick that I found revolting. I hated spit on my ear.

"Well, if we do, we won't be friends anymore, and I value our friendship," I mumbled unconvincingly; after all, it was not as if we were *close* friends.

"No. Intimacy will enhance the friendship we share," he countered. "Our friendship will stand on a more solid foundation. Love doesn't destroy. War does that."

He had a point. Sex was not a big deal; it wasn't worth arguing about, ruining the good vibes of the moment, or ending the whole encounter with negativity. The dingy room was dim, my legs were shaved, and there was nothing to lose.

But when I saw him standing there in his skivvies, I broke into laughter. Maybe it was the grass, or the oddness of the moment. I had never imagined being in bed with this cat. He laughed too, and then literally pounced on top of me, quickly undoing my bra.

A short time later I was dressed and ready to leave for my parents' home. I would visit with them, drink sweet red wine, eat platter after platter of luscious foods, then accept my father's offer to drive me back. All along I would avoid my mother's red eyes, ignore her sighs, and behave as if nothing had changed.

I HAD GROWN UP in a secular society, but the holidays had meaning, and a gray-bearded God was, if not my constant companion, a *presence*, a *confidante*, a nebulous spirit whose existence was not yet suspect. Holidays had a different aura about them, as if more sunlight and oxygen were infused into the air. From the sweet apples and honey of Rosh Hashanah, to the straw baskets lined in grape leaves and filled with fruit and green confetti on Shavuot, each holy day had its own palpable air. You woke up in the morning and knew that it was not an ordinary day, but one that was adorned in finery, perfumed by orange blossoms.

After dinner, my father and I would walk past the field, past the bushes of colorful marigolds that grew wild along the path, past Luna Park, locked up for the holidays, the Ferris Wheel high in the sky unmoving as if stopped in mid-song, and continue towards the clock tower on the main street of Jaffa, the two of us blending in with the dense, loud crowds.

Even late in the evening, bent, thin old men, their leathery faces etched with sun and years, were hawking falafel, bagels, shish kebab, doughnuts, sunflower seeds, and, of course, filling the air with smoke. Old women in head scarves guarded store fronts that sold everything from shoes, spices, olives, hookahs, candle holders, and Hebrew and Arabic books, to gilded *mezuzahs*. My father would ignore most street vendors, their tempting offers, discounts, pleas, and wit usually falling on deaf ears. Once in a blue moon he would rustle the few coins in his pockets and decide to go for sunflower seeds, treats that came in a newspaper cone and were salty, crunchy, and simply perfect.

If we were out early in the day, we would often walk as far as the mostly vacant Jaffa shoreline, stepping over jellyfish and seaweed on

the bleached soft sands, behind us dilapidated, abandoned old factories, warehouses, and tarred shops, and, in the near distance, the white
Bauhaus buildings of Tel Aviv, shining with light.

To keep my father's interest, I would ply him with questions, asking whatever came to my mind. "Abba, is there a person in the world
who knows all the languages?"

"I don't think so. There are too many. But some people do know
a lot."

"Abba, why is there a law against eating pigs?" The thought of eating pigs was revolting, but I could never visualize what was meant by
'hooves', 'cloven', or the other terms discussed in class.

And he, my father, gave me the only explanation that made sense:
"Jewish religious laws are based on health and cleanliness. Pigs carried
disease and made people sick. God decided it was easier to forbid Jews
from eating ham rather then get into explanations that the ancients
would not understand."

"What about the Gentiles? Where did *they* come from?"

"From Jesus, who was a Jew. Jews are always involved in getting
themselves in trouble. Communism . . . revolutions. Jews are always
attracted to new ideas, always ready to pick up causes that embrace the
poor or the underdog; but at the end, this liberal philosophy got them
hated. We Jews influenced the whole world with our religion and our
philosophy. We created Christianity. We created Islam. We created
Communism. But we are despised anyway!"

Although I heard his criticism, I also felt his pride. And, yes, I was
proud to be Jewish as well, believing that we Jews were people who had
been shown to be on the right and just side of history. Even while subjected to anti-Semitism, pogroms, evictions, wars, slavery, and cruelty,
we had remained a moral and compassionate society, knowing right
from wrong and practicing ethical tenets that have withstood the test
of time. We were a nation unified by the sheer strength of ideas and

intellectual thought, despite the Diaspora, when we were disseminated like unwanted weeds to all four corners of the world, orphaned and ousted from our Motherland. Until now. I was a Jewish girl in Israel, and thanks to the bravery and survival skills of my strong and handsome father, I had come into being with my future as promising as the sand dunes of Tel Aviv, miraculous as the rebirth of Hebrew into a living, pulsating, dynamic language that we knew so easily and so well.

On Purim my mother sewed exotic, thrilling outfits that I was proud to show off. I was usually a gypsy with long embroidered skirts, peasant blouses, and layers and layers of beads. My braids would be undone, my long, thick, wavy hair decorated with colorful ribbons. On my eyelids my mother would apply blue eye shadow that made me feel like an American movie star. Sometimes I was Queen Esther, dressed like a bride.

At school we learned the origins and stories surrounding the holidays, which we celebrated in the custom handed down to us by countless generations. We sang, danced, ate, dressed, and prayed in a manner befitting each unique holiday. We believed in them; everyone I knew believed in their essential truth; everyone I knew revered each holiday, a testament to our ancestors' wisdom, bravery, and strength.

Passover was definitely my favorite holiday. The house would smell of fresh paint, wild flowers, parsley, onions, carrots, and dill. I would get new patent leather shoes, a new white blouse, and a blue skirt that I would wear to school and to the Seder. On the eve of the Seder, my female cousins and I would pick yellow and white daisies that grew wild in the fields. Seders were boring. My father, in a singsong voice, read much of the Haggadah, although blissfully he skipped some sections, and my mother and grandmother, if she was there, hovered around him, obeying each command. Once my mother and grandmother, at the end of the table closest to the kitchen, got into a good conversation about someone they both hated, and I was dying to hear the rest, but with one look my father put an end to the gossip.

I liked the Passover fare, but only on Passover, and did not miss bread, my favorite food, until almost the end of the holiday. On that seventh day, the minute that the North Star appeared in the sky, my family, and what seemed like all of Tel Aviv, would rush into the busy city streets to buy and bite into freshly made bagels, rye bread, pretzels, and pastry, the aroma of freshly baked goods as intoxicating as opium. Men with sacks of fresh bread on their backs could hardly keep up with the throngs of leaven-deprived folks dying to sink their teeth into a piece of hearty, crusty rye bread, chewy and still warm and soft in the middle. Bread, the staff of life: We missed it the seventh day of Passover with a craving that couldn't have been greater if we had been stuck in the wilderness for no less than forty years, begging God for sustenance, praying for divine Manna.

THEN I CHANGED. I was no longer that prepubescent girl holding her father's hand on long strolls, seeking his approval, adoring his looks, awed by his intellect. As the years passed, I could hardly keep track of the major holidays; I never considered observing any of them, except for the major ones, for which my parents expected me to be present. I never agonized over the change in my attitudes. I was Jewish by race but nonreligious by choice. I was never wrought with guilt, misgivings, or existential angst over my gradual disbelief in the usefulness of religious practice. Neither was I proud of my ancestry; if anything, it made me feel like an outsider. I didn't give a damn if my friends or boyfriends or co-workers or neighbors were black, brown, Chinese, Buddhist, or Catholic. Yes, I cared how Israel fared in all its wars with the Arabs. I always wanted Israel to win; but I usually found politics dull and boring and, at any given time, would not have been able to name the president or prime minister of the country that had once been home.

My interests were limited, and my general knowledge of the world as well. My English was ungrammatical and accented, my Hebrew almost forgotten. I had no sense of direction or purpose. I wanted love and looked for it in boys; but boys couldn't possibly love me, I knew. *No one* could love a hairy girl, and if someone did there would be something wrong with him, I thought without a snicker. Before I became Suzie, I'd had dreams, but the dreams had been left behind on the coastline of a country always at war. Bracha did have potential: She was sweet, pretty, and bright, loved reading, and spoke well. She had loving parents, a loving grandmother, cousins, aunts, and uncles. Suzie was another story: a high school dropout, a tramp, and a daughter who did nothing but inflict pain and sorrow on her parents. What's more, she snared boys under false pretenses; if they had seen her nakedness as it was, they would have run for the hills, would have left on the next train, would have jumped into the driver's seat, waving good riddance to that he-she person whose pretty blue eyes belied the beast within.

JOHN WAS MY LATEST love, the object of my adulation and daily make-believes. "And then they married" was a phrase—no, a voice, repeating itself in my brain, like an old song that allows no peace, like a melody that sours with endless replication but leads nowhere. Of Polish ancestry, nineteen-year-old John had those high Slavic cheekbones, slanted blue eyes, blond hair, smooth muscular body, and striking good looks of a movie star that absolutely turned me on. He was the perfect representation of the lover I had always imagined, my Jungian *animus*, my ideal man who without a doubt fulfilled an idea that, up to then, I had not consciously understood. But upon introduction, I knew that here—through some other-worldly force, through an unconsciousness that had been ancestrally bequeathed to me, bound to my DNA as concretely as the color of my eyes—was the man for me. If I had believed in past lives, I would have said that he and I must have known each other in previous incarnations, in the dark ages, in disease-infested Europe, in the jungles of Africa, in prehistoric caves. I might even have gone as far as to say that we had known each other in the bubbling muck of the briny, frothing sea, before space or time, before history. In some distant place or time, we could have been lovers, enemies, siblings, mother and child. We might have wronged each other or loved passionately, it didn't matter; we were destined to meet again and again until the end of time. Such was my insanity.

When we met he was already in the air force, playing trumpet in the military band. He came to see me on his days off, invariably stoned either on grass or LSD, acid in sugar cubes, hallucinations forced through man-made concoctions, trips shaped by odd rearrangements of natural elements out of control. He was perpetually tripping and turning me on to high notes, to non-existent flowers, to shapes, designs, sensations hitherto unknown but titillating and frightening at the same time. Maybe, I would think, we had no business going where the trips took us, no license to wander in the garden, obeying vermin and snakes. We were testing boundaries that should have been left pristine and untouched.

"I gotta split," he would say at some point after making love, and I would listen to his footsteps fading down the stairs, never sure that I would ever see him again, never sure of his thoughts, never knowing whether I was Alice in Wonderland, Dorothy on the Yellow Brick Road, or, more simply, a fucked-up chick, a dumb broad. I was shy around him, saying little lest I would sound ignorant, following his lead as if I were a pious Muslim female walking several steps behind her man. In my journal I wrote sentences such as *He kissed the most intimate part of my body last night.* What I could not write was that his fucking was hard and furious, or that, while on top of me, heavily pummeling his body against mine, holding himself up on his muscular arms and going in and out without a break, he could come up with something like, "Hey, have other cats ever fucked you like this?"

In my naïveté, when I noted his testicular sac I had incorrectly concluded that John had only one ball, a terrible anatomical deformity that in my judgment had probably given him a lot of grief. Childishly, I had assumed that each testicle was supposed to be contained in its own pouch. I said nothing to embarrass him, feeling rather magnanimous about being willing and able to love such an unfortunate and flawed male. As it was, I never said much. Not until I missed my period.

"You think you're *pregnant?*" he exclaimed in disbelief, his tanned face turning pale.

"Well, I never missed a period before in my life."

"Don't jump to conclusions," he said as he tried to collect himself. "Let's see what happens. I bet you're just a little late and freaking out too soon."

I disagreed but didn't dispute his reasoning. He looked as if he were working hard to cheer himself up, pushing aside the negative crap I had just laid on him, shit that could pile up like scattered, unpaid bills, traffic tickets, or lousy, cacophonous high notes.

The next time we were together he greeted me at my door with, "Did you get your period?"

"Ah. . .not yet. I'm three weeks overdue."

"Shit! Let's smoke a joint."

We got stoned, listened to a side by Art Blakely and his Jazz Messengers, and watched the candles as they flickered and shone, forming strange silhouettes on the walls, dancing, gyrating, casting spells, drawing shadows on the Indian bedspread, illuminating the beaded curtain, playing with the large blue oil painting, one moment concealing its lines and shapes and the next revealing the dark eyes of a misshapen female face. A flush of radiance settled over the room, and forgetting all else, we ended up as always, naked and breathless on my narrow couch.

"I don't know if I'm stoned or tired," John said afterwards. "Probably just tired." Yet he made no effort to rise and dress.

"By the way," he continued as if having an afterthought, "Can you do anything artistic?"

I blushed, wondering what had brought on that non-sequitur. Was he judging my worth as a girlfriend or as the mother of his child?

"Well, I'm pretty good at drawing."

"No shit! Can you draw a picture of me playing trumpet?"

"Sure. I think so."

For the next few days I played around with charcoal, pen, pencil, erasures, hour after hour, as if working on a masterpiece for which I had been generously commissioned and therefore was striving for perfection. At last I had it: John solo on the bandstand, improvising a Maynard Ferguson piece, perhaps, his face contorted with effort, beads of sweat on his brow, his eyes shut as if looking inward, listening to the music, coaxing his trumpet to produce the melodies in his mind, coaxing the high, elegant, lyrical notes to rise even higher, while in the background the drummer, bassist, and pianist seem to be listening intently, tapping their feet to the beat, looking at him with approval, as if to say, "I hear you, man!"

I was happy with the drawing and couldn't wait to show it to him. But when he came the next time, the first thing out of his mouth was, "Did you get your period yet?"

"No, I didn't. I think I'm pregnant." My nipples had been sore the last couple of days, and I'd had one episode of nausea.

"Shit! What are you going to do?"

"Hey, maybe I'll move near your base. Me and the baby. Maybe I'll move to New York City. I don't know. Maybe I'll run away and start a new life."

Had I listened closely I would have heard him mutter, "Yeah, just what I *need*."

I worried but didn't worry. I imagined my little girl Pamela, my beautiful Pamela for whom I'd give up my parents, my past, everything that was known and familiar. I would be Pamela's mother, and John—well, I had no illusions. I didn't for a moment believe that he'd marry me, and besides, I *couldn't* marry him. I couldn't live with him day in and day out, secretly attending to my strange routine. It would have been impossible to keep up the façade. It would be better if he were to remain my boyfriend. And Pamela's father. My pretty girl would have the best mother in the world.

A few days later John suggested, "You should see a doctor."

"Whom should I see? I have no idea how to go about this."

"I know a gynecologist, a friend of my mother's. Here's his number. Call him and make an appointment right away. You need to find out soon." I detected a gentleness in his voice that was usually lacking. The word *pity* came to mind.

"Okay, I will," I promised, scared stiff at the thought of having to confess my condition to an absolute stranger. He had the doctor's business card in his wallet and handed it to me. I put it in my pocketbook, not looking at it, impressed by John's efficiency and determination. By then he appeared much calmer, like a murderer who had a plan to dispose of his victim's body, I thought. He rolled a joint, inhaled deeply, coughed, and passed it to me.

"I'm hot and sweaty. Let's take a bath," he suggested.

"You can go ahead. I'm okay," I said. That was the *last* thing I needed.

"Come on, take a bath with me," he insisted peevishly. "I want you to scrub my back."

"I don't *want* to take a bath now. I'm not in the mood," I practically begged. I couldn't imagine myself in the well-lit bathroom, naked but for my excessive body hair. It would have been easier to walk out naked into the dark, seedy streets of Newark. It would have been easier to be swallowed up in an earthquake. But he was relentless.

"Come on," he snickered as he walked through the beaded curtain, past the kitchen, and into my incandescent bathroom. I could hear him beginning to fill the tub.

"What's *wrong* with you?" he asked, his voice loud with irritation after he turned around and saw me standing in the same spot, not making a move.

"Nothing." I stood up and draped my long black robe over my shoulders, attempting a casualness I didn't feel. Finally I entered the bathroom holding a small candle. I immediately turned off the overhead light, as if creating ambience was the only thing on my mind; but all the while I was feeling dumb and brainless as I climbed into the tub, hoping I could pull off the act, waiting for the nightmare to end. Had he complained, I would have been at a loss for an explanation, but he didn't say anything. We sat soaking in silence. When he got up, I grabbed my towel and followed suit, almost breathing a sigh of relief, as if I had gotten away with something akin to laying a loud fart in public. Back in my living room, he was already putting his clothes on.

"I hope you're not leaving," I said, concerned.

"I am. I'm tired," he replied.

As much as I didn't want to make a fool of myself, I couldn't help it. Involuntary tears flooded my eyes, and within seconds I was sobbing loudly, bawling as if I were a kindergarten child watching my mommy walking away.

"What's *wrong* with you?" he demanded, annoyance in his voice.

"Nothing," I whimpered. "I guess I'm just being typically female."

"*Female*? *Look* at you!" He was laughing as he pointed to my arms, my face, my legs. "You don't exactly *look* that female!" Again he laughed, as if proud of his wit and humor.

I stopped making any sounds. In a flash I realized that I had not succeeded in pulling the wool over his eyes; he had *seen* me. He *knew*. He was rightfully revolted by me. *I wish the floor would open up and swallow me whole*, I prayed. *I wish I could melt into nothingness, like the Wicked Witch of the West!*

The towel was still wrapped around me, and I hugged it tighter, trying to shrink into myself, wanting to not *be* myself, wishing to metamorphose into Kafka's cockroach, into something small and furry, a frightened creature on the run.

"I'll come by soon," he said unconvincingly. "I have to split now. Don't forget to make an appointment with the doctor later."

After he was gone, I lit a cigarette, turned on the lights, blew out the candles, turned off the red lamp by the sofa, and studied the oil painting I had recently acquired. It was good. Although abstract, the artist had captured the alienation between the two figures seated in an ordinary kitchen, a married couple undoubtedly, he discreetly glancing at the folded newspaper on the table, she holding her coffee cup and staring beyond her husband, thinking of God knows what. Suddenly, I remembered: my charcoal drawing! He never saw it! And there it was, crumpled between the cushions on the sofa. John must have unwittingly sat on it with his bare wet ass! The charcoal outlines were nothing but gray shadows, bleeding all over the page.

A FEW DAYS LATER, sitting on the toilet and absentmindedly scratching my itchy pubic area that for some reason had been mildly bothering me for a while, but especially so in the past two or three days, I noticed that beneath all that curly dark hair, my long, sharp nails had drawn blood. Instinctively, I knew something was wrong. Looking closely, I thought I imagined movement. Then I saw them: multiple creepy, crawly small, reddish, living things, lice or some other pestilence, crawling on my pubic area, sucking blood. I picked one off and crunched it between my fingers, the way my mother had done when I had lice. I could almost smell the special shampoo she used and feel the teeth of the small black comb running through my hair, making me cry out in pain. Back then my scalp itched, and now, unbelievably, it was my pubic area! With a small comb, I attacked the area, alive with the damn critters that seemed to be lice but were larger than the lice of my childhood.

Even after spending a long time combing and picking out the parasites, I had made only a small dent. Tired and frustrated, I tried to go to sleep but sleep never came. The telephone rang but there was no one on the line. It was probably the same creep who had been doing that on and off for a couple of months. I took the phone off its hook, but after a few minutes it began beeping like a living object seeking attention. Just as I thought the beeping was about to cease, a loud recorded message spoken in a female voice came on the line, telling me that my phone was off the hook and reminding me repeatedly to hang up or try my call again later. *Nothing* I did worked. Trying to trick it by dialing a couple of numbers didn't work; the beeping busy signals resumed, followed by the automated message. The fucking telephone was a presence that wouldn't keep still! Even placing a pillow over it couldn't stifle the clamor. It was me against the machine, and I was losing! I could imagine going stark raving mad, even jumping out the window. Finally, I hung it back up on the wall. Immediately the damn thing sprang to life. Although it was already past two a.m. and there was no chance in the world that it would be John, after about ten rings I picked it up anyway, just in time to hear the nut breathing heavily in my ear.

"Goddamn it!" I screamed at the top of my lungs. "I know who you are, you jive, fucking son of a bitch! I'm calling the cops and having you arrested!"

He hung up. Daylight was seeping in through my heavily draped windows, but sleep was as elusive as a childhood lullaby. I lay back down trying in vain not to think of the creatures sucking my blood.

SHORTLY THERAFTER, I HAD an appointment with the gynecologist, John's mother's friend.

"You have beautiful breasts," the doctor whispered while fondling them. "You should be proud."

A couple of squeezes later he finally came around to the issue at hand.

"To get an idea of what's going on inside you, we are going to have to admit you to the hospital for a procedure called a D&C. It's a fancy term for a very simple and effective way of diagnosing why you're not getting your periods. But your mother will have to sign a consent. Can you convince her to accompany you to our next appointment?"

I made up some inane story to my mother about my feminine health problems, and to my surprise she asked no questions. Maybe she guessed. More likely, she had no desire to learn the details.

The day of the procedure, I woke up before dawn. It was a cold spring dawn that bore bad tidings. A D&C! I couldn't imagine not being in agony. I was scared of needles, of knives, of steel instruments, of the astringent odor of alcohol. I didn't want to go to the hospital, although I wanted to know if I was having a baby. I wanted to follow John's instructions. I wanted him to be pleased with me. Although I knew I could never face him again, I missed him so much. I wanted his love and his baby. Motherhood would make me a complete woman; there would be nothing masculine about me. All that nonsense about superfluous hair would simply go away.

The sun was slow to rise that morning as I was desolately walking to the bus stop, where I could see a solemn bunch of tired people—nurses, waitresses, security guards—wiping sleep off their eyes while checking the horizon for the bus that would take them to another day of mind-numbing work. I sat all the way in the back of the bus, dying for a cigarette and a cup of coffee. Twenty minutes later, in a state of utter distress, I found myself in a sterile hospital room, dressed in a hospital gown. A girl about my age was in the other bed. They had already given me Demerol, and I was floating up towards the ceiling, almost touching the tiny cracks in the plaster, listening in spite of myself to the Muzak version of Miles's *Sketches of Spain*, wanting to dance, to fly away like a songbird from this perilous place where death was no stranger—I could sense that—and from surgery and pain and whatever invasive plan they had in store for me.

"Why are you here?" asked my roommate.

"To find out if I'm pregnant," I replied. "And you?"

"I'm having a legal abortion," she replied offhandedly, as if I had asked her directions to the nearest bathroom.

I burst out laughing way too heartily, and she joined me instinctively, infected by laughter as if it were a yawn. "Legal abortion" made no sense; it was incongruous. I certainly wouldn't want that. My doctor had told me I had pretty breasts, and said he would offer me legal advice and care. I was no longer afraid: I was willing to surrender, go under on command!

When I came to, I wanted a cigarette. A nurse stood by my bed. "You may have a cigarette," she promised, "but I need to see you stand up first. Also, I want you to empty your bladder now."

I stood up, lit the cigarette, felt a bloody pad between my legs, and, clinging to the nurse's arm, attempted to reach the bathroom. A few steps later I felt dizzy, the room swayed, and I knew that I was going to pass out. Alarmed, she quickly and efficiently placed me back in bed, where all I could think of was, *I miss the baby I never had.*

Many hours later, perhaps a lifetime, I was deposited in a cab and delivered back to my apartment. I called John but couldn't reach him.

I called him the next day but still couldn't reach him. I tried phoning him for several more days, with no results. My apartment felt hot and oppressive, and so, when my abdominal cramps abated and the bleeding subsided, I decided to get out of my private hell-hole and stay with my parents for awhile.

My relationship with John was clearly over, but "hope springs eternal," as they say, and despite all logic I kept expecting him to return every time I heard footsteps on the stairs, every time the phone rang or a car screeched to a halt below me on the street. Reminding myself that he had seen me in my true nakedness and had ridiculed me did not succeed in crushing my longings; it only made me hate myself. I wallowed in self-pity.

ONE GOOD THING HAPPENED: I tweezed my eyebrows apart and the hair over the bridge of my nose never grew back. The rest of my eyebrows could be tweezed normally; it was the only area of my face that I felt comfortable treating by myself. No electrolysis for my eyebrows; tweezing them was socially acceptable, after all, and I tweezed them into very thin arches that I was proud to show off. There was one upside to having all this hair: my lashes were dark and long, accentuating my large, blue eyes, my best feature by far; my hair was thick, wavy, and manageable. On the other hand, my shaved legs were never smooth, their stubble always an irritant. Cuts, bumps, rashes, nicks, and scratches were acquired characteristics of my scabrous skin, my Achilles heel, which was not only hairy but sensitive, easily offended. Skin, the largest organ of the body, the first line of defense, was my ignominy, my anathema. There was never a reprieve or respite from the physical and emotional attention it demanded. My affliction always took center stage in my mind, taking up space, time, even reason. No matter how I fought, the sickening, gross, unwanted hair persisted like an aggressive tumor, resistant to treatment, unfazed by blades, tweezers, lotions, dyes, or electricity; on the contrary, everything in my hair removal arsenal appeared to rather invigorate the growth. It was indeed a war.

I MISSED JOHN TERRIBLY for about two months. I wrote silly poems and mourned the baby I never had. I missed the little girl who'd never had a chance. I missed Pamela and cried over John. A few months later, I did see John, but by then he was a stranger, an acquaintance among familiar faces in a downtown nightclub, and I was an impulsive girl planning to follow Steve, a guy I barely knew, to Washington, D.C. Steve, a pianist, had a vague opportunity to perform at The Bohemian Caverns, a popular jazz spot; as I had nothing in the offing, I had nothing to lose by going with him. After the music ended and the band started packing up their instruments, John meandered over to our table, ignored Steve, and whispered in my ear: "Man, I did a hit of acid. I am *so* stoned!"

ALTHOUGH I VISITED MY parents frequently and even stayed overnight now and then, I had no intention of moving back home. During one of my visits, my parents ceremoniously requested a talk. This caught me by surprise, as it was very much out of character for them: In my family talks were not scheduled; they just *happened*, and were invariably accompanied by arguments, recriminations, tears, accusations, yelling, and name-calling, all of which generally erupted like sandstorms in the desert, pelting dirt and dust over everyone within earshot. But this time we sat down formally around the kitchen table. My brother was out, so I had to face both of them alone.

My father began the conversation in a reasonable and mellow tone usually reserved for strangers. "Bracha, you have been on your own for a year already and have achieved nothing. Your mother and I have been talking, and we think that this is a good time for you to come back home."

Is he kidding? I was speechless. There I was, about to make the move to D.C., and he was coming at me totally from left field! Asking me to return home was like asking an ex-convict to return to jail just for the heck of it. I had intended to explain my upcoming move, but now they'd made it impossible. There was no way I could admit that returning to their house was not only out of the question, but, worse, that I was moving much further away for no apparent reason.

"I am not moving back here!" I declared, even as my mother's tears tugged at my heartstrings. She allowed the tears to run freely and copiously, as it was not in her nature ever to modulate her emotions or withhold moans, groans, gasps, even burps and farts. When we were children, she would call to us from the bathroom at least twice a week, "Shlomo! Bracha! Someone bring me some warm water! I need to wash my *Shmondo!*" the crude Yiddish word for the vagina.

"What are you going to do, then? Run around with *shkutsim?* Never marry? You are getting older, you know," my mother piped in, blowing her nose. "You are almost twenty and unmarried. You have to find a husband before it's too late. You have to wash yourself and wear clean clothes. A girl like you should smell of perfume and hold her head high. You should watch every step, because the world doesn't forget. Your father and I know what is best, and you can't run away from the truth. You can't be a liar and a tramp and expect a future!"

All that was pretty much the crux of their argument. It was me against two people who in a hundred years could never have understood me, nor would they try to do so. They knew what they knew and could not be convinced otherwise. I was of marriageable age. I was running around in the sewers with God knew whom. As parents, they had to redirect me towards the right path; that was their duty. It occurred to me that they might have received professional advice, perhaps from their rabbi. It was totally off the wall for them to initiate the talk and carry it through as if we were a family of debaters, truth seekers, or Talmudic scholars doling out wisdom and charity learned from ancient books. But soon enough, after they realized that their recalcitrant daughter would not budge, they reverted to their usual modus operandi, threatening, mimicking, yelling incoherently as if speaking in tongues.

I had no choice but to say that, with all due respect, I was not coming back home. I even added unnecessarily, "I have no interest in getting married, having kids, and all that bullshit. I want something different. I want to paint or draw or do something that will make me happy. I've never been able to excel in anything, but I have one talent and I want to develop it: I want to be an artist."

"We should never have come to America!" my mother wailed; my father called me a moron. Since civilized discourse was no longer an option, I walked out the back door, contemplating going insane. I laughed loudly, made faces at them, grunted, honked like a boar, and sang off key on top of my lungs. Finally, when they fell silent, I stopped the theatrics and walked off alone.

STEVE HAD ALREADY GONE to Washington, and I was in the process of following him there. He wrote long, meandering letters daily and phoned collect every evening, as if wanting to stay on top of me lest I lose momentum. He had already found a cool place for us to crash, he promised, as well as a steady gig for himself at the Bohemian Caverns. Washington was a gas. It was a hip city, full of jazz, poetry, art. We would have a ball!

On a cold spring morning I was on a train, reading *Atlas Shrugged*, ready to start my hip, artsy existence in a city I had never seen, with something like twenty dollars in my wallet and a few clothes in my suitcase, basking in optimism and ready for adventure.

LIFE LESSONS

AS HAIRY AS *I already was, more was yet to come. At the time I arrived in Washington, D.C., I had yet to have hair around my nipples, on my chest, and on my abdomen. There were still small areas on my inner thighs that did not require shaving. Gradually hair attacked those hitherto smooth spaces, often catching me by surprise and filling me with dismay. Eventually, I would have to attend to a vast area of my body, from my toes to my head, and in the hidden, private, revolting places in between. Even my butt was not spared.*

If the devil were to approach me now, right here, alone in this room, and offer a deal: "Okay, woman, after a lifetime of bitching and moaning, would you exchange this elderly, wrinkled, blemished, sun-spotted, thin-skinned, veined, saggy form for that previous one, the hairy young one? Would you do it? Could you?" my answer would be no. A resounding no. I couldn't manage all that work again. I couldn't manage the fear of looking in the mirror and seeing yet more hair on my face, on my cheekbones, for God's sake! When you are old, you are old in the dark as well. Nothing can hide it. Someone once said to me, "There ain't nothing uglier than a gray pussy!" a phrase that stands out in my mind as one of the ugliest I've ever heard. I am still the Bracha who yearns for unattainable beauty; but I am also Suzie, an aging woman past her prime, who is still interested and interesting but fears the loneliness at the end of the day, checking and rechecking the day's messages, waiting for deliverance, while at the same time feeling alarmed by another's touch and cold to the idea of it.

The joke is exactly that: Once the hair no longer mattered, neither did the elasticity, the muscle, the collagen. When I am dead, they will have to cover me from head to toe—or better yet, close the fucking coffin! I am tired and a little high, a little drunk, very much frightened at the prospect of going on without a road map, without directions. No guide. No friend. No mother or father to point the way home.

I have spent a lifetime doing nothing. *There is* nothing *to justify this gift that was wasted, this life that was spent in the bathroom, preening and grooming for the sake of sex appeal, for the sake of a man who never came—a man who never gave a damn! On second thought: ah, to be young! And I wasted all those years. Damn!*

THE PAD THAT STEVE found for us turned out to be one cheerless room on the second floor above a bar, Tasso's. It was a proper place for misfits like us, who had dropped out, too stoned to do anything meaningful, too uninterested, rundown, disillusioned, and fucked up yet clinging to the notion of artistic superiority. Everyone we knew was into *something.* People ran around DuPont Circle stoned on amphetamines, looking to cop more cheap drugs, or cheap sex, or grass, or whatever the wind blew in. In 1967 Washington D.C. was *not* San Francisco, was *not* the capitol, *not* a city, but a *state of mind* into which I could crawl and tell myself, "Man, I'm *so* cool! I *love* my hip existence!"

Steve and I shared a bed but were hardly lovers or, for that matter, friends; in fact, I didn't particularly know him or even like him. Physically, he was repugnant—short, dark, stocky, hairy, and asymmetrical, with a crooked mouth, a deviated septum, and uneven eyes. All in all, he looked meaner than he probably was.

The morning after my arrival, he fried eggs on a hotplate in the room and sprinkled them with garlic powder, the only condiment on hand. It was the worst breakfast I have ever had. Neither of us had any money, but while Steve looked at the *Washington Post*'s want ads for a waitressing job for *me,* he no longer gushed about his *own* gig at the Caverns, or anywhere else for that matter.

"Look," he said, when I asked for an explanation, "I can't talk to the owner now. The cat's mother died, and he's totally broken up. Y'-know, since black cats don't know their fathers, they're much more attached to their mothers than we are. Way *too* attached. I just have to wait it out and be cool. Leave it to me, baby—when I get the right vibes, I'll know what to do."

In the interim, it made sense to Steve that I pick up the slack. I should find a waitressing gig to get us through the rough patch, and he would concentrate on the music business.

I didn't agree, however. I hung out in the bar downstairs, drinking, meeting people, listening to music, and getting high on grass, speed, or whatever came along. I congratulated myself for being cool, for ending up in the coolest, hippest place in town. Besides juicy burgers, cheap drinks, and a choice of one-night stands, Tasso's greatest appeal was its jukebox. Where else could one play Horace Silver's *Nica's Dream,* Miles' *Sketches of Spain,* or Ellington's *Take the A Train,* and at the same time, in between jazz takes, holler along with the Beatles, "Get Back, Get Back, Get Back to Where You Once Belonged," and dig the lyrics and the music and the din of the crowd that made the candles on the dark wooden tabletops flicker and sway? It seemed to me that fate had steered me into the center of the universe. Serendipity, fortune, luck were all on my side.

In 1967 the war in Vietnam was escalating, civil rights issues were coming into focus, and activists and war protesters were descending upon the capitol in droves, while I, there in the nation's capital, was unaware, unlearned, apolitical, unguided, and uninterested in unconscious actions or motives. Events followed one another, and things just happened, and not necessarily in any type of rational order or cause-and-effect manner, not even in random motion. John had left me, Steve had asked me to follow him, there was nothing special going on in Newark, home was out of the question, and I had no sense of connection, no feeling of being bound to a place, no nostalgia for anyone or anything.

Five years or so after stepping off the ship in New York City—wearing an Israeli folk dress, speaking little English, gawking at the skyscrapers, crying for my grandmother, already missing my eucalyptus tree, aching for the streets of Tel Aviv, even for the huge billboard of Brigitte Bardot above the crowds, yearning for the crowds themselves, upon which I had fixed my stare from the taxi taking us to the port in Haifa, trying hard to imprint their shapes on my mind, knowing that it would be a long time, if ever, before I heard and saw the only place on Earth that was my home—I had become Suzie, a hip chick in a hip place, who feared nothing and thought she knew the score.

Within a couple of weeks, or perhaps months, Steve had decided to return to Newark to see his old man and try to cop some bread. He would return within a few days, he said. After he had gone, I rummaged through a pile of papers left on the floor and found a postcard from someone named Nellie dated a day or so before. Nellie wrote, *Steve, I'm so sorry you got gangrene and can't work. I'm broke right now, but I'll try to help you out as soon as I can.*

It was January, and the weather was unusually warm. In the evening the thermometer had climbed up to seventy degrees. Everyone was out in the Circle, taking advantage of the winter thaw.

In my room I could hear the drumbeat coming from Tasso's jukebox. Our place was a disaster, dust and grime covering everything—the bed, the linoleum floor, the chest of drawers, the hot burner on which Steve had cooked. Clothes were piled over an unsteady chair, and on the wall was the eye chart that a previous tenant had left behind. The whole place reeked of cat urine. The communal bathroom right outside the door smelled of sex, smoke, and various unidentifiable, better-left-alone odors.

The room was large without being spacious. The windows faced the street but collected no sunlight; the drab furniture looked like Salvation Army discards. But very late at night I could hear the guys in the next room discussing Dostoevsky, I could listen to someone playing Chopin on the piano down the hall, and I could pat the stray cat that would sneak into my room whenever I left the door open.

The bar closed at two in the morning, and when I couldn't sleep I would read poetry out loud to myself. I discovered Sylvia Plath and Anne Sexton, among others, and made believe that I needed no other company. I did meet some very forgettable people, and overall, sought nothing—that is, of course, until the money ran out. The pathetic sight of salami and cheese left out on the fire escape in the absence of a refrigerator filled me with nausea, and, worse, a longing for home.

To add insult to injury, I had inadvertently locked myself out of the room at three in the morning, having gone out to use the bathroom, and had spent the rest of the night outside my door in my threadbare flannel nightgown, bored, tired, and cold, until early the next morning, when I spotted a neighbor and his dog ambling down the stairs and asked for help.

The first thing I did after my rescue was phone my parents to ask for bus fare home. As if someone was fast-forwarding my life, in a quick succession of events I found myself being spirited away from my love affair with DC and my days of poetry and freedom, frame by frame, moving at high speed, in a blur of colors and sounds, skipping over some details, accentuating others, until there I was, on a Greyhound bus, getting out of Washington, D.C.

Although I had been on my own for more than a year, as far as my parents were concerned nothing had changed; all previous rules were resurrected, and the oppression returned with a whopping force that almost knocked me off my feet. I didn't even bother going out at night; I was too tired to deal with the arguments such acts would evoke. It was better to bide my time until I felt ready to return to Washington.

I had some phone numbers, knew some people, and this time knew where I was going and where I would get off. Or so I thought.

THEN MAURICE CAME INTO my life. I had initially met him through Steve in one of the jazz clubs in Georgetown. Maurice, a local jazz celebrity, had played piano with some jazz giants. People compared him to Art Tatum or Monk, but he had his own distinct, original style. He was a tall black man, in his early thirties, almost handsome, though his long black beard and Afro concealed the outline of his features, making him appear older, foreign, an avatar of an earlier century. But his piercing brown eyes and his slow, cautious, commanding manner of articulating archaic, multisyllabic words cut right through space and time, immediately placing his listeners at attention.

We were visiting Josie, an artist with a pretty, light-skinned face devoid of makeup, and sporting a "natural." Everyone was smoking grass and listening to John Coltrane's "A Love Supreme." We were all stoned, and the music sounded sacred, holy, like a prayer. When it was over, I stood up to leave; Maurice jumped up and offered to walk me home.

Around Dupont Circle the streets were deserted and the bars locked up for the night. The music I had just heard for the first time washed over my whole being, Coltrane's vocal chant echoing in my mind: *A Love Supreme, A Love Supreme, A Love Supreme*. Maurice was silent, apparently still listening. At my door he gave me his address, 26 Meridian Place, and whispered, "I will be waiting for you. When you come to me, my love, don't knock. Just walk in."

And so I did. I walked into his place on a cool but sunny day in early spring; it might have been any day of the week, but it felt like a holiday, a Sunday. The wide avenues felt fresh, renewed, and cleansed after the winter cold and slush. I could smell the cherry blossoms and admire their fleeting beauty. I knew that I was young and free, on the precipice of falling hard for Maurice; I was walking on air, feeling as light as a snowflake in December, prepared to surrender. On a whim I walked into a liquor store and bought a green-glassed bottle of Chianti; though I knew nothing about wines, I had seen such bottles used as candle holders. I was wearing jeans, a man's sweatshirt, and a dark pea jacket that someone had given me. When I saw my reflection in a shop window, my mother's trite advice popped into my head: "A woman should always wear clean, pretty clothes and smell of perfume." I almost laughed out loud. *She has no idea*, I thought.

In my wildest dreams I couldn't imagine that my parents, the same people who had been the objects of anti-Semitism, prejudice, pogroms, hatred, and all manner of evil, would consider a black man equal to other men. In their minds, I knew, he would hardly qualify as a *human being*, much less their daughter's future lover. Yet I could forgive them, because I had no other expectations of them, and, more importantly, I was bubbling with excitement, almost dizzy with the premonition that I was stepping over an invisible border, running through a field of possibilities, reaching for a cloud way over my head.

Of course, I didn't knock, not only because he had said it would be unnecessary, but also because it felt appropriate to just walk in. He was at the piano, completely naked, playing around with an original tune evocative of green forests and beautiful maidens. He had been waiting for me. He knew I would come, he told me, and he was prepared to wait an eternity. That was how it began, with no introductions or formalities or unnecessary words.

Afterwards, we went out to a small jazz club on Fourteenth Street, where everyone knew him and wanted to hear him play. And he did. As I listened, I noticed the other men trying to get my attention and the women looking at me with curiosity. When he returned to our table with a slow, confident stride, nodding to me, I gushed, "Being here makes me wish I were black, too."

And he, looking sanguine, remarked, "I'm glad you put it like that. Previous chicks have said that as smart and as talented as I am, I should be white."

Later that night, in his apartment, one shabby room and a bathroom on the second floor of a tenement building, one of his friends came by, and the two of them played chess all night. Maurice won each game. While they played, I fell asleep on the narrow couch against the wall, listening to Duke Ellington and the Modern Jazz Quartet and incorporating the notes into my dreams.

In the morning I fried eggs on the greasy stovetop burners. I knew how to scramble eggs, but that morning the eggs were terrible: the yokes stuck together in glutinous, runny lumps, and the egg whites were burnt. Maurice took a small bite and commented, "Only a bride would fry eggs this badly."

And indeed that's how I felt: like his bride. Maurice welcomed me into his life with the grace and finesse of someone born and raised in a universe where music, art, and poetry infused the tedium and grayness of ordinary days, and altered the rough woolen fabric of normality into woven silk tapestry that would last for centuries, like heirlooms that babies yet unborn would one day revere and admire. He was larger than life: gifted, capable, by dint of a salvaged out-of-tune piano, of drawing beauty from the mystic realm, beauty as acute as a Shakespearean sonnet, blessed as a passage from the *Songs of Solomon*. I believed in him, and I believed that the rest of the world would sooner or later know him for the genius that he was.

"You are so young and innocent," he teased. "How many springs have you had in your life?"

"Springs?" I had to count, "Nineteen—no, eighteen. And you?"

"I am thirty-two and a dirty old man who wants to eat your pussy."

We didn't leave the room for two days. As much as I wanted the world to stop, and my obsessions and worries to just leave me alone, I couldn't ignore my legs. Black stubble reappeared as always, and my skin took on the unwelcome texture of rough sandpaper. I was glad to be going home to my small hotel room; I needed a razor, bleach, my whole arsenal of depilatory objects to reverse the clock and transform my appearance to that of someone ordinary: a run-of-the-mill female, a woman who could be held and caressed.

IF YOU LEAVE BLEACH cream on the skin too long, the hairs become almost invisible and brittle. They break off, and things look pretty good, until a couple of days later, when the black roots start showing. I had to keep all that in check. Though I was short of money, finding an electrolysis practitioner in Washington was one of my first orders of business. There were a few in the yellow pages, and I picked the one whose address was nearby. She was a thin, taciturn, middle-aged woman who wore all white like a nurse, as if to give her profession legitimacy. As soon as she started on my upper lip, a piercing shot of pain went through my face. The shock alone brought involuntary tears to my eyes. This was no Merle. For each small prick and electric shock, one hair was tweezed off. I was glad that I had scheduled only a fifteen-minute session, although it would have been more economical to spring for one thirty minutes long. Thirty minutes would have *killed* me, I thought.

Over the years I have noted with unexpressed fury that each and every electrologist shorted me by at least five minutes. I felt ripped off on the one hand but happy to be done with the ordeal on the other, and therefore I never complained. I soldiered on, hoping that, after a few treatments, the hair would disappear for good. That was not to be.

This silent professional in her white lab coat worked on my face the whole time I lived in Washington but hardly made a dent. The hair returned gradually, initially unseen, moving invisibly like the second hand on a watch, only to return with a vengeance—a fact of life I had to learn to accept.

Hair or no hair, I fell in love. As the sun rose on Rock Creek Park in Washington, D.C., that first spring we were together, we could be found holding hands at dawn, staring at a piece of sculpture that would appear out of the bushes without prior notice, as if it had been placed there at that very moment just for our eyes. I was taken aback, not only by the loveliness that surrounded us like a Garden of Eden, but by the overwhelming flow of feelings that I had hitherto never known could exist in me for another human being. *I love this man*, I'd say to myself over and over again.

"Maurice, I love you."

"Baby, I love you, too. *Je t'aime toujours.*"

I moved in with him, into his shabby, roach-infested place, feeling as if I had won the jackpot. In his single room there was a kitchen, a convertible couch, and a grand piano with all manner of junk on the floor beneath it: cracked leather shoes, girlie magazines, sheet music, socks, moldy clothes, books with torn covers, chipped dishes, hardware, and a myriad of unknown objects in cardboard boxes.

The worst part were the roaches, which roamed freely and undisturbed. They were even in the bathroom, all over the tub and medicine cabinet. I had not seen American roaches until then.

"Oh, no, there are worms all over the table!" I hollered at first. Maurice, looking amused, explained: "Baby, your naïveté is absolutely charming. These are cockroaches, not worms. You had to be thinking of the word *vermin*, that is, from the Latin *vermis*. Worms are another species altogether. . . ."

Coming from Israel, I was no stranger to all manner of bugs, but Maurice's roaches differed from the water bugs I had known in my childhood, and which my father had easily crushed with his feet. Sometimes in bed at night, I would watch green lizards crawling on the ceiling; they were very slow and improbably soothing.

These new American roaches were much less intimidating, but they were numerous and, as they lacked natural enemies, there was little for us to do but ignore them. As Maurice would say, "You kill one, and all his brothers and cousins come to the funeral."

We learned to ignore other facts of life as well. At least *I* did. In 1967 I was still naïve, youthful, and green, easily captivated by the strangeness of Americans and still enthralled with everything new and untried, often misreading social cues as if I were an alien from a different plant, which was exactly what I was. Walking home on Fourteenth Street one wintery Saturday evening, when all the bars were still open and the streets crowded with cars and pedestrians, we were stopped by two white policemen as we were crossing the street. I was dressed in a white fake fur coat, my hair teased and sprayed into a beehive do, my eyes made up in dark charcoal, while Maurice, in his usual eccentric, mismatched outfit, already looking peculiar and too hip in his long, natural hair and beard, was holding my arm.

"Hey, man, you blind?" the younger cop bellowed at Maurice. "Can't you see you are crossing against the light?"

"No, I am not blind," Maurice responded in an even tone, "but the lights were changing as we were crossing on momentum. Sorry, Officer."

"On momentum," the cop mimicked. "Yeah, on momentum. Did you hear *that?*" he addressed his partner, and the two laughed. "Get the hell to wherever you two freaks are going, or I might arrest both of you on momentum."

In a little restaurant where we loved the crab-stuffed shrimp, an elderly waitress practically threw the food at us. "What's the matter with *her?*" I asked Maurice, but of course the question was rhetorical. When we were finished, Maurice paid the bill, then handed her a crisp five-dollar bill and, in a pleasant and unhurried manner, looked her in the eyes and said, "Please give this with my compliments to the cook."

"The cook?" she sputtered between pursed lips, unable to conceal her surprise.

"Yes, the *cook*," he reiterated. "Give him the tip with our compliments on his culinary expertise."

"Yes, sir," she snapped. "I will give it to the cook."

For a short time, I worked behind the counter in a general store in Maryland, right across the border. The other girl was a prototype of an older, hardened, bleached-blonde career waitress, in a pink uniform, name tag over her left breast, blue-veined, overworked hands and long, pointy red nails, welcoming regulars with her Southern-accented endearments and exaggerated friendliness. As soon as there was a break in the flow of customers she addressed me, and upon learning I was from another country, Austria, I said, she wanted to know why so many foreign women date coloreds. "For the life of me," she drawled, "I cannot fathom touching one of them people." I kept my mouth shut.

Then there were the neighborhood kids. Since we were only on the second floor, I could hear them at play in the alley between the tenements: "Fuck *you*, man! You are a jive turkey!"

"No, motherfucker, *you* are a jive turkey! Fuck *you*!"

Every time they saw us on the street they would chase us, laughing, "Hey, there they go, beauty and the beast!" Maurice, who always stopped to say hello and chat with young kids, found the children amusing.

Maurice was at the piano day and night but had no paying gig. I had no idea who paid the rent. I harbored the notion that he might secretly work as the janitor or superintendent, although there was no evidence of it. On the contrary, I knew that it would be out of character for him to sneak around shamefacedly; housekeeping was not his forte. I never saw him sweep, scrub the tub, or engage in other such tasks. Eventually, when I learned that his two older sisters were, by necessity, taking care of his affairs, I would have another explanation. He tried to find gigs, but none lasted more than a few days. As for me, since there were many clubs and bars along Fourteenth Street, all the way from Meridian Place to the center of the city where the tourists congregated, I tried each and every joint along the way, but all of them asked for my ID, and I was not yet twenty-one.

Then my luck changed, and I was hired on the spot at The Speakeasy, a barn-like joint modeled after the speakeasies of the Prohibition Era, replete with vaudeville acts and barely clad waitresses prancing around in high heels and fishnet stockings. The cocktail waitresses, costumed like Playboy bunnies, were expected, not unlike the painted pigs of an earlier era whose role it had been to lure men into seedy joints, to be part of the entertainment, a smorgasbord of vaudeville acts, songs, dance routines, and comedy. Among the routines was an old man's sentimental rendition of "Danny Boy" and a band that got the crowd going with "I'm a Yankee Doodle Dandy" and "Dixieland," a major crowd pleaser. Above the whole place was a skinny girl on a swing. The clientele, mostly men, among them many service guys either on their way to Vietnam or back, whooped and hollered, got drunk, and threw away their money on a vague hint or expectation that sex was the promise they saw in the girl's blank eyes as she stuffed bills under her breasts. In time I learned to sell the free peanuts to the drunks, re-sell pitchers of Schmidt beer, give out fictitious phone numbers to guys who kept on tipping, and pretend to accept expensive drinks that were, in fact, nothing but ice water.

The very first night, I felt I was at some kind of other-worldly ball; I could see men doubled over with laughter, but there was nothing particularly funny going on. All that mirth and glee, looked at from a tilted perspective, could be easily confused with horror. What was it all about?

The other girls looked at me suspiciously; they were civil but not particularly friendly. They were all shapes, nationalities, and ages. There was a Vietnamese girl who was short and hungry for cash. There was a beautiful girl from Roanoke, Virginia, who became a good friend but would get on my nerves because she dumped more and more toilet paper sheets into the toilet bowls after she peed but would never flush the damn thing. Her name was Lee. She had long, wavy dark hair and the face of a movie star; she could have been the Black Dahlia. In Roanoke she had left her child and lover after she was seen making out with a black cat. Her lover had threatened to kill her, and the result was that she wanted nothing to do with white men. "Ooh," she complained, "a pink dick is so *ugly*."

There were the two German sisters, Heidi and Helga, who also became my best friends. They were two beautiful bad girls who both hated their father, a Nazi. Each girl had a different mother. I met Heidi's mother once when she came to visit. She was loving and sweet. She looked at my bare hands and commented, "Darling, you don't wear any jewelry?" I didn't know what to say; it had never dawned on me to wear jewelry on my shaved hands.

Helga was tall and regal, her long brown hair always pulled away from her face in a tight ponytail. Her only visible flaw was her ankles, which were thick; some people called them "piano legs."

Heidi, her half-sister, had a deep masculine voice that belied her classic blonde beauty. She was a Marlene Dietrich all the way. In Germany she had married a black man named James Brown when he was on his way to Vietnam. A few months later, she received a phone call telling her that he had been injured, and she was flown to the United States, to a military hospital somewhere in the South. "They treated me like *shit*," she complained in her husky voice. "They referred to me as 'the white female' and gave me nasty looks." James ended up a quadriplegic, paralyzed from the neck down, while Heidi ended up with a beautiful apartment in D.C. and a pink Cadillac.

Each girl at the Speakeasy had landed there with an interesting story. There were girls who had babies to support, girls who were impossibly thin, girls who were beautiful, girls who came and went and talked about Vegas and Hollywood and making it in New York City, but when they stopped showing up they were never missed or remembered.

When I had received my assignment from our supervisor, Margaret, a tall, handsome, stiff woman in her thirties wearing a tight, extremely well-groomed bun and an expression that suggested an aversion to her surroundings, I learned that I was to work as far away from the stage as possible, in an area the girls called "Siberia." My mentor for the evening, a thin, flat-chested girl who wore little makeup, quickly taught me the tricks of the trade. "Don't walk away till they put some money in your tip tray," she explained. A pitcher of Schmidt cost two fifty, and the customer was expected to leave, at the very least, two quarters change. Likewise, for a seventy-five-cent glass of beer, we could easily pocket the quarter. Guys expected that. I was taught to wrap bills around my left index finger the way everyone else did, and to smile and flirt with the men and ignore their girlfriends, if they were there, because women were terrible tippers.

Fortunately, my first night was a slow one, and I managed to deliver drinks, make change, and smile, ignoring the taunts, noise, frenzy, music—a cacophony that permeated the entire enterprise. By the end of the night I was pleased. I had made fifteen dollars!

In the dressing room at two in the morning, when one of my colleagues, a tall, beautiful girl, asked me in her German accent what I had made in tips, I noticed that the others, at least eight young women in various stages of undress, were looking at me with relief and amusement. I was no threat, I guessed. Of course, I noted the smooth, hairless skin of every girl in the dressing room. I could not see myself in league with such beauties, but I learned how to make believe. I learned how to become the object of lust. It was important to be wanted, because it made a huge difference. A girl could make fifteen dollars or a hundred; it was all part of the same game.

Eventually I learned to hustle. I did fairly well, taking money from horny, drunk servicemen; it was easier than taking candy from a baby. Although we had a dressing room, I always came with my costume under my clothes, or, at the very least, my stockings on. We had some regular customers, admirers of a sort, and I remember one commiserating with me, saying, "I know how hard you girls work—it's blood money."

Girls did all kinds of things for tips. One girl sold a bit of her pubic hair to a sad, lonely old man; others sold their panties, garter belts, even tampons. Some, of course, sold their bodies. My German friend Heidi once told me, "Suzie, I took this black guy home, and he told me I was his dream come true. I was his angel. He gave me a hundred dollars, came right away, and fell asleep. I felt bad for him and tried to wake him up."

But I did learn how to hustle for dollars, cutting corners here and there, selling and reselling pitchers of beer, selling for a dollar or two bowls of peanuts that were free, selling bogus phone numbers, selling fantasies to young guys who were coming back from Vietnam missing a limb, a jaw, or a bit of their minds. But the whole time I was faithful to Maurice. Maurice had been happy for me to have the job. He knew a lot about cocktail waitresses; I had entered the world with which he was, as a musician, quite familiar.

WHEN I RECEIVED ASSURANCE that I had been hired to work and was given the address of where to purchase the required costume, I hadn't allowed shyness to encroach on my will. I had chosen a low-cut, gold lamé piece that flattered my thin shape and gave me room to pad my breasts. It was one of the more expensive pieces, but I couldn't wait to model it for Maurice.

When I came home, I was surprised to discover that he had company, a girl about my age or maybe younger, named Evan. The name "Evan" in Hebrew means *stone*—that was my first thought—but Evan was not made of stone; she was made of soft, smooth flesh and blonde hair. In the bathroom I changed into my costume, still energized by my new look, and even put on my highest-heeled shoes. When I returned to the room, Maurice and Evan exclaimed, "Hey, you look great!" At that point I started feeling a little silly. He was still at the piano, and she was humming along. I sat there in my outfit, wishing for her to disappear; I didn't like the way she looked at him; it was pure adoration, and I didn't understand the nature of their friendship. At the same time, I maintained a calm demeanor; after all, he had many friends, and at any given time anyone could walk into the room.

After a couple of hours or so, Evan left. "How did you feel about her being here?" he asked as soon as she was out the door.

I was taken aback. How did I *feel*? Well, jealous, undoubtedly, but too proud to admit to that. "I felt fine. She was nice. Who *is* she?"

"Just a friend. But since up to now the only competition you had was the piano, I wonder if you minded sharing me with another girl."

"What do you mean, *sharing* you?"

"Sharing my attention, obviously."

"I'm okay. I don't need your undivided attention all the time. It was fun having company."

"And you have no other thoughts or qualms that you might wish to articulate?"

"Not really." I started to feel a pounding on the left side of my head; a migraine was coming on.

He looked at me thoughtfully, lit a cigarette, inhaled deeply, and, as if preparing to impart some words of wisdom, gravely nodded and said, "Well, I would never cheat on you, my love. When a relationship ends, I go through a period of decontamination. I will not have sex for at least a few months, until I feel cleansed. That's what I did when Ana and I broke up. I came home after a gig and she was in bed with some cat. She looked up at me and said, 'Oh, he's just a friend.'"

"So what are you saying?" I lit a cigarette, knowing that it would make the migraine worse. But I could deal with *physical* pain.

"What I mean is, Evan is sensual and loving," he continued. "The three of us can have sex together. We will feel even closer to each other after sharing our love and our bodies."

I was totally stunned! I had heard of a *ménage a trois,* more often as some pathetic joke, but I didn't know that *normal* people participated in such a decadent and unnatural act. The thought of seeing him making love to another woman was beyond appalling; it was worse than a slap in the face—worse than breaking up! I expressed my feelings while crying, still wearing the silly costume and feeling degraded, absurd, and totally ridiculous. I kicked off my heels and buried my face in my hands.

It was an argument that would come up from time to time over the next two years, but a notion that would never be consummated. Not with Maurice anyway.

IN ADDITION TO SEX lessons, Maurice taught me how to fry chicken by double-dipping each piece in whipped eggs and flour; how to play a decent game of chess—as long as he gave me queen odds; how to read Henry Miller, in particular *Sexus*; how to differentiate between making love and fucking; and how to cry without making a sound. But he revealed very little about himself or his life before I had inserted myself into it.

"I am a widower," he answered when I wondered about his wife.

"What happened to her?" I asked, wanting to know; but he would never answer.

He admitted that his first wife had been German, a woman he had met while he was in the service, and that they had a son, Moritz. About his stint in the service I knew nothing, except for a story he told me: While on the bus with a bunch of white servicemen, he had found himself singing out loud, "You make my brown eyes blue," and suddenly everyone had turned around, looked at him, and laughed.

He had once been busted in Manhattan.

"Let me see your arms!" a cop had ordered.

"Leave me alone, pig! I have no tracks!" he had protested.

And that had led to an admission at Bellevue.

"Why did they do that to you?"

"Well, in court I heard 'The People vs. Maurice J. Gaston.' They asked me if I understood the charges, and I said, 'Certainly, I do. It is *The People vs. I.*' And so they diagnosed me as a schizophrenic and secluded me at St. Elizabeth's. The mother of my son came to see me in the hospital, gave me a polite peck on the check, and said, 'Maurice, take care of yourself.'"

And then he showed me a pamphlet of poems, which he had composed in the hospital, entitled *Skits o' Phrenia*.

The poems, which he read aloud to me, were clever but lacked emotion. They could have been written by someone dead—someone in whom rigor mortis had already set in.

Who was this man I was crazy about? He was both an intimate and a stranger. His speech was peppered with words that I secretly looked up in the dictionary: *benevolence, comeuppance, fortitude, desolation, decontamination*. Many people were impressed, while others commented on his eccentricity and grandiosity. I thought he was the cat's meow, even as I didn't know whether he had graduated from college or sat up nights memorizing the dictionary. I *did* learn that there were rules.

I was not permitted to eat or purchase pork products.

"Are you a Black Muslim?" I asked naively.

"Well," he laughed, pointing at his skin, "one thing for sure: I *am* black."

"So why can't we eat bacon?" I asked.

He said nothing.

"Don't wear makeup," he ordered.

Another rule.

"Why not?" I protested. "I don't feel pretty unless I do. Especially when we go out."

"It's gilding the lily," he scolded.

"Don't smoke on the street," he insisted.

Yet another rule.

NOT WEARING MAKEUP, PARTICULARLY around Heidi and Helga and my other female friends who were beautiful, made me feel like the ugly duckling in the bunch, a plastic dime store flower among long-stemmed roses. It was reminiscent of the early hassles I'd had with my parents over makeup.

My father would fly off the handle whenever I lined my eyes with black pencil, which was fashionable in the 1960s. According to him and to my mother, who agreed with everything he said, I looked cheap, a tramp advertising her availability. It was such a taboo that, at my friend's house, I'd apply thick eyeliner above and below my eyes, giving them a cat-like look, then wash it all off before coming home. Once, on my way home, I realized I had forgotten to remove the eye makeup. Panicked, I tried to wipe it off with the black snow piled at the curb, so great was my fear.

AFTER WE HAD BEEN living together for a while, Maurice commented on my hairy legs. It reminded him of a previous girlfriend who had been hairy but sexy. When he told me that, I changed the subject immediately, and, miraculously, allowed myself to be seen naked in the daytime. Still, there was no way I would allow him to know about the electrologist or about the bleaching-and-shaving routine. When he was not home, I would apply the bleach to the mustache, sideburns, cheekbones, chin, arms, and the rest of the problem areas, then stand still as a soldier on patrol, ready to wash off everything at once lest I be caught. Sometimes, after rinsing off the dried bleach, I would find that I had rinsed it off too soon and would have to reapply the stuff and begin all over again.

Once, after leaving the apartment for the Speakeasy, I recalled that I had inadvertently left the empty bottle of bleaching cream by the toilet bowl. Throughout my shift I worried that Maurice would discover my secret, as if I were covering up some ugly, infectious, sexually transmitted disease. Actually, gonorrhea would have been less embarrassing. And speaking of gonorrhea, in his refrigerator Maurice kept penicillin vials of indeterminate age but of obvious utility. It was not a secret; when I asked, he was happy to explain the wisdom behind the prophylactic antibiotics.

THERE WAS NOTHING ABOUT Newark or my family that I missed; I would have been happy to be left to my own devices for a long, long time. But they decided to visit me. I was working at the Speakeasy six evenings a week from 6 p.m. to 2 a.m. I couldn't even *imagine* the hysteria that would ensue were my parents to witness me prancing around the place in a bunny uniform; but much worse would happen if they were to see Maurice and me shacked up in our ghetto pad, the bed in the center of the room attesting to how far down I had sunk. There was a lot of preparation to be done. I was afraid of my power to inflict pain on those two people; I knew that a swelling of guilt would haunt me for the rest of my life, keep me awake nights, chain me to words and deeds that should not have seen daylight, should not have been disclosed. I believed that, if they knew my living circumstances, my mother would commit suicide and my father murder!

The Speakeasy's supervisor blithely informed me that I could not take a week off; she didn't give a damn about my issues with my visiting parents and fired me on the spot. Maurice reluctantly agreed to stay away.

A friend who, miraculously, was going out of town that week allowed me the use of her apartment. But when my parents arrived hours earlier, in the morning instead of later in the evening as they had originally planned, Maurice was just getting out of the shower.

I whispered to him, "Don't move. They're here," and prayed that he would not do anything crazy. They knocked repeatedly, impatiently, and I thanked God that a long corridor separated the front door from the main room. I sat motionless at the kitchen table, waiting for the knocking to cease. Maurice was almost dressed. He had on a long-sleeved white shirt and rolled-up jeans—an uncool look when bell-bottoms, colorful shirts, bandanas, beads, and sandals were on the verge of becoming the fashion statement of the decade. He was in the process of putting on his dress shoes when he looked up at as if he'd just had an epiphany. In a hushed voice he said, "Look, I'm your old man, and I should meet your parents. I'll go up to your mother and speak to her in Polish. I *know* that would break the ice."

Yeah, right. The look of horror on my face was enough to convince him his plan wouldn't work.

Maurice left shortly after the knocking had ceased, just in time to miss my parents' return. Though temporarily relieved, I felt a gnawing tug at my soul: I feared I had emasculated him; I was on the side of evil. My actions made him into an Uncle Tom, into half a man. I was responsible for perpetuating the long, grim history of hatred, and for what?

The next day, my parents returned to Jersey satisfied and as much in the dark as they had been before their visit. They had been mesmerized and revolted by the spectacles in Dupont Circle: overt homosexuals flaunting their sexuality, long-haired guitar players, half-naked girls—but most of all, the sight of mixed couples, beautiful young girls arm in arm with the blacks.

I knew little about politics in general and even less about the civil rights struggles that were going on in the country. Yes, I had heard that blacks were rioting, and that a cloud of violence threatened large cities, but I had no idea that it was only in 1965 that Johnson had signed the Civil Rights Act, or that in some states it would have been illegal for Maurice and me to marry. I didn't know that legal discrimination was a fact of life; from my naive point of view, prejudice belonged in the past, along with slavery and all other evils committed by uncivilized societies. In the sixties, I believed, we were living in a modern society that eschewed primitive notions of racial superiority, at least publicly. Prejudice was practiced among toothless, illiterate, hapless poor whites who knew no better. Nazism had been an aberration, as the slave trade had been, but modern America was indeed the New World.

On April 4, 1968, Dr. Martin Luther King, Jr. was assassinated in Memphis, and all hell broke loose. Washington was burning, and for days the two of us were unable to leave the confines of our room. Maurice played the piano while I read Henry Miller or perused his *Playboy* and other girlie magazines. We had no phone, radio, or television. It was only when Maurice's sister dutifully came by that we learned of the looting and rioting on Fourteenth Street uptown, our neighborhood. "If you smell smoke, leave," she only halfway joked before leaving. Phyllis and Anne, his older sisters, looked after him, I later learned; in fact, they were the ones who were paying the rent on the apartment.

Stores were on fire; the National Guard was patrolling the streets. When we finally ventured out, it saddened me to see that the new Mays department store, where I had only recently bought a bathrobe for my mother, had been burned and looted, and the local grocery stores abandoned. Some merchants placed signs like *Soul Brother* in front of their stores, hoping that the rioters would spare them as God had spared the Jewish homes in Egypt. Someone hung a similar sign from a window in front of our building, not that anyone who lived there had anything to steal.

Living as we did, day to day, hand to mouth, politics held little interest for either one of us. Frankly, I knew very little about Dr. King, and Maurice behaved as if none of that had anything to do with him. He referred to the riots as *mass hysteria*, a phrase I found elegant, erudite. I thought people were stupid for burning down the neighborhood in which they lived, because we who lived there suffered the consequences: To buy a carton of milk, you had to travel all the way downtown. Maurice and I knew many of the cats who participated in this "mass hysteria," and, in fact, afterwards we were given opportunities to buy some gold jewelry for practically nothing, but Maurice refused on principle. I had no jewelry, and for some time afterward a part of me regretted turning down some of those offers.

As a white girl, I did not feel threatened living in that part of Washington. Although I rarely saw any other whites on the streets before or after the riots, I was never singled out for any sinister reason; if anything, many people bent over backwards to make me feel at home. In the beauty salon I asked for French curls, and they did not grimace, laugh, or behave in any way that suggested that I was probably the first one asking for that particular style. The other women were getting Afros or straightening their hair, and my beautician struggled with mine, even speaking to my errant locks: "Now, you stay there like you're supposed to!" No one told me to get the fuck out, no one tried to steal anything from me, no one ever tried to rape me, and no one ever assaulted me. Except Maurice.

7

BEAUTY AND THE BEAST

O NE MORNING I WOKE up with chills, muscle aches, sore throat—all the familiar symptoms of cold or flu. Instead of saying something to Maurice, who was lying next to me lost in thought and smoking a cigarette, I preferred suffering silently, hoping that he would telepathically recognize an oncoming acute illness and immediately cosset and coddle his baby, offering me succor and nursing care just as my mother would have done. I wanted hot tea with lemon, a cold compress, an extra blanket, a fluffed pillow, a concerned, loving person anxious about my health and well-being.

"Baby, will you go down and get the mail, please?" he asked when he heard me cough.

"What for? You expecting money?"

"No. I don't expect to find any remuneration or reward in the mailbox, but I *do* expect honor and obedience from my old lady."

Wordlessly, I pulled on my terrycloth robe and went down the one flight of stairs. There was a letter addressed to me from a girlfriend in Newark, nothing special.

Back in the room, I jammed the letter into my pocketbook without even looking at it and immediately returned to bed, pulling the blanket up almost over my head. *Let him think what he wants*, I silently answered his questioning look. *Let him think I got a letter from an old boyfriend*. As I felt sorry for myself, involuntary tears began to flow, a little at first, until, for no reason, I was weeping and crying as if I had received terrible news in the mail.

"What is *this* about?" he almost shouted.

"I'm okay," I whimpered. "I don't want to talk about it."

"But I am standing here asking you a question, and I desire to be informed. What's going *on* with you?"

I wanted to say that he should have gone down to get the mail. I wanted to say that he should have nursed me, treated me solicitously, kindly, gently; he should have made me toast with honey and a drink to sooth my throat; but I couldn't demean myself. I couldn't tell him what I had hoped he would do. He should have done those things without detailed directives. He should have been sensitive and empathetic, as I would have, had the situation been reversed. In the wake of those thoughts, another stream of tears, sniffles, and choked-up whimpering ensued. My nose was running, my throat hurt, and I was shivering, probably coming down with a fever.

The crying was cathartic, however. I buried my head in the pillow and, after twenty minutes or so, sat up, ready to make peace. He was seated at the piano bench where I had seen him last, his head tilted a bit to the left; he appeared preoccupied, lost in thought. I called his name, and he abruptly jumped up, as if awakened from a deep sleep, and to my confusion and disbelief began pelting me with blows to the face and chest, knocking me back down onto the bed where the night before he had licked my anus until I almost screamed with exhaustion and boredom.

"*Now* you have something to complain about!" he yelled, revulsion and loathing spewing out with the words. I said nothing. I remained on the bed as he had left me, attempting to become nothing, no more and no less than a fixture, afraid for my life.

From the corner of one swollen eye I could see him dressing methodically and unhurriedly; he even put a white handkerchief in his jacket pocket and spit-polished his shoes. He looked for all the world like a man ready to start his day, placing his best foot forward. An eternity later, I heard him leave the building.

After a few moments, fairly certain he was gone, probably traipsing down Fourteenth Street, whistling a jazzy tune, I imagined, I slowly stood up, mindful of my beaten body, threw my clothes, books, and toiletries into a bag, ran out of the building, avoiding stares, caught a bus on Fourteenth Street, and rode it to the end of the line.

THERE WAS MORE TO Maurice than met the eye—I'd known that from the start—but I wanted to know more: I wanted to understand what demons controlled his thoughts, what forces drove him towards unpredictability, towards rage and violence. I wanted to find excuses. I wanted him back. I wanted to know that he and I could reignite the dawn in Meridian Park, replay *A Love Supreme*. I hoped that the violence would fade with the bruises.

The prospect of being without him was untenable, but going back was risky. I spent hours in a Washington public library, reading all I could find on schizophrenia but understanding only a fraction of the psychiatric mumbo jumbo. Like many back then, I believed that schizophrenia meant having split personalities, good and bad. I recalled his odd and unreadable facial expressions when smoking grass. After a few tokes, he would look absent, as if tuned to inner sounds only *he* could hear, voices only *he* could decipher. "Ah, so," he would mutter, a half-smile on his face, a secret.

Everyone who knew him, who had seen him smoke dope, knew his highs were odd and discomfiting, even hinting at something sinister.

The usual heightened sensations—laughter, merriment, sensuality—or wasted observations—"Wow, look at this bottle of shampoo! It's out of sight!"—were silenced by an inchoate fear, an unnamed anxiety that hinted at dark spaces, alternate reality, unknown and unwanted discordance. No one dared speak, only he, and all he ever said was, "Ah, so," to which there was no response.

I became obsessed with his second wife. Who *was* she? How had she died? Had he harmed her? I tried to recall what he'd told me about her initially, but I couldn't. His responses had been convoluted, tangential, unemotional, and I, embarrassed for prying, left the mystery untouched, dead and buried. But now it was in the forefront, and I was *scared*. Had she met with foul play? After her death, did he practice his version of decontamination and cleansing of the soul and hands? Knowing what I knew, and chilled by what could happen to me, all that should have given me pause, should have driven me away to the ends of the earth! Self-preservation, an instinct that even a *cockroach* knows, should have kept me running from danger; either that, or I should have been crouched among library stacks studying my *own* psychology, instead of torturing myself with his schizophrenia, a word I could not even pronounce.

I RETURNED TO MAURICE on Meridian Place and stayed there on and off for about a year. We had no money. Once in a blue moon Maurice would get work, but the gigs always ended quickly and on a sour note. People said he sounded like Monk. Local musicians admired him; artists couldn't get enough. But in the noisy, smoke-filled local restaurants and dives where the patrons expected a sound that they could hum along with, a beat that they could bump and grind to on the dance floor, his playing missed the crowd, filling the air like rare perfume, the riffs and rhythms so many snowflakes floating against gravity.

"I am *not* going to play 'Misty'," was his response to being fired from the chic Italian restaurant that catered to businessmen in town for a night or two, who, after a long day in a conference or in the venerable halls of Congress, wished to relax with a bowl of spaghetti, a bottle of Chianti, and a black man at the piano cheering them up with good-time music. Maurice didn't mind going hungry or living in a dump surrounded by old newspapers, girlie magazines, and all manner of junk, and wearing the same seersucker suit season after season. At home he played his out-of-tune piano, smoked Viceroys, wrote beautiful melodies with titles such as "Snowflakes in the Spring" that could have assured him immortality had he sought the accolades.

I loved Washington in the spring, the warm air full of promise. But I wanted to go home for Passover. I wanted my room, where I could sleep through the night without the constant fear of assault or worse. I wanted relief from walking on eggshells, from editing every sentence before expressing it to Maurice. I also wanted to see Shlomo, my brother, who had graduated from high school, gotten drafted into the army, and been fortuitously rejected with a diagnosis of hypertension. He was doing nothing, according to my mother, but in fact, I knew he was weighing his options and seriously considering returning to Israel.

Maurice was upset. "I don't want to go for a whole week without you. Your place is with your old man."

"I know, baby, but please don't lay all these changes on me. You know I'll be back. I have to see my family."

I was contrite but resolute, holding my ground. I could already feel the solace of the ancient Passover hymns, taste the crisp-textured almond macaroons, savor the syrupy sweet red wine, revert back to childhood, and bask in parental love. The past took on a pinker and gentler glow, and as it turned out, the visit went well. Fortified and expecting the familial bliss to shatter sooner or later, I was ready to return to D.C.

The night before my flight back, I had a strange dream, full of details as dreams often are, but with one that impressed upon me a distinct feeling of reality: I was homeless, lonely, sleeping on the street like a bum, with no place to go.

The flight was rather uneventful until we reached Washington, and there, suddenly, an odd atypical whistle, like an alarm signaling a tea kettle boiling, sounded throughout the cabin. The captain immediately announced something unintelligible; I felt a bout of diarrhea coming on. This is *it!* I thought as I lit one cigarette after another.

The other passengers appeared mildly concerned; the stewardess who rushed from the back of the plane to the front appeared hurried but hardly frantic. At last I understood the captain's repeated assurances, and tried to ignore the noise, which I understood as air coming in through the siding, whatever *that* meant. But that was not all: The airport was crowded, the plane couldn't land, and we were circling the sky, spinning around the city, around and around, as if stuck in someone else's horror movie script.

After at least an hour and a pack of Marlboros, the plane finally landed and we were on solid ground, an expected and anticlimactic end to what later would appear like a minor glitch, a story not worth telling. But it would leave me forever afraid of flying.

I had given up the slight hope that Maurice would meet me at the airport, and as soon as I breathed the humid D.C. air I waved down a taxi and, from the back seat, shouted instructions to the driver, imploring him to drive faster. At last I reached Meridian Place. I was wearing a short-sleeved, China-red, A-line silk dress, sexy and bouncy. My hair was long and thick, worn partially up, my eyes made up with green shadow, dark liner, and mascara.

I knew I looked hot as I reached his apartment and flung the front door wide open. As I did so, I found Maurice in bed with another woman, caught, as it were, *in flagrante*. This scene—indeed, this shopworn cliché—took my breath away; I was crashing through thin air, falling at great speed without the benefit of a parachute, once again feeling the wind whistling through the siding, against my will playing a role in someone's else's horror movie!

What I did next was completely out of character: I hit her with my pocketbook. Repeatedly. If it had been a movie, this scene would have provided silly comic relief, despite my tears, her fears, Maurice's rage. The naked brown-haired girl with small breasts and baby-smooth skin wasted no time grabbing her clothes and getting the hell out of there. She even left behind her leather jacket and, in the ashtray, a lit cigarette.

With alacrity, Maurice jumped into the fray, and with one aggressive motion shoved me against the piano. "What's *wrong* with you!" he hollered, and punched my face simultaneously. His violence surprised me. *Can't he see that he has already hurt me*, I thought. *Doesn't he know that I care?* It didn't make sense; *he* should have been the one on his knees crying, begging my forgiveness. I didn't feel the force of the blows or taste the blood filling my mouth. I said nothing as I walked out, in my sexy red dress and clutching my pocketbook, into the night, homeless, alone, bereft of emotion.

I couldn't stand the sight of women. All women became that brown-haired girl, my anathema, my enemy. I didn't want to think of her but, like an annoying jingle, her image clung to my mind, pecked at it. I could practically *feel* the texture of her smooth thighs, the downy softness of her face, her naked femininity a slap at my wretched, pitiful struggle to be like all other women, to be like *her*.

My vanity, under the blow of true nakedness, had been struck, beaten to a pulp, bloodied, spat on, despised. She had lain with him in *daylight*, smoking a cigarette, hiding *nothing*, her female charms flaunted as she grabbed her clothes and ran, unaware that she was envied. I wanted what *she* had: the luxury of un-self-consciousness, the taking for granted of love in the afternoon, sunlight showing off the glow of her porcelain skin, her flawless form. This nameless girl unknowingly became the embodiment of my sorrow, my fury, my hate. I could not destroy her image by pelting it with whatever was on hand any more than I could actually efface her with my pocketbook. I was like an old woman idiotically trying to fight off a tough young intruder, all to save a couple of dollars and a tube of lipstick. Too funny. Too sad.

I didn't know what to do, so I got drunk. Alone, in a rundown hotel room, I drank Pernod, a licorice drink in a cobalt blue bottle that I had bought because I thought it sophisticated, something from a Henry Miller novel. It didn't take long for the room to reel, the ceiling to wobble, and all the objects around me to lose form and structure. The yellow-flowered bedspread rife with unmentionable stains, the linoleum floor worn and cracked, the bedside tables etched with cigarette burns, the rusty sink, the spider webs and flypaper, and the dusty, lone light bulb hanging from the ceiling cried for their senseless, dilapidated, decrepit state of being, and I shared their shame and grief. It was all disgraceful, unbecoming, and for naught, including the unending retching and vomiting. In the midst of all that, I called my mother, as if an insane situation required an insane response. My father handed the phone to my mother. They both sounded like people awakened out of a sound, well-earned sleep.

"I just found my boyfriend with another woman," I wept. She must have been utterly taken aback: This was not a sentence either one of us expected to hear coming out of my mouth.

There was an excruciating pause. Finally, having recouped, she said, "So, what do *you* care? He is not your *husband!*"

"That's right," I agreed, hanging up the phone and forcing down another gulp of Pernod. Soon I passed out, and neither my mother nor I ever mentioned that phone call. It was as if it had never happened.

THE NEXT TIME HE attacked me, he pulled me by my hair out into the corridor. I was down on the unwashed, cold tile floor, appalled, frightened, scared for my life. I was saved by the unwitting intrusion of a tenant who walked past us and into his own apartment. The guy, dressed in a heavy coat, didn't look at or say anything to us; he probably assumed that whatever was happening was a private matter between lovers, and he was not stupid enough to insert himself between two consenting adults. But he broke the spell. Maurice's rage consumed itself, imploding into ash and rubble.

Back indoors, things were said, plans made, nothing memorable. Whatever it was that had set Maurice off on that occasion must have been a garden-variety domestic squabble. Maybe I had refused to shine his shoes; maybe I had overcooked the meat, fried pork bacon instead of beef, refused to give him head. Whatever the root cause of that latest fearsome episode, it couldn't have been monumental. He could have at last killed or maimed me over spilled milk, literally. I could search for insights into his behavior forever. I could try to avoid the acts or words that I knew could potentially set him off. If I was smart, I could keep my mouth shut, zipped from corner to corner.

But I could also walk away forever. The madness was not *mine*; I hadn't inherited it, hadn't contributed to its formation and growth, hadn't been there through the early traumas that cultivated and watered the rage until it reached its adult potential, its ability to destroy. I was an innocent bystander, a foreigner, who had adopted an untamed fury, an evil twin of the musical, lovely man whom I adored and from whom I should have run at first light. I was, I had to believe, devaluing my *own* life, treating myself as worthless.

Where was Bracha, the advocate for the underdog, the girl who touted free will, who loved cats, trees, I. B. Singer stories, who fought her parents tooth and nail for autonomy and self-determination? I was living unchained in a mine field, relying upon a man whose demons and *dybbuks*, I dare say, could rear their ugly heads, extend their tentacles outward, any time day or night, without prior warning and without provocation. I knew of no woman, young or old, who would tolerate such conditions and still speak of love.

A girlfriend who happened to come by uninvited and got a good look at our living conditions later asked how I could tolerate sleeping in that roach- and rat-infested place even *one* night; and she asked that not knowing the half of it. It was *I* who was becoming divided: I longed to stay, and I wanted to go. I wanted one part of him and despised the other. I longed for his music, love, poetry, but feared his dark side. Schizophrenia, despite what the medical books said, was indeed contagious. It was *I* who was split in two; it was *I* who became clinically crazy.

ONE MORNING, A COUPLE of weeks or so after the last outburst, I walked to the corner grocery store, filled my shopping cart with milk, fruit, steaks, and some non-perishables, and thought about returning to his room and cooking dinner with him. I imagined him at the grand piano, with all the junk beneath it, a cigarette dangling from his lips, his brow furrowed in concentration, his eyes cold and black, composing something sweet and melodious while shooting dark looks at me. Instantly, I felt dizzy, overcome with nausea, and gasping for clean air. My legs felt as if they belonged to someone else, and I was afraid they would lead me out of the supermarket, down the street, up the stairs, and straight into his room and into a tight, cavernous, dangerous free fall from which I would never recover. I thought of finding a bathroom in the store in order to splash some water over my face but never got that far. A fast-moving dream in a collage of purples, greens, and reds sped through my unconsciousness and then vanished into nothing, almost taking me with it.

While still trying to resurrect and understand that dream, its magic and perplexity, I came to on the hard tiled floor and found myself the center of attention and concern. I heard someone say, "She just suddenly fell out. I saw her head hit the floor." I was not surprised to realize that I had fainted. An ambulance came and whisked me off to the emergency room at George Washington University Hospital, where they expeditiously admitted me into a medical unit for tests and observation. I had never felt better in my life!

The next morning, while I was lying in bed in my hospital gown, a team of doctors and medical students entered the room and began a conversation about my fainting episode, which they called *syncope*. They said nothing to me, and I felt self-conscious, particularly with my revealing gown showing off my day-old stubble. To add to my ignominy, one of the doctors reached down and, ignoring me as if I were lifeless, lifted one of my hairy arms that had not been bleached for two days. Turning to the others, he smugly proclaimed, "She is definitely hirsute, and I would wonder if there is any underlying adrenal disease that we should consider."

Another guy removed the top of the gown and checked my nipples. "No," he observed, "there's no hair around the areolas." The others agreed, and the topic was dropped. After some more medical poppycock, they disbanded, leaving me alone with my shame.

What an ignorant bunch, I thought. *It never occurred to those arrogant bastards that my nipples might have been tweezed!* Not that I would have admitted to that had they asked. Even if my *life* depended on it! I could have more easily jumped off the stretcher and performed a belly dance than explained to the doctors why my areolas were hairless on that day! It had never occurred to me that my hairiness could be more than just a cosmetic problem; I didn't know that, although in most cases hirsutism was idiopathic, there could be a small chance that it was due to a medical, and even *curable*, abnormality.

Somehow I knew innately that nothing had gone awry with my

adrenal glands, neurotransmitters, pancreas, brain waves, lymphatic system, or any hormonal or lymphatic fluids in my body. There was no medical reason that could be responsible for unwanted hair growth. My hirsute nature was my legacy, my inheritance, my cross to bear. It was there just for its own sake; it did not augur worse conditions, did not threaten my life in any way, and did not diminish my chances of getting through my youth without physical trauma or abuse. It was just one of those things.

Later, Maurice would tell me that he thought I had run out on him, and in my own meek way, of course, I *had*, particularly since I was relishing my freedom, lying by the window on the clean hospital bed, feeling safe and secure. Hospitals had always made me feel safe. They were places where life and death met, where mission and heroism intersected. I liked the hustle and bustle of the hospital's interior, even the disinfectant smell, the sounding of alarms, the slamming of doors. It was a place of healing, even if the price required being poked, prodded, and palpated.

It didn't bother me that the doctors were puzzled by my lab results, or that they were ruling out diseases that I couldn't even pronounce! I had books to read, television to watch, and best of all, menus to fill out. I could circle whatever I wanted. It was a luxury to be served meals in bed, to be spoken to kindly and offered nightly sleeping pills and a back massage; I felt like a princess. After about two weeks and multiple vials of blood drawn each morning, I was told that I needed a kidney biopsy.

I eagerly called my mother; nothing could get her love and attention more than a medical emergency, a genuine disease worthy of concern. She already knew I was in the hospital, and had sent me sheer baby doll pajamas that I couldn't wear because they revealed too much unshaven skin. But my father answered the phone.

"I'm in the hospital for tests," I said, "and the doctors say there might be something seriously wrong with my kidneys."

There was a palpable silence. I heard him clearing his throat, and felt his uneasiness over the miles of telephone wires. "Your mother and Shlomo left for Israel only yesterday," he reported, as if it were an explanation for his awkwardness. "They will be back in two weeks."

What was he thinking? I had the unpleasant feeling that he equated my being hospitalized with something sexual, unclean, female, venereal.

"Your mother sent you a present. Did you get it?"

"Oh, yes. . .well . . . okay. . . ."

"*Zei gezint.*"

"Yep. You, too."

IN THE MORNING A couple of aides brought heavy sandbags and placed them by the foot of the bed.

"What are *those* for?" I asked, virtually shivering.

"Oh, they're just to keep you from moving," said the nurse, who had walked into the room carrying a tray of sharp and forbidding instruments—needles in various sizes, scissors, scalpels, the works. "You'll have to lie on your tummy and keep still."

They placed the sandbags on my ankles, and I expected the worst, lying on my stomach and not knowing what was happening right behind my back. They stuck me with Novocain, and I hollered in pain; then they snipped off a piece of tissue from my kidneys. A few days later I was provided with a solid verdict: Chronic glomerulonephritis. Finally I had something *concrete* to focus on, and my problem had a *shape* and a *name*. This illness, *whatever* it implied, offered me credibility. It would have been embarrassing to come home with nothing. I was happy to offer the doctors a disease as proof that I was a bona fide patient who merited the time and attention they had showered upon me. Most of all, I had something to show Maurice. My diagnosis was my ticket to a better relationship, I hoped.

Since he had no telephone and I had made no effort to reach him, all he knew was that during a routine trip to the grocery store I had disappeared. The possibility of a kidney problem had never crossed my mind before; if it hadn't been for the biopsy, I wouldn't have known the function or location of those organs. Having a diagnosis written down on a doctor's prescription pad gave me, and my unscheduled hospital vacation, legitimacy.

Years later, during hypochondriacal episodes that would occur from time to time, I endured genuine panic attacks. Fear of dying claimed my mind and robbed me of sleep. I made doctors' appointments just to hear reassuring words. But as time passed and my kidneys continued to function without my awareness, the memory of the biopsy and diagnosis became distant and vague. I even questioned the veracity of the diagnosis, my trust in my recollections, and my prior fear of mortality.

THE NEXT VIOLENT EPISODE struck soon enough, and that time it was clearly I who had instigated it. While I was taking my rest in the hospital, Maurice had met a girl who played classical flute, and according to him their relationship was platonic, based only on their shared passion for music. The girl happened to have obtained two tickets to a rare performance by Vladimir Horowitz and wanted Maurice to accompany her. I became furious, overcome with jealousy and disbelief.

"*Please* don't go. How would *you* feel if *I* had a date with someone else?" I pleaded for a good two weeks.

"It's not a date. It's about the music," he insisted.

"Right. But I don't dig this chick and can't imagine why she'd ask *you* instead of one of her friends," I said.

"I *am* her friend."

When the night of the performance arrived, and he, bathed,

cologned, and outfitted in his Sunday best, so to speak, jauntily bounced out of the apartment, leaving behind a cloud of cigarette smoke, I didn't say a word, though in my head there was enough venom and fumes to set the concert hall on fire!

Later that evening Heidi and I went to a jazz club on Fourteenth Street where, through Maurice, I knew the musicians. We drank wine, smoked cigarettes, and tapped our feet to the jazzy, hip rock beat. I was interested in the guitar player, a thin, bearded, long-haired white guy. He had a habit of twisting and distorting his face into odd, comical expressions while playing, at times looking as if he were in agony. Fascinated, I watched his face and noted his eyes smiling at me. When the band took a break, he sauntered over to us.

"Ladies, it is a pleasure to meet you here. What can I get you?" he asked.

"More wine!" we both cried in unison. The bar was crowded and festive, and while the band was on break, the juke box blasted James Brown's more recent mantra, "Say It Out Loud, I'm Black and I'm Proud." The guitarist offered us a joint, and together, Heidi on one of his arms and I hanging onto the other, we strolled out of the bar toward the curb, where his car was parked—at which exact second I saw Maurice coming toward us, head bent down and tilted to one side as if listening to internal commands, probably ordering him to kill. He didn't hasten his step, nor did he slow down. He came towards me as if he didn't see me and, wordlessly, struck me in the face. I saw stars.

There were people all around, but no one came forward, no one intervened. In the chaos I lost sight of Heidi and the guitarist. Maurice pulled me into the middle of the street and struck my face again with his fist, then pushed me away and resumed his walk uptown in the same measured, even footsteps. The whole scene had taken only moments. I could feel and taste blood streaking my face like tears, but all I could think was, *Oh, no! He's mad at me! We're breaking up again, and I don't* want *to break up!*

I chased his dark, disappearing figure, calling his name and crying. He stopped as if startled, looked me over as if he had never seen me before; then, like a stern father, he upbraided me. "*Look* at you, bleeding in the middle of the street!"

We were not far from Meridian Place, and I chased him all the way home. Upstairs, like a solicitous father, he cleansed the gash above my eye with an antiseptic, then covered it with gauze pads he had lying around. It took about twenty years for the scar to fade.

My fear of his temper never abated, nor did my instinct for self-preservation, but my craving for him knew no bounds. And I feared *myself* as well: I feared that, alone, without his love, I would sink into an abyss of depression that would squeeze my breath away. I feared my own dark reactions. I feared the bleak moods that would overcome me, particularly at night, if I knew he would not be coming home. I had no idea how I could possibly cope. I knew I would not cut my wrists or ingest poisons, the histrionic behaviors I had resorted to in my adolescence, which had been meant for an audience and had served to silence my parents. But the pangs of loss would be too unbearable, particularly alone at night, when the austerity of my surroundings and the weight of my own company would bear upon me, crush me, drown me in waves of hollow, free-flowing panic worse than a cardiac infarction, worse than a torn artery, leaving me lying in my own shit and blood. I craved him like an addict craves his fix. Maurice was my heron, my smack, my scag, my white horse, my poison, my animus, and I knew no way out.

BY THAT TIME I had acquired a cool one-bedroom apartment, again in the Dupont Circle area that I liked, and made some effort to decorate it, hanging heavy navy blue fiberglass drapes on the bedroom window to prevent future boyfriends from noticing my skin, and buying some second-hand furniture. Maurice built me a coffee table from a door he picked up on the street.

We were still together but slowly drifting apart. Although I *did* give him a set of keys, he didn't like to spend too much time in my place since I didn't have a piano. Unbelievably, I not only entertained thoughts of buying or renting one but actually walked into a Steinway showroom to get a feel for the cost. Since I couldn't play even a rudimentary tune, I felt like an imposter in that formidable space, where real buyers were testing sounds and creating a classical cacophony of singular renditions. Then there was the cost. I was out of my element and couldn't leave there fast enough, apologizing to the tall, well-dressed salesman on my way out.

It was not unusual for us to hang out in Tasso's, although we were not drinkers. We would always run into people we knew, and of course, like everyone else, we would drop quarters into the best jukebox in the world. It was there that I heard Donovan's "Season of the Witch" for the first time, and even went out and bought the album. In the future each song would conjure up Tasso's ambience, cigarette smoke, and french fries, and would bring back the scent of Shalimar, the pungent odor of incense, the velvety texture of black paintings being sold by street vendors along Connecticut Avenue.

On such an afternoon, after buying the album I drifted into a bookstore and directly scanned the poetry section. I ended up with a collection of William Carlos Williams' work, particularly since I loved his short poem "Forgive Me." Closer to home I splurged on a bouquet of hot pink tulips and a bottle of rosé. Life felt good.

When Maurice and I entered the bar, we found my friends Helga and Heidi, two drop-dead blonde beauties, and a bevy of men sitting at a small table. Maurice joined the men, becoming one of the crowd, fawning over the women, complimenting their hair, clothes, German accents, all the while ignoring me. When Helga complained that her current lover was away and that she was horny enough to call over a regular from the Speakeasy, Maurice appeared baffled. "You don't have to *do* that, sweetie," he said in front of me. "*I can always accommodate you.*"

Bored and jealous, I doodled on cocktail napkins: princesses in ballroom gowns, girls on the beach, irate faces, diagrams, and then a short poem, a haiku of sorts, that had been in my head:

> *Loving, hating you and I,*
> *Allowing vows to go awry,*
> *You don't care & I don't know why.*

He glanced at it as if it were a bad report card, scowled, took out his pocket pen and scribbled, *Confidence entrusted. Later disgusted.* He turned his back and continued the spectacle of shamelessly flirting with my girlfriends. There was no question in my mind about what was on *his*; for two years he had badgered and bothered me over one topic: He wanted to sleep with me and another woman. He had a theory that neither he nor I should have sex outside the relationship, but that it would be ethical and moral for him to fuck another girl in my presence. Sometimes he would joke: "The plural of *spouse* is *spice*." Our conversations about a *ménage á trois* never went well. "I am *not* a lesbian," I would argue. "I don't *want* to go to bed with another woman!"

"I am not *asking* you to do anything with another woman. I am asking you to please your man, to provide pleasure for the *two* of us that would enhance our intimacy and love. You will never again feel cheated."

"Yeah, right. Well, I won't! Stop asking me to do something I find upsetting and revolting!"

When he followed me out of Tasso's, which was practically across the street from my apartment, and entered my bedroom, I ignored him as I began to dress for bed. I had to work the next morning. I was tired and disgusted.

"Why did you stop them from coming here with us?" he complained. "They *would* have if you weren't stuck in your Puritan, uptight, bourgeois bag!"

I answered before I could think. "If *you* spent as much energy on *music* as you do on *women*, you'd be *rich!*" And that was that. I'd hit the right target: stepped on the eggshells, on glass, on the most exquisite, fragile taboo. Fear almost knocked me backwards as he lunged at me, and like a trapped animal I ran towards the nearest door, into the windowless bathroom, trapping myself further into a definite No Exit predicament.

It took him seconds to break down the door, then grab my neck and start squeezing. Unable to speak, of course, I looked directly into his eyes, trying to establish some contact, trying to connect to some aspect of humanity. Trying to save my life. The person into whose eyes I stared was not Maurice, was not even *human*; it was as if he had been taken over by a demon, by that other dark, fetid, raunchy, schizoid persona that was always just under the surface.

I continued staring into his eyes, pleading silently, *Stop killing me.* I felt my knees buckle. I began to feel light-headed. I began to accept that I would die in that bathroom on that beautiful spring night while everyone was still at Tasso's partying, jostling each other, trying to talk over the jukebox blaring the latest Blood Sweat & Tears number:

> *What goes up must come down*
> *Spinning wheel, got to go round*
> *Talking about your troubles it's a crying sin*
> *Ride a painted pony*
> *Let the spinning wheel spin.*
> *You got no money, and you, you got no home*
> *Spinning wheel, spinning all alone*
> *Talking about your troubles and you, you never learn*

Ride a painted pony
Let the spinning wheel turn.

Suddenly he changed his mind. His hands stopped squeezing my neck, and I could breathe. Lying limply on the bathroom floor, my head spinning, I watched him as he ran to the closet, and I knew that he was still under the spell, under the impulse to inflict pain. In a rage, he threw out clothing, shoes, bags, until he found what he was looking for: a noose made of twine. He held the noose in his hands as if contemplating its function, then flung it back toward the closet. He stood undecided for a moment, then hurried to the kitchen. I was already out of the bathroom when I saw him coming towards me with a steak knife. I didn't feel like a character in a Grade B film. I didn't feel the bruises around my neck. I didn't feel weak or strong. I didn't feel *any-thing* except the urge to *live*.

"I love you, Maurice," I whimpered and sobbed. "I'm sorry. Please forgive me. Please come to bed with me. I want to make love to you. I want to take care of you. Please, please come to bed with me."

It worked. He put the knife down on the bedside table and got into bed, becoming more or less himself, the rage spent. I had to lie with him, suck his dick, fuck him, pretend to love and adore him until morning, when the sun finally rose and the bruises on my neck began turning black and blue.

ALMOST IMMEDIATELY, I SOLD the furniture I had acquired, packed up, and took the Greyhound bus to New York City. I had no plans, no address, no acquaintances in Manhattan, but I was toting my baggage, real and imagined, to The Big Apple, to a place where I could be anonymous. I was ashamed of my life and humiliated by the physical abuse, as if I were still the newest kid in second grade, kicked around by my schoolmates for being shy and unpopular. Again I felt like that child: abused, bashful, unworthy.

FOR YEARS AFTERWARD, I was afraid of running into Maurice. My fear was not unfounded, in part because it was *I* who kept up the communication. I sent him a postcard, and he in turn sent me a birthday card along with a small book of original poems inscribed in perfect penmanship: *To Suzie, Hope & Cope. Maurice.* On the cover was a photograph of him sitting at the piano. His beard was longer and grayer than before, but the concentration in his eyes was familiar.

In the early 1970s there were many long-haired, bearded guys in the Village who looked just like Maurice. Once, while at the movies and about to watch *Jesus Christ Superstar*, I was certain that he was sitting two rows ahead of me. Another time, I saw him, in a blue seersucker suit, dozing on a park bench in Washington Square Park, squinting against the glare of the afternoon sun.

I saw him *everywhere*, as if he were my personal ghost etched upon my psyche. A few paces nearby, a band was doing Jimmie Hendrix. Maurice listened only to jazz, but once in a while a rock band would catch his attention. For about a year he was humming "Son of Suzy Creamcheese," by the Mothers of Invention:

> *Suzy Creamcheese, oh, mama, now what's got into ya?*
> *Suzy you you were such a sweetie*
> *Yeah, yeah, yeah*
> *Once you were my one and only*
> *   yeah, yeah, yeah*
> *Blow your mind on too much Kool-aid*
> *   Yeah, yeah, yeah.*

He told me that the group was great, their lyrics original, their sound the most creative on the scene. I liked to hear him sing, especially when he was in a relaxed mood and we were walking arm in arm through the hustle and bustle of Fourteenth Street, ignoring the crowds or the cats nodding to him with approval, "Right on, brother!" he smiling to himself, squeezing my hand. For some reason that's how I always remembered us: my arm hooked in his, he on the curb side of the street, protective, tall, solid, a pack of Viceroys in his shirt pocket, humming the melody or lyrics of a song, a jingle, or a tune that was taking shape in his mind, chiseling and refining it into a composition, each note adding its weight and uniqueness upon the entire whole, creating a symphony that only *he* would hear.

NEW YORK

AT AGE TWENTY-TWO I reached a dubious milestone in the daily routine of eliminating superfluous hair growth; the routine, or rather chore, took an hour at least. I hated shaving my thighs every day. I felt I was damaging my skin irrevocably while simultaneously and inadvertently energizing the follicles to spawn hardier and healthier growth. My thinned-skinned thighs were always nicked and irritated, the dermal cells resenting the cold chafing of the razor's edge. Battling hair growth became a full-time occupation, worse than ever. For one thing, I now had to tweeze my nipples even more and dye the hairs between my breasts and on my abdomen. Although I had discovered a new and improved bleaching product, the burning and itching for the first ten to fifteen minutes were so unbearable, it was as if I were being scrubbed with a poison ivy extract. Tweezing my nipples was a fact difficult to acknowledge even to myself. Although I had endured for years the curse of my hairiness, my ego still had difficulty coming to terms with the image of me in front of the mirror, holding a nipple in hand, plucking black hairs that surrounded that apex of female beauty.

My skin was my nemesis, my shame, my secret; hairiness, my identity, my affliction, lay at the core of my self-image. I was a minority as a woman but did not belong to a group or a subset or a sect that could fight for rights and acceptance on my behalf. I was a minority of one, hiding in the closet as if I had mischievously violated social mores, ignored decorum, and muddied the line between the genders. I was a woman whose femininity was eerily hideous, a definite blow to my sense of self.

I did not belong to a racial minority, but my skin nonetheless held me back. I didn't have the right to compare my cosmetic woes with the suffering of a people who had been enslaved and violated, raped and tortured for centuries because of the color of their skin, but I understood how a biological trait could invite ostracism, bullying, and ridicule. You can't hide your racial identity or your features or the size of your body, for the most part. But an affliction like mine can be relatively invisible for short periods of time, allowing a certain sense of normalcy and respite, only to return later, often at the worst moment, to reveal its true nature. I was an alchemist who fooled and betrayed men. I could turn sisal into silk and back again; I was the great pretender.

Not all women are blessed with beauty, I reasoned, but whatever they lacked did not render them a freak of nature sporting a beard, mustache, and sideburns. If nature or God had created me, I would have been normal; I must have been created by the devil, or by a creature with a sense of humor, someone who'd done a half-assed job in a hurry, someone like me, too impatient to pay attention to detail. I would pay a bill, and forget to sign my name on the check; I would jot down an address and arrive at the wrong destination. I would buy a dress only to discover it was the wrong size. I would mop the kitchen floor but miss the bread crumbs under the stove, or iron a shirt and leave the cuffs still wrinkled. Yes, I had trouble with detail, and the devil was in the details, indeed; in the follicles of my female skin.

It didn't help to remind myself that my condition was cosmetic in nature, undeserving of empathy, public forums, or twelve-step rehabilitation programs, and particularly of self-pity. Other women, fortunate enough to have smooth and lovely skin, might view my hairiness as not worse than bunions or hammer toes, particularly if these women had other cosmetic faults that could not be shaved away. And yet, just as unseen germs have shaped the course of human history, I believed that my unseen genetic hand-me-down had the gravitas and force to shape the course of the rest of my life. My inability to overcome a predestined and haphazard confluence of amino acids, which on a basic level had no secret agenda or nefarious whims, left me at the mercy of mere chance. It seemed that all of life was due to mere chance, a matter of serendipity. What if my parents never met? That was a question, an idea that, as a child, my friends and I often contemplated. Would I have existed elsewhere? But I knew, of course, that I could only be me, with all my ancestors intact and my history unchanged. I also understood that the root cause of a situation was not to blame for any given individual response; life could not have been predetermined. I alone had chosen to have a benign, literally skin-deep defect to marshal my life in a direction that it would have otherwise not taken. I was unable to regard hairiness as a minor disability. That was the crux of my problem: I had made a mountain out of a molehill. I wallowed in angst befitting an existential crisis, a moral dilemma, an ethical ridge. Yes, to my shame, I made everything worse.

IN NEW YORK I tried to find waitressing jobs; once I even danced in a club in Greenwich Village called the Purple Onion. They had outfitted me with silly-looking pasties to cover my nipples, and I donned hot pants, black panty hose, and high heels. Not a great dancer to begin with, I was worse on the small elevated stand where all I could do was concentrate on the faces of the tourists, male and female, gawking at me as if I were the symbol of everything gone wrong in our generation: hippies, drugs, sex, long hair, and rock 'n' roll. When I took a bathroom break, a girl from the audience jumped on the stand and showed off her moves to the crowd as if suggesting to me, *See? This is how it should be done!*

Even so, as if to boost my morale, the bandleader asked me to go on the road with his group. It was a complimentary offer, but unthinkable. I was impulsive and daring, but not to that degree. I couldn't see myself on the road with a rock 'n' roll band, going from town to town, sneaking around to perform my beauty ablutions. Worse than that, I couldn't imagine explaining my whereabouts to my parents. They had been greatly relieved when I came back to New York. As clueless as they felt about my love life, my intellectual and artistic interests, or even my newly found hip fashion style—bell-bottoms, wide leather belts, tasseled vests, and all the rest—they preferred to have me reside close by. I didn't have the heart, or whatever it took, to dump more bad news on top of all their disappointments, pleadings, and admonitions.

AFTER THE PURPLE ONION, with only a few bucks in my pocketbook and no invitation from the owner for a repeat performance, I returned to my hangout on McDougal Street feeling dejected and lonely. An unpleasant thought struck me: You are nothing. Not smart, not educated, not an intellectual, not an artist of any sort; and not even good enough to be a sex object. I had only recently overheard a cat tell his friends, "Dig this, man. I had sex with this girl who had a glass ceiling, and I noticed how hairy my ass was." Everyone laughed, as the guy laughed at himself. Well, I too had a hairy ass, but did not need a glass ceiling to confirm that fact.

People say that, if you make it in New York, you can make it anywhere. New York City in 1969 was superficially abuzz in good vibrations, but there was a real estate shortage. As a twenty-two-year-old girl, it was not really a question of homelessness; there was always a place to crash, but hardly a place that would be conducive to a complicated morning routine or to any kind of comfort and privacy. People said you had to get the *Village Voice* the night before general distribution and start the apartment hunt immediately before everything got snatched up. Another well-known method was to peruse the *New York Times* obituaries, rush over to the deceased apartments, and slip the super a few dollars.

I had no luck with either method. Only once I was actually shown a place: a sixth-floor walkup in the East Village, a small efficiency apartment, a kitchenette dating back to the forties if not earlier, a toilet with no shower, and plaster hanging by a thread from the ceiling. While I was there, several more people came by, and one couple took the place, offering more money for the dump than I would ever have considered reasonable. It looked like a kind of place where a murder could happen, despite the police lock on the door and gates on the fire escape window.

I couldn't imagine what it would be like to have a boyfriend come by unexpectedly, such a small thing but huge for me. I always noticed such details in movies or literature, since for me spontaneity was out of reach. Still, I was a naturally impulsive person; if something seemed like a good idea, I wouldn't persevere, wouldn't weigh the pros and cons, I would just leap ahead. Perhaps in some ways the fact that I couldn't leap into some thoughtless sexual silliness prevented some untoward and unpleasant consequences. Once I stopped by during lunch at a co-worker's place. He had been flirting with me for some time, and I enjoyed the attention. I was working in an office, typing labels all day, and he was a Ph.D. candidate, working on basic scientific research for an Ivy League college. We were making out in the middle of the afternoon. His high-rise apartment faced the Hudson River, and light washed over the room in a sweet, warming way. It got hot and heavy, and he asked me to take my clothes off. Of course, I couldn't undress, and I probably would not have even if my body had just been waxed; I needed the cover of dark.

"I thought you were hip," he complained. "What difference would it make if it's today or Friday? We are going to see each other more and will eventually fuck. Do we really have to wait the compulsory three dates?"

It was not a rational argument, and I could have responded in various ways. I could have said, "I'd like to know you better," or "The timing is wrong," or "I have my period," but instead I was tongue tied, thinking that he had no idea what I look like underneath. I hadn't shaved my legs in a few days, and the stubble on my thighs could be felt through my light linen pants. If he saw me naked in the unforgiving daylight, he would more than likely recoil in revulsion. Or he might, out of pity and good manners, try to get rid of me as politely as possible. I could imagine such a scene as the premise for a situation comedy: A beautiful, sexy girl finds men in bars and clubs, brings them home, and then shocks them upon undressing, at the moment when they are most aroused, revealing her revolting, hairy body. The name of the show would be *The Pink Unicorn*.

I was obsessed. I felt the whole situation was unfair, but there was nothing negotiable about it. Unwanted, ugly hairs burrowed their way out of my skin as if they were parasites, escaping my inner body. When they were removed, they left my defoliated skin weeping with abrasions. The unwanted hair always looked and felt foreign, alien, a "not me," other entity —and yet, like all my features, it was a component of my genes, in the small arrangements of my DNA, in the chromosomes that made me uniquely me; and therefore, my hairiness, like gender, body type, shyness, temperament, eye color, bone structure was destined, and it became me, intolerably me, a trait and its sequelae, like a fatal, chronic, parasitic disease that I could not escape nor cure. Somehow I was at fault, through carelessness or superficiality or sheer stupidity, and therefore it was I who had to deal with this handicap alone and tame it at all costs. I could show myself only after dark and like a vampire, rely on darkness and shadows to gently polish off the jagged edges and render me lovely, feminine, smooth. Self-pity, obsessive thoughts, ruminations on the topic, began to bore even me.

And so I dimmed the lights. But even with dim lights, making love to a guy could prove a challenge. In the midst of an erotic moment, I might notice some long dark strays that I had missed earlier, and immediately, instead of focusing on the moment, enjoying sexual satisfaction and the pleasure of a man's touch, my objective would be to get through the ordeal with my secret safe. If someone suddenly turned the lights on, I would grab the sheets and cover up, as if a night chill had suddenly permeated the room. The memory of John's sneering at my hirsute body was the stuff of my nightmares. I would see him in my dreams amused at my reference to myself as feminine. I would see myself drowning in the bathtub, my skin defoliated, superfluous hair clogging the drain, never again to stand up to reveal my anti-femininity by candlelight. I would run barefoot on craggy hills, slicing my feet on broken beer bottles; I would run at sunset by a river rife with malarial mosquitoes; I would crawl on buckling knees in a vast desert; I would shower outdoors in sub-zero temperatures, snow turning my hair gray; I would do anything but allow anyone to laugh at me again.

THIS IS WHAT HAPPENED once: There were a bunch of us sitting around, getting high, acting silly, when someone started a game. The guy picked a girl volunteer to put a blindfold on, then asked, "On your honeymoon, what is the first thing you take off?" If she removed the correct item, she would win and the game would be over. Anyway, I was nominated to be the volunteer. The blindfold was placed over my eyes, and I began taking my clothes off, starting with the easiest, shoes, socks, sweater, shirt. I knew the room was dim, so, although I was nervous, I kept taking off clothing. Finally I was stark naked, but even with the blindfold on I could see that someone had turned the lights on. I threw off the blindfold and looked about me frantically as everyone stared, gawked, and chuckled. "On your honeymoon, the first thing you take off is the blindfold," laughed the guy who had orchestrated the whole game. My friends were all dressed, and I was standing naked in the incandescent brightness as if I were in a classic bad dream. As if running for my life, I grabbed my clothes and left the room. I didn't know what people saw; most likely, they didn't notice anything, just a naked girl. It was all done in good nature, but it was a worse scene than anything I could have dreamed up. I was humiliated, not only by revealing my hairy body, but by the necessity of having to act modest, uncool. Maybe there was a moral to this story. Maybe the moral was that you don't ignore whatever it is that is in front of your face. Maybe it was that you don't complicate things, don't look for hidden meaning. Years later I figured it out: The guys just wanted to look at naked girls.

I NEEDED TO MAKE money. This was New York, and I was alone and broke. In desperation I called Jerry, a man who was a regular at the Speakeasy. Jerry could have been in his forties or fifties, there was no telling. His face was scarred by adolescent acne, his hair gray and thinning; he was neither tall nor short, neither fat nor skinny, just one of the nondescript regulars who got his kicks sipping beer and waiting to get lucky. He was a good tipper, drank at least a dozen beers without signs of intoxication, and all the girls liked him, thought of him as a harmless old fool. When I told him I was moving to New York, he had given me his telephone number.

"Suzie," he'd said softly, "I am happy to hear that. What you are earning here is blood money. It ain't worth it."

"Well, it's a job. What's more I have never gone out with a trick. I am not a prostitute," I had countered.

"I know. You're a good girl, but being friends with Helga and Heidi is like taking the first step in that direction."

When I called him from a bar on Seventh Avenue in the Village, he was surprised to hear from me, but just the same offered to come all the way to the City the following weekend and help me out in some way. Both he and I knew what the way was, and his fatherly warnings were panning out even without the German sisters to pave the way. True to his word, he came the following weekend, and I agreed to meet him at his West Side hotel. I packed a light overnight bag and saw him at the bar as soon as I entered the lobby. When he spotted me, he jumped up, held both my hands, and kissed me on the mouth. I joined him for a scotch, and he held a lighter to my cigarette as I fumbled with my mini skirt, striving for the most flattering pose. Hungry, and concluding that Jerry didn't have dinner on his mind, I ate a few bowls of pretzels and washed them down with more scotch and water.

"There is something I have to tell you," Jerry said the second we entered the hotel room. The large bed was well made, and his tattered valise lay open on the pretty brocade spread, revealing its messy innards, looking more like a dirty laundry bag. For the first time I also noticed that his clothes were rather shabby: his white shirt wrinkled, its collar shiny; his black polyester pants worn at the knees, his shoes scuffed at the heels. Jerry wore a mawkish expression, as pitiable and as his attire, and I braced myself for bad news. He continued, "I've been robbed. Somebody broke into this room earlier today and stole my gold watch and all the money that I had in the suitcase. I have barely enough to get me home."

I wanted to laugh and say, "Yeah, I was robbed, too," but contained myself. For the sake of not looking like a whore, I stuck around with him that night; at least the bed was comfortable, and I had no other place to go.

Later, I worked in one midtown bar where I was expected, not only to serve many drinks, but to allow customers to buy me a few and to play along with their pick-up lines as if I were a hooker. I stayed there for the duration of the evening and walked out with maybe a couple of dollars to my name. Another bar had a great jukebox but there were no customers, and no money. I stayed for a few minutes, had a drink, listened to Billie Holiday doing "Travelin' Light," and left. As I was walking west on a seedy mid-town street, my high heels tapping too loudly, I noticed the street walkers looking at me, some enviously, some maliciously. I wanted to holler, "Hey, don't worry about me, I'm no threat. No competition." Soon enough I felt the presence of a man behind me. He was an obese person in his forties in a rumpled gray business suit.

"Hey, baby, would you like to come to my hotel room? It's just around the corner." No preliminaries or niceties to break the ice, straight to the point.

I should have explained that I was not a working girl, but instead I heard myself ask, "How much would you give me?" and there it was. As if I were a wind-up toy, I followed him robotically through the luxurious lobby, noting the crystal chandeliers, uniformed staff, and well-heeled guests. In his room, he took off all his clothes, lay down on the large bed, and waited for me to service him. Half-dressed, I climbed on his erect dick, put it inside me, and seconds later it was over. His copious cum leaked down my thighs, and it could not have felt more sickening than vomit or feces. I ran to the bathroom, lifted the toilet seat, turned the faucet on, and threw up everything I had eaten all week. I rinsed my mouth and reemerged to find the man blissfully dressed.

"Baby, would you like me to call my friends in? They're staying here too for the convention. They'd love to meet you." He winked.

"No. No." I didn't want to betray the panic I felt.

"Okay, I hear you. I'll just leave the room and get us some ice."

I didn't believe him. I thought, Busted. He's a cop, and my life is ruined. As soon as I heard the door slam behind him, I jumped into the shower, scrubbed myself, toweled off quickly, dressed, and ran out of the room. The elevator took forever to come, but seconds later, I was jogging towards the train, breathing a sigh of relief as if I had just eluded a lifetime behind bars. I was out of there, not having received money for my ordeal, but I had been a real whore nonetheless and a stupid whore at that. A posse of young black males whistled as I hustled by on West Forty-seventh Street. "Hi, baby," one called out. "Looking good."

I turned around and looked at them; they looked like thugs. "You look good too, kiddo," I retorted, staring boldly at the adolescent with a smirk on his face. Very little could have scared me that evening; I had already crossed the line. Like a dope addict who proceeds from sniffing to mainlining, I had already crossed over to the wild side, like millions before me. I became that archetypal young person lured into the big city, into a web of neon lights, then chewed up, spit out. Like Holly in Lou Reed's "Walk on the Wild Side," I plucked my eyebrows, shaved my legs, and went from a he to a she. I became one of the lost souls in the unforgiving city, broken and broke, easily seduced by glitter and wishful thinking, then succumbing to naiveté, bad luck, bad men, bad ideas. I had been raised in the Promised Land, crossed the ocean on a large ship, arrived at the place of opportunity, seen money grow on trees, but landed in a back alley where neither opportunity nor promise could coexist.

DURING THAT FIRST SUMMER, in 1969, when everyone was talking about Woodstock, I managed to lose my suitcase and all my belongings, catch a dose of gonorrhea, drop acid, and sleep in Central Park. In Woodstock, hippies rolled around in the mud for days, listened to live rock bands, showered in public, got high, made history. There was no way in hell I could have participated, even if I had been a rock fan or active in the anti-Vietnam peace movement. By the end of the weekend, my hairiness would have been obvious to everyone. My legs would have guaranteed second looks, my natural state, seen by others, have fomented a shame that even the best acid could not have alleviated.

For a while I, and the other disaffected characters, crashed in squalor in a dreary place on top of the Feenjon restaurant and hangout. It was a dump lit only by strings of Christmas lights, and reeked of cat pee. Actually, the fact that the only source of light was generated by the colorful, flickering bulbs was a blessing. The stained mattresses, breeding roaches, filth, and a the motley crew of misfits and drop-outs, coming and going, sleeping, jerking off, fucking, collectively looked better in that gloom.

Someone suggested that I could become an airline stewardess— and I, with my fear of flying, decided that it was a great idea. I rose early one morning and tried to clean myself up at the cold water sink as best as I could. I put on pantyhose stockings, a blue mini-dress with long sleeves, and high-heeled shoes. As I was dressing, I excitedly discussed my plans with one of my so-called roommates, who was still in bed under the covers. Just as I was ready to walk out the door, I heard him heave a loud sigh of relief, then gasp, "God, oh God, baby, that was good." He was asleep by the time I found my keys.

At the airport, I had no luck. Nobody seemed interested in hiring me on the spot, perhaps because I had no permanent address. My name, in care of "The Feenjon," on my job applications bore no results, and after two weeks, I gave up hope. Something had to change, and in a resolute moment I purchased a conservative blue suit, sensible shoes, and without much effort found a job as a clerk-typist for a large national bank.

I had hoped they would hire and train me to be a bank teller, which had a modicum of glamour in my opinion, but I was assigned to a back room, piled with cabinets and office machines, behind the common area where auxiliary staff, accountants, secretaries, and managers performed their duties, and given a desk where I sat alone day after day filing papers and typing numbers. A couple of secretaries made some friendly gestures towards me, but I rebuffed them. I was comfortable in my cluttered surroundings and preferred my solitude, happy to be left alone. My daily routine was monotonous. I became part of the rat race, part of the crowd running down the subway stairs at the end of the day, eager to jump on the next train home.

Yet despite my own refusal to be involved with others, I became morose and bitter. When I heard the staff outside my filing office laughing or making after-work plans, my bitterness turned to hatred. Suddenly I was the unpopular high school student again who barely spoke English and didn't use deodorant. I was the kid in third grade whom the teacher put in the corner, facing the walls, arms raised. Only God knew what evil deed I must have performed to warrant such ignominy. Resurrected memories of grade school, replete with scents, texture, and sound, put me right back among the eucalyptus trees behind the school, where I was the only girl in class unable to follow the simple steps to the *hora*. There I was, lagging behind the other girls, awkwardly prancing around on two left feet, making up my own steps as I went along, as if I had been dropped into the mix by accident. I was the kid rarely invited to birthday parties, rarely asked to dance, rarely included in conversation.

In class, even the teacher knew to either ignore me or say something biting and hurtful. Once when I had my arm up for permission to go to the bathroom, she looked at me in disdain and asked if I was prepared to answer her question. I hadn't heard the question; I had to urinate. "Teacher, may I go to the bathroom?" I asked bashfully.

"I should have known that that's why you have your arm up." Everyone laughed, and I dragged myself out of the class, my head hung low. It would never have occurred to me to come up with a retort or a smart-alecky answer. We had been told to raise our arm for bathroom permission, and I always obeyed the rules. I left the classroom and went down the hill to the white building among the eucalyptus trees that was the girls' bathroom. Once there, I didn't move fast enough; I had held my urine for too long, and my bladder exploded. Urine streaked down my legs, and my pink panties and blue skirt got soaked. I had no choice but to stay in that bathroom, hoping the desert-like heat would dry my skirt in time to go home. There was time to kill, and a murderous, killing impulse overcame me. I reached into my book bag, found my crayons, and got to work. When I was finished, I had defaced the walls and doors in each stall, there were about four, with curse words, obscene drawings, and pornographic comments attributed to my classmates. In the rush of the moment, I didn't give a damn about being found out, and when I was completely spent, a wonderful sense of accomplishment washed over me. The next day, a big deal was made over the graffiti, particularly due to its vulgarity. I never owned up to my crimes, and no one ever suspected that Bracha was the culprit. From that point on, I would always identify with the bad guy; I knew how it felt to be guilty and to pretend otherwise. Innocence was nothing but an act.

So I was not part of the office clique, although as an adult I could see how I myself had created the situation and had only myself to blame. Once I rebuffed their early, friendly overtures, I'd become a kind of social pariah and remained one for the two years that I worked there. But working alone in a large room with files, counter spaces, and a desk with good lighting provided some fringe benefits: It afforded an opportunity to tweeze my hands and fingers, pluck away nasal hairs, and at the end of the day, feel a sense of fulfillment, having completed work and personal chores all at the same time. I'd had to be acutely attuned to people coming and going; getting caught tweezing my hands was not an option. The hairs on the hands were black and strong, growing even above the knuckles, but they were easy to tweeze as long as I allowed a week or two in between. Nasal hairs could be tweezed or yanked out if I had a good grip with my finger nails. After I started tweezing in the file room, I transitioned to bleaching my face, arms, and the newly growing hair between my breasts and on my abdomen in the small bathroom stall of the ladies room. Since there were enough stalls, I could disappear into one for a half hour without anyone noticing, particularly during lunch hours or, better yet, after the end of the day. Knowing that I had such a chore ahead of me usually ruined the day completely. I dreaded the whole ordeal. There I was in the toilet with a toxic, ammonia-based paste practically all over my face, arms, and torso, counting the minutes, while women came and went, peeing in the stalls next to me, farting, and sighing. Sometimes, to make time pass more enjoyably and quickly, I'd play with my clit, forcing myself into an odd, insipid orgasm, a shallow, localized gasp, a comma between separate thoughts in a sentence, followed immediately by self-loathing and disgust. After the bleach cream dried and the hair turned platinum blonde, I wiped the drying paste off with toilet paper and, when the coast was clear, dashed to the public sink, and fixed myself up as quickly as possible. After the successful execution of the ordeal, relief and accomplishment would follow me home, as if I had gotten away with a crime. I would reach the apartment with my arms renewed, my femininity temporarily restored, and my unsightly black roots pulverized.

Eliminating superfluous hair at times felt akin to de-weeding a garden, being a good neighbor, a responsible citizen. But weeds, unlike masculine hair, could be lovelier than orchids, depending upon one's perspective. What could be lovelier than a field of blue cornflowers, forsythia in the spring, black-eyed Susans along the highway, dandelions, clusters of orange and yellow florets briefly reflecting sunshine, ensuring life goes on, year after year after year, disseminating their fuzzy seed to the wind, seed as downy as feather, light as air. No, masculine hairiness on a young woman was unlike weeds, it was rather akin to a curse—not to a leper's curse, not a plague, but a comic, absurd, meaningless yoke, a random, unintended burden.

ABU-KABIR WAS ALWAYS in my dreams. Even after returning as an adult tourist, visiting friends and family, flaunting my gold ornaments and outlet-bought clothes as if they were advanced university degrees, and rearranging my early, young images into the new reality that was the neighborhood, I always dreamt of it as it had been in the past: lemon trees in the fields by my grandmother's house, the scent of budding citrusfruit, opium. After the late sixties, my childhood fields ceased to exist. Progress took over, and the streets, which literally had no name (ours actually had a number—17 it was), strangely caught the attention of some government bureaucrat who came up with the idea and funds to rip out the ancient citrus trees and replant the fields with evergreens instead. The few impoverished souls, two of my cousins included, who remained in the makeshift, dilapidated structures of mortar and cement were paid to move away, the so-called houses were torn down, probably with a grand scheme of beautifying the area, a plan which never materialized. Only a few stones, ancient staircases leading nowhere, partial brick walls, a ceramic tile or two, remained.

The Russian Cloister looked abandoned and desolate, its bell tower never to toll again. The nuns who had laboriously climbed its steep stairs were never seen again either, except in heaven, if there was such a place. As a child, I would fear the church, and the silent nuns in their black habits and heavy crosses were particularly chilling and forbidding. Of course, I had no idea who or what the nuns were, only that my mother told me they were extremely pious and pure but nonetheless hated Jews. The massive iron gate was always locked—always except when, by chance, someone entered or left that mysterious holy ground. Once, only once, the gate was open when Shlomo and I happened to pass it by. Terrified but curious, we hung by the entrance and peeked in. We could see clear paths of well-manicured gardens. After a little while, an attractive, blue-eyed, well-dressed adult male spotted us and, in broken Hebrew, invited us in for a tour. He spoke to both of us but looked only at me. Primitive instinct almost made me refuse, but my curiosity was too great, and Shlomo as well jumped at the opportunity. The man, to my mind was very elegant and polite, the ideal grown-up, educated, cultured, a representation of my future husband, the way I would always imagine him: tall, thin, wearing a dark suit, a top hat and a suggestion of a smile. I must have been about nine or ten at the time, and although I had always admired and loved my father's dark, sullen good looks, even at that age I knew that my father lacked the gentility and refinement that this Russian exuded without effort. He taught me a few Russian phrases and introduced me to various people who smiled warmly at me and my brother. They seemed amused by our presence, particularly by our attempts to speak Russian, but before we knew it, the tour was over and we were spirited out of the Garden of Eden, unbitten, unstung, and unharmed.

On my rare, touristy visits back to Israel, it was hard to mentally restore and rearrange the landmarks and recall what was where, and I could tell where our house stood only in relation to the eucalyptus tree, but even the tree appeared aged, its branches sparser. Someone had surrounded its base with small rocks, as if to create an illusion of a well-cultivated, intentionally designed landscape. In winter, after being pummeled by rain and hailstorm of biblical proportions, the fields turned lush with wild green growth; to the east, the route to school, more fir trees showed off their evergreen presence, thwarting the citrus and even the stately eucalyptuses.

Once, on the way to school, I walked through a beehive and was attacked by the entire hive. I ran back home to my mother, who had no idea what to do for me. My eyelids suffered the brunt of the attack. The next morning they became swollen, red, and tightly stuck together, as if glued. I lay in the dark on my parents' bed, doing nothing but listening to my mother and her mother chat as if I were not there. They discussed important things, such as my father's infidelities, or the tragic fate of relatives who had been left to perish in Poland. When I think about it, I am saddened that I never had a mother with whom I could have had a meaningful conversation. I am saddened that my mother never matured, never grew up. Forever she remained the child who had fled Poland, who followed others' commands, who remained fearful, inadequate, barely literate, expecting nothing out of life but grief and disappointments.

Quite often I dreamt that shallow inlets of the Mediterranean Sea waters had flooded our house, and that I could easily swim and float in the warm water. Those were good dreams, but when I woke I was filled with longing for the cactus plants and their sweet, danger-filled fruit, the abundance of marigolds, daisies, and anemones, especially anemones, blood red, fragile, plentiful, common, and mysterious.

A NEW LIFE

P AUL, MY NEW BOYFRIEND, was not exactly a slob, but rather a pack rat, saving anything he ever owned, accumulating more junk as he went along: *New York Times* op-ed pages, clothing, shoes, junk mail, receipts, light bulbs, unpaid bills, chipped china, rusty tools, his grandmother's frying pan, college textbooks, just to mention a few. He referred to all those items as "my possessions," which no one was allowed to trash. He had his own storage system, and a fantasy that he would eventually go through all of it and discard items of no value.

You entered and were immediately overcome by the cat box stench that permeated the entire apartment. Infrequently, he'd empty the entire contents of the box, ammonia-soaked litter wafting up and through the hallway like a mini-sandstorm, adding to the layers of poisonous dust already thriving in that long, narrow, and gloomy entryway with its makeshift bookcases crammed with outdated textbooks. The toilet with the pull-chain tank was right there by the front door; it did not have a sink. In order to wash your hands, you had to walk to the kitchen, where the sink and bathtub were located. The kitchen sink was always cluttered with dishes, the bathtub in need of a good professional scrubbing. Off the kitchen lay a small bedroom with windows facing the kitchen windows of the next building's tenants. The room smelled of tomatoes and garlic and was occupied by Zoe, Paul's female roommate. Zoe was an artist, but I never knew what she did for a living. She paid the rent and minded her own business, Paul said. The living room had one brick wall, sort of charming, except for the large abstract oil painting that Zoe had given him. On a huge canvas, she had painted sloppy horizontal sections of yellow, blue, and green, and called the piece *Reflections in Yellow, Blue, and Green*. The pink sofa was a street find, something salvaged from a burning building, which, except for the smoky scent it exuded and the back pillows it was missing, was in fairly good shape. A good maple dresser and a couple of solid bureaus were gifts from Mom and Dad, as were all the utensils, dinnerware, linen, and towels. The bedroom, off the living room, was large enough for a double bed, nothing else. As the room was wall-to-wall mattress and quite a challenge to maneuver, it was basically left undone and unchanged.

That apartment was home to Paul, Zoe, the male cat, Bruce, billions of cockroaches, and it was that apartment that I chose to move into and unhappily live in for at least two years.

Yet it was an improvement over the rat hole with the Christmas lights above the Feenjon. It was there that I'd met Paul, a law student, among the professional chess players, playboys, amphetamine fiends, out-of-work actors, NYU students, lost children, young musicians, misfits, and street beggars. Paul's blue eyes and long, wavy, thick brown hair were charming. But his best asset was not his intelligence, trim body, and kind affect, but the fact that he was Jewish and could be introduced to my parents. He was someone I could marry and live happily ever after with, without grief and mourning from them. Best of all, Paul was on his way to becoming a lawyer.

Like all young denizens of the Village and its sister communities all over the country and the world, Paul wore bell-bottom pants, a hip leather belt with a large, thick silver buckle, wide ties, un-ironed shirts, sideburns, and an attitude of superiority. In his pocket he carried his grandfather's onion watch, like some nineteenth-century fop. When the soles of his shoes wore down, he bought leather strips and spent hours repairing them himself. He carried around a paperback copy of Philip Roth's *When She Was Good*, not to show himself off as a reader, which he was not, but in the eternal belief that someday he might actually read the novel.

Paul's parents were professional, educated people who lived in the Midwest. Coming to study in New York had been a culture shock, he told me. He had never seen the ocean until attending college in New York, never known that there were poor Jews like my family in the world, and had trouble reconciling my "free spirit" existence with my Jewishness; and, in the beginning, incredulously, he forgave me for giving him the clap, saying, "I am happy to have the experience." In due time, he collected more hard-luck experiences, dropped out of college, dropped acid, grew a beard, learned to smoke everything, and stopped bathing. His parents came to visit once. I had thought they would approve of me, but they were not impressed by my Jewish credentials; on the contrary, they saw me as unsophisticated and uneducated, a symptom of their son's maladjustment. I had my own problems, though: the lack of privacy in that apartment, particularly the location of the tub in the kitchen, created many grooming challenges. For example, I might come home from work ready to bleach, shave, pluck, etc., but be unable to attend to my duties because either Paul or Zoe was home. I bought an electric razor that I used during every brief chance, always watchful and on guard, lest someone catch me in the act. Even exhausted, every unexpected free moment was a golden opportunity not to be wasted.

Depilatory activities trumped all other considerations. They were a state of being, a state of mind, a state of existence that never ceased to require attention. There was never a moment when I could lay down my tweezers or razors and say to myself that the work was done. I had read somewhere that there was a full-time worker out there whose sole responsibility was maintaining the light bulbs on the George Washington Bridge. There were so many bulbs that by the time the whole span from New York to New Jersey was complete, the cycle had to begin anew.

In my very early twenties, I erroneously believed puberty was behind me, and, more importantly, that I had grown all the superfluous hair I was to grow. I was wrong. The hairiness was the very first indication of puberty and would be the last to signal full maturity. As the years progressed, I was forced to accept the fact that the ordeal would require more time and ingenuity. It became akin to a chronic disease that wreaks more havoc on its hapless victim as time moves on—a nemesis that had no awareness of its nature; a virus that had no agenda except to blindly replicate itself, with no regard to its host; a parasite, mindless of its selfishness, simply doing what came naturally, responding to its own intrinsic fear of annihilation. The hairiness had no meaning. Each unwanted hair had its own desire to exist. Maybe every living organism was a spiny thorn in God's smooth, perfect universe, superfluous and unsightly. Extinction would come, but at its own speed. People constantly succumbed to infectious diseases, accidents, wars, hemorrhagic strokes, cardiac infarctions, pneumonias, old age, diabetes, and violence, yet continued to rebound and multiple. Eventually all my hairiness might be a thing of the past, and I might have the smooth legs of an aged man whose virility was but a distant memory. Eventually nothing would remain the same. Nothing would remain, period, except probably bacteria feasting on a stray hair.

In my teens, unshaved areas could be hidden in the dark, but once shaved, my sand-paper, prickly thighs always felt coarse to the touch, no matter the effort and time I had expended on the process. When I moved in with Paul, a good man whom I wanted to be with, I had to persistently remake myself into a feminine, love-worthy girl, a mission that required a good deal of planning, scheming, and calculation. Attending to my niggling needs was a burden that never paused for vacations or holidays. I had to remain mindful and on guard at every moment lest I miss a long, dark, curly hair or hairs around my pink nipples, or permit nasal hairs to grow beyond and down towards my lips. And, of course, facial hair, the most obvious and ugliest scourge, from my forehead, upper cheeks, over and below my lips, by my ears, forming sideburns, and on my chin, all the way down and including my long neck had, without question or apology, to be eliminated at any price. In short, I had to admit to myself that, like an animal, almost all my skin surface was covered with hair. I lived in an untenable situation in which even acknowledging to myself that I was always, each day, each hour, preoccupied and obsessed with unsightly body hair was a direct blow to the kind of person I would have wished to be.

On one of the first days in New York, I found myself wandering in the Lower East Side, a part of the city that had been formerly Jewish and that still contained remnants of its earlier incarnation. The streets teemed with small shops and merchants in one great cacophony of business being conducted noisily and openly. Most shops, their front doors ajar, revealed crammed, dark, cluttered spaces, where merchandise consumed every inch of space. The owners and hawkers gathered in front of their stores or stalls, stuff strewn over makeshift tables or hung on laundry lines within colorful tents. Elderly Jews were selling and buying all manner of things: leather goods, books, underwear, used clothing, sheets and towels, glass wear, dishes, tablecloths, ladies' garments, even freshly baked *challas* and fruit. I could hear Yiddish spoken everywhere. It was August, the streets were crowded, and body odors and perspiration mingled with the scent of tobacco, urine, gasoline, bus fumes, fried foods. Manhattan, more tropical in August than any coastal sea town in the Bahamas, but devoid of sea breeze, was sweating humidity. The hot air, the steam rising through the ground vents, the thunder of a passing train down below, lent itself to a vision of Dante's inferno. At the same time, the city that never slept rock 'n' rolled, its heartbeat pounding, its arteries delivering oxygen, removing trash, open for business.

I was in love with New York, with each cobblestone, each alley, each dusty tree. The entire landscape of skyscrapers made me feel safe, as if I were in a valley protected by rigid, concrete, indestructible mountains.

I wanted to exchange my long-sleeved shirt for something light and summery, but as my arms needed bleaching, I was too embarrassed, full of pity and sorrow for myself. And then, in front of a cluttered hardware store, I saw two vendors, an elderly man and a younger one, possibly his son, engaged in an animated Yiddish conversation. I couldn't make out what they were saying, but I knew from the few words that I did hear that they were arguing about Spinoza, the existence of God, and the nature of good and evil. I stopped in my tracks, mesmerized. The older man was clutching a prayer book, the younger one absorbed in a massive tome spread over his entire lap. They stopped talking, and the older man looked at me informally and asked if I wanted anything. No, I didn't want anything they had for sale. I didn't need a faucet, or a screw, or a light bulb. I didn't need paint brushes, hooks, or cans of varnish. What I needed just then was to be one of them. I needed to move out of my skin-tight prison cell and enter their world of thought and contemplation. I needed to be the kind of person whose mind was not occupied only with daily minutiae but who was capable of reasoning, reflecting, and thinking, not out of necessity or narcissism, but out of inquisitiveness, a thirst for knowledge, and an appreciation of art. I was only twenty-two but growing increasingly apprehensive that I was allowing youthful idealism to slip through my fingers and to evaporate like boiling water.

I had often thought of the larger picture, tried to imagine where I, a tiny organism in the whole scheme of things, in the unimaginably vast universe, could possibly fit in. Perhaps my own being, not larger or more significant than that of a bacterium or an invisible germ, a living thing made up of only a few strands of DNA occupying space in my body, was a speck in some godly thing, a bacterium in a heavenly laboratory. Who knew? Perhaps I, and the whole universe, were nothing but a toy to an unimaginable mammoth child-god object that arranged and rearranged us at whim. His second would be our eternity.

Fearing my shallowness, I attempted to lay meaning in the context of the silliness in which I dwelt. I didn't believe in the supernatural or in magic. I didn't believe that religions, any of them, had answers that were not based on pure conjecture: They were all pretty much the same, offering hope and eternal life in order to make this life and its certain mortality bearable. But despite my admiration for intellectuals, musicians, artists, and writers, I didn't read the philosophers' treatises, did not sign up for adult education, and did not even have the patience to read a newspaper. I might have wanted to wax philosophical, but my all-consuming passion was the superficial nature of my skin. I concerned myself, not with finding the ultimate meaning of life, poetry, or God, but with my cosmetic affliction. As a child I had loved to draw. People had said I had talent. I could easily duplicate in charcoal, pencil, or ink whatever image presented itself to me: a person's face, an imaginary young beauty in long lovely tresses and romantic clothing smiling at the viewer from an otherworldly distance, a still life of layer-chocolate torte resting on a delicate Worcester bone china dessert plate, elegant silver utensils formally placed on a white cloth napkin, and a crystal glass filled with dark red-purple wine behind the dessert, vying for attention. I had learned to paint in watercolors after I won a set at a birthday party of one of my second-grade classmates, the only time in my life that I won anything in a raffle. I loved art classes in elementary school, not only because they made me feel proud of myself, but because it was in those classes that I learned how to create depth in a drawing, how to take a blank page and, with a few brush strokes, create distance, shape, mood, and color. Later, I learned to use crayons, and much later to paint with oils on canvas or wood. But to my inner shame and regret, a palpable, almost physical pain would rip through my heart at the recollection of my early love of art and its later abandonment. I did not follow my bliss, nor did I make attempts to resurrect any talents I might have had or develop those that lay dormant. But I doodled—on napkins, on envelopes, on tabletops, wherever. People would say, "Maybe, after high school, you might go to art school and become a dress designer," but I had lost momentum. I came to focus on my hirsute body, my cosmetic flaws. In sober moments I would realize that I was throwing away gold in my quest for glitter, choosing trivia instead of Torah, cartoons instead of culture. But sobriety and reason had nothing to do with it: I was preoccupied with the absurd. I was preoccupied and crazed with my perceived and real disfigurement of my skin, the embarrassing body hair that in my head had assumed the proportion of a calamity. I, the daughter of Holocaust survivors, the child of the new land of Israel, knew nothing about perspective, was unable to laugh at the absurd.

IN EARLY SPRING, WHEN Paul and I lay in bed together, both in pajamas, a defense against the cold night, a glorious feeling would overcome me. I could snuggle up to him, allow him to touch me anywhere, and feel cozy and secure. My skin was no longer a barrier, an untouchable organ, a potential end game. Under covers, I morphed into an ordinary girl, a thrill, a welcome negation of my grandiose life-long fantasies of being special, a rebuke to my younger self who had shunned the notion of mediocrity. I could only imagine what it would be like to feel at ease in one's own skin, an experience I had never had.

For summer, I bought a light, cute terry cloth robe to wear around the house; but as soon as the days grew warmer, it became impossible to wear anything in that airless, un-airconditioned tenement apartment. Paul could walk around with his shorts on; he had a nice body, with normal hair distribution, and no weird, embarrassing physical flaws. Zoe, who slept through the days, had nothing to worry about, as far as I knew.

I INTRODUCED MY PARENTS to Paul shortly after he dropped out of law school and was well on his way to becoming a bona fide drug addict. He met all their criteria for a suitor: He was Jewish. Starting at age seventeen, my parents' most singular, repetitive demand of me was that I should marry, and marry a Jew. In their worldview, I was becoming an old maid, and I had better snag someone before running out of time. I could bring home a doctor, a charlatan, a known womanizer, a senator, a sixty-year-old curmudgeon, or an obese shoe salesman; it didn't matter, as long as he met that one requirement: Born Jewish. There was nothing about the passage of time or distance from the *shtetl* that could alter their fundamental, fixed notions regarding a woman's role in life. As far as they were concerned, an unmarried daughter over eighteen was nothing but a curse: a hopeless, unwanted, discarded object of grief and disgrace.

"Bracha," my mother cried, "you are not getting any younger. You have to think. Wear pretty clothes and splash on perfume. There are boys in the Jewish Center who would drop dead just to look at you."

"Yes," my father would chime in, "a girl in her twenties, especially one with a reputation, might as well kill herself."

Paul's father was a college professor of astronomy, and his mother a smug housewife who thought herself educated by proxy. I had told Paul that I'd grown up poor in Israel, that I came from very humble circumstances, so I was startled when he later asked, "What does your father do?"

Before I could think, a lie escaped my lips. "He's an electrical engineer."

"Really," said Paul. "He must be an intelligent man." Yeah, right. It never occurred to me that the two would meet.

I knew that, when they did, my lie would be as apparent as daylight, but I took my chances. I wanted to make my parents smile for a change; I had a chance to undo the past, to soothe their worries, and to bring home a peace offering, an olive branch. Paul, who was neither a blue-collar worker, nor an entrepreneur, nor an artist, nor an heir to a fortune, could, by his mere presence, bring a measure of relief to my long-disappointed, suffering parents. My diminutive mother was growing in reverse, becoming shorter every year, and her once-beautiful blue eyes, opaque with permanent tears, could, without much effort, inject remorse into every fiber of my being. This child-mother, who had endured her husband's infidelities and verbal abuse in her youth, had lived long enough to see her daughter become a stranger with no *mazel tovs* and wedding bells in her future.

Paul and I visited my parents again on a Labor Day weekend, on a gorgeous Saturday afternoon when the thermometer hit the 80s, but the cleansing feeling of fall was already palpable. Paul looked at my father and said, "Yosef, what is it you do?"

My father proudly told him about his plumbing and heating business. I had hoped that Paul would not remember the electrical engineer lie, but he had.

"Your father is not an electrical engineer," he informed me the first

moment we were alone, quite pleased with himself. "He's a plumber."
As if I didn't know.

EVEN AS A CHILD, I had been ashamed of both my parents' lack of education, and particularly embarrassed by my father's occupation. "I am the plumber's daughter," I would tell myself in moments of self-deprecation, an objectionable personal identity that was reinforced forever after my grandmother took me to see Clark Gable, whom she adored, in *It Happened One Night*, and, there on the screen, to my private disgrace, Gable's suave character made a couple of supposedly humorous references, comparing the crass, loud, cheap stereotypical plumber's daughter to the gorgeous Claudette Colbert character, the elegant, refined, articulate, morally superior rich banker's daughter. In any language, plumber, "installator" in Hebrew, sounded unclean, more than vaguely suggestive of shit, piss, crap, sewage, menstrual blood, and overflowing, polluted, runny waste, better not left to the imagination. My father, however, was proud of his work, his attitude suggesting that he had never aspired to, or been made aware of, loftier careers; education, art, literature, none of that had ever crossed his path, no curiosity or thirst for knowledge ever stirred his imagination. As a child, I never saw him read a book, except those thin Polish periodicals that arrived in the mail monthly, always depicting the same scantily dressed blonde on the cover, lying on her back on a classy divan, smiling suggestively at the reader, her long, shapely, smooth white legs raised impossibly high, asking to be touched.

As soon as we arrived in the States, people had said that plumbers make good money, and that, being sometimes true, had increased my father's good opinion of himself. He did not find Paul's questions objectionable. My father thought himself wise, and was completely unself-conscious opining in public, showing off his lack of education and superstitious convictions. He was a man who never doubted himself, never second guessed his decisions or apologized to anyone in the world. He was also a pathological liar. If caught in a misstatement or a downright fib, he would rearrange words and phrases, like a politician trapped in a downright lie.

We were with my family that entire long, official end-of-summer weekend, but what I dreaded most was the scheduled trip to the Shore. I had hoped for rain or some natural disaster, an act of God, but the temperature remained high and the sun bright.

I tried at the last moment to squirm out of the ordeal. "I really don't feel like going to the shore with my parents. It's too far, and it's hot, and I don't like my bathing suit."

"Come on, I can't wait to get to the water. You know, for me it's a gas."

"But I don't feel comfortable with my parents," I peevishly went on, "and this weekend I feel fat."

"Well, at least you have great legs. And you are *not* fat."

People always assumed that being thin was enough. Paul had never seen my nude legs in the daytime, and the prospect of revealing them under the hot sun, with no cloud on the horizon, was less inviting than a bout of pneumonia or a day in the hospital. But I was trapped in that position, and had to make the best of it. Sunday morning, after a sleepless night, I rose before dawn, showered, and shaved, and bleached, and tweezed until all was done. In my brother's room, I could hear Paul stumbling around, getting ready for breakfast.

As soon as we staked out our piece of territory, and my mother and I spread a faded blanket on the sand, I jumped out of my sundress and ran into the water. From there, pretending to enjoy myself, I could see everyone already devouring the food my mother had prepared in advance: fresh rolls, chopped chicken liver, boiled eggs, plum tomatoes, cold tea, grapes, bananas, left-over pound cake, and home-baked sugar cookies. Apparently sated, I could see Paul sauntering off towards the boardwalk, then stopping in front of an ice cream stand. That was my cue. Although the water had felt cool and refreshing, I wanted to reach the safety of the towel while he was a distance away. As I jogged towards our spot, my thighs began to chafe and burn. An angry rash had appeared on my newly shaved skin, and the seawater had literally added salt to the wounds.

Paul reappeared licking on a vanilla ice cream in a large waffle cone. He wore a red-and-blue-checkered bathing suit, and his legs looked strong and solid, but his face was flushed.

"I just heard that Louis Armstrong died."

"Really?" It was hard to put the news in any kind of context. I loved Louis Armstrong but hadn't given him a thought in ages. I was reminded of the day, a few years earlier, when I heard that Marilyn Monroe had been found dead. It was bad news but far removed, sad but impersonal.

My mother looked displeased. Although I had insisted that it was rude to speak Yiddish in front of Paul, she blathered on, not even trying to throw a couple of English words his way. She was offended that my boyfriend didn't have the courtesy to offer ice cream to all of us, and particularly to her, the matriarch. The joy and relief at finally seeing her prayers possibly come to fruition had lasted only a few hours before baseline disaffection and alienation resumed their habitual position in her mind. After I dried off, careful to hide my sore legs, I put my long dress back on, where it remained for the rest of the day.

Louis Armstrong, who had been a legend, was now dead, with one last breath putting an end to a whole era, but as always, among all my thoughts and feelings, despite all the news in the world, I was more obsessed with the changing status of my skin. Fortunately, no one commented upon my lolling around on the blanket fully dressed, but I resented the gods and my luck to be in a no-win situation: If I had shaved the night before, I would already be showing stubble, but when

I shaved in the morning, my skin broke out in excoriated trails of razor burns.

There were more forays to the beach, but I learned how to cover up. When we were invited to a weekend at a friend's house in Fire Island, I successfully prayed for rain, and we spent the entire weekend playing board games. Other times, I would wear my bathing suit under a long hippie dress that I kept just for that purpose. Cover-ups had not been invented yet, but cover up I did. I tried leg makeup, thinking that the darker look would smooth out the shaving bumps, but the result was a bigger mess: The makeup streaked, and the battered follicles stood out even more, like a chicken pox breakout in the wrong place. When we were invited to someone's backyard pool party, everyone was in bathing suits or shorts but me. I often donned a long, white, sleeveless cotton dress and felt like a fish out of water the entire time. We were once invited on a picnic, and again everyone wore shorts but me; I was in jeans despite the summer heat, sweating in secret. I didn't own shorts and owned only one one-piece black bathing suit for more than ten years. What was the point spending money on a bathing suit? It could not hide all of me. Summer no longer tasted of cold watermelon sold on the streets by hackers hollering "sugar, sugar," it no longer smelled of lemon popsicles and ice cream, nor did it augur weeks of long days running barefooted with my cousins, climbing fig and mulberry bushes for their fruit, pulling ripe bananas off my uncle's trees, and falling asleep to the rustle of the eucalyptus tree when a small breeze blew and the night was silent. Instead, summers became the season of the blade.

Paul was a mediocre lover but, in fact, perfect for me. He didn't mind when I turned off the lights, nor did he insist on stroking, hugging, or much foreplay. If by chance he came near my bristly thighs, I would guide his hand away, and he wouldn't care or complain. Sex didn't take too long, and it did not require compromising positions.

When he reached orgasm, it was over. As for me, since I had to be on guard at all times, my physical pleasure was of lesser importance. Even during the height of passion, I could not allow myself to lose total control, to be less of an observer. Total physical abandon and recklessness were luxuries I could not afford, period. It's a good thing that I'm not gay, I would think. There's no way a woman would be fooled. A woman would see me for what I am: a hairy beast.

It seemed that I managed to negotiate my grooming needs and a relationship. Paul thought I was pretty, and during the time we were together never ridiculed my appearance, never behaved as if he knew or cared that I was physically abnormal. Possibly he was too stoned to notice. On occasion, he would tease me pleasantly about my "beauty treatments" or "fuzzy-wuzzy" face, harmless banter that I ignored.

After two years, the relationship began to wane, and we seemed to be slowly heading towards its inevitable conclusion. I freaked out about the proverbial uncapped toothpaste tube, the raised toilet seat, and began day-dreaming of other men, fantasizing about passionate and urgent embraces and lovemaking, comparing Paul's tepid moves to others' in the past, in reality or in my imagination. We had stormy fights, back and forth accusations of infidelity, incompetence, inertia, ingratitude, lassitude, and misbehaviors new and old.

We were strolling towards the apartment on a Saturday evening, after seeing Bergman's *Persona* for the second time. We were each in our own thoughts, still under the spell of the film's melancholia. "What do you think was the underlying message?" Paul asked.

"Well, it was far out. Two crazy chicks in that dark place. I don't know." I had found the film confusing but didn't want to sound ignorant.

"Well, what Bergman laid on us here is the existential question of what is reality."

"Yeah, I'm hip. But did he mean to say that the two chicks were one?"

"No. Not necessarily. If that's what you get out of it, that's cool. If you want to dig it as a reference to female sexuality and immorality, that's another reality," he answered, taking a deep hit on his joint.

Paul had introduced me to "cinema"—to Bergman, Antonioni, Fellini. We watched Max von Sydow, in his role as a medieval crusader playing chess with death, at least three times and talked about its meaning for weeks. In exchange, I introduced him to jazz and Knut Hamsun's *Growth of the Soil*, one of my favorite novels.

We continued an animated discussion, seeking *Persona's* hidden meanings and ambiguous analogies, walking along a deserted Eighth Avenue, its sense of danger and gloom mirroring the film's mood.

All of a sudden, Paul stopped. Transfixed. In the gutter were bags containing pieces upon pieces of fur, no larger than 3-by-4s, and in various shades and textures.

"Wow. Unbelievable shit!" he excitedly shouted, as if he had just discovered a pot of gold. "I can sew these together and make something out of it."

"Oh, come on," I responded. "You don't need more crap. Leave it here."

"Are you tripping? How often do you think you run across a shit-load of real fur? And I bet you they have more inside."

I resigned myself, knowing that, when it came to "stuff," there was no winning, but I was pissed. We walked into the storefront.

Two elderly men were sitting at a cluttered desk. "Hey, hey, we are closed," they shouted in unison.

"Yes, sorry to interrupt. But do you have more of this stuff that you don't need?"

The two men looked at him as if they knew the type. "Yeah, you can have these two bags in the corner." They looked at each other, snickering, as Paul grabbed the sacks. One of the men spat out the words "another *shlepper*," not even bothering to conceal his contempt. Paul didn't give a damn. He proudly *shlepped* the heavy bags of fur to his apartment as I walked next to him, silent and hostile.

At home, Zoe was at the kitchen table, busy cleaning out seeds from a pile of marijuana—a barefooted hippie, replete with a paisley headband, beads, beard, long hair, and colorful clothing assisting.

"What the hell is all that?" she shrieked. "Wow. I am grossed out."

"Don't you want me to sew you a mink stole?"

"Fuck, no." They took their drugs and slammed the door to their room. I could hear them laughing and felt victorious.

"See, Paul?" I taunted, "even Zoe and that cat think you are off your rocker."

"I don't need all these bad vibrations," he muttered. But he was satisfied. He had his stuff and didn't give a hoot for others' opinions. The former law student had won his case. His bags were intact, and he placed them in the kitchen corner, between the bathtub and the stove, where they remained forever, as far as I knew. Although we continued going to movies, one of the few things we enjoyed in common, we never again referred to Bergman's *Persona*, a masterpiece that would forever, in my mind, lie dormant under piles of useless swatches of fur.

Among all his possessions Paul also owned, as I have mentioned, a jealous, evil, long-haired gray tabby, a present from a former girlfriend, named Shat. As if maintaining loyalty to the ex, the cat definitely had it in for me, spraying on my laundry, attempting to scratch and even bite, marking his territory on the couch and with his heft pushing me away. Paul had refused to "fix" Shat, empathizing with the animal's male aggression, and ignoring my constant bitching. And I had considered myself a cat lover until I met Shat, who eventually broke my heart after all. Paul, planning to move, had arranged for Shat to live on a farm upstate. The cat had peed in fear as we struggled to bring him down the stairs and into the car. He had whimpered and cried all the way to the farm. Much later I'd learned his fate: Shat had disappeared in the house the first day he arrived there, and all the goading and pleading could not entice him to come out and eat. He had stayed hidden about a week, then slunk out of the house and vanished into the outdoors forever.

Shat brought to mind the fate of the dog we'd had in Israel—a vicious mutt that my father, for some unknown reason, brought home and of whom I was scared to death. The dog was kept on a leash by the front door and barked like a demon every time anyone came and went. A few months after acquiring him, it began vomiting, losing weight, and appearing listless. My parents, who spoke in Polish whenever they didn't want us to understand, discussed the dog's fate as Shlomo and I were in bed feigning sleep. The trouble was that, by then, after years of hearing the language, I understood it even if I couldn't pronounce a single word. In vain, Shlomo and I begged my mother to save the dog, and when she tired of our pleas she promised that she would. But instead, one bright day, she placed the dog in a sack, boarded the bus to the beach in Tel Aviv, and when no one was looking, left him on the hot sand to die. I cried for weeks.

As in most relationships, money was always an issue, but in our case things were pretty grim. As a clerk I never made much money, and Paul worked odd jobs that only sometimes paid off. His excellent elementary and high school education had prepared him for various crafts and hobbies: carpentry, interior design, painting, plumbing, ballroom dancing, drawing, even electrical wiring. Once he had decided to drop out of school and out of the establishment, he preferred to do nothing. Nothing but smoke pot, that is.

Zoe decided to move out. She found an apartment in our building where the previous owner, a known bag lady with no family, had suddenly died, leaving behind about forty years of accumulated stuff. In what must have been a lapse in judgment, Zoe engaged Paul in the formidable task of clearing the place and making it habitable. It never happened. He became absorbed in the deceased's life, attempting to recreate it and to erect a timeline of events that had led to her lonely death. Night after night he perused her books, diaries, pictures, clothing, and all manner of the detritus of a life long lived, forgetting or ignoring all other obligations. Much of her stuff he took with him: 1920s sewing patterns, knitting and crocheting pamphlets, small pottery made in occupied Japan, a crystal vase, Depression-era cookbooks. If Zoe hadn't thrown him out, Paul might have spent the rest of his life there. Paul taught himself knitting, and I embarked on an heirloom crochet-lace tablecloth. The mercerized ecru cotton cloth, a collection of square doilies hooked together, turned out too small for my mother's French provincial dining-room table, and, sadly, I didn't own a dining-room table then, or later.

10

CHANGES

LTHOUGH I HAD NAGGED and harangued Paul, like Xantippe in the marketplace, for all his character flaws, including lethargy, slothfulness, perpetual tardiness, and pot use, I was not prepared for an end of the relationship. I had hoped that Paul would get his act together, get a job, agree to get married, and rescue me from my parents' disappointments. They were waiting for a marriage announcement, my mother fantasizing about the pink dress she would purchase. Each and every time we spoke, she never neglected to ask me, "*Nu*, what are you going to do? You are wasting your time on a man who will never marry you. What's wrong with you? Don't you want a husband and children like everyone else?"

Truth be told, my hopes for my future were not as disparate from my mother's as I would have wished them to be. I began yearning for motherhood, and although it was hard to admit even to myself, I wanted to be married. I couldn't understand why I'd been having sex for years without protection yet not conceiving. Naturally, I suspected that I was too masculine to become pregnant. The same factor that produced my hirsutism had probably worked on my ovaries and uterus to keep me barren. Perhaps I was not a real woman; perhaps I was some kind of pseudo-hermaphrodite, a thing stuck between genders, unable to decide which way to go. But I had breasts, I was getting my periods, and most of all, in my wildest dreams I couldn't imagine myself a man. At five-five and 110 pounds, I would make a rather puny man, a man who had no interest in fishing, hunting, heavy lifting, building, fast driving, or women and sports. I liked too many things labeled feminine; I even loved frilly, romantic clothes, fresh flowers, and sweet perfume. If I had been a pious or religious Jew, I'd be truthful thanking God during Morning Prayer, "Lord, and thank you for not making me a man." In my mind's eye, I could easily erase all the superfluous hair from my toes to my temple, and imagine my skin as pure, fluorescent, good to the touch. In my mind's eye I could wish all the hair away, but only in my mind's eye.

I made an appointment and met with fertility specialist who happened to be a woman. "You are telling me that you are living with a man, unmarried, and you are wondering why you can't get pregnant? Am I getting this right?" she asked, staring at me as if I were out of my mind.

"Well, we are *planning* to get married," I apologized, "but I really want to know if there is something wrong with me."

"Well," she huffed, "we are not going to do a fertility work-up on a single woman. If you *do* get married, make another appointment."

I was flabbergasted. It was 1971. The Sixties were over, the women's liberation movement was on in full force, the sexual revolution and the pill had changed sexual behavior and sexual mores, and nobody expected a woman in her early twenties to be a virgin. But the doctor made me feel like a tramp. I left her office, and my fertility, to fate.

EVEN IF I HAD wanted to, it would have been impossible to find the words to explain to my parents my relationship with Paul. An odd vocabulary between my parents and me had evolved since leaving home: We no longer had a common language, literally. In Israel, I had spoken Yiddish with my mother and, after I entered grammar school, Hebrew with my father, but both my Yiddish and Hebrew had become rusty, while my parents' English remained poor. At some point, my father and I reverted to speaking Yiddish, which seemed childlike, awkward, and intimate. Speaking to him in my mother's tongue seemed practically incestuous, as if we were resurrecting a childhood intimacy that had no business in the adult world. My father had become more a stranger than a relative, more like an ex-husband or ex-lover who had once been the beloved object, then the hated object, and then finally just a pain in the neck.

One evening Paul came home, his long, wavy hair all shaved off but for a small patch in the back of his head. His eyes were glazed over. I thought that grass and uppers had finally pushed him over the edge, and perhaps they had. He calmly informed me that he had at last discovered true reality within the Hare Krishna, and as if to prove his point, he began chanting: "Hare Krishna, Hare Krishna, Hare Krishna, Hare Hare," a catchy chant that I had always liked. Whenever a group of Hare Krishna devotees appeared on the street in their saffron robes, chanting and striking their cymbals, I would feel cheered up. Their insane joyfulness was contagious. They were Americans with an exotic tilt, but, just the same, I thought of them as a bunch of lost souls, nuts, hippies with money and too much leisure time on their hands. They amused. Their mantra never failed to leave its stamp on my brain cells, like the trail of musky cologne, or rather patchouli oil, long after the perfume evaporated.

THE CORNER OF MacDOUGAL and Bleecker had almost become a tourist attraction, the parade of stoned hippies as colorful as peacocks flowed aimlessly, a river of bodies without destination.

It was there that I met Anders. I was the hippie and he the tourist.

"May I offer to buy you a drink," he inquired politely in heavily accented English. I loved his blue eyes and fair complexion. Over six feet tall, he seemed to rise above the crowd, his reddish-blond hair like a rare spot of light in a dark ocean. Almost everyone I knew was out of town, on their way to Woodstock. When people talked about going, I'd had no interest. I could never have camped out for a few days; I would have changed from a girl to a werewolf by the end of the weekend; moreover, it was to be a rock concert. "Not my bag," I had said, "I'm into jazz."

"Sure. I'd love to have a drink. Would you like to go to the Village Gate and hear music?" Both Thelonious Monk and Miles Davis were performing that evening. He'd offered only a drink, but I'd seized the opportunity to hear the two great jazz giants. Hearing Monk play made me think of Maurice, and an unexplained sadness came over me for myself, for him, for Anders. I was accompanied by a stranger with no interest in the music, who reached for my hand awkwardly, who appeared like a nice guy but certainly, despite the blue eyes and hair the color of straw, was not my type. When we left the Village Gate, we walked to the Waverly Hotel, where Anders was staying. He was in New York to visit a sister dying of breast cancer at St. Vincent's Hospital, and was eager to return home to Copenhagen. When he spoke of her, his eyes moistened and his body trembled. Once in his room, he continued telling me about his sister's illness; he showed me pictures of his whole family, including a picture of his dead mother laid out prettily in a steel coffin.

Anders, at age twenty-seven, was still a virgin. Walking up to me in the Village had taken every bit of strength that he could muster; women scared him. Confessing his weaknesses made him seem weak and naive and made me feel older, more sophisticated, and more jaded as well. I pitied him. Right then and there I decided that it would be a *mitzvah*, an act of altruism, to release him from virginity. Since he had never been with a woman before, I was less conscious of my hairiness; he wouldn't know the difference, I thought, and, for the first time, I had the upper hand in a romantic relationship. I could handle this guy. And when he asked me to go to Copenhagen with him, I saw no good reason to refuse.

A few weeks later, as summer was winding down, we left the rowdiness and clamor that was Greenwich Village and home. I packed all my depilatory armaments, clothing, and layers upon layers of raw guilt, believing my mother's tearful claim that I was putting her in an early grave.

Anders lived in a small, rented house on the outskirts of the city and commuted to his clerical job in the city square by bicycle, as did everyone else. The two bedrooms were small, as was the kitchen and living area. The place, like all the others in the neighborhood, had a temporary, fragile, shed-like feel to it, as if it had been built cheaply and on the run. Leading to the house was the garden: a patch of grass, blue cornflowers, a single rose bush. Inside, the furniture was broken down, fixtures were in a state of disrepair, and the appliances hardly functional. We slept on a bed that had coils sticking out of its thin mattress that was all dips, hills, and valleys. In order to obtain a good night's sleep, I had to internalize that damn mattress so that, even in sleep, I would know how to turn. It was a challenge. Sometimes I would wake, startled to find myself in that foreign place, lying next to a man I hardly knew. Mornings I would wave as he cycled off to work, ashamed that I had never achieved the ordinary feat of riding a bike.

When I was twelve, my father had decided that it was time for me to have bike-riding lessons. One of my earliest and most pleasurable memories was of being a passenger on my father's bike, holding his waist, feeling the air on my face, secure in knowing he could be trusted with my life. As long as he was in charge, there was no injury to fear, no peril to overcome. My riding lessons went well. Once, when I thought he was behind me steadying the bike, I realized that I was riding alone, pedaling on those thin wheels that belied my understanding of the physical properties of nature.

"See?" he shouted with joy. "You biked alone. You did it."

I was elated. Shortly after, he took off to England, and my lessons ceased. That was the end of that story. Until I was living in Copenhagen, I had forgotten all about bicycles.

ALTHOUGH I WAS HOME a lot, I never saw or spoke to a neighbor, and still everyone's garden seemed neat and well tended. Before long, Anders and I settled into a routine, a bourgeois life style almost, he the breadwinner and I the loving housewife who bought groceries, cooked dinner, and cleaned the house, more or less. And I did love him, somewhat, but knew he was only a respite from real life, a lull in my manic, unfocused existence. I knew that I would return to New York, pick up where I had left off, and face growing older, hairier, poorer, all by myself. In the meantime, I didn't share my thoughts with Anders, my gentle, melancholy Dane who never failed to cater to me, to treat me as if I were precious, and to thank me for turning him into a regular guy.

But there was little to talk about. We had no common language, literally and figuratively. I never saw him read a book, and when I thought I could inspire him to read, at the very least, a Hans Christian Anderson fairy tale, just so that we could share ideas, he laughed.

"You like my mother talk now. I not a good student. Never."

If I tried to pick a fight, I couldn't succeed. We were not on the same wavelength; we were rather two unrelated objects on a collision course in the middle of nowhere.

"I know you don't love me. For you, it's just that you finally have sex."

"Suzie. I love you, my way only. I know only Suzie. You are only woman I know. And I know my heart has for you all my love."

The irony was that I loved his physicality; the touch of his hand on the back of my neck could send shivers up and down my spine. His body, a foreign country, was, nonetheless, an oasis. I was a woman to him, there was no other, no comparisons, and I did not fear being discovered as a fraud. And we were in Denmark, where tall, svelte blondes with silky limbs and white teeth graced the landscape naturally, unaware of their luck, born on top of the world, fair, light, diaphanous, smooth as ice. I envied each and every girl I saw. In a hundred years I could not have imagined myself walking among them, I and my unsightly Jewish hair, Jewish troubles, holding the tanned arm of one of their men, having the temerity, the moxie, the sheer *chutzpah* to insert myself into their midst, as if I were their equal. And yet there I was.

Needless to say, in Copenhagen, there were no bleach creams, depilatory gels, or advertisements for electrolysis in drug stores or magazines. I wrote to my mother and asked for several boxes of bleach cream. My brother was the go-between, translating my words to Yiddish and composing dictated letters to me. I could imagine her chasing him with one of my missives, and he, annoyed at yet another chore, reluctantly agreeing to write a few rote and meaningless sentences back to me. But to my relief she did send me several containers of bleach in a brown paper package, on which, as required, the contents of the package were spelled out for the entire world to see. BLEACH CREAM. BLEACH CREAM. To my sensibilities, these two words were an obscenity that should not be elucidated or printed; Bleach cream was to be hidden in the back of the medicine cabinet, behind the antifungal ointment, the jar of witch hazel for hemorrhoids, or the extra-absorbent sanitary napkins.

TO ANDERS' CREDIT, HE did his best to entertain me, to show me some of the highlights of his home town, although he would have preferred downing a few bottles of Carlsberg beer on Saturday afternoon than gadding about the countryside looking for museums, castles, tourist attractions, or the like. But he uncomplainingly agreed to traipse all over the place just to humor me. Using public transportation, we hit most of the touristy sights: Rosenborg Castle, the National Art Museum, the botanical gardens, even the Assistens Cemetary, the burial site of Hans Christian Anderson. Anders' affect during those long labyrinthine strolls through sculptures and paintings was flat and pained. As a companion, he was as exciting as a piece of wood; in fact, he looked wooden, taciturn, and introverted. There was no telling what was going through his mind, although I suspected, nothing much. Yiddish words—*putz, goishke kopf, yoyno, shmuck*—would enter my head uninvited. I hated him for that. He was a *tabula rasa*, a blank board, for me to mold and carve, but aside for learning to fuck, he was unteachable.

The weather was always gray and dreary. At the deer garden in Klampenborg, I shivered in the bone-chilling cold and wind, and actually tried to warm up against the trunk of a tree. When a herd of deer came running, I panicked. The Little Mermaid was indeed little, and unimpressive, a big ado about nothing, I thought, remembering the formidable sculpture at Rock Creek Park in D.C. or the Central Park reservoir in Manhattan; and I missed New York every day. Copenhagen was beautiful, I had to admit, with its closed-to-traffic shopping street, its town square, the royal gardens and theaters; but my heart was not there. Our longest trip was a ferry ride to Malmo, Sweden. I couldn't believe that, in the time it takes to cross the George Washington Bridge from New York to New Jersey, I could be in a new country. "I'm in Sweden," I kept repeating to myself. A little old lady, perfectly groomed, dressed beautifully in a mink jacket and expensive kitten-heeled shoes, sat on a park bench holding her pocket book, smiling sweetly. She represented poise, civility, old-world charm. "I am in Sweden," I kept repeating, looking at my boyfriend who had nothing to say.

STEPPING OFF A PLANE or boat to a new country was as exciting as opening a new novel, one that I knew I would love and that could transport me out of this world and offer unknown plots and action. A new place presented the opportunity to be a child again, to see anew native plants, food, people's mannerisms, coins, styles, buildings, foreign rhythms, and the cadence of a previously unheard language. No experience could be as awe-inspiring; however, this time I had failed to anticipate that I would be homesick for New York, that I was older and more jaded. From the moment we landed in Copenhagen, where a grayness and apathy settled upon the city like lava, I hated the place.

Being in Copenhagen was unlike the adventure of sailing from Port Haifa, crossing the sea through the formidable Gibraltar Straits, docking in Athens, or climbing up Mt. Acropolis, where it was easy to imagine that, up at the summit, the gods resided, even as the ramp up was punctuated by cripples, pregnant women with their tiny nurslings, malnourished men lacking teeth or proper clothes, all holding their tin cups, begging. Nor was it as joyous as strolling the streets of Naples, studying the features of passers-by, listening to the trilling accordion players, standing next to my mother while she haggled in Hebrew, Yiddish, and sign language with a doll vendor. That infant-size pink doll in frilly clothing was eventually placed on the couch at home and became my mother's loyal companion. She sewed her new clothes, spoke to her, and eventually bought her at least a dozen doll friends.

The winter days were very short and icy. The Danes all looked the same, and despite their friendly smiles, I sensed coldness in their blue eyes. I had a heavy wool winter coat I had bought on sale at Stern's the year before, but it could not hold up to the miserably long

Danish winter. Even the Hamlet Castle lost its allure in the below-frigid temperatures and punishing winds.

But when spring arrived, the city seemed to emerge from hibernation. A circus came to town, cherubic children chased each other, girls sunned themselves braless in the parks, the ice in the river melted, everyone seemed to congregate at the city center, and tulips in every color of the rainbow bloomed everywhere the eye turned. Copenhagen, like my mood, lifted its spirits and glowed, and even Anders seemed brighter, more engaged. One day he brought home a record player. At last we found something we had in common: He loved Joan Baez. Nights became shorter, and the birds by our window woke us up earlier and earlier. I didn't mind. I loved their songs and the daylight at night. I still loved Anders, but I loved the notion that he loved me and not any of the Danish girls, many world-class beauties.

ALMOST TWO YEARS PASSED in that fashion, and by then I was itching to get back home. I was sick and tired of the foods: greasy Swedish meatballs, bacon saltier than the Dead Sea, herring and onions, preserved eel, thin crackers topped with elaborately crafted smidgens of cucumbers, radishes, slivers of meat, elevated to the status of sandwiches that could hardly whet the appetite. Even the epicurean cheeses and dark-roasted coffees couldn't make up for the steady diet of sardines and warmed-over, well-done meat patties.

I feared telling Anders that I was leaving. A quirky but ghastly notion had been brewing in the back of my mind for months until it became a concrete thought that took hold day and night: He would kill me rather than let me go. I had a friend, Ruth, a German girl whom I had met at the National Gallery on one of my solo trips. She was an art major at the university, and we would meet rather frequently either at the dorm room where she lived, or in one of the small restaurants near the town center. She laughed when I clued her in on my paranoid musings.

"Has he ever shown you and signs like a violent person?" she asked after her laughter died down.

"No. Never."

"So what makes you think he could do something like that?"

"He's too attached to me. And you know I'm his one and only lover. I think I've heard of stories like this. Guys freaking out in situations of this sort. I heard something like this in Israel. You know it can happen."

By that time, my fear was no longer just an intrusive thought; I had convinced myself that he would kill me. He would say, "If I can't have you, no one will," and he would strangle me to death and dispose of my body in the backyard, among the boroughs that the hedge hogs had dug.

IN THE STUDENT HOUSING where Ruth lived, there was a popular co-ed sauna that I had hitherto avoided like the plague. But the evening prior to my flight home, weeks after enduring Anders' long, mournful face, heavy sighs, and wordless pacing, I took Ruth up on her invitation to the sauna. To me, she seemed like an older woman, at least forty or fifty, and when she said something about having her period, I was surprised. She was short, with chubby legs and small breasts, and completely un-self-conscious in that well-lit locker room where we undressed and showered before entering the sauna. I hadn't known that the sauna would be dimly lit, a pleasant surprise, or that two male students would be seated comfortably naked on a bench across us and continue a conversation in that guttural, foreign tongue, as if our presence didn't faze them at all. And, I was sure it didn't. The Danes never whistled at a woman walking down the street, never gawked at bare tits, didn't seem to utter crude, scatological comments in mixed company. There was much pornography, casually compartmentalized and consumed in its proper space and time. The men were occupied in an animated conversation. I understood nothing, of course, but for the name D. H. Lawrence, and wished I knew what they were saying. Although they saw us, there was nothing in their affect to indicate interest.

In cowardice, I had decided to spend my last night in Ruth's studio. She went to sleep on the narrow couch while Anders and I made love on the floor. When he reached orgasm, he squealed, "Oh, oh, oh, I went," and I could hear Ruth stifling a chuckle. She told Anders he could call her from time to time, but I believed he never did.

On the SAS jet the following day, I couldn't get the song out of my mind:

> *At my window the leaves are falling*
> *A cold wild wind will come*
> *Sweethearts walk by together*
> *And I still miss someone.*

BACK IN THE CITY

HE NEW YORK I had left only two years previously was gone, changed, unrecognizable, as if in my absence a cataclysmic event occurred and emptied a whole faction of society: long-haired hippies, pot smokers, black Muslim incense peddlers, chicks in colorful granny dresses, cats in tight jeans and wide leather belts sporting huge, heavy buckles, the steel drum musicians in Washington Square Park, the whole patchouli-oiled carnival, all vanished. In their stead, the village teemed with hostile, menacing gangs of youth who roamed Sixth Avenue and the New York University neighborhood streets as if they held the city keys. Hookers, sporting white high-heeled boots and longhaired blonde wigs, brazenly hustled the streets along the West Side Highway, flamboyant gays in multi-colored jeans and leather jackets wiggled their asses at strangers and blew sweet musky smoke at tourists' stunned faces. At twenty-six, I felt old, out of it, a misfit in granny dresses and disapproving affect. Jimi Hendrix was dead. Janis Joplin was, too. The music on the streets sounded an odd beat; a new fad, graffiti in garish colors and meaningless flowing swirls, arches, geometric patterns and hidden symbols indiscriminately defaced building facades, automobiles, trains, even sidewalks. The letters and numbers clearly implied that only a chosen few were privy to hidden codes, and that those few were up to no good.

Standing on a subway platform, I looked in amazement as even a brand-new subway train roared into the tunnel soiled in graffiti. The subway cars, thus subjected to vandalism, appeared to be vulnerable, unstable, sad. A train roaring towards the station would sound strong and confident, but then, the doors would open, people would spill out, rush in, while the graffiti, like dirty laundry, would expose to the world the pathetic state of affairs, the disorder and disarray that should have been observed by those in authority and acted upon. It really bothered me.

When I was a child I used to doodle and scribble on walls. On the credenza in the kitchen I engraved in Hebrew a little message to myself: "I'm having a bad day. Suffering from catarrh." That was probably the summer my father disappeared to London. On the walls in the two others rooms, I wrote notes or drew pictures whenever the spirit moved me. For some strange reason, my parents never objected to the scribbling; it was not commented upon. It never occurred to me that graffiti was not acceptable, particularly in one's own home until I visited a girl friend living in a chichi part of Tel Aviv and observed that all the walls were beautifully painted.

And here in New York there were hundreds who didn't mind treating the whole city as their private wall. Strolling down McDougal Street in the Village, familiar faces were inexplicably gone. Down on their luck former artists smoked pot on building stoops, descending into a facsimile of earlier Bowery lost souls. The naïve mental image of an urbane and sophisticated Manhattan that I had envisioned in my youth gave way to an ugly, dirty city.

I developed panic attacks: trains could derail, tunnels could crumble, bridges could collapse. All trains became vessels that could lead to disaster, and I would suffer the rides with my eyes closed, my heart beating fast and out of whack as if I were about to have a heart attack. I tried to avoid all trains that ran through tunnels or over bridges. Manhattan outer boroughs became completely out of reach. I had to imagine that the city extended to the end of the world, and that no rivers, lakes, bridges or railroad tracks existed outside of its perimeters. Elevators, particularly in buildings I didn't know, scared the hell out of me. If possible, I would walk up twenty flights of stairs, just to avoid the sense that I was about to sink into an abyss. Crowded elevators, particularly those in the subway were out of the question. I would simply have to walk or take a taxi. I became obsessed with being murdered. One night I slept on the couch at a friend's place but, in the middle of the night woke in alarm, recalling something that the friend had said earlier and arriving at the crazy conclusion that he might murder me; a part of me knew this was paranoid and wacky, but, at the same time, another part of me saw the logic in that fear.

Through a friend, I found a place on Eighth Street in the Village. It was a one-room apartment on top of a men's clothing store, and the windows opened onto a ledge where I could grow plants. But when I crawled out the windows to water them, I realized someone could just as easily get up on the ledge and crawl in. At once I was tormented by that thought. It took a while, but I was able to convince the landlord to install bars on the windows, thus effectively getting rid of my "balcony," the apartment's unique feature. After my potted tulips dried up and died, I hung dark blue drapes to avoid facing the products of my neglect.

I met the man I would eventually hate at one of the hangouts on Bleecker Street. I was sitting alone at the bar one Friday night, drinking a glass of wine, smoking cigarettes, pretending to be comfortable at that setting. I was the only unaccompanied female in the entire place. Whenever I went to a bar or restaurant by myself, I would get into a funky mood; but, it was important to get out, not so much as a political statement, but also because the alternative, sitting alone, was too depressing. But if people asked, I would say that I believed that women had the same rights as men in the work force, at home, and on the streets, including the right to eat, drink, go out unaccompanied to restaurants and bars, wear sexy clothing without being hassled, hit on, degraded, or raped. I recalled that in my late teens I was legally prohibited from sitting at the bar with the guys. Even back then, I found it odd, though in a million years I wouldn't have thought of challenging that law.

"May I buy you a beer?" was Charles' opening line. A beer, I thought, what an asshole. Out loud I said, "I'll have a chardonnay." He bought me the drink, after digging deep into his jeans' pockets and cautiously paying the bartender with loose change. He looked kind of cute, and I was thankful to have company. At first glance, I could tell he was Jewish. He looked like an NYU professor: middle-aged, a bit pudgy around the middle, with thinning gray hair gathered in a loose ponytail, scruffy, gray beard, intelligent blue eyes behind round glasses, wearing clothes that didn't look dirty but not clean and crisp either. Despite the clichéd opening line, he impressed me with his educated, articulate manner of speaking. He drank two or three beers, a couple of vodkas, smoked a hundred cigarettes, and regaled me with stories that made us both laugh, while complimenting every aspect of my appearance, listening to every word I had to say. I knew we hit it off.

"Want to go for a ride?" he asked when I was about to order another wine. I was surprised that he was in the Village with a car, but I agreed to go for a ride. It turned out that he'd grown up in Newark, about half a mile from my parents' house, and that we had a friend of a friend in common. His father, who'd died only a few months earlier, had owned a furniture store and the car. Charles had inherited both. He'd also inherited his mother, he said playfully, who at seventy- something was senile and unable to live on her own.

"You want to see where I live?" he suggested, as if it were an innocuous thought that had just entered his mind. He noted my hesitation and added, "You really don't have to be concerned. I won't molest you. Promise. I told you my mother lives with me."

He took the Henry Hudson Parkway, always a magical ride, with the City's skyline lit up to the east, and the Jersey cliffs on the other side of the wide river, but, that spring night evoked every lyric about the night, and the stars, and falling in love ever written. He passed me a joint; I took a hit and passed it back to him. He took a hit and passed it back to me and, as if in a dream, the George Washington Bridge appeared, greener and grander than Emerald City, spanning elegantly between two shores, thwarting even God's earthly creations, standing tall as if to say, "I know who I am. I know where I'm going, and I'll be here long after you are gone."

His huge fifth-floor apartment on Riverside Drive provided unparalleled views of the Hudson. His mother was indeed there, but, after introductions, she mumbled something to herself and disappeared. Looking out the bare windows in the living room, my eyes following the pace of a lazy barge moving north up the river, and feeling the dizzying touch of his hands, I was more than simply intoxicated: I felt that I had crossed over to nirvana. I was in paradise, as close to heaven as possible without dying. And then, I realized he was unzipping my tight jeans, his hand trying to reach between my legs, and without warning paradise was pulled away and reality hit me like the morning after. Except that it was not the morning after, and that, ostensibly everything in the room remained the same.

I pushed his hands away and straightened my clothes.

"Okay. Cool. How about another drink?" he asked as he strode towards the kitchen. "I don't have any wine, baby. But have some vodka with me. I hate drinking alone."

"Okay. I'll have one drink, but after that you are going to have to drive me back home. You promised."

"And I will," he chuckled. "I will. But you are so enticing, so pretty. I love holding you, feeling your silky skin, playing with your hair. You turn me on. Believe me, I am not usually this easily captivated."

"Me, too. I am glad we met. It's been a wonderful evening," I responded, actually at a loss for words or explanation. "But I really can't stay. Really."

We had a few more drinks. Listened to Elton John, John Lennon, Dylan's latest album on the radio, talked about jazz and the cats we both wanted to hear live, smoked more grass and cigarettes. Made out a little more, cautiously; I didn't want him to think I was a cock-teaser. It was way after midnight when I gathered my things to go.

"Next time," I promised, applying lipstick without a mirror, combing my hair with my hands.

"Wow, baby, are you sure you want to leave? You can stay here, you know. You can have my room, and I'll sleep here on the couch. I promised I won't molest you. We Princeton men keep our promises. We are gentlemen, you know."

"Come on, Charles. Please drive me home. I really have to go home," I pleaded. And I did: I needed to shave my legs. I needed a pair of tweezers for my nipples. I needed bleach cream for all the rest.

IN THE BEAUTY SALON, they told me that, in order to wax my legs, I had to avoid shaving for at least two weeks. Shaving had become easier and safer thanks to new disposable razors, but once I decided on waxing and made an appointment, I had to tolerate the inevitable stubble. They also said that my legs would remain smooth for about six weeks, which turned out to be, at least in my case, an exaggeration. Unchecked, my hair would thrive like Kudu down south, like well-watered grass in the spring, like a cancer. I couldn't stand having my thighs touch each other; the sensation of stubble against stubble felt as painful as an electric current that could ignite fire and re-create in my mind every offensive sense that my body ever experienced. To the office, I had to wear a dark shade of ecru stockings, and even then, I could feel the stubble sticking out through the nylon mesh. I was lucky, though, that wearing pants became permissible, and that from time to time I could cover up in my blue bell-bottom pantsuit.

I showed up for my waxing appointment, which luckily happened to fall only a few days after meeting Charles. The procedure took place in a midtown salon. It was akin to torture, bringing to mind the Little Mermaid fairy tale I had loved in childhood, and my own interpretation of its moral: A girl must suffer excruciating pain to have beautiful legs and the love of a prince. The lady in the white lab coat waxed my legs in sections, applying the warm beeswax on a small area, covering it in some type of cloth, and then in one furious gesture, yanking off the cloth and the stubborn hairs with it. One thing about my body hair, it was not only thick but also dark and strong, like the stubble on a swarthy man's face.

"You do have a lot of hair," she commented needlessly between yanks, which were painful on my lower legs but agonizing on my thighs, particularly the backs of my thighs. When she was done waxing, she tweezed the hairs that had refused to submit to the honeybee wax, and there I was, standing with my legs on fire but with no stubble or unsightly hair for the first time since childhood.

Once my legs were waxed, I was confident that, when Charles and I saw each other later in the week, I would not have to ward off his touch. He could stroke my legs or my thighs with his own hands or with his mouth, and I could respond like a normal woman. I wouldn't have to be on guard, policing his every gesture. This one time, I could bask in the imaginings of my girlhood—luxuriate in a world of fairy-tale endings, eternal love, unwavering trust, a far-away land where kindred spirits skip joyfully through life's journey, down, down the yellow brick road. But even as I could dwell in make-believe, I always knew full well that I could never admit my hirsute condition to anyone, not a girl friend, not a colleague, not a one-night stand, not even to my mother, let alone to a man I had a crush on, a man I wanted to keep. It was out of the question. If I wanted Charles to love me, I had to do whatever it took, whether a king's ransom or a lifetime of monotonous pecking and grooming.

And, in fact, later, again on his couch, I could show off my body in the dimness of the room, where lights and shadows intersected, reveal the new red bra and lacy panties I'd bought just for him.

"Mmmmm, I love your matching, pretty, sweet, sweet little unmentionable fine little things," Charles cooed. And later, "I love your body. I love your long, wavy hair cascading off your shoulders. Yeah, I love the curly hair on your mons pubis, the smoothness of your translucent, white, fair skin."

But even as I felt that I was unworthy of his compliments, that I was pulling the wool over his eyes, I couldn't help but judge his body and note his masculine shortcomings. I had never been with anyone in his forties, and if I were to sum him up from a slightly different angle, from a point of view that didn't include his total humanity, I could be startled by his aging appearance. His middle-aged body was pasty white and flabby, his chest soft, his ass flat, his short legs varicose veined. His teeth were discolored, almost yellow. When he opened his mouth too wide, I could see a couple of naked gaps where teeth should have been. But, unlike my usual squeamishness, his body still turned me on; my desire for him transcended his physicality. Instead, I was sick with worry about my hairiness. I felt forced to find more ways to fight my constant upward battle with my skin, which in a way was becoming second nature. It was my private world.

"I don't know what it is that turns me on so much about a garter belt and stockings on a woman. It is unbelievably sexy to me," he explained as he told me where to buy Frederick of Hollywood-type lingerie. Having only recently shed those garments in favor of the more liberating panty hose, having had my consciousness raised by the women's movement and having absorbed to some extent the lessons of the 1960s, I resisted dressing up in such a way. But it was either that or nothing. As he said, "When you fight with me you can't win, because even if you win you lose."

I would ride the A train from the Village to the Heights, once or twice a week, and stay with him all night, then try to wake up for my typing job in lower Manhattan. He couldn't leave his mother alone, she might set the house on fire, and so the commuting fell to me. Also, once his car was parked, he was unwilling to go through the hassle of moving it and then searching for a new spot. I was always sleep-deprived, always tired. Charles, on the other hand, made his own schedule, giving music lessons only in the late afternoons or evenings. I actually heard him on the phone, telling a prospective student that he had a day job and no openings until after 4 p.m. He drank cheap vodka and drank it all the time. He even had the local liquor store deliver. He would be sober in the early evening, but as the night progressed the vodka would put him in an expansive mood, and he would, not only engage me with his sexual fantasies, but wax philosophical on unrelated and disparate topics such as the Crusaders victories, the genius of Paul Simon, the assault of Islam on ancient Europe, the life cycle of an e-coli organism, the emergence of the microcomputer, world inflation, the price of oil, the health benefits of smoking pot and drinking vodka.

He had run across a book on horse racing, and as smart as he was, he actually believed he could beat the odds and make a fortune. If not at home, he could easily be found at the Off Track Betting storefront in the bus station in his neighborhood. One day he said, "I had a dream that a dying horse was dragging away my car."

"That's an easy one to interpret," I laughed, not knowing that he had already had the car repossessed. And then there was the business with his mother, who, in a demented state, wandered around the house, not only without medical care, but with no care whatsoever. Once or twice she almost set the kitchen on fire, preparing dainty sandwiches for an imaginary luncheon and forgetting to turn the oven off. Often she broadcast her thoughts out loud, saying things like, "Well, he's got a lover now. Or is this one his wife?" When we took her out, at my insistence, to a Japanese restaurant, she took one look at the waitress, and then broke into an aria from *Madame Butterfly*, prompting Charles to lose his temper.

"She has not had a bath for about a year," he confessed one evening. "I don't know why she doesn't stink; I guess because she walks so slowly."

Secretly, I harbored the notion that, as a little boy, Charles had seen his mother in her lingerie, and that that was the root of his kinky erotic fantasies, and as I watched her shuffling around the house in her soft slippers, well-worn beige suits, and pearls, her gray hair pinned up, and her reading glasses tied to a string around her neck, I tried unsuccessfully to imagine this shapeless heap of a woman as a sensual young mother sitting on the edge of her bed, clamping the lacy garter strap to the top of the silk stockings, then standing up, turning her watchful eyes to the back of her legs, adjusting the seam snaking up from the top of her high heeled shoes, up her shapely legs, to the garter straps. But the two images were discordant, even in the world of fantasy where everything was possible.

Charles complained bitterly that his older brother in Philadelphia was not sharing the burden.

"What does your brother do?"

"He writes rebuttals."

"He does what?"

"He teaches math to high school students. But he's always in trouble and always writing rebuttals. That's what he is good at, rebuttals."

"Well then," I suggested, "how about putting her in a nursing home?"

"I can't," he explained patiently, as if he were speaking to a child. "I need her social security money." After that, I never asked again. After all, it had nothing to do with me. His mother never interfered, for one thing; and I didn't want to know anything that could break the spell.

SHORTLY AFTER WE BECAME lovers, Charles welcomed me at his front door holding a small package in a white shopping bag.

"I bought you something. I bought you a present," he exclaimed, giving my nipples a quick hard squeeze.

"No, no peeking," he teased. "Come in first."

I tossed out the tissue paper and took out my present. While he sat across from me beaming, I held in my hands a new beige garter belt, size 34, and a pair of sheer nylon stockings.

I was surprised and even anxious. In my awkwardness, I attempted to make light of the situation:

"Oh, you shouldn't have."

"You are wrong. I should have. You have no idea what I had to go through to get you this. I walked into the lingerie shop and asked for a ga-ga-garter belt for my wife. I was as nervous as a teenage boy buying rubbers."

"Your wife, eh?"

"Yes, after you put this on, you will be my wife."

At last I was being proposed to, not on bended knees, not with a diamond ring, but with a fetish, and a proposal to be signed there and then on the spot on a page torn out of a notebook: *Hereby the undersigned agree to join each other in holy matrimony.*

He signed. I signed.

"But I'm wearing jeans," I protested laughing. "How can I wear this?"

"That's okay. Put these on under your jeans, and when we come home after dinner, I'll ravish you."

Wearing thigh-high stockings did make me feel sexy. My legs felt smooth, and I loved the expectation of freedom that being partially dressed promised. During dinner, during conversation and wine, I knew that he knew that, under my jeans, belying my tough-chick red platform shoes and leather jacket, I had on a secret garment that would turn me into a sensual, erotic replica of the 1950s model woman. But for me it meant that I would allow him to touch a good portion of my legs; I would be able to let my guard down, at least for a little while.

If the declaration of marriage was a playful antic on his part, it was similarly a game for me. Despite the relentless pressure from my parents, particularly my mother, my father had already given up on me and declared me an old maid, I knew from the start that I could never marry Charles even if he did beg on bended knees. He came with too much baggage, too many dirty sheets, too many bed crumbs, too many rules, too little money. He was as bad as all his predecessors, if not worse. Therefore, instead of sensibly dismissing him even as boyfriend material, I obsessed about my hairiness; I didn't want to be called, fuzzy-wuzzy, wooly baby, furry, hairy or worse. I dutifully went along with his capriciousness, his drunken 4 a.m. phone calls, OTB gambling, his rules, rages, disloyalty, and all his fetishes. I tolerated the dirty dishes in the sink, the funky bed sheets, or the revolting toilet. I fell in love with him who played the flute, who quoted Kant, Descartes, or Shakespeare, and who made me laugh. His intellect was a turn on; his character, a rough terrain, was left unexplored. I refused to read the writing on the wall.

When I complained that our long marathon nights left me drained and sleep deprived, he plied me with amphetamines. When all the cigarettes and pot were smoked, and the empty Smirnoff bottles littered the entire place, adding broken glass to the general disorder, and morning was not far off, and he still lay there unable to get hard on or achieve orgasm because, as he complained, "I want you to put this negligee on the right way, and you just lie there doing nothing," and I, on the defense, whined, "but I did everything you asked earlier, and its very late, and I'm exhausted. Besides, can't you just get off on having a naked woman in bed with you?" and I would think, there is no way I could ever live with this man and do this every day.

A girl friend advised: "Tell him to jerk himself off and be done with it in five minutes." Later the same girl friend revealed that, when I was out of town visiting my parents, he had phoned her asking for sex. That friend was not a shrinking violet, but Charles' uninvited, presumptuous, bold phone call had left her offended and outraged.

"Yes, I made a mistake, I know." He made no attempt to deny any of the accusations. "Go ahead, hit me. Go ahead, tear my skin off. Whatever you want to do is okay. I deserve it."

I didn't hit him. I went away, only to come back a few days later "on bended knees," to paraphrase Billie Holiday, my favorite singer. And nothing changed. He was a fountain of knowledge, a walking encyclopedia, and he wallowed in it. The fun and games continued: I could sit on the toilet minding my business and he would burst in launching into a detailed, critical analysis of *Jaws*, a film he raved about or the latest best seller, *One Flew over the Cuckoo's Nest*. He didn't mind criticizing my favorite writers; when I shared a poem I had written with him in mind, he dismissed it with the words, "not great art." I believed him and stopped writing, even though writing was cathartic and healing. But if I wanted to go to the movies, he'd huff, "But I have only a couple of bucks in my pockets." He'd wake me in the morning speaking a made-up language and encourage me to play along with him. Sometimes he would ask me to pretend to phone another man and play with myself while he did God knows what in the other room. Once, however, the game turned ugly when, instead of make-believe, I actually called someone I had met earlier that evening, a lead singer in a band called Kinky Kandy. Charles picked up the phone and heard the man say, "It was so good to feel your pussy in that sleazy bar," and stormed into the room with fists clenched, and attacked the phone, ripping it off the wall, as if the phone were the embodiment of *Kinky Kandy*'s lead singer.

After coming, instead of smoking the last cigarette of the day, turning off the lights, and going to sleep; he'd continue dragging the night out, squeezing as much out of a minute as humanly possible. He might reach for his clarinet, turn the television on, or read out loud demanding my attention, treating me like the captured audience that I was. But inevitably, the thrills that excited me in the beginning faded and were replaced with hostility and irritation, almost in exact proportion. As Maurice had put it years earlier, "Confidence entrusted, later disgusted." But there was more to come.

ONE WEEKEND EVENING, AFTER having spent several hours at the end of each weekday tweezing out unwanted hair, after attending to all the rote, mundane, and painful tasks that my body demanded of me, I arrived at his place in a good mood despite the heavy rain, the long train ride, the walk down the mean streets from the subway station to his building. All that time and money I had spent making myself into a feminine object of desire were worth it, I knew. I'd managed to liberate myself from ugliness, even if in the process I had ignored the bills that were piling up, the dishes in the sink, laundry, letters, phone calls, and all the other mundane necessities of daily life.

He waited for me in front of the building, wearing a hostile affect, with one look diminishing my expectations. We rode up the elevator in silence, but the second he slammed the door behind us and we were in the privacy of his apartment, with only his demented mother ambling about, speaking to her imaginary guests, he hollered, "Listen, bitch, you are fucking late. Can't you count backward so you don't keep others waiting? You think I want to stand downstairs like a fucking asshole, waiting for some fucking Dominican to stick a gun in my head, blow my brains out?"

"But I couldn't get a train," I protested.

"Please, I'm sorry. Please calm down."

"Right. You have me sitting here on my ass, twiddling my thumbs, waiting for my one true love to show up. Fuck you. I expected you two hours ago. Fuck you. Get the fuck out." His face was red. He wasn't joking.

"But, Charlie, it's not my fault. How can you yell at me when I am standing here wet and cold? I'm here because I want to be with you."

"You enrage me. Got it? Get the fuck out of here." He bared his false teeth, like an animal displaying his superiority, staring at me contemptuously, as if I were his arch enemy. I began crying. I cried not only because of his cruelty, but out of shame for all my useless juggling and damn maneuvering. I didn't want to be thrown out, sent back home. For all he knew, however, all I had to do was don the required garter belt and stockings, dab a little lipstick and rouge on my face, jump onto an express train, and arrive as scheduled, fresh as a daisy, absolutely ready and willing to give him head, prance around like an idiot all night, following directions: Okay, now bend over—no, not like that, the other way. Put on the black shoes, not the red ones, I hate those. Leave your bra on—no, take it off, but not all the way, let your tits stick out, spread your legs so I can see your cunt, let me look at your asshole, stick this up your cunt, no not a little, all the way, stick the fucking bottle up your cunt, yeah, that's good, now put your panties back on, walk with the bottle in your pussy, let me see you walk out the room, that's good, no come back, pick up the phone, I want to hear you talk dirty, okay now stand in front of the mirror, watch me fuck you in the ass, spread your cheeks, stick it out, more, bend your head more, now down on your knees, beg for cock, lie down on your stomach, scream while I smack your ass, turn over, lift your ass higher, put the pillow under it, spread your legs wider, don't move, beg to be whipped with my belt, yeah, baby, take it, take it, wait till I'm done whipping you, now lie still while I tie you up. You want to get fucked? Don't move while I tie you up. Okay, now stand up, dance, wiggle your ass, squeeze your nipples—okay, hold them, don't move, hold your nipples so I can squeeze them with the paper clips, now dance, don't let the clips fall off, move, turn to your side, don't let the fucking shoes come off. Put your finger up my ass while I'm fucking your cunt, lie still, take it all in, take my cock, put the dildo in there too, squeeze my balls, suck my cock, ouch, no teeth, suck it hard, let me see your head move up and down, suck harder, lick the shaft, jerk it off, get the Vaseline, swallow my cum, get my cigarettes.

Even as I was riding down the elevator, I hoped he would come after me. But I faced the dark and seedy streets of Washington Heights alone, afraid of getting jumped, raped, killed. Eventually I flagged down a gypsy cab, negotiated the fare, and found myself back at my apartment, alone, going out of my mind, afraid that my sobs would frighten my neighbors.

Early the next morning he called and begged my forgiveness. As usual.

If I hadn't been in love with him, I would have been turned off by his appearance, and particularly by his teeth. I read somewhere that erotic love was the absence of revulsion to another's body, and that statement resonated with me. Some nights he kept those damn teeth glued in place to his mouth by bubble gum. When we were out in public, I was afraid of running into friends. Eventually, of course, his dental woes worsened, and he ended up with dentures. I begged in vain to be spared the sight of his toothless mouth, but he didn't care; his self confidence in my presence was not affected by his physical shortcomings. It was I, the female, who had to maintain a façade of hot sexuality, dolled up in garters and silk. My worth was in proportion to my feminine charms; my bedroom dress code was dictated by his mandates.

Once I showed up wearing cotton panties.

"How can you come to me with those on?" He looked at me as if I were unclean.

"I have my period."

"That makes it even worse. You should have put in more effort then."

"Okay, man. Next time." I had already put in more effort than he could possibly imagine. But that was my problem.

"I refrained from jerking off all day. For your benefit, I might add. It's perverse."

I was afraid he would launch into a tirade or into one of his rages, but instead he turned back to the television. The Mets were winning, and he was in high spirits, drunk but not yet out of control.

It was, of course, a given: no garter, no erection. And from time to time no erection, no matter what.

"But it's your thing," I later protested. "It's not my fault that you are difficult to please."

To my girlfriends I said, "I feel like I do all the work. He expects me to stand on my head at 3 a.m. He wants me to dress up when I have almost no strength to pee."

It took time, but eventually I became sick of the whole thing.

I CAME TO MY senses after two years and after a three-week summer vacation in Tel Aviv. Lying on the beach, squinting my eyes against the sun, feeling my skin gently burning, listening to Hebrew in the background, a language simultaneously foreign and familiar, to the life guards warning swimmers from straying too far out to sea, a hitherto unacknowledged insight roused me from reverie: I was no longer in love with Charles. This plain insight had, of course, been brewing all along, but there on the beach it assumed shape and form and came upon me with the relief that one feels when a toothache is finally gone, when health is restored, and fear of loss subjugated. His supremacy over me in the absence of my willingness was no more, nothing but sea foam on the white sands under my feet.

He didn't know it yet but it was over. And I did get to have the last words: "I no longer love you."

GROWTH

AFTER I HAD STARTED tweezing my thighs and overgrown pubic area, it became a routine thing—if not exactly enjoyable, satisfying nonetheless. I could pluck while talking on the phone, listening to music, even watching television. I had tweezers with me wherever I went, as if they were my lifeline. With the night stand's high-intensity lamp on, I would reach for the tweezers at the sight of a wayward hair. I had been tweezing my hands for years, but up until then I didn't think that thighs would be doable; there was too much skin surface area to tackle. But, with gratification, I could create a bald spot and enlarge it within only a couple of hours. All I needed was determination and anger; anger at the hair that did not belong. And the anger allowed me to pluck the hair, let it fall out by its roots, dead. But in the end, the hair won. It would grow back under the skin, as if hiding from me, cause the follicles to become enlarged, red, and infected. Sometimes, if a follicle became too large and swollen, I would puncture it with a sewing needle and then pull out the offending hair, which with disgust and fascination I could see uncoil sometimes to at least six inches. At the end, I was left where I had begun: forced to keep my body under wraps.

Electrolysis, like all other methods, was a temporary solution, providing temporary relief, but the mustache, sideburns, goatee reappeared as certainly as cobwebs on the ceiling and dust on everything else. Each time I studied my face closely and objectively, I would be shocked all over again to see hair on my neck, cheekbones, forehead, unusual places for hair growth, even on a hairy male. The hair was blonde thanks to bleaching, but it was there always demanding attention. Sometimes I would tell myself that the mirrors were lying, exaggerating images that no one but me could possibly see. Knowing that there were worse things in the world never made me feel better about myself. Earthquakes, tsunamis, wars, famine, affected the whole wide world, but large catastrophes never negated or attenuated my own private hell. My own headache, I reasoned, was worse than someone else's brain tumor. I could hardly admit to myself that my preoccupation with my bodily self went beyond the Pale. My ancestors might have fought for liberty, autonomy, freedom from oppression, whereas I lived my life in America, voluntarily chained to vanity, surrendering my will, time, and money to a self-imposed, skin-deep despot that ruled mercilessly, and defined the course of my life, my destiny.

Others had their own hang-ups, but I was hairy. Hairy. The word itself made me cringe: It reeked of testosterone, sweat, athlete's foot, halitosis, unwashed laundry, excrement; indeed it was a shitty word, a shitty condition. Comparison to other women's maladies was not possible; my empathy could barely extend to those with life-threatening abnormalities.

"I can't wear shorts because I have fat knees," a friend once complained. "Well, I too avoid shorts as much as possible," I happily joined in. But ugly knees, fat thighs, eczema, saggy breasts, pimples, psoriasis, flab, cellulite, wrinkles, hair loss, flat chests, big noses were open for discussion in polite circles without inviting too much laughter, pity, or revulsion, but hairy? Who except other exquisitely hairy women could even begin to understand? Being hairy was more a comedy than a tragedy, a punch line rather than a drama, a joke not an affliction, an admission of guilt rather than a plea for help. Who could possibly help? An expert on gender identity? A psychiatrist in fifty-minute sessions twice a week? An electrologist in fifteen-minute painful intervals? A friend upset with her fat knees? None of them could do anything. The bearded lady's place was in the circus or a freak show. She had no business looking for love.

Bracha Holtz, who had pretended to be a ballerina even as she couldn't dance the *hora*, who had dreamt of becoming a princess although not even her father or mother treated her as such, who had longed for acceptance but was been beaten in the school yard, who had sought love but hid in the closet, that girl, the former me, could not possibly accept a distorted femininity. Neither Bracha nor Suzie, none of me, could say out loud, "I couldn't have *been* a contender," without lying.

And so I soldiered on fighting hair as if it were the enemy, as if it were a battle that could end in either peace on earth or the extinction of our species. I barely followed politics, news, current events. I had no idea who my senators were, nor cared. My generation had protested the war in Vietnam, engaged in revolutions, walked on the moon, but I, to my shame, barely lifted my head to look around. As a matter of fact, I twisted myself in a knot trying to see the back of my body, trying to evaluate the situations with my butt. I was aware that my ass was hairy, but the mirror not only confirmed that, but by the light of the reading lamp, I could clearly, without denial, see the outlandish spectacle of coarse dark hair on soft white skin. I had seen men's naked asses, and mine was as hairy if not more so than theirs. If any man were repelled by that sight, I would not blame him. That very day, I bought a tube of Nair, as if it were a life-saving potion. As a teenager,

I had once or twice tried the stuff on my legs and found the stink unbearable and the results unsatisfactory; but now after more than a decade, I held hope that the New and Improved lotion would deserve its new motto and work wonders on my virgin anal hair.

After coating my butt with a generous amount of the foul substance, I had to sit on the toilet, my legs spread high and wide, my hands holding my buttocks apart, while the noxious concoction was percolating on my raw anal skin. Adding insult to injury, the harsh chemical odor burned my eyes, nose and throat, probably my lungs, as well. The entire ignominious process would be a secret that I would never reveal to a soul, even under threat of torture or death by electric chair; I would remain mute maintaining a dignified silence.

"So what if I have hair on my ass, who needs to know?" a dormant small voice in my head asked. I could afford the ambivalence once the chore was completed and I could admire my work with satisfaction, just as an artist might after setting the final brush strokes of on a particularly complex work of art.

"But I don't want hair on my ass," I apologized to no one.

"Right. But now you started something that will just add to the routine."

"So what. We all do what we have to do."

"Who else do you know who does that? It's gross."

Gross. That's what it was; but no one had to know, not even myself.

I would fall asleep ruminating about my options: I could make my life easier if I were to become celibate, like a nun. Or I could wear long sleeves all the time as if I had track marks. I could wear pants to work, avoid the beach, never kiss anyone. Or, I could just grow up, forget about the whole business. Pretend it ain't there; let others gawk. Fuck it. But I could no more change my personality than my hairiness—I knew that.

I had an ugly wart on my right middle finger, centered right above the knuckle. I didn't always have it, of course, but by the time I became aware of it, it had been there for a few months, at least, and I couldn't pin point its beginning. As large and repulsive as it was, it didn't bother me; in fact, I rather liked its rough texture. But when the girls in the office advised, "hey, be careful. It might get caught in the file cabinet and rip off your finger," I went to see a dermatologist who came highly recommended. When I walked into the upscale doctor's office, I was befuddled by its loud, colorful décor. The entire place was wallpapered in various geometric patterns, and the furniture, paintings, *objets d' art,* were a collection of ornate avatars of previous centuries. Fitting the decor, the doctor reminded me of Liberace in dress and manner. One glance at my wart, he got into action, and within seconds it was gone. It didn't even leave a mark.

A few months later, I felt several pea-sized lumps on the inner aspect of my forearm, right under the skin. In panic, I palpated my entire body, and sure enough, discovered a few more on my neck and abdomen. Sudden dread swept over me like a winter chill, annihilating any thought in my brain, erasing all the day's events. I was sure I was dying of cancer. The dread I felt got worse by the minute and when I called the doctor's office the next morning, I was hysterical, begging for an immediate appointment. Within hours, I found myself perched on the tip of his exam table, trying to distract myself by focusing on the purple wallpaper. He took one look at all my lumps, and cheerfully declared: "You have benign subcutaneous angio- lipomas. If they don't bother you, we should just leave them alone." And as soon as those words were out of his mouth, everything returned to status quo and my attention shifted back to everyday, garden-variety worries.

Soon after, I noticed a small skin-colored bump on the right side of my nose, close to my eyes. As with the wart, I knew that the bump had not always been there but couldn't pinpoint the first time I had seen it. It didn't bother me and I ignored it for years until, one morning, when I looked in the mirror, I saw the thing encrusted in blood. Cancer. Skin cancer, I was certain. The now familiar panic hit me with a ferociousness that only fear of extinction could bring on. Skin cancer was certain death, particularly in my case, I believed, since that cyst had been there for years, long enough to metastasize into every major organ in my body. Again, I called my dermatologist, hysterically demanding an immediate visit.

"What you have is not a big deal. We see it all the time," Dr. Berman declared after a quick glance at my source of terror. "We can remove it right here. It will take only a few minutes."

"Right now?" It was great news but I wasn't ready for a painful medical procedure.

"Yes. It will be quick. Let's do it, and send it to the lab for a biopsy."

"Biopsy? I thought you said it was nothing."

"It *is* nothing. But we routinely biopsy removed tissue."

I knew that I would go nuts waiting for the biopsy results. I wasn't sure that he was being truthful. Maybe, I thought, he was calming me down because he knew that I would otherwise freak.

A few frenetic days later, "Looks good," the doctor said after removing the small bandage. "Let's make an appointment for follow-up in two weeks."

"Is it cancer? What did the biopsy show?"

"Well, it was not cancer, exactly," Dr. Berman patiently explained. "Whatever it was, it is now gone, but we have to follow it for a couple of months or so."

"But was it malignant?"

"No. Absolutely not. Just stay out of the sun, and let me have a look at it in two weeks."

I left his office initially reassured but upon further reflection, on my way to the bus stop, doubt and panic literally stopped me in my tracks. The sunny September morning had become ominously gray and cloudy. Rain was threatening. I leaned against a building and remembered that my mother who also had a cyst removed at one time told me that she didn't require follow up visits. I saw people rushing to catch cross town buses, others waving down taxies. Traffic was almost at a standstill, and the impatient honking of horns signaled the arrival of evening. Healthy throngs of men and women were hurrying home to children, parents, spouses, or roommates; dinners, television shows, lovemaking and to other everyday, routine activities in their immediate future; while I was so far removed from all that jostling, I might as well have been on the moon.

"I have skin cancer," and "I'm going to die," were two refrains that overtook my mind like maddening ditties that refused to shut up.

Skin cancer: It made sense. My skin, my anathema, had worked against me all along, and now it had really fucked up, created a tumor that would travel throughout my blood stream, spread and grow in distant places, metastasize like wildfires. This would be one flame that would not respond to my own slash-and-burn hair depilatory techniques; this cancer would eventually end my life. Those were my thoughts, and there was no one to share them with, there was no one that could provide succor. I went through the motions of my daily routines in a state of sheer despair: I stopped eating and lost ten pounds; my hair began falling out. Everywhere I looked, pillow, bathroom floor, sink, brushes, I saw long strands of my dark hair, fallen, as if already anticipating its fate. But each time I asked, Dr. Berman presented the same answer:

"Well, I would not call it cancer."

"What *would* you call it then?"

"A cyst."

"Why do I need follow-up, then?"

"Because I like to err on the side of caution."

And that was the crux of the dialogue between us, there in his cheery office, amid the wallpaper patterns that had no rhyme or reason. But deep down inside, I preferred the euphemisms, as that what I thought he was employing, to some naked truth that could send me spiraling down straight into the bowels of a snake pit, if such places still existed.

But after about three months, my doctor, pleased with my progress—there was hardly a scar where the cyst used to be—unceremoniously, and obviously unaware of the hysteria his patient had endured, blithely informed me that there was no need for further follow-up, unless, of course, a new cyst were to form.

"Basal cells do occasionally return. You should avoid the sun and wear dark sunglasses outdoors both winters and summers," he advised as I was walking out the door.

Basal cell. I finally had a name for my own private hell. I stopped at the library and looked it up. "Carcinoma in situ," I learned, rarely metastasizes. If left untreated, it destroys only surrounding tissue. And it was often related to spending too much time in the sun.

The dermatologist's warnings against sun exposure lasted only as long as the cancer scare. Unfortunately, my skin had a tendency to burn rather than tan. Even the pain of my first sunburn was no deterrent against my belief that the sun was good for my hairy skin. That first sunburn: I must have been about seven or eight when my father, on leave from the Army Reserves, took me to the beach in Tel-Aviv. It was just him and me, and I was thrilled to be in the water, jumping over, with what seemed to me at the time huge waves. As long as he was holding me, I felt safe. I didn't know how to swim, but like all kids, I loved the water. After a while, he brought me back to our preclaimed patch of sand, spread out the blanket, and said, "I'm going swimming. Don't go anywhere. I'll be back soon." I watched him walk away in his tight blue swimming shorts, proud of his confident stride and strong, thin, body. He had left me some change, and when the ice cream hawker walked by for the hundredth time calling, "Eskimo, Eskimo," I bought a lemon popsicle that dripped and melted before I was even half-way finished licking it. I had nothing to do but wait for my father, my eyes glued to the water's edge where everyone, adults and children, were frolicking, having a blast. Nearby, some men were playing ping pong, and from time to time I had to deflect a speeding ball. The lifeguard whistled and screamed over his megaphone, "Ladies and gentlemen, protect your belongings. There is a thief on the beach."

I tried to imagine the thief: a lank, mustachioed guy with darting eyes and dark skin, dressed in a shiny black suit and patent leather shoes, lurking around furtively. Time passed. A fat, red sun was slowly beginning to sink beyond the waters on the horizon, creating a cascade of red, orange, and yellow skies. People stood in awe watching the sunset, but there was no sign of my father as yet. I didn't panic. I knew my father would not abandon me. When the beach was practically deserted, at last my father appeared, looking dapper, and accompanied by Uncle Immanuel, my mother's older brother.

"Sorry, little girl that I took so long. But your uncle and I went swimming and lost track of time." He brought me home and immediately left to return to his military base. The next morning, my mother came in to wake me up for school. When I stood up, my skin was on fire, I became overwhelmed with pain, and I passed out cold. Seconds later, I regained consciousness, as my mother was wailing and keening, cursing my father, and splashing cold water on my face. I was to have more sunburns in the future, but that first one had to be the worst. I was in exquisite pain for at least a few days. Back then, there were no steroidal ointments, no panacea for sunburned skin. Like everyone I knew, the pain had to be endured until the skin blistered and could finally be peeled like the outer layer of a boiled onion.

The diagnosis of skin cancer convinced me that the foundation for the errant cell occurred then, while my father was swimming and I waited patiently under the hot Asia-Minor sun. At any rate, I didn't mind blaming my parents. If it happened to me, they had to be at fault, and there was comfort in that thought.

The same was true for my latest woe: alopecia. My mother's life-long bemoaning of the thinning of her hair was passed down to me. Dr. Berman instructed me to collect all the fallen hair, and count them, one by one. If there were more than two hundred in one day, he explained, then I was definitely losing more than my normal share. And so I did. But hair being hair, it was impossible to keep track or to count, and the doctor treated me with injections directly to my scalp. After several treatments, I had a sense that I was losing fewer hairs. The doctor managed to make light of my questions and I never learned what the injections contained. Plain tap water, I suspected; or his own formula for making a killing. One way or another, it didn't matter; I wanted to believe.

I became one of Dr. Berman's most loyal patients until the day I received a notice from his office announcing his retirement. In all those years, and through all my frantic consultations, it never once dawned on me to ask his opinion about my hirsute predicament. Not even once.

The business of the basal cell carcinoma continued to drive me crazy. I couldn't trust my body to function normally on its own steam. It had already permitted a cancerous cell to thrive and multiply, and there was no telling what could happen next. In fact, it was a minor miracle, to my thinking, that my brain, internal organs, circulatory system, etc., could be trusted upon to function harmoniously day after day, year after year. Every physical symptom, every pain and ache, assumed ominous potential: a muscle spasm became a heart attack, a fever, tuberculosis. I began spending all my time running to doctors.

Aside from my dermatological issues, my hypochondria spread to include blindness, cardiac failure, renal dysfunction, colon cancer, sudden death. I became convinced that a deadly disease lurked right below the surface and only reassurance from doctors and surrender to various blood tests and x-rays could quell my worries, albeit temporarily. I expected bad news at any moment, catastrophes around the corner. Indeed, there was no reason for why the worst might not happen; there was no god in heaven, there was no cause and effect on earth, there was no one to hear prayers, and no one to give a damn. Life was a crap shoot. I was insignificant, nothing but a speck of dust in the whole scheme of things, an idiot shrouded in self-pity and petit melodrama.

I was an unmarried woman, an old maid, childless, with no career or education, typing dog labels for a living. I would lie in bed at night in my basement bedroom, listening to snippets of conversation up on the sidewalk, trying to imagine to whom the voices belonged. Friends or lovers would call or come by from time to time, but nothing was ever enough to fill the void, to allay the loneliness. My girlfriends were married, raising families. Other women were climbing up career and social ladders. The world was changing, and I seemed at the stand still. In the throes of self pity, I wrote:

IN THE DOG HOUSE

Sitting in the secretarial pool,
unable to swim or take diction,
my heart beats as if it had its own clock,
disconnected from these keys
or these words that have no definition.
What happened?
What am I doing here,
lady in black,
orphaned, widowed, abandoned,

an alley cat no longer wanted
at the end of the summer season,
left to say Kaddish for myself
again and again in one lifetime.
What gods have I offended?
Disallowed to atone
or dwell in sacred places,
left to fuck up over and over again,
never to know the sleep of the just
or the glory of divine redemption,
I walk this way all alone.

I read the poem to whoever would listen, but no one seemed to make sense of it or to offer true positive feedback. Their tepid responses became embarrassing, and I filed the poem away, putting an end to awkward moments.

13

BAD BUSINESS

I MET TONY, A swarthy, slightly overweight, mustachioed, good-natured guy of Puerto Rican descent, at a bar. Somewhere I had read that the chance of developing a relationship through such circumstances was about one in a million; I had a better chance of meeting Jesus Christ and his twelve disciples. But it was a Friday night, and for lack of anything better, I was drinking alone, engaging in meaningless, repetitive exchanges with different guys, smoking cigarettes.

Shortly after we met, maybe after a couple of weeks, we were in his miniature Upper West Side third floor walkup, preparing to go out for dinner, when his phone rang. I could tell immediately he was talking to a girl, and my heart sank.

"Hi." He held the phone to his ear awkwardly. "Yes, me, too. I love the beach."

He looked at me while she was saying something, smiled and said into the receiver, "No. But thanks for asking. I really appreciate it. Yes. I'm seeing someone."

I was flabbergasted.

"Sorry about that," he explained after replacing the receiver. "It was a girl down the street whom I dated a couple of times before I met you. She wanted to go to Jones Beach."

"Really?" I was beside myself with joy that he didn't want to see someone else, but, at the same time overcome with jealousy that another girl could ask him to go to the beach. I wanted to be that normal-skinned girl, living down the street, who could don a bathing suit, a bikini no doubt, and traipse merrily on the fucking beach, sand between her pretty toes, un-self-conscious; on the contrary proud of her physique like a young gazelle speeding away on the shores of Africa. That girl down the street whom I didn't know, but knew enough to know she had no unsightly growths, no anomalies, no creepy, itchy ingrown pubic hair, no turn offs, no angry rashes, no ingrown hairs, no razor bumps in all the wrong places, no bullshit like me.

Moreover, that girl probably didn't have parents like mine. Mine, the objects of anti-Semitism and hatred, the products of the Holocaust and all its subsequent pain and loss, ironically didn't bat an eyelash at their own religious and racist attitudes. If they themselves would not have enslaved anyone, they still, in a million years, could not imagine that someone black or brown or yellow had the same humanity that they had. When it came to "goyim," en masse, they felt religious superiority, but they also felt envy, resentment, and begrudging respect. They had non-Jewish friends, back in Poland and in Newark whom they highly regarded and whose company they enjoyed. But, their attitude towards Puerto Ricans, Blacks, and other colorful minorities was undecidedly prejudiced, and that despite the fact that neither the Puerto Ricans nor the Blacks ever conducted pogroms against the Jews, nor built extermination gas chambers; those indignities were invented by sophisticated, white Europeans. History, however, had nothing to do with what they wanted from me. Already heartbroken by my brother's marriage to a *shiksa* (for that was who Shlomo, who legally changed his name to Shawn, had married: a high school sweetheart named Shannon who bore him two freckled, red-haired girls, Allison and Morgan, who looked just like their Irish mom), my parents, more than ever, longed for Jewish grandchildren; a wish that only I could fulfill, even though hope that I would do that was fading with each passage of another birthday. I had no doubt that Tony would never be the answer to my parents' prayers; they would never regard him as a godsend. But, at the same time, their influence on my emotions began to wane. I was on my own and could do whatever I wanted. Their last white, Jewish hope was Paul, who did not become my husband, and to whom they henceforth referred to as "a piece of *drek*."

I did introduce this brown-skinned man to my parents. On the bus to their suburban home, for Passover Seder, I found myself stealing glances at Tony, as if he were a stranger I had just met. I was trying to imagine my parents' reaction, and nervously I noted that Tony was definitely not a white man. Perhaps his ancestors were Moors who settled in Spain and then ended up in South America. Perhaps they were Hindu, but, whatever they were, they were not Caucasians. Although Tony saw himself as American as apple pie, my father and mother who never learned more than rudimentary English, might see him as a foreigner, I feared. But after more than a decade in America, it was also possible that their own foreignness would lessen, and that their old-world views would shrink and give way to a more modern outlook, I hoped.

The first words out of my father's mouth were: "You are older than he is." My parents could say anything they wanted because they spoke Jewish.

I answered in Yiddish, "And what difference does that make?"

"It's an *important* difference," my father asserted. "The man is supposed to be older and the woman younger. The world works in a certain way, and don't think that you can go ahead and change it."

"Well, I'm only four years older, and he doesn't care."

"He doesn't care now, but wait. He'll never marry you, and you don't have time to waste."

My mother then chipped in, "You know, Bracha, he is not an ugly man, but he is too young. What does he need with an old-maid Jewess?"

Tony just stood there comfortably, waiting patiently for someone to address him. He could tell at a glance that he was not among learned Jews, the living room alone gave them away, cluttered with bric-a-brac in haphazard arrangements: doilies under crystal vases containing plastic roses, my mother's dolls seated like fossilized babies on the brown, velvet couch, photographs of Moshe Dayan on the fridge among pictures of Shlomo and me, postcards from Israel, and Jewish-themed prints displayed on the dining room table, and among all that junk, not one book in sight.

"Please let's all speak English," I interrupted, "I want Tony to be included."

From time to time my mother would ask me the meaning of a word that she had repeatedly heard on television or on the street, but it never occurred to her to learn how to use a dictionary. My father showed no interest whatsoever. He knew what he knew, and that was enough. If he couldn't make himself understood, he would become furious—not at himself, but at the "idiot" who couldn't understand a sentence that combined words and elements from Yiddish, Hebrew, Polish, Russian, and English in a bizarre combination that came out sounding more like utter gibberish.

Being away with Tony that weekend, and every other time for as long as we were to be together, presented serious hair-management problems. To shave in the bathtub in my parents' bathroom was necessary, but even the thought was mentally exhausting; it would be so good to be away from my body, even for a little while. In their house, everyone would notice that I was showering and wasting water for longer than necessary, plus my mother could barge in to the bathroom at any moment without knocking or prior notice. But after not shaving for two days, my body felt as if it was sheathed in sandpaper, particularly my thighs. I was ready for all kinds of excuses about why he couldn't come near me, but when he lovingly stroked my back and urged me to come to bed, I not only wanted him, but couldn't think of what to say. I was not fit to be bedded and loved. After all, this was the same old crap; I needed to shave, tweeze, bleach, the whole nasty routine that I could never accept but had to execute. I required at least two hours pruning and primping my uniquely odd skin in order to feel half way up to standard. This state of affairs was definitely enough to ruin my libido, to extinguish the fireworks and to render me an observer, not a participant, in the act of making love, having sex. I was terrified that Tony would notice my stubbly thighs, would be grossed out by my masculinity, and would find some excuse to leave. Yet I had to pretend to be an ordinary woman. My movements were calculated to avoid his feeling my skin, my goal was for the act to be over without unthinkable embarrassment. As always, I had to take charge of the lighting: a candle or red lamp had to be placed just so, to show off only shapes and shadows. A sheet and a robe had to be within arm's reach for sudden emergencies. My own pleasure had nothing to do with it. It came, in a sense, when the whole thing was over and I felt that I pleased him and got away without losing face; such was my sex life, more or less.

"What are you going for? Are you trying to look like an egg?" teased Ann, my electrologist at that time. She not only worked on my face, but on my abdomen as well. In order to encourage her to do a thorough job, I promised that, after my face and abdomen were completed, I would have her attack my arms, which I was very tired of bleaching. It was a way of guaranteeing her that I would be her perpetual client or at least a client for the foreseeable future. I trusted Ann as much as the other electrologists, but obviously it was not in their best interest to actually destroy hair follicles, even if they could. I had long ago abandoned the thought that electrolysis was the permanent solution they promised; it was a maintenance program as far as I could see, but the best game in town. My apprehension with every electrologist, starting with Merle, was that she would worsen the situation by tweezing hairs without applying an electrical current, intentionally or not, and thus strengthen hairs and increase growth. My fear was not unfounded as I could feel hairs on my upper lip, neck, chin, etc., being yanked out manually by tweezers. I knew the difference between a current actually hitting the follicle and the motion of the hair coming out easily versus the tweezers pulling on a resistant hair. But I never said a word to any of them. I never complained or asked questions. Sometimes the procedure was so painful, particularly on the center of the upper lip that I didn't give a damn what they did; I just wanted to get out of there. I never really worried about the money; fifteen-minute sessions usually cost about $30.00 plus tip, but there was no choice—it was akin to paying whatever they charged for a loaf of bread. If I had to skimp on eating out or buying clothes, then that's what had to be done. Ann, a middle-aged Jewish widow, struck me as fairy competent but, every now and then, she herself sported a mustache. If she couldn't totally eliminate her own hair, then it couldn't be done, I concluded. On the other hand, the fact that she too struggled with hirsutism, maybe even more than I, considering she made a career of it, allowed me to feel a kinship with her. I'd be suspicious of an electrologist who had entered into my world of the hirsute only to profit from it and at the end of the day leave and re-join the world of femininity, maybe even joke about us, the poor bewhiskered creatures. Most electrologists I knew had some type of certificate on their wall, boasting of their training and affiliation with their society. I often wondered how they got into that business and knew I could never be one because that would be equivalent to publicizing my own burden.

"You do *what* for a living?" I imagined people's surprised looks, and then I would notice their gaze freeze on my upper lip with shock and pity.

When Ann worked on the center of the upper lip, involuntary tears would run down my face, the pain being exquisite, as if I were being subjected to some type of medieval surgery without the benefit of anesthesia. I would think about those poor souls depicted in medical encyclopedias that had limbs chopped off. I could visualize the doctors in their white coats standing around observing the procedure, attempting to focus only on skill and technique while the patient shackled and restrained screamed on top of his lungs as his leg was being lopped off, right there in the operating theater or in the middle of the town square. At those moments, I would stop worrying about the mustache, and beg for relief. "Well, if we don't continue working on the center," she'd argue reasonably, "you are going to end up with a Hitler mustache." And of course she was right.

Tony, like any normal male, expected a feminine girl friend, not a freak, and to that end I had to jump through hoops, scale high walls, climb rocky mountains, walk on water, create miracles. In other words, I had to breathe and think hair elimination in order to make magic, turn a beast into a girl. Well, that was the story of my life. I didn't need an audience to hear in my head the refrain "hairy, ugly bitch." But once everything was done and I climbed out of the shower I felt that to some extent I had received temporary admission to the female world where I rightfully belonged, except for a quirk of nature.

14

FUN IN THE SUN

I CAUGHT THE JOGGING bug and started running, a sport even I could do, except that it required wearing shorts. It was impossible to wake up mornings hung over, work all day, come home, shave legs, and go running; I had to learn to run in long pants even in the heat of summer. It occurred to me that, if I ran fast enough, no one would notice my hairiness, but, still, I knew the ugly, black stubble was there, and I didn't dare take any chances.

In passing, a friend of mine who emigrated from the Soviet Union told me that back home where she was from most women had very hairy legs. She blamed that on the sun.

"It makes everything grow, including hair."

"But Africans live in the sun, and they are generally not hairy," I pointed out.

"Well, maybe the melanin in their skin affects the hair growth," she further explained, "but in the Caucasus we have hair all over. When you put on a pair of stockings, the plastered hair underneath looks gross."

I was transfixed; no one I knew had ever talked about hairiness so openly, but I also observed that her own skin was translucent and clear. But she continued: "The most embarrassing thing that ever happened to me was when a man once said, 'I don't know why you women shave your legs. Hairy legs are so sexy.' But I definitely disagreed with him."

I laughed when she told me this story; everyone always laughs when talking about hairy women. I also thought that virgin legs, that is, unshaved legs, were sexy providing the hair was soft, light, and downy. Oh, how I longed to have smooth skin, virgin skin untouched by the razor nor burned by formulas.

Often, when someone invited me for an outdoor event that required revealing clothing, I would readily accept the invitation, but secretly pray for rain. Like a vampire I came out only at night; daylight was my nemesis, my ruin. When Tony and I began talking of taking a vacation, I had an ongoing invitation from Uncle Richard in England; I never expected the plan to materialize. Not that I would have to show my body in London in October, but I would not have the privacy to perform my beauty ablutions, I feared. But, I couldn't get out of that one; moreover, I wanted to travel, particularly with my boyfriend. When we got off the plane in Heathrow Airport, tired and jet lagged, my first thought was: I hope I can find space to bleach and shave on this ten-day vacation. Even on the plane, and even as I clutched Tony's arm for fear of crashing, my mind was on my skin at every moment.

Uncle Richard arranged for a tour guide to chauffeur us around to all the tourist highlights of London: Westminster Abbey, Big Ben, Carnaby Street, and The Thames. We fed the pigeons at Trafalgar Square, admired the grandeur of the palaces, saw *Jesus Christ Superstar* on stage, even stood at a pub eating fried fish and drinking warm ale. London was atypically sunny and beautiful, not even hinting at rain or fog. Uncle Richard resembled my father, but unlike my father, had poise and elegance. Proudly, as soon as we had arrived at his home and after we met his wife, he showed us his garden in the back of the house. "Imagine," he chuckled, "Moshe Yankel's son tends his own English Garden." Moshe Yankel, the grandfather I never met; he had perished in the Crakow ghetto, was a religious man who never posed for photographs as befitting a pious Jew. I had heard that he was a drinker with a dark, violent streak, a fact that I never doubted. I also learned that he had encouraged his sons to flee Crakow just in the nick of time, hours before the Germans erected their infamous ghetto in the heart of the city. Uncle Richard, his oldest son, was the one who had generously funded our move out of Israel. But my parents, true to form, were critical and hostile after Richard's recent second marriage to a Polish-Catholic woman, Basha, twenty years his junior, a former opera singer from Lodz, who in London made her living as a cook. My uncle was amused by my parents' disapproval. "I never thought my little brother was so narrow-minded," he laughed.

After a couple of days, Tony rented a car, and we took off by ourselves out of the city. I always had trouble sleeping, and, coupled with jet lag, I hardly slept at all. It was a blessing in disguise: Before we left my uncle's house, while everyone was still asleep, and the house was filled with shadows, I snuck into the bathroom to attend to my unique grooming needs. The cacophony of snores in the house was music to my ears. As if committing an illegal or unnatural act, I worked quickly with the alacrity of a professional, keeping vigil over the bathroom door, attuned to every sound, every breath outside. When I was almost done, I sprayed the bathroom in perfume to mask the malodorous fumes of bleaching cream, and basked in the glory of a job well done.

In an indulgent and expansive mood, when we arrived at Stratford-on-Avon, we rented a room in a hotel that looked as grand and formidable as a real palace. The bathroom alone, with its Jacuzzi, was larger than any hotel room I had ever stayed at in my entire life. As soon as he took his coat off, Tony poured himself a vodka from our mini-bar, offered me a glass of wine, made dinner reservations in the hotel's highly recommended restaurant, and stretched himself on the bed, television tuned to a British sit com. As casually as possible, I walked into the bathroom, all my necessary tools with me, and in my best nonchalant tone announced, "Oh, I am going to relax and take a long, hot bath.

As soon as I finished shaving one leg, Tony barged in.

"Sorry I disturbed your beauty bath, baby, but room service called us down to dinner. They are actually waiting for us. They reminded me that our reservations were for 7 p.m."

"Jesus, every since we got here everyone has been rushing us." It was true. Even the bed-and-breakfast proprietors awaited our arrival at specific times.

Did he see the razor? I obsessed as I jumped out of the tub, dried hastily, and put on a pair of black stockings, black heels, and a black clingy dress I had bought at a cheap dress shop in Tony's neighborhood named "Sexy Girl." All the while Tony was enjoying his drinks and laughing along with the sound track on the television screen, as if he had no care in the word. Alcohol was beginning to do its magic on me as well, and although I didn't get a chance to complete the all too vital grooming routine, my spirits were rising; the thrill of being away in England and in love, surrounded by luxury and anticipation was as acute and as titillating as the trill of church bells, the scent of almond trees in bloom, the warnings of fog horns at dusk. Tony looked great in a dark suit and red tie, revealing the inner businessman that he actually was but also showing off his strong body and confident stride. Arm-in-arm, we ambled down to the cavernous dining room, only to discover that the elegant restaurant and solicitous waiters were completely at our disposal. Only one other couple, about a mile away, was in sight. We laughed about our English hosts' hustling us out of our room in order to be prompt for dinner, but, I didn't find it funny that I had gotten to shave only one leg. It was an annoyance hanging over my head, like a clothesline of wet laundry on a gray day.

After dinner, we joined an elegant couple at their table in the hotel bar. At midnight, many Hennessey's, cigarettes, stories, and chocolates later, it was time to leave. We bid goodbyes to our new friends, both married but not to each other, all of us knowing that we would never see each other again, but exchanging addresses nonetheless, for decorum's sake. Barely able to make it up the elevator to our room, Tony was forced to almost drag and half-carry me up until we entered and I fell fully clothed on the bed. The TV was still on, and I was listening to words and sounds but could not follow a single sentence. In a state of hypnogogic dream-sleep I thought I was on a derailing train and braced myself for impact when Tony, another drink in his hand, shook me back to the present moment.

"Oh, no. I've been looking forward to this. I wanted to fuck in this medieval room. I wanted to fully enjoy what we have here. I wanted to fuck in the whirlpool bath, on the bed, on the floor. We are going to get our money's worth. Don't you dare pass out on me, baby." Somehow I managed to go along; feeling like a one-legged woman jumping jacks.

Tony and I went away to a few more places during the years we were together: Israel, France, The Bahamas, Puerto Rico, and Italy. And one thread that strung these discrete events together, the common denominator, was my obsessive-compulsive maneuverings to destroy and hide my villous state. Going away was almost not worth the effort.

Before a trip to Puerto Rico, I had timed my hair removal efforts to the last detail, but to my frustration the flight was postponed a few days due to inclement weather. To say that I was wild with impatience would be an understatement.

"Don't worry, honey," Tony tried to reassure me, "we are both off for a couple of weeks and even if we leave tomorrow or the next day, we would still be able to stay the whole six nights."

But for me the clock started ticking from the moment that the beautician yanked off the last strip of cloth off my waxed arms; from the moment the electrologist applied witch hazel to my sore face. I worried that the hair would return before we even got off the ground. I would be back to my normal ape-like hairy self, gripped with my constant fixation on my body hair, unable to enjoy the beach or the rainforest or evenings on the veranda sipping piña coladas. While waiting for news on the next flight, I went for a walk in the snow. I went to the store. I hid in my room with my tweezers, listening to the foreboding weather forecasts and praying for a god to intervene. In a few days I would become undone, and all the previous exertion would be for nothing. I kept examining my arms every half hour; sure that I could feel hair follicles recovering from the recent assault and doubling their effort to produce a stronger, hardier growth. Three tense, long, anxious days later, at last, the storm passed and we were cleared to take off.

Magically, my arms and legs remained smooth the whole week we were away. I was able to go into the water without worrying about razor burns or unsightly bumps. I didn't have to wear long sleeves. I didn't have to get up before Tony, lock the bathroom door and pray that he did not have to pee while my face and body were covered in white layers of cream reeking of ammonia and chlorine. I was a normal woman. At least, for a few days, like other women, I could lie on the beach, read a novel, have a drink, hug my boyfriend, pose for pictures, squint against the glare of the tropical sun, shake my ass at the handsome young guys, walk proudly like any young woman with long dark hair, pretty face, and sensual body. I needed that kind of vacation.

Vacations, weekend trips, long weekends with friends all challenged my hair removal capabilities but at least held promise and reward as well. But events away from home and my beauty routine were a hassle just the same. A point in fact was a weeklong hospitalization for a bunionectomy. The surgery was considered elective, but it was less a matter of vanity than practicality. No matter what shoes I wore, I was always in pain, always in some kind of foot discomfort. The surgery required a few days' stay in the hospital, which would have been okay if no one had come to visit. But Tony, considerate as he was, treated my minor orthopedic procedure as if it were open heart surgery. "I'll see you every day," he solemnly promised, and he did.

Naturally, I had had the foresight to pack the bleach, tweezers, and razors, but to execute my routine I had to be quite ingenious, being that I was in a two-bedded room, literally unable to ambulate to the bathroom, and in constant apprehension behind the hospital curtain lest someone walk in and catch in me in the act—but I had to attend to my routine, there was no negotiation. It was no easy task to bleach and shave while lying down in bed, drugged with shots of morphine, attuned to footsteps on the other side of the flimsy curtain. But it had to be done. Each evening, Tony tracked over to Mount Sinai Hospital, bringing me Cuban sandwiches, *café con leche*, bananas, strawberries, and chocolates, plus compilations of *Crossword Puzzle* magazines and copies of the *Times*.

I was in bed for a week before they approved my discharge and sent me home on crutches. Tony brought me to his apartment and waited on me hand and foot. While he was at work, I schemed and planned my beauty regimen. He would leave early each morning, out to duke it out with the sharks in the volatile real estate market, while I slept till at least noon, waking in time for his solicitous late-morning calls. It was impossible not to be crazy about that man. He was good to me in a way no one in my life had ever been, and truthfully I had no idea how I'd lucked out like that. He never expressed anything derogatory about my physical appearance and was always quick and generous with his compliments. Somehow, he found me bright and exciting, sexy and smart. When the lights were low, I was always a willing and obedient lover, wanting nothing but to please. . . and to keep him in the dark.

But in my head, in my inner life, there was a vacuum where a dialogue should have been. How much time can a person spend in self-talk without thinking of mega-issues, of coming to realizations about life's goals and the purpose of one's being. My inner life was preoccupied with utter and complete trivia, nonsense about shaving and tweezing, and the superficial aspects of my skin. What had happened to me? As a young girl, I'd had the lofty and ambitious hopes and dreams that all children have: I would be an actress and set the world on fire, I would write great novels and make a name for myself. Or I would be a ballerina dancing on her toes in pink tutus. Playing on the porch underneath the clotheslines, I would imagine myself a grown and sophisticated woman as I pranced around under my mother's drying lingerie, my father's shorts, and my own T-shirts as, like flags, they danced in the breeze. Who had that me been before the hair grew in, before a non-life-threatening cosmetic mishap rendered me a woman in a man's skin. I could wallow in self-pity forever and at the same time keep on plucking away at my problem, like a cat scratching its back with its paw.

I HAD BEEN BACK to Israel only once since we emigrated and was dying to see the country again; moreover, I wanted to show off the country that I still felt patriotic about while disabusing Tony of his image of Israel as the Holy Land, a place of piety and prayer. He loved having fun, had long been known to be the last to leave a party, loved crowds, music, festivities, vodka, beer, wine, pizza, and fried foods. The minute we entered the promenade in Tel Aviv, breathed in the salt air, fried falafel, and cigarette smoke, he sighed in contentment: "Ah, I feel I died and went to heaven. I can spend the rest of my life here."

That was exactly what I had hoped for. In the residential northern Tel Aviv streets, along well-tended gardens of cactus flowers, gladioli, shrubs, and the ever-present scent of sycamore, sea air, and unrelenting humidity, we held hands and fantasized about retirement in one of the Bauhaus-style white houses, sipping white wine from the Galilean wineries, dining on fried St. Peter's fish, freshly baked, hearty Israeli sour dough rolls, biting into tomatoes bursting with flavor, and filling up on apricots, grapes, guavas, figs, and dates, intoxicating in their pure essence—indeed the land of milk and honey.

It was a dream. It was only a dream to be buried under the sand dunes sooner or later, but golden for the time being.

By then I had found a new device, a depilatory gadget that looked like an electric razor but that, instead of shaving, tweezed off even short coarse hairs by the dozen, rendering large areas of skin fairly hairless and smooth—a miraculous invention deserving, in my view, of a Nobel Prize. It was my wonder drug, my penicillin. It was my dream come true: that I could spend an hour or so with this object and achieve results that, in the past, had required hours of manually tweezing and straining was a godsend. To be in Israel with Tony was heaven on Earth, and to have an instrument to make me feel whole was beyond my wildest expectations.

Practically as soon as we settled into the Marriott, right on the beach, I rushed to the room service desk to obtain a converter for my device. It was a matter of life and death, as the converter I had spent fifty dollars on back in the States had nearly caused an electrical fire in the room. Fortunately, they had one. For a few wonderful days, I spent the mornings on the beach with Tony, soaking up the sunshine and the view, and writing in my journal; I'd leave before him, quickly return to our room, take care of the hair business, and, once depilatorized and bleached, enjoy the rest of the day in relative comfort. One time the maid knocked at the door while I was shaving; the damn thing made a lot of noise, and, panicked as if I were the intruder, I opened the door, hoping to get rid of her at once.

"Excuse me," she apologized in broken English, "but I noticed yesterday you have this electric shaver, and I wonder if it really works."

I looked at her and immediately empathized. "Yes, it's great," I answered in Hebrew. "It works for me." I was definitely feeling at home.

On a nostalgic jaunt to Abu Kabir, I discovered that nothing was the same as I remembered. That one large unpaved street, surrounded by fields and abandoned houses, smelling of sewage and eucalyptus trees, was smaller, quieter, the Arab concrete ramshackle hovels in which we conducted our lives mostly empty and more run down, if that was possible. Kiryat Shalom looked more like a ghetto this time around. Growing up, I had always hoped my parents would have enough money to move us there, as many of our European Jewish neighbors had done. The new development of identical white four-family houses with flower gardens in front and back, paved streets, streetlamps, and a few grocery and candy stores had, in my youth, a serene, pleasant, safe appeal. Practically all the kids in elementary school lived in Kiryat Shalom, except maybe a handful of ne'er do wells who were our neighbors. My parents were even more broke than the poorest Jews. Once, when I was invited to a classmate's birthday party, my mother rummaged at the last moment through our large cedar closet and found a scented soap that I could present as a gift. I don't remember whose birthday it was, but I do recall the gales of hearty laughter that shook the room when my odd gift was unwrapped. I was mortified, unable to say a word, and shortly after walked home alone.

And there I was, a few years later, certainly not rich but still able to stay at a four-star hotel, eat and drink decent white wine in a string of restaurants on the Promenade in Tel Aviv, the same Promenade along the beach where the sunsets were so dazzling that people stopped in their tracks to watch the fat, red sun sink and disappear gradually behind the distant horizon, and where, to my child's mind, only very special, wealthy people could congregate and mingle in the open-air restaurants while their children ate banana splits, and they danced to the samba and tango late into the night. My parents and I could only afford to gawk and admire from the other side of the wrought-iron gate, from where we could hear the band quite clearly but knew they were not playing for us.

MY GRANDMOTHER WALKED WITH a limp. She had explained to me that she was had been born a twin with one leg shorter than the other. The twin had died at birth, and my grandmother had accepted her lot in life. Born and raised in Lodz, she would have been an anachronism in the abandoned Arab fields outside Tel Aviv, except that I'd never known her before, and to me my *bubbe* was Abu-Kabir. Standing there, literally among the ruins, I could see her in my mind's eye, shabbily dressed in a soiled housedress and slippers, running down the street, with one leg shorter than another in that particular jump-skip-skip-jump manner that was uniquely hers. She didn't give a damn about her appearance, but to my mortification, kids chased her. Later, when I thought of those boys, a few words from Lawrence Ferlinghetti's poem came to mind:

Johnny Nolan has a patch on his ass. Kids chased him.

And I, pulled along by her strong arm, had no choice but to ignore the jabs being hurled in our direction and march on. My grandmother, not exactly a shrinking violet, had at her disposal about a hundred juicy Yiddish curses, which she did not hesitate to unleash at anyone regardless of gender or age.

In first grade, to my mortification, I saw her in the school lobby, standing in a line with other parents, probably to pay a bill, as I was walking out of class alone. She smiled and waved, motioning for me to join her, speaking to me in Yiddish, calling me "Bruchalo." I walked on as if deaf and blind, not quickening or slowing my step. I walked out of the school without saying a word, hoping none of the kids had heard or noticed that the crippled, Yiddish-speaking old woman was addressing me. By the time I reached home, I had almost forgotten the incident, until later, when it was almost time for supper, and both my grandmother and mother were sitting on the kitchen floor peeling potatoes, discarding the mountains of skins on old newspapers and placing the clean potatoes into one large pot, while I was nearby, day-dreaming, listening to the two women gossip. "Have you seen Fat Sonia lately? It looks like she gained another ten kilos since she started exercising."

"Yes, I saw her this morning," replied my grandmother. "She was on the porch eating a loaf of bread stuffed with salami." Both women laughed. "I was on the way to school when I saw her. She said that the exercises boost her appetite. By the way, can you believe that the girl pretended not to know me in school?"

I froze. And while my mother looked at me in disbelief, my grand-mother added, her sharp blue eyes focusing on mine, "So, you're ashamed of your *bubbe*, little girl?"

I didn't answer; I had never loved her more than at that moment. I was mortified, ashamed, and remorseful, and for many years I was haunted by that memory. It felt like the original sin, or something close to it, as if I had broken a universal commandment or a biblical taboo held dear by all societies: "Do not negate your grandmother's presence," or "Sorrow shall befell those ashamed of their elders."

Yiddish was not spoken by Israelis back in the 1950s, not only be-cause it was the language of the Diaspora and of the ghetto, but because everyone was encouraged to learn Hebrew, the new official language of the new country. I could hear snippets of conversations in Arabic or some European language from time to time, but rarely Yiddish outside of my family. When I did hear it spoken on the Yiddish radio station my parents listened to, I could not recognize it as the language I knew, nor understand a single whole sentence. In fact, it sounded so elegant, so Germanic, that I was convinced my family spoke a crude and boorish dialect that was unique to them. Other adults, all those people who had escaped violence and hatred from all over the world, managed to speak, read, and write Hebrew; only my parents, as far as I knew, didn't bother to study, attend evening classes, or improve their education. They never ceased to embarrass me with their broken Hebrew and guttural Yiddish, while my schoolmates' parents expressed themselves in a quiet, articulate manner. If I told my mother to call me Bracha, not the Yiddish, "Bruchale," in public, she looked on the verge of tears, as if I were a traitor. Never mind that other girls were addressed by their families in their proper Hebrew names. I was Bruchale in front of my peers and alone suffered the derision that accompanied that moniker.

Worse than being yelled at was being belittled and bullied. I couldn't handle taunts without breaking into tears, couldn't fight back physically or think of a witty, ass-kicking response. I couldn't ignore them either. I was, to my disgrace, like my mother: meek and bashful, scared of my own shadow. I was a little girl whose most prominent emotion was shame. I was ashamed of living in Abu-Kabir, a place with no name, a place with an open sewage system, overflowing with human excrement and urine infusing the hot, dusty air, the medicinal scent of eucalyptus, the gasoline vapors from the only gas station, with the malodorous stench that was the smell I thought of as home. While our European-Jewish neighbors managed to improve their lot and move out, we remained in our ugly, dilapidated Arab-built dwelling, our new neighbors being dark-skinned Persian Jews who blasted Arabic music over their radios, laughed too much, and fried pungent eggplant that made my mouth water. And, of course, they all spoke Hebrew.

I was ashamed of my parents' language, of my grandmother's illiteracy—in public situations she insisted on signing her name with three "x"s—of my clothes, of my appearance in general. My little toe looked funny to me; my brittle fingernails grew upward and broke; my hair was long and braided while everyone else's was either short or worn in a ponytail, which we called "Koo Koo." Most of all, I was ashamed of what I could not do: I couldn't do a headstand, like other girls. I couldn't follow simple dance steps, I couldn't sing to save my life, I couldn't speak in class without blushing, I couldn't joke and kid with other students or be part of the crowd. In classes, I barely got by. In second grade, I either forgot or didn't do homework, only to be in trouble the following day. When I was told that I would have to stay for an hour after school, working on the homework that I had failed to do, fear of my parents' wrath reduced me to tears, and I kept my head on my desk for hours and whimpered, tears and snot and saliva ruining the wood finish, until the teacher, fed up, changed her mind and allowed me to go home. My teachers publicly criticized me. In third grade, in an attempt to quell disagreement, name calling, and arguments, she urged the students to find a way to become friends and get along with each other. However, to prove to the class that she was not a dunce but an understanding and fair teacher, she went on, "We don't have to go to extremes. I don't expect that Eliza (the most popular girl in class) should have to invite Bracha to her parties, but, overall we should respect one another." That was the same teacher who, as a consequence of some misdemeanor during a lesson, forced me to stand in the corner, and face the wall with my arms up. My arms, naturally, grew tired and heavy, but worse was hearing the titters and chuckles from classmates I couldn't see. I have always remembered the humiliation but not the reason for the indignity. Certainly, I was not one of the loud kids who jumped over desks, participated in practical jokes, or tormented the teachers. I was a quiet child, inferior to everyone around me. And then, of all things, I grew into a hairy adolescent, a hairy adult, my face to the wall.

We had the same teacher until sixth grade, whereupon she was replaced by a kindly, plain-looking woman who once took me aside when the kids were teasing me and I had no clue why, and whispered, "When you get home, tell you mother to shorten your pretty new skirt." It was a pleated, dark woolen skirt that my mother had been proud to buy me. The teacher's name was Chaya, and she had thick black hair that the students assumed was a wig. The rumors were that she had probably lost her hair in a concentration camp. There was no basis for that rumor, but it gave the class something to laugh about.

BITCH

I N KNUT HANSON'S MASTERPIECE, Growth of the Soil, *the heroine, that heart-wrenching character whose life has been shaped by a harelip, a minor birth defect, comes to learn much later that, had she had a simple surgical repair, her whole life would have taken a different turn; she would have been pretty and would have been able to collect all the benefits that come with good looks.*

I am she. Lying in bed alone, listening to random songs on the music channel, I am waiting for my Klonopin to take effect. The standards bring back memories. I listen to "Fly Me to the Moon," "I Did It My Way," "My Funny Valentine," "A Foggy Day in London Town," and wish there was someone, some special someone, to wrap my arms around. Each old-school song evokes a place, an event, a bar scene full of music and laughter, a time in the past that I wish were the present. Most of all, I wish to be held.

But what difference does it make at this juncture? I'm free of the whole game, lying in bed staring straight at old age and a crumbling ceiling. There is no bright future ahead, no years and years of blinding sun and long summers among the orange groves. It has all been a waste: waste of time, waste of space, waste of priorities. People I have known are gone, some dead, some dying, some still believing in dewy mornings and breezy evenings that will come but not for them. Here it is almost time to end the book, close the chapter, stop drinking that red wine. It does no good anyway. It can dull some things and magnify others. It can conjure up words that should never have been spoken, thoughts that should never have taken place. Nobody knows a good thing until it is gone;

after the eulogies come the tears, come the regrets, come longing for what might have been. Always too late. I'm waiting for the sedative to take effect, and I'm listening to music. Abbey Lincoln speaks to me:

> *The world is falling down*
> *Hold my hand,*
> *It's a lonely sound,*
> *Hold my hand.*
> *We'll follow the breeze*
> *And go like the wind.*
> *and look for a place*
> *where the willows bend*
> *The world is falling down*
> *Hold my hand, hold my hand*
> *Hold my hand, hold my hand*

TWO OR THREE YEARS into the relationship, every move Tony made rubbed me the wrong way.

The proverbial uncapped toothpaste tube, the toilet seat that was left up, the socks on the floor, the way he chewed his food, became, not merely annoyances, but calamities to which I reacted as if the world were coming to an end. "You left the toilet seat up again during the night. I almost fell into the damn thing and broke my ass," I would exaggerate without qualms. He was getting a potbelly that literally rubbed me the wrong way. It created a distance between our bodies. Yet he kept on drinking and eating. His eating habits were repulsive, and he seemed to ignore any common-sense notions about nutrition. The cupboards were stuffed with bags of various salty chips, crackers, instant mashed potatoes, candy, chocolate-covered nuts, sugary cereals, and all manner of junk food. He spoke about his hearty appetite as if it were a gift, and I could notice his mouth salivating at the mere suggestion of dinner. I began to think of him as a sensualist, as a boorish peasant who derived joy and fulfillment through the most primitive human needs.

Sex had been great at first, but soon I tired of long marathons and the entire machination that was part of the ordeal, his ample abdomen revolting. I began to notice that he chewed with his mouth open, producing revolting smacking sounds with his lips. "Close your mouth, man, or I'm going to throw up," I'd say, though that, and comments like it, never seemed to do much good.

"I'm sorry," Tony would say, and continue to chew, and chew, and chew.

My emotions, particularly anger, became unmanageable, as difficult to modulate and control as a quick-spreading pandemic. I was Pandora, unable to contain ills, rage, hostility, all those feelings that, once spent in a nasty, violent diatribe, decreased my self-esteem far more than my hairy legs. But he never lost his optimism, I had to hand him that. And if he did despair, he never let on. Rapidly, I morphed from a sweet, loving girlfriend to a wench, losing my temper if he was ten minutes late, shouting and complaining as if he had done me a great injustice. And yet I didn't think he would be fed up. I didn't think that he would be hurt. I didn't think that he would find life with me not worth living. I didn't think, period. I believed, however, that it was vital that I keep shaving, waxing, bleaching, tweezing; it never dawned on me that I was focusing on the wrong malady; I was worried about shadows while ghosts were lurking deep in the closets.

Once, after a particularly nasty argument, looking in the mirror the following morning I saw my eyes were swollen, my nose red, and my mustache more pronounced. Some nasal hairs were protruding, which I tweezed automatically, then the hairs over my eyebrows and, in a growing frenzy, my cheeks, my nipples, the hair above and below the surface area of my underarms, the hair way over the pubic area, my toes and feet, and finally my fingers and hands. Tweezing calmed me. I bleached what I could, used Neet for my behind, and finally jumped

into the shower and shaved the rest. Feeling pleased with my accom-
plishments, I promised myself to be a better person next time, and
next time, and so on until all time was lost, and it became too late.

Despite all my hang-ups, I still longed for the ideal, that is, marriage. I had hoped that after we were together a year he would present
me with a diamond ring, but instead I received a steam iron. When
he went on a business trip to Hawaii, he brought me back coral jewelry
set in a yellow metal which was not gold. For my birthday one year, he
brought me a bouquet of long-stemmed roses, which I considered a
last-minute, piss-poor present. I even told him so. And I was furious
the rest of the night.

It continued. And it seemed that the fights, the disappointments,
the displaced anger, the blackouts, the ups, the downs, the love, the
loathing, the excuses, the sleepless nights, the self-recriminations, the
complaints, the promises would continue forever—until they stopped.

ONE NIGHT, I WROTE a haiku:

Death grins toothlessly,
His lungs drowning in water,
Calling on the phone.

It was after midnight, and I was struggling in vain to fall asleep, a
sleep I hardly deserved. My bedside telephone was ringing incessantly,
but I didn't make the slightest effort to pick it up. I knew who it was
and what he wanted, and it couldn't be good. If only I could ignore
the cravings that were ascending like waves in the midst of a winter
storm, I would get through the night. If I could endure, wait for the
wave to reach its plateau, I'd be home free. The jitteriness and growing
sense of doom were beyond physical pain; I felt like jumping out the
window, while my heart, imprisoned in its ribcage, was beating irreg-

ularly and forcefully, as if to accuse. But the cravings for relief were in-humanly long, as I hugged myself under the covers, trying to shrink into a non-sensing, non-thinking entity.

Then I'd think of my connection and his product, and finally the phone. At once, even before the fine powder had a chance to bind unto the depleted pleasure cells in my brain, before the hit, before the knock on the door even, my mood was hope, and despair was forced into a back seat behind a curtain that sooner or later rose and revealed the cluttered stage behind. Such was my experience with cocaine, a drug considered innocuous when I had stumbled upon it, a coincidence that seemed predetermined by everything in my past and my parents' past, and their parents, all the way back. It was my perfect storm, and I was lucky to survive it, especially lucky because I was split into two per-sonas: one who knew better, and another who didn't give a damn.

Drugs had been on my periphery almost from the beginning of my life in America. Starting with my uncle's dire warnings, and my par-ents' premature alarm and threats, the notion that a substance, a pill or a drink, for example, could alter a person's perceptions, thoughts, and behavior intrigued me to no end. I couldn't imagine losing control to an object, couldn't understand losing grip on reality. I would hold on to myself, I childishly thought, no matter what.

I saw my father drunk only once. We had visited my parents' friends earlier in the evening, and we were trudging up the unpaved, muddy street to our house. It was already after dark, and no one was on the street. Shlomo and I were holding onto our mother's hands. A few paces ahead of us, my father was ranting and raving; he looked as if a Jewish incubus had suddenly taken possession of him and at any moment he might howl like a hyena or bark like a rabid dog.

As we were passing the white house where my friend Leah lived, he stopped in midstride, banged on the window, and bellowed: "Come out of there, you damn whore. Come on, Hanka. Hanka. Bitch, I'm calling you to come out. Whore. Come out if you dare."

Hanka, my friend Leah's mother, of course didn't come out, nor did any of the neighbors. My mother, covering her face with her palms as she would during Shabbat prayer, tried to grab my father's arm, to lead him home, all the while cajoling, "Jozef, Jozef, please, I beg of you, for shame, stop."

Minutes later, we were in our living room—that is, my father was lying on the couch and my mother was standing by the entrance, shielding us.

"Come over here," he gestured to her, his index finger beckoning. It looked comical.

"No. I'm afraid," she answered truthfully.

"Afraid?" he roared. "I should be afraid, you whore. You are all a bunch of whores."

I used to think of Hanka as pretty. She was a blue-eyed blonde, generous with her smiles and with hard candy. Her husband, Marion, was a handsome man who never spoke to us kids and carried himself in a dignified manner, like a senator or lawyer. Hanka had been one of my father's lovers, and, naturally, my mother's nemesis and object of curses. And those curses were serious incantations purported to in-flict cancer, shingles, madness, leprosy, smallpox, poverty, boils, death. Those were curses for the vengeful, angry Genesis God to inflict upon Hanka—a great and loving God who punished sinners and took care of his chosen, righteous people.

My mother's curses didn't materialize; instead, Hanka bade so long to Abu-Kabir and sailed off to greener pastures in America. She took her children—Michael, the oldest, a terror at ten, and Leah, my friend with the blonde pigtails. For some reason, Marion stayed behind, and all of the neighborhood children were certain that he was running a house of ill repute from his ramshackle stone living quarters, which as far as anyone knew might have been built during the Ottoman Empire.

Miriam was two years older than I, and in first grade my mother had paid her to walk me to school and back. It was an Orthodox, all-girls school, quite a distance from our house but, unlike the local public school, willing to enroll me in first grade at three months short of my sixth birthday. To get to school, I had to walk through a field where cows grazed and past a house where a gaggle of geese honked and chased after me. I was afraid of all animals, and particularly afraid of the geese. Miriam was untamed and afraid of nothing. She looked tough: Her long red hair was rarely combed, her freckled face smeared with food and grime, and her scrawny arms and legs always scratched and bruised. She knew every Arabic curse phrase and didn't mind showing off even in front of adults. Her father owned a horse and wagon and was known as the town drunk, and her mother was vague and invisible.

One day Miriam suggested we peek through the gate of Marion's house. We crept past the iron entrance and up the few stone steps that lead to the enclosed cemented open area in front of the place. Immediately, and with delight, we saw ladies' underwear hanging out to dry, but then, to our discomfiture, a beautiful woman in a sheer pink negligee and an amused look emerged from the kitchen, a lit cigarette between her painted lips.

"Girls, do you need anything?" she asked in a mellifluous voice, blowing a cloud of gray smoke.

"Who is it, Nava?" called Marion from inside.

Miriam was quick on her feet. "We came to play with Leah."

"Oh, little girls. Leah's friends."

"Tell them Leah is in America and not coming back."

The following year my parents took me out of the Orthodox school and enrolled me in Givat Hashalom, "Peace Hill," a site engraved in my mind like a bad case of the flu that lingers. But among the pious in first grade, I did learn an important lesson: I was considered middling to less than fair in the hierarchy of popularity and brains among my five- and six-year-old classmates. Our teacher, a youngish, plain Orthodox woman in a wavy blonde wig and long-sleeved blouse, devised a four-tier seating system—the bright kids in a row on the right, the mediocre ones in the second row, the less then mediocre in the third row, where I was placed, and the really stupid, ugly, and obnoxious ones in a row on the left. I wanted to be where I did not belong, all the way on the right among the confident, smart, outgoing girls, but the teacher, in her infinite wisdom, had designed her own plan: "You, stupid, to the left; you, to the right."

And that's how I came to be the new kid in school in second grade where the others pulled my braids, chased me in the yard, even tore my clothes. My teacher took pity on me and allowed me to hang onto her skirts during recess, the worst time of the school day—until, inexplicably, the assaults ended and were replaced by benign neglect. At times I was practically invisible, fading into the shadows.

Years later, I ran into Miriam in a Jaffa street market. She was hanging out with a fried-meat vendor, a brown-skinned, tall young guy, either Arab or a Sephardic Jew, I couldn't tell. The fried meat made my mouth water.

"What kind of meat is this?" I wanted to know.

"Fried testicles," she cackled, doubling over with laughter.

BACK IN WASHINGTON, D.C., Heidi and I were offered heroin. Heidi was not into the drug culture. Even as everyone was smoking pot, she remained satisfied with good scotch, champagne, and caviar. But on that occasion she surprised me by agreeing to try some. As for me, I had never even seen heroin before, and temptation, coupled with adventure, came over me with a sense of enchantment, as if I were about to discover a new galaxy or walk on the moon.

We both snorted the white powder and waited for something to go off. Nothing much did, and we returned to my apartment. As soon as we walked through the door, Heidi dashed to the bathroom and began throwing up. Soon, I was doing the same. We stayed there, sick and nauseous, for the rest of the evening. The next day, Heidi swore off drugs. I, on the other hand, felt that I had opened a very hip page in the story of my life.

But my drug of choice was cocaine, not heroin. I couldn't fathom sticking my skin with needles; moreover, cocaine wasn't an addictive street drug, I believed, but a sophisticated substance used and advocated by the rich and famous. The first time I snorted cocaine, nothing major happened; it seemed that I was looking at the world through new glasses, that was all. The grass in the field looked greener, the music from the car radio sounded clearer, my own thoughts were mellow and pleasant, as if coated in cotton candy. Cocaine didn't cause the wooziness, disorientation, lethargy, madness, and mania, emotions that I had at one time or another had attributed to drugs. It induced a state of mind grounded in the present, and a sense of well being that I imagined was the norm in people less neurotic than I. But it was not a substance to be had as easily as alcohol, it was not waiting for me around the corner, and so I didn't give it a thought. . .until, that is, it became available on *every* corner and was just waiting to be had.

"Want to go for a walk on the wild side?" my gay friend Raul would call me and ask. My answer was always yes. He was the one who had discovered the street dealers in Spanish Harlem, but I became the one who was unable to maintain a recreational stance. The dealers and street runners recognized me the minute I set foot on their turf. They greeted me, "Check it out, lady. Check it out." Checking it out meant walking up several flights of well-worn stairs in a six-story tenement building, past crying babies, ear-piercing televisions, pungent cooking odors, dead chickens, and God knows what else. But the mostly ordinary, everyday sounds of the families living their lives behind the locked and double-locked doors of those grimy staircases belied the fear and danger that rattled in me with each step towards the dealer's door. Inside, the rooms were usually barren, except for the essentials: a statue of the Virgin Mary or of Jesus, a table upon which mounds of cocaine were sitting out in the open, and a small scale. Often there were several people in the room, all speaking Spanish, and, if Raul was with me, we could chat about the weather, the business at hand, or the latest news from the Dominican Republic. It wasn't much different when I was alone. They were interested in money, and I was interested in getting high.

My favorite activity while high was cleaning the apartment and attending to my beauty routine. Cocaine made chores fun.

Fortunately, my love affair with the drug didn't last. The cops cleaned out the neighborhood, and my bank account was cleaned out by cocaine. In a few months, I was totally broke, exhausted, and almost suicidal. I smoked too many cigarettes, imbibed too many glasses of wine, and, as could have been predicted, made too many dumb decisions, brought home too many guys, and trusted people I shouldn't have.

HOW DO YOU EXPLAIN the passage of years, a decade or two, without anything to show for it? Well, not anything worth showing, that is. I managed to break my nose on the bathroom floor when I had trouble finding the toilet. I also fractured my four front teeth during a blackout, in a fall I couldn't for the life of me recall. Driving someone's car, I damn nearly lost my life on the Henry Hudson when I lost control of the wheel and rammed into an embankment near 125th Street. The physical toll of that accident was a torn upper lip and permanent scar tissue that affected the symmetry of my face; financially, I ended up with a mound of tickets that took three years to pay off. But my face remained attractive, my body trim, and my skin hairy.

I preferred one- or two-night stands, as in that way I not only didn't risk exposure but also didn't have to devote all that effort to my appearance. I had a brief relationship with a guy I had met at a jazz club on the Upper West Side. He was a short, bearded Jewish man about my age who hated his job, playing guitar in various orchestras on and off Broadway, hated his apartment, hated his parents, hated his ex-wife, in short, an all-around misanthrope who for some unconscious reason turned me on. He also hated his skin, which itched non-stop even while he was sleeping. After sex, a brief interlude from his torment, he would start scratching and continue to scratch, groan, twist, and turn for the rest of the night. Because we smoked a lot of pot, I would drift into a weird space where his scratching started to make some existential sense. He showed me the bottles of medications, creams, ointments, soaps, bath oils, lotions, and the rest of the junk that might as well have been snake oil for all the good it did, and in a self-pitying voice ripe with resignation and disgust, said, "See the load that I have to bear."

After seeing him on and off for a few months, I developed his symptoms, as if in solidarity with his pain. My dermatologist prescribed Atarax, a nasty medication that definitely stopped the itching but rendered me a walking zombie. Half an hour after one pill, my head would grow heavy, my eyes close, and I would feel as if I were submerged in water. The next day would be hell; eight hours of sleep could not wipe away the inertia. Once the side effects abated, the itching returned with a vengeance. The cure was worse than the disease.

We informally stopped seeing each other: He stopped calling, and I let it go. In due course, I forgot about him and the itching. I ran into him a couple of years later. He was with a pleasant-looking woman, and he was pushing a baby carriage. When I stopped to admire the baby, his wife continued walking ahead a few paces, generously giving us a moment of privacy, and he whispered, "So you see, this is what my shitty life has come to."

He would have thrilled my parents, had I married him.

Instead, I was married to my wine. I not only drank it but studied wines, read all I could find about food pairings, vintages, grapes, soil, bouquet, Napa Valley. With friends I would joke, "I'm not a wino, I'm a connoisseur." Alas, my expertise was limited to bottles under ten dollars, and after a couple of glasses, I would drink anything, even Kosher for Passover wines that had somehow ended up in my cabinet. And when I drank, I didn't eat, didn't sleep, didn't want to see anyone, particularly not myself. Still, hung over or not, I had to wake up every morning and face an office and colleagues that looked to be lopsided aliens from another planet. Eventually those awful mornings caught up with me; I was fired and ended up with lots of time to drink but with no money to buy even the cheapest burgundy.

Drugs took up little space in my head. Where I dwelled, there was not much that could trump my life-long fixation; there was no drug or alcohol that could undo my self-image or actual one. After almost two decades of battling facial and body hair, I still could not accept that I was a hairy woman. I was a woman who was ashamed to even shop with girlfriends, try on clothes in front of them. I feared their pity or amused comments. No one knew the machinations I suffered to avoid being seen naked and hairy. My skin was my prison, my weakness, my Achilles heel, my *bête noir*. It was the burden I had to carry with me at all times, my ball and chain, my letter "A"—as stupid as it seemed even to me.

I was not a depressive or a pessimist, but I had no clue, no idea of what to do with the rest of my life. What was the point of all this? My skills were minimal: I could type sixty words a minute, which was my only so-called talent. When I searched the *New York Times* Want Ads, I realized I couldn't even be a secretary or gal Friday. I wasn't terribly organized; I didn't have a good phone voice, given my accent and my nervousness: I didn't know anything about office machines and had no desire whatsoever to learn. I hated filling out employment forms and facing some well-scrubbed young secretary who could instantly sum up my whole sad gestalt. All that sad state of affairs pretty much kept me in the category of "clerk-typist," a job title that pretty much said it all: minimum wage for minimum skills. No child says, "When I grow up, I'll be a clerk-typist." Growing up, I'd never imagined that I would sit in a large room, pounding away on typewriter keys day in and day out, forgetting childhood fantasies, forgetting that there had been a time when I anticipated a future as sweet and pink as fine rosé.

I WAS HOME ALONE watching *Kojak*, drinking cabernet, when I decided to give up sex and men. It was raining, and the raindrops on my window made a playful sound, like a children's song. When I was a child, I loved walking in the rain, wearing a cape-like, hooded raincoat that smelled of rubber and sodden earth. Only grown-ups used umbrellas, inadequate and awkward things that provided only minimal coverage and could possibly cause serious injury in crowds. But the raincoat was sheer bliss. I loved the colors and cheerful patterns, but most of all I loved being able to walk in a field of tall grasses during a winter storm and feel completely warm and dry.

Without a man, my life would be simplified; my time would be my own. My body, my overgrown pubic hair, my prickly pear- textured thighs, the whole damn mess, would be a non-issue, erased, unattended, unworthy of the *Sturm und Drang* that had defined my being. I would become a single woman again, like Pearl Buck's Madame Wu at forty. But unlike her, I had no husband and grown children to protest my choice; I didn't have to endure a husband's concubine or give up my home. No handsome stranger was about to walk up the path to my apartment and whisk me off into a tumultuous and magnificent love affair. All I had to do was find harmony in solitude. I would sublimate the need for physical contact with art and literature. I would study each page of the dictionary; I would draw and paint in water colors and acrylics; I would study French or Spanish; I would take up ballroom dancing; I would save my money and travel to exotic places; I would read history, science, medical books; I would go back to school and get a bachelor's degree in fine arts; I would become a regular at the Museum of Modern Art, I would subscribe to the New York Times, the New Yorker, and Time magazine, and stay abreast of politics. I would be a brand new me: a well-rounded, intelligent woman who could discuss Ulysses at cocktail parties, debate the latest Supreme Court nominee. Indeed I would lift myself above my physicality, rise above the superficial and mundane, get out of the bathroom and enter the world of ideas.

It was time to be the real me, Bracha, the girl who dreamed of life in America and imagined it through a kaleidoscope of shapes and colors brimming with possibilities. I would not be a movie star, a poet, a writer, as I had told myself so long ago. I would not be married to a handsome man in an elegant dark suit who would love and adore me. I would not be a mother to a sweet, ponytailed, blonde little girl with big blue eyes for whom I would buy flouncy, short, girly dresses, and ballet slippers, arrange dance and piano lessons, and paint her nails bright red. I would not have a little girl named Melina, Orley, Ariella, Leah, or Navah. But I would have a life that mattered. I would avenge myself in front of the image of my former young tormentors who had envied me when they learned that I, Bracha, had been chosen to go to America. Girls who never gave me the time of day had sought me out, given me their addresses, and extracted promises that I would write. One popular girl, Dahlia, who had Mediterranean olive skin and was as pretty as the flower, pursued me more than anyone else for weeks before the big move. She wrote in my scrapbook, drew pictures of red hearts, trees, and sun rays. She reinforced the Hebrew letters of her name and address in red, green, and blue pen.

I was flattered at the time but I also knew that I would never write. All her declarations of friendship left me cold; I knew I was being manipulated but didn't see any harm in playing along; there was no need for unpleasantries, tears, or confrontations. In America that first summer, sharing a bedroom with my cousin Barbie, I thought of Dahlia from time to time but still didn't feel compelled to write; there was nothing to say.

A few months later, Varda wrote to tell me that Dahlia had died. While alone in the house babysitting, blood had begun pouring out of every orifice in her body until she bled to death, was what Varda wrote. That was the story. For a long time I imagined the death when I least wanted to, particularly at night. I imagined the baby crying in her crib while Dahlia lay on the sofa, blood pouring out of her vagina, rectum, nose, mouth, ears, her eyes, and all her large and small capillaries. I imagined her panic as the life was draining out of her, unable to find any help, waiting in vain for the adults to return from their party, dinner, or movie, and rescue her. Dahlia, such a pretty name: Had I had a daughter, I would have named her Dahlia.

In the meantime, I needed a job. Most of my clothes came from second-hand shops, and my furniture was virtually junk, odds and ends that did not conceal their vintage. When I called my parents for money, the answer was always negative until my begging reached a feverish pitch that would soften their hearts, particularly if I complained of feeling sick or not having enough to eat, and I would eventually receive an envelope in the mail, my name and address misspelled, and within it would be a check for a hundred dollars, carefully wrapped in layers and layers of baby blue toilet paper.

Since I lived near a large city hospital, I decided to try my luck there. Hospitals had always intrigued me and made me feel safe. They were noble places whose purpose was to care for the sick and the weak; their mission was to cure, to restore to health unfortunates struck by disease or bad luck. My interview in the Human Resources office was brief, and I passed the required typing test. I would have liked some interesting position, in a lab or in an admissions office, where I could be privy to the drama of life and death, but ended up being a clerk on a busy medical-surgical unit, where life and death became routine, and what was lacking in drama was made up for in the petty histrionics of everyday life. On the totem pole of hospital workers, I was pretty low, particularly for a youngish white woman who, despite an accent, had a fairly good command of the English language, but I swallowed my pride and kept the patient charts neat, left lab values for the doctors to contemplate, ordered supplies before the nurses and aides freaked out, answered the telephone, and complied with a million requests from doctors, patients, and nurses. I didn't mind paging a doctor even if he was known for his temper, nor did I argue with Housekeeping or Dietary. I became one of those nondescript women who exist all over New York City and follow an exact schedule day after day after day. I woke up early, made my own lunch, took the bus to work, and often stayed late. I was a known, reliable fixture on my unit who, at the end of the day, cheerfully wished everyone a good evening or a good week-end, then walked to the bus stop, consumed with an inchoate fear that threatened to overcome me, render me less than real, a snowflake in the desert, as I undertook my journey to a tiny place I called home, preparing to face a lonesome evening looking at the color television, drinking at least a bottle of cabernet sauvignon.

Once in a while, I would jot down a poem or feel inspired to draw a face or a fantasy I had had in a dream. I even tried my hand at short stories and resumed keeping a journal to vent my feelings. Over the years, my drawings and writings accumulated in a yellow manila folder that I regarded as more precious than gold. The poems would usually write themselves; they didn't require much rewriting and were composed strictly for themselves. An idea would register in my mind, and the idea would foment related thoughts that would simmer and bubble in my head until the words emerged on paper.

I did that year after year after year, the seasons coming and going as regularly as the beat of a heart. Around me the world, the city, the crowds, remained static, but I was changing, growing older, neither happy nor tortured. I had entered middle age, ashamed of the label, went through menopause in the blink of the eye, and then came home one day to find in my mail an invitation to join AARP and realized that I was already on the other side. I took the magazine with me to the bathroom and studied the smiling celebrity face on the cover, until the tears flowed and flowed like water. Where had the years gone? How had I gotten to be fifty years old? I had not been with a man for ages and loved the hiatus from the plucking and bleaching. After so long without sex, I began to feel practically a virgin, scared that I would not be able to ever again experience an orgasm or a passionate embrace from a man:

PRACTICALLY A VIRGIN

Practically a virgin,
Years and years after chasing promises
Hollow as tall reeds along the creek,
Along the railroad tracks
Where no train whistle blows,
No terminal lights flash or beckon,
At the cross sign by the weepy road.

Practically a virgin,
clinging to shopworn warnings
abandoned long ago,

Jayne Mead

trailing behind on all fours,
yearning for a shudder, a frisson,
a reason for being in the dark
late at the end of dusk or dawn.

Practically a virgin,
post-wisdom, no longer taut,
as hardened as stainless steel,
gray, bent, blind, and clueless,
waiting for that train that no longer passes
no longer thunders, rumbles, or shudders,
for a love that is dead and gone,

I do believe I will be there soon,
under a glorious wedding canopy
adorned in pearls and silk organza,
made up in sheer white powder,
pure as cold newborn snow,
drinking wine as freely as water
at last, deflowered, unburdened,
good to go.

LAST CALL

A S A WELL-SEASONED HOSPITAL clerk, I could do my work with my eyes closed, so to speak, deriving no fulfillment, expecting no accolades, achieving no gratification, looking forward to nothing except my paycheck. I was protected by the union and didn't fear termination, suspension, or a supervisor's unmerited criticism. Job satisfaction came from other sources. I would endlessly peruse patients' medical records, looking for misfortunes, catastrophes, orphan illnesses, incurable cancers, dementia, homelessness, and all the ills in the *Merck Manual*. I had a sense of life outside the hospital walls as one amazing race: hordes of people running as if under threat of the devil's whip; others, malnourished, frail, and ill, dropping along ditches and alleyways stricken, unable to continue through the arduous trek, awaiting transport to either the morgue or hospital. The runners, blinded by fear and denial, focused only on their own existence; they were aware of Darwin's theory of evolution. Their goal was to stay upright among the mob, push onward despite the absence of rhyme or reason, compelled to survive at any cost. There was simply no time for reflection. But in the hospital rooms, behind the plastic curtain, aware of coughing, farting, moaning, Cheyne-Stokes roommates, time stood still, time stood waiting like a sentry at the queen's palace. After a while, the overflowing medical charts became redundant. The patient in Room eight, Bed two, was just another asthmatic, infarction, deep vein thrombosis, sickle cell disease. The narratives by nurses, doctors, and the rest of the team sucked the life out of their patients' humanity. The patients possessed no histories, thoughts, or feelings. They presented themselves as an array of symptoms, side effects, diagnoses to be ruled in or out, compliant or resistant, submissive or threatening. Their passive, medicated bodies were jabbed, probed, palpated, manipulated, auscultated, biopsied, x-rayed, irradiated, fed, turned this way and that, all in the name of medicine, science, and recovery.

Around me, year after year, new batches of young doctors and nurses came and went, to quote Sylvia Path in one of my favorite poems, "Tulips":

> *The nurses pass and pass, they are no trouble,*
> *They pass the way gulls pass inland in their white caps,*
> *Doing things with their hands, one just the same as another,*
> *So it is impossible to tell how many there are.*

I spent my workdays in the nurses' station performing mindless tasks, tending to wallow in self-pity, ruing the years that had passed like minutes. I wanted to find someone to blame for my failures while I hated and envied the confident professionals around me and thought I could have been them. What if I had been born in America instead of in an Austrian refugee camp; would I be sitting here robotically stamping charts, or would I be doing meaningful work? When people asked what I did for a living, I would answer, "I work as a clerk-typist." The "as" applied to blue-color work only; professionals identified themselves by their careers. "I am a psychiatrist," one might state. What if I had

been born to moderately sane and intelligent people instead of to a couple of frenzied teenagers overwhelmed by war, famine, and loss, would
I have overcome my inane, impulsive, immature, and self-destructive
behaviors and instead been a studious and ambitious girl, spending my
evenings reading texts about the Reformation, the Roman Republic,
the Invasion of 1066, not tweezing my thighs, filling my bedroom with
smoke and my head with flimflam elevated to the status of a state dinner
but as memorable as a muddy cup of coffee at the corner luncheonette?
Would my life have been different? Hard to tell. I was aware that there
were doctors, lawyers, senators, academics, whose early circumstances
did not portend a successful life but who overcame hurdles nonetheless.
And there I was in the hospital, not saving lives, not offering solace, not
healing the sick, not holding a hand, not even adjusting a dying man's
pillow, year after year, watching time fade away like images on the com-
puter screen after logging off for the night.

It was sobering to realize that the medical residents were younger
than I, and that I had absolutely no chance of attracting a good-looking
doctor and living happily ever after. I was shy around everyone and at
times too loud in a feeble attempt to overcompensate for that shyness,
and I was particularly shy around articulate, smart people. I would
stumble on words, misuse or forget the very ones I was reaching for,
as if they were stuck to the tip of my tongue with Crazy Glue.

Early in my so-called career, I'd had some fantasies, illusions rather,
of meeting a good-looking physician, quitting my dead-end job, and
finding happiness, status, and stability. If I were married to a doctor,
I would live in a nice apartment that I would decorate with my artwork
and antique pieces that I would find during weekend jaunts to the
country. I would shop at Bloomingdale's or Saks, and appear at charity
events at the Museum of Natural History. I would learn Spanish and
attend night classes that I would ace, and earn degrees in literature and
art. All those dreams. Simple, girly, unattainable—because, while fan-

tasizing, an intrusive thought, ugly as sin, would shatter the fantasies: No damn doctor was going to marry a hairy woman. How could I possibly imagine living with a doctor or any upscale, professional man and manage to attend to my depilatory activities? For a man to live with me, he had to be wanting. He had to be a slob, a pauper, a maniac, or a schizophrenic like Maurice. That was the hand that I had been dealt, and, screaming and kicking, I had to deal with it.

Had I married a Jewish doctor, I would have brought happiness to my parents. I would have given my small, inadequate, fearful mother a modicum of joy, a hint of silk thread in the dour tapestry of her life. As time went on and there were no proposals, no *mazel tovs* or phone calls with the news that they had hoped to hear, they lowered their expectations of me. "Isn't there anyone where you work that you can go out with?" my mother would ask.

"No one Jewish," I'd respond as if to exonerate myself.

If my father were present, he would jump in immediately: "No. It must be a Jew. I will never allow my daughter to bring a goy home." But I didn't believe his proclamations. They were evoked as an offering, a talisman against God's wrath. My father, as he became older, became a cautious person. He followed his doctor's orders, stayed attuned to his health, prayed more frequently, and attended Shabbat services every week. He took no chances. I knew intrinsically that, if I were to bring home an x-ray technician, a lab worker, a widower, a one-legged man, a man with one foot in the grave who had never heard of Judaism and prayed to Jesus and false idols every day of his life, he would have been more welcome than my "old maid" status. They never expected that their beautiful Bruchale would not be showered with marriage proposals. "Only homely girls are left sitting," was a line from a Yiddish song my father used to sing to me at bedtime. As to my brother, there was not so much *naches* there either.

"Shlomo," my mother spat. "He's a *dreck*. A *cacker*." For years, they had called him a *yoyno*. I had no idea where this word came from, but I understood its connotation. In my parents' world view, a man who gives in to his wife, who does as she bids, is a worthless *schmuck* of a man. My brother was such a man. Tolerant and gentle, he had refused to participate in, or agree with, the constant stream of criticism that my parents had hurled at his wives. They'd despised the first one, in fact accused her of adultery, and despised the second one, whom they accused of snobbishness, selfishness, arrogance, and so on. As they got older, they created a united front; it was them against a world where everyone was either a thief, a liar, or a whore. They seemed unable to derive joy, not even from their granddaughters.

Once or twice, at least, I had brief flings, no longer than perhaps twenty minutes at a clip, in the on-call room of some resident or another. I liked those semi-nude quickies; they required less prep time than a real date. I could maneuver my clothes or the bed linens so that not much of me was visible or palpable, play the role of a sex kitten who had been around the block a few times, and find a frisson of relief in the moments of heavy breathing and sweating and the sounds of bodies coming together, the unlikely place and time adding to the thrill. Afterwards, I'd quickly wash up and scurry off back to my desk as if nothing had happened, and indeed it was nothing, certainly nothing to write home about.

I didn't give up on men entirely. I had a stupid affair with a Haitian orderly, someone much younger than I, an affair that lasted long enough to devolve from passion, lust, and adoration to disgust and revulsion. If I hadn't been drunk so much of the time, that affair would have never gotten off the ground. Intoxicated, I lost my self-consciousness and judgment. I could turn off the lights, and there, under the skies of an alternate universe, pretend I was other than who I was. I was no longer the hairy woman who was afraid to be seen. I was sexy and uninhibited and female. I could don sexy underwear, threadbare remnants from previous relationships, turn on the music, move to the rhythm of an Elvin Jones drum beat, wiggle to the hot, holy, heart-wrenching sound of Coltrane, perform a striptease to Brubeck's *Take Five*. The music and sex brought back my youth minus its scrapes and sorrows. The past was then whitewashed, perfumed with patchouli oil, smoothed by distance and the web of time. With the Haitian, his accented English, paucity of words, and all the pretentions he wore like armor against his insecurities, which were many, I could play the smart, sophisticated, older woman. I called him my boy toy, and yet, even with him, I would panic if he called at the last moment and my legs were unshaven. Many times, I shaved my legs in the hospital's filthy public bathrooms, cutting myself, hating myself.

A few years later, in 1981, AIDS came on the scene and, shortly after I learned about the five "H"s, the high-risk groups for spreading HIV: health care workers, homosexuals, hemophiliacs, heroin users, and Haitians. My former lover belonged to at least two of the high-risk groups; I was filled with panic: In a dream I was making love to a gay man, and when he injected his sperm into my body, I felt I was given a strange infusion of power. I was inoculated with life and death forces at the same time; I had achieved a higher state of understanding.

I fretted, worried, and ruminated over every real or imagined AIDS symptom. A red spot on my thigh became Kaposi's sarcoma, a cough pneumonia. I'd lie in bed at night, reviewing my licentious history, almost certain that I had done enough to deserve this incurable plague. All my previous hypochondriacal fears didn't match this new and horrid panic. Because in the beginning I didn't know that the disease could strike women, I had thought myself immune. My sympathies lay with the gay community. With my friend Raul, I'd even joined in fund-raising marches, dances, and pleas for community awareness—that is, until I thought that I too could be a victim. After Raul left my house, I poured bleach on every surface that he might have come in contact with, at once ashamed and frightened.

Eventually, I stopped making myself crazy over fear of AIDS; kidney disease; cardiac arrhythmia; skin, colon, throat, or ovarian cancers; multiple myeloma; early-onset Alzheimer's, new emerging infections; or sudden death. It was as if the whole litany of troubles simply vanished, disappeared into a black hole of infinite nothingness. Even fear of flying became a thing of the past. "If it crashes, it crashes," became my motto—that is, if I happened even to entertain the thought. I could hardly relate to my younger, fearful self except in one domain, in one area that haunted me, that followed me like an armed stalker practically all my years: superfluous body and facial hair. That, and that alone, was a topic that could not be broached with others. There were no opportunities to vent, no sharing my secret with girlfriends, no advice columns or support groups, no twelve-step meetings or prayers to a higher power.

It became culturally acceptable for celebrities and everyone else to open their hearts and souls to the media, to mourn publicly, to expose long-hidden family secrets, to revel in past indiscretions and present redemptions. On television, they boasted about their battles with alcoholism, spousal abuse, anorexia, obesity, cancer, borderline behavior, incest, sex addictions, and other real or imagined addictions and personal stories from sin to enlightenment. I could never do that. I have always cringed at displays of weepy emotionality, self-pity, or grief. Yet what if hirsutism were a social issue? What if it were discussed openly, as if it were obesity or alcoholism? To this day, the thought of publicly admitting such a flaw is unthinkable for me.

The problem with my affliction was its uncommonality. My plight, my orphan malady, to the degree that I was affected by it, was rare. My hairiness was not just a minor nuisance to be joked about, it *was* my pink unicorn, my calamity.

Jayne Mead

I AM ON JONES *Beach, Long Island running, allowing the waves to crash at my feet, breathing the salt air that is like pure oxygen, reviving me, providing me with momentum, urging my body forward on the sand formed and hardened by water ebbing and flowing each day, every day, until the end of time. Every now and then a wave hits hard and my pants become soaked, the bottoms soggy with water. Underneath I'm wearing animal print, bikini panties which can pass for real bikinis, I am certain, and in one motion pull off my wet jogging pants, drop them on a bush of white beach roses in bloom. Hardly skipping a beat, I continue running, past the guys casting long fishing poles, past the sea gulls and the albatross, past the Muslim women in their modest dress and head coverings intently guarding their children at play, past the chatty adolescent girls and their roaming eyes, past the obese mothers in skirted bathing suits and their rowdy kids, past the young couples kissing on the dunes, and past the gay lovers filming the sunset. It is already past seven p.m., and behind me the sun, a fat red star spewing fire, is beginning to sink and slowly disappear from the shore, promising a quick return.*

If I look down at my legs, I see loose skin, saggy knees, varicose and spider veins, age spots, broken capillaries. Whether it's there or not I don't see superfluous hair anymore; aging has shifted my focus, amended priorities, devalued life-long fixations, leaving them lacking spark. Aging has also diminished my eyesight's acuity and if I choose, I don't have to see anything close. I don't need a close shave. What mattered yesterday is shopworn today, its energy consumed by year after year of angst and anger. At last, I have become invisible, even to arthritic curmudgeons leaning upon their walkers; and I feel good. But I still look back, now that I know where one chapter ends and another begins, reviewing, retelling, reminiscing; I am obliging the text-book expectation, the role assigned to my generation at this stage of life.

Eventually everything is water under the bridge.

CPSIA information can be obtained at www.ICGtesting.com
Printed in the USA
BVOW021541240412

288519BV00002B/4/P

9 780984 953646